EX LIBRIS
VINTAGE CLASSICS

D1427740

THE L-SHAPED ROOM

Lynne Reid Banks was born in London in 1929 and was evacuated to the Canadian prairies during the war. On her return to England she studied at RADA and was an actress in the early 1950s; later she became one of the first two women reporters on British television. Her first book, *The L-Shaped Room*, was published in 1960 and was an instant and lasting best-seller. Lynne Reid Banks is also a best-selling author of books for children and young adults. Her classic children's novel, *The Indian in the Cupboard*, has sold over ten million copies worldwide. She lives in London.

LYNNE REID BANKS

The L-Shaped Room

VINTAGE BOOKS
London

Published by Vintage 2004

13

First published in Great Britain in 1960 by Chatto & Windus

Vintage
Random House, 20 Vauxhall Bridge Road,
London SW1V 2SA

www.vintage-classics.info

Addresses for companies within The Random House Group Limited can be found at: www.randomhouse.co.uk/offices.htm

The Random House Group Limited Reg. No. 954009

A CIP catalogue record for this book is available from the British Library

ISBN 9780099469636

The Random House Group Limited supports The Forest Stewardship Council® (FSC®), the leading international forest-certification organisation. Our books carrying the FSC label are printed on FSC®-certified paper. FSC is the only forest-certification scheme supported by the leading environmental organisations, including Greenpeace. Our paper procurement policy can be found at www.randomhouse.co.uk/environment

Printed and bound in Great Britain by Clays Ltd, St Ives plc

FOR PAT
WHETHER SHE LIKES IT OR NOT
AND IN MEMORY OF
JAMIE

Chapter 1

THERE wasn't much to be said for the place, really, but it had a roof over it and a door which locked from the inside, which was all I cared about just then. I didn't even bother to take in the details – they were pretty sordid, but I didn't notice them so they didn't depress me; perhaps because I was already at rock-bottom. I just threw my one suitcase on to the bed, took my few belongings out of it and shut them all into one drawer of the three-legged chest of drawers. Then there didn't seem to be anything else I ought to do so I sat in the arm-chair and stared out of the window.

It was a greyish sort of day, which suited the way I was feeling, and it looked greyer because the window needed cleaning. I registered this vaguely and thought I'd buy some Windolene tomorrow and give it a going-over; then I thought, what the hell, no one's going to see it. I had an empty sort of feeling and wondered if I was hungry. If so it would be the first time for a week I'd felt like eating. I thought about various sorts of food, but they all struck me as quite unattractive until I came to coffee. Almost all I'd had for a week was coffee. I got up and felt in my trenchcoat pocket to make sure I had my wallet and keys, and then went out, carefully locking the door.

My room was five flights up in one of those gone-to-seed houses in Fulham, all dark brown wallpaper inside and peeling paint outside. On every second landing was a chipped sink with one tap and an old ink-written notice which said 'Don't Leave Tap Driping'. The landing lights were the sort that go out before you can reach the next one. There were a couple of prostitutes in the basement; the landlady had been quite open about them. She'd pointed out that there was even an advantage to having them there, namely that nobody asked questions about anybody. She dropped her eyes as she said that. Not out of modesty. She was looking to see if I were pregnant. Just because you don't ask questions, her look said, it doesn't mean you're not curious. But I had only been pregnant a month, so of course there was nothing to see.

I was curious, in a remote sort of way, about the prostitutes. I'd never met one; I'd never wanted to. They'd seemed like strange animals from another part of the forest with whom I had nothing in common. Now, since my own father evidently considered me one, I had to think again. After all, they were people. It might be rather interesting to talk to one.

However, they weren't around now. It was mid-afternoon and I supposed they were sleeping. As I left the house and walked past the area railings I looked at the basement windows, but the curtains were drawn.

The neighbourhood was completely strange to me. If I'd been in any mood to make judgements I'd have judged it to be pretty grim. The shabby houses fronted almost right on to the pavement, though some of them had front yards stuck with a few sooty bushes. Most of the windows lacked curtains and that gave the houses a blind look, or rather a dead look, like open-eyed corpses. They were decaying like corpses, too. Some of the front yards had dustbins instead of bushes, which would have smelt if it hadn't been drizzling. But the drizzle didn't do anything to reduce the dog-smell, which was foul. You had to watch where you walked. It hadn't been raining long and the pavement had that sweaty look.

I walked automatically in the direction of the only landmark I knew in the district – the paper-shop where I'd seen the advertisement for the room. The advertisement was still there, behind the cracked glass among the other cards advertising second-hand prams, as new, and French girl gives lessons, phone after 6 p.m. Some rain had leaked into the frame and there was a yellow stain on the corner of the card; it looked as if it had been there for a long time.

The proprietor of the shop came out to put a new card into the frame. He was bare-headed and after a minute his scalp shone with rain through his thin unwashed hair.

'That room's taken,' I said, pointing to the card. It was the first time I'd spoken since I made the arrangement with the landlady at noon. My father and I hadn't said a word to each other when I went home for my things. He'd told me to go and I was going; he didn't care where and so why should I tell him?

The old paper-shop man looked at the card, and then at me. He wasn't very interested in either. 'I expect it is,' he said. 'It could be. They come and go,' he said indifferently.

He stuck the new advertisement up with two tarnished thumb-tacks. It said: 'Photographer's Model free evenings. Special poses.' And a phone number. I looked at the phone number to see if it was the same as mine; perhaps one of the tarts in the basement had decided to invest sixpence a week in the hope of attracting new custom. But I couldn't remember what my new number was; I could only remember my old one. I'd had the same telephone number for the whole of my life; twenty-seven years with the same telephone number. I said to the old man: 'Have you got a telephone?'

'Not a public. You could use it, though. Cost you sixpence. It's in the back.'

Sixpence was what it cost to telephone from the big hotel in the West End where I worked. But still, it was too cheap for this call. Because I was wondering what would happen if I called my father and said to him, 'I've found a place to live, Father. It's one room in the worst part of Fulham. There's one bathroom for the whole house, and two tarts live in the basement. Is that what you wanted? Is that where you think I belong?'

The old man stopped in the doorway and looked back at me. 'Well, do you want to phone, or don't you?'

'No, I don't think I will after all.'

He turned to go in and I said, 'Aren't you going to take the card down?'

'Which?'

'About the room. I told you, it's taken.'

'How do you know it's taken?'

'Because I've taken it.'

He came back to where I was standing in the rain, and put his face close to mine. 'You didn't put that card in, did you?'

'No,' I said, puzzled. 'I just saw the card and went about the room, and I took it. I live there now,' I said, the funny, unlikely truth of it coming real for the first time, 'so it's not vacant any more.'

'Who's paying for that card to be up there?' he asked me, jabbing at it angrily. 'You or somebody else?'

'Not me,' I said.

'Well then,' he said triumphantly, 'who are you to tell me to take it down? When you have a card up there, then you'll have the right to tell me to take it down. And when you come to tell me to take it down,' he went on, angrier than ever, 'maybe you'll pay me the twelve-and-six you owe me for having it up there twenty-five weeks since your deposit ran out. I'm not a bleeding charity, you know,' he said almost snarling through his little grey teeth, 'even the chippies pay up more regular than the bloody landladies. Those chippies, they know what it means to have a living to make. You can say what you like about 'em, that much they do know. These old faggots letting off rooms to God knows what riff-raff, black riff-raff too, doesn't matter so long as the rent's the right colour – they think their lousy dirty houses are the whole world, they don't stop to wonder if there's other people outside trying to keep alive. 'You want to use the phone?' he asked in the same aggressive voice. 'Cost you sixpence, it's in the back.'

I shook my head and he looked at me curiously. I doubt if he'd really noticed me properly before. 'You can shut the door,' he said more kindly. 'No one can hear you.'

'No thank you,' I said. 'Can I get some coffee near here?'

His face closed again. 'I ain't running a cafe,' he said, but grumbling this time, not snarling.

'I meant –'

'Nor a bleeding information desk, neither.' He looked at me again in the same sharp way. 'You say you're *living* in that room?'

'Yes.'

He stared at me a bit longer, sucking his teeth. 'Bloody Commies,' he said suddenly. 'Why couldn't they leave the middle classes alone? Never did no real harm as I could see. Live and let live, I say, all except the bobos, you have to keep them in their place. *And* the old faggots with their bleeding houses. Sorry, miss.'

I realized with surprise that he was apologizing for saying bleeding. It was as if he were in the presence of a corpse – the corpse of the middle classes. He was looking at me as if I were its last twitch.

'Don't you go on paying your rent on the dot, miss,' he went on in a very kindly, confidential tone. 'You keep the old cow waiting, like she does me. And wait she will, don't you worry. It's not as easy as it used to be to find people so down on their luck they'd live in one of her rat-holes . . .' He went on staring at me. I clenched my hands in my pockets. I felt like a piece of flotsam.

'I must go,' I said awkwardly.

'That's right, miss. You go and have a nice cup of something hot. There's a place about five minutes' walk from here. Round to the left at the lights. Not the first place you come to, don't go in there, the stuff she calls tea's nothing but dust, and the milk's tinned. The second place. Frank's, he's a pal of mine; give you a good cuppa, Frank will, and you don't get the rough types there like you do some places. Frank won't have bobos in, and you won't find none of the girls there this time of day. Shouldn't go in there late at night, though. He does his best, Frank does, but you can't put a sieve on the door, can you? You have to take what comes, same as the pubs. Pity they don't divide cafes off into saloon and public, if you ask me. People like to be with their own sort. Not as how you'd find many of your sort around here . . .' He went on staring at me and sucking his teeth. We stood there for a moment waiting for the conversation to start again, and then I nodded and turned away.

I found Frank's. It wasn't a bad place. The tables had yellow Formica tops which Frank wiped after each customer. The lights were yellow too, warm in the drab afternoon, not like the cold white neon ones. I was the only person there, except Frank, who was the same age as the old man. At first glance, he could have been the old man. I sat down at the table furthest from the door and Frank came and wiped my table. He didn't ask what I wanted.

'Could I have some coffee, please?'

He said nothing and didn't nod, but finished wiping the table and then went behind the counter and drew off a cup of milk-coffee, turning the tap off very suddenly at just the right moment. He carried it over without spilling any, and brought a bowl of sugar to the table.

'Didn't want it black,' he said, without a question-mark.

'No, that's fine.'

'Sixpence.'

Everything seemed to be sixpence. Again I heard myself asking:

'Have you got a telephone?'

'No. Two kiosks in the main road by the cinema.' He went away and started wiping tables again.

I sat stirring my coffee. So far as I was capable of liking any place, I liked Frank's. It reminded me of a similar place where I worked once.

It was years ago, when I was trying to be an actress. In spite of what my father thought, and said, I'd got my first job, in a repertory company up North – what they used to call a commonwealth rep before Actors' Equity got teeth in its jaws and forbade such things. 'Ever so common and no wealth,' we used to tell each other. Commonwealth meant no one got a salary but at the end of each week we divided the profits equally. That was a very democratic idea, except that there never were any profits. We didn't care. We got parcels from home and shared them, and money too if we had the right sort of parents, which I didn't, but I made up for it by not smoking. Kind people in the town who believed we were starving thought we'd be insulted by offers of food (they were wrong) but were always pressing cigarettes on us. I used to say, 'Thank you, I'll take it for later.' Then, when we all met at the theatre, I'd empty out my pockets and hand round my loot, bent at odd angles and leaking tobacco. In exchange I would get a share of the tinned soup or spaghetti somebody's sympathetic mother had sent.

Of course my father didn't know about that side of it. I wrote to him during the weeks when I was stage managing, sitting in the wings waiting to strain my insides winding down the curtain which had a faulty counterweight. I told him I was acting big parts and that the producer was pleased with me, which was true some of the time, and I sent him cuttings from the local paper when I was mentioned there. I was extremely happy.

Then, one night, there was a terrible scene.

A man who was in the company, a queer called Malcolm, was in love with another of the actors. This actor wasn't a bit queer; he was in love with me. Malcolm rather pathetically thought nobody knew he was queer, and was very ashamed of it; actually, of course, you only had to look at him to know. I liked him otherwise, and he liked me; but he loved this actor, and that I found disgusting. So did the actor, and one evening we let Malcolm catch us kissing in one of the dressing-rooms after the performance.

We didn't think how he might feel. We just thought he would stop mooning about the actor when he saw how normal he was. It wasn't until I looked up from the kiss and saw him standing in the doorway that I suddenly got frightened.

I've always played a game in which I decide what kind of animal or bird or insect people look like. Malcolm always reminded me of a cat. A female cat, soft and affectionate but with something hidden deep that you couldn't get to know. As he stood in the doorway with his snub-nosed cat's face gone white, I knew suddenly that that hidden something was the savagery all cats have, even the very tame ones.

He came flying at me with his nails clawing and his mouth snarling. I was too scared to move, and the actor didn't move either. I still have two faint long marks on my cheek where his nails went. They don't show under make-up but when I'm upset or angry they come up red and nothing hides them. I was lucky, really, because of course he was after my eyes, but he missed them through being too crazy to watch what he was doing.

When I felt the pain on my face I screamed and caught hold of his wrists, and then the actor gave a sort of jerk like someone waking up and threw himself against Malcolm, who fell over, and we lay on top of him until he stopped struggling and lay still.

It was very quiet then, all except the sounds of our breathing; I felt uncomfortable, lying half on the dressing-room floor and half on Malcolm's body with my face pressed against his chest. He smelled of paint and dust from the theatre, and of the talcum powder he put under his arms. I lifted my face away and left two streaks of blood on his woollen shirt.

He was lying on his back with his eyes open and his mouth panting and there was a little froth on his lips. Suddenly his face screwed up like a little girl's and he began to cry and say, 'I'm sorry, I'm sorry, I'm sorry, I'm sorry . . .' The actor and I got off him very quickly and awkwardly and stood up, as if we were children caught by grown-ups doing something indecent.

I went quickly out of that dressing-room and up the stairs to the one all the girls used. I washed my face in cold water; then I was sick into the basin. Afterwards I washed my face again and put some peroxide on the scratches out of a bottle one of the girls used to bleach her hair. The scratches looked very bad because my face was so white; it looked frighteningly ugly, like someone else's face. I was crying and the tears kept running into the scratches and making them sting; but the peroxide stung so much worse that I couldn't feel anything from the tears after that. But I kept on crying while I was packing my clothes and stage tat into my big trunk. I didn't do it very carefully, but one spreads around a lot in three months so it took a long time to sort all my things out. I wasn't finished when Malcolm knocked on the door.

He came in and his face still looked like a cat's, a cat that's caught in a trap and wants you to let it out. I didn't say anything and he leaned back against the door and watched me packing.

'You're going, then.' His voice had that gasp in it that comes after a lot of crying.

I didn't answer. I wished he'd go away. I thought if he stayed I'd have to tell him that we'd let him catch us purposely because we wanted to rub it in that we were normal and that he disgusted us. He didn't disgust me now; I disgusted myself. But he made it worse, standing there so defencelessly with his red eyes and hurt mouth. I rolled up the stained towel with my greasepaint in it and put it in the top tray of the trunk with my shoes. Then I picked the tray up. It was quite heavy.

'Let me help with that.'

'No,' I said sharply. 'Leave it alone.'

I put the tray on top of my things in the trunk and closed down the lid.

Behind me, he gasped again and said, '*Please* don't go.'

I faced him so that he could see the scratches. 'How can I stay after this?' I said. He looked at me. His soft, helpless face seemed to shiver. I felt sick again.

'Have you put something on them?'

'Yes,' I said, 'don't worry, I'm not going to risk getting blood poisoning.' His face became a shade more wretched, if possible, which was what I'd wanted. I wanted to punish him for making me feel so guilty.

He began to cry again, quite openly. He came towards me with his face screwed up and put his arms round me and sobbed, 'Please, don't go, I'll never forgive myself, please . . .' As I stood there with him hanging on to me, pleading and crying, I could imagine how, in a day or so, I would relive this scene and wish I had petted and comforted him and forgiven him and agreed to stay, making it all his fault. But at this moment I knew it was my fault, and so I stood there with my arms not moving to cuddle him and what I said was, 'Will you ask two of the men to help me out with my trunk?' And the way I said 'men' stopped his pleading because it was so insulting, and he let me go and walked out with something like dignity.

So I left the company, and as I'd expected I regretted it next day, but it was too late then. I gave a week's notice at my digs and sat around in them wondering where I would go when it expired because the season wasn't due to end for another two months and I couldn't go back to my father before that. In a small town like that everyone knows the local actors and speaks to them in shops; there was no question *there* of having no curiosity – everyone was bursting with it, starting with my landlady and spreading to the street my digs were in and from there all over town. I couldn't go out for a walk without being asked a hundred times why I'd left the company, and what had happened to my face, and was it true what Mrs Whatnot said, that this or that? The most widely accepted story was that I'd had a fight with one of the other actresses over a part, and I didn't correct it. As to what I was going to do, I didn't know, I only knew I couldn't go home for two more months.

The actor who had thought himself in love with me wasn't in love with me at all, and I wasn't in love with him either. We discovered that when he came to see me. I wasn't glad to see him although I tried to be, and he felt the same. We sat in the kitchen of my digs on the blue plush settee in front of the stove. We talked and drank the tea which my landlady always made for every visitor, and we didn't touch each other or look at each other much, because we felt like two people who've committed a crime together but are trying to behave as if it weren't important or had never happened.

He asked if I were going back to London and I said no, I couldn't tell Father what had really happened and I couldn't tell him a lie either because he always knew when I was lying. So the actor said, 'Well, what are you going to do?' And I said, 'I'll have to stay in this town because of the postmark on letters to Father.' That was the first time I'd thought of that.

The actor asked what I was going to live on, which was a good question, because at least the rep had paid for my digs as part of the get-out and that had included one meal a day and all the tea I could drink. I said, 'Obviously I'll have to get a job,' and the actor said, 'You mean, not acting?'– incredulously, as if there weren't any other kinds of job, which is how all actors feel to begin with, and how I felt too until that moment.

That night after it was dark I went for a walk to a part of town I'd never been to, on the other side of the river. People around there didn't go to the theatre much and nobody knew me. I saw a notice in a café window saying they needed a waitress. I went in and sat down at a table, and watched the proprietor wiping the table-tops with a damp cloth. They weren't Formica. They were coloured oilcloth tacked under at the corners. There was a cruet and a bottle of Worcester Sauce on each table, and a bowl of sugar. I couldn't decide whether I should apply for the job or not, and I thought, *I'll order some coffee and if the cup's cracked or there's lipstick on it I'll pay and walk out.* It wasn't that I cared too much about things like that; at the theatre we'd drunk coffee out of jam jars and cooked in paint tins on top of the remains of what the person before had cooked; it was just a way of deciding whether to ask for the job or not, like tossing a coin.

I ordered the coffee and it came. There was none spilled in the saucer and the cup might have been brand new for all the cracks or lipstick I found on it, though I looked carefully, half-hoping there would be. I drank the coffee and then went to the counter and applied for the job.

I'd played the daughter in a Yorkshire comedy the week before and I told the proprietor my name was Millie Braithewaite, speaking in a Yorkshire accent, but he said who did I think I was having on? I was the young lass from the theatre, the one all the pother was about; he'd spotted me right off as soon as I came in.

It took a bit of talking to convince him that I needed the job, and that I could do it if he gave it to me, but in the end he said I could start tomorrow. A day's unpaid trial and after that a week's notice on either side. I was to get £4 10s. a week, my hours being from ten in the morning till the customers went home at night. Four-ten sounded like a lot and I was very grateful, thinking he'd engaged me out of pity. What I didn't realize was that what I'd done was the local equivalent of Ingrid Bergman getting a job as a hat-check girl in the Regent Palace Hotel right after the Rossellini scandal.

The first week was a nightmare. The whole town came across the river to have a look at me. The café had never done such business. The proprietor gave up wiping the tables between customers: there wasn't time. He just stood behind the cash-register and grinned whenever he caught my eye.

I didn't try to hate all the interested gawpers who sat and joked and whispered while I fetched their egg and chips, tea, Tizer, and bread and butter; I just hated the proprietor. I hated him quietly and steadily while I worked as I had never worked in my life before.

Every night I would hang my overall away in a little cupboard off the café kitchen and look at my face in a bit of mirror propped over a coat-hook. I would think about how I hated the proprietor because he was fat and because he had engaged me not out of pity but as a sort of side-show, and I would watch the two scratch-marks standing out redly as the humiliation thickened in my throat and the tears of tiredness came at last.

I would tell myself to go and tell him I wouldn't be coming

next day; but at the beginning I thought it was too soon to give up, and after the third day I was too tired to say anything to anyone. I told myself I'd stick it till the end of the week and get my four-ten out of him before I told him I was never coming back.

Saturday was the worst day of all. Apart from the looks and remarks, the work itself went on for nearly twelve hours without a break, except half an hour at seven when I was supposed to have supper. I sat down in the smoky, greasy kitchen, and pushed the plate of fish and chips away and put my head down on my arms where it had been. I didn't go to sleep. I just lay there thinking over and over again, *Only five more hours. Only five more hours.* I had no other thought in my head at all. When the proprietor put his hand on my shoulder to tell me my half-hour was up, I opened my eyes and sat up suddenly. I must have been partly asleep because everything reeled and sparkled for a minute and the proprietor's face in the middle of it looked exactly like my father's.

It was after eleven when the last of them went. After the door slammed behind him there was a beautiful ringing silence. I stood in the middle of it and it was like bathing in warm milk. Then the proprietor opened the cash-register to put in the last customer's eightpence-halfpenny and I thought that breaking that silence was the best reason I'd ever had to hate him.

I walked to him, where he stood behind the counter, gloating over the overflowing cash-drawer, and said: 'While you've got that drawer open, may I have my wages, please?'

He counted out my money, less insurance, very slowly, and, it seemed to me, grudgingly. Then he passed it over to me, but when I reached to take it he drew it back. He held it where I couldn't reach it, and weighed it in his hand, smiling at me.

I could feel the scratches burning on my face and I saw him looking at them. I wanted to open my mouth and scream until I had no lungs left, to scream right into his face until just the noise made him stop smiling that fat smile. But, unbelievably, he couldn't see from my eyes how much I hated him, because he said in quite an ordinary voice, 'Ah well, I suppose you've earned it,' and he gave it to me.

As soon as it was in my hand I saw that his smile was just the smile of a fat Yorkshireman who's had a good week's business and is having a joke to celebrate. It wasn't a torturer's smile at his victim. I put the money in my pocket and walked round the end of the counter to go into the kitchen for my coat. Then I remembered I hadn't told him yet that I wasn't coming in again. I turned to him but before I could say anything he said, 'You could have thirty bob more if you'd come in tomorrow.'

'Tomorrow's Sunday,' I said stupidly.

'Well, I know you're tired. But you won't be a novelty for ever. We want to strike while iron's hot. Then you can take it easy when the rush dies down.'

There was quite a long pause and I must have started swaying on my feet because his expression changed and he said, 'Are you all right, lass? You look a bit poorly.' I suddenly shouted at him, 'You can take your thirty bob and stuff it, you bloody thick-skinned slave-driver!'

He looked at me for a second with his mouth open, and then he started to laugh. He laughed until he grew weak and had to lean on the counter and wipe his eyes. 'Ee well,' he said at last, 'Ee well, happen you're right. Happen it's a bit much to ask. Take your thirty bob and stuff it, eh? Ee, you'll do, lass, you will. See you Monday. Don't forget to turn lights out and lock door.' And he went out, chuckling and shaking his head.

I went into the back of the café and took off my overall and put my coat on. Then I looked at myself in the piece of mirror as I always did. The red had died right out of the marks: they showed, but only because they had scabs on them. The skin round them was clear and they had a healthy look. I thought it was Saturday night, and at the theatre they'd be striking the set after the last performance of this week's play. They would all be scrambling about on ladders and uncleating the flats and packing the borrowed props in boxes ready to be returned next day to their owners. The new little girl stage manager would be brewing coffee on the gas-ring in the cramped scene-dock, the ring that was used for cooking meals and heating up the foul-smelling size and boiling the kettle for tea. Throughout the work of the night, someone would keep feeding records to the panatrope.

I wondered what the actor would be doing. He hadn't been to see me in the café. I had hoped he wouldn't come, but when he didn't I had been disappointed. I hadn't seen any of the other rep people since the night I left. My landlady told me they'd got a new girl from Birmingham to replace me. During the week I'd been in the café, she'd been rehearsing Christina in *The Silver Cord*. On

Mondays she would be playing it. It was two-for-the-price-of-one on Mondays to make sure of a good first-night house; there were a lot of regulars who always came on Mondays and didn't mind about the missed lighting cues or prompts or people trying to open doors the wrong way, because they'd got in for half-price. It was always a full house on Mondays, even for a drama. I wondered if the new girl understood what a wonderful and difficult part Christina was.

I left the café, turning out the lights and locking the door. Then I walked back to my digs and asked my landlady if I could stay on. She was very pleased because not many people wanted that sort of accommodation and she hadn't found anyone else. She said I looked right fagged and that he had no business keeping me so late. She got a hot potato pie out of the warmer by the stove and dished some of it on to a plate of cold meat. I felt calm and very hungry; my landlady sat on the arm of the plush settee and chatted to me while I ate, passing me the ketchup and the bread and butter and the raisin turnovers to follow. It was very nice to be waited on for a change. She mentioned that her sister had happened to be passing the café and had popped in to see how I was getting on. She said her sister had said that I worked like she didn't know what, and that I'd make a grand waitress if only I smiled a bit more. She said I always smiled so lovely when I was taking a funny part in the plays, but that I looked so rain-faced in the café it fair put her off her poached eggs. I said I quite saw how it could. Then we both had a cup of tea and my landlady made me a hot water bottle because she said I looked shivery. She'd let me sleep in in the morning, she said; I could sleep all day if I liked. She'd bring my lunch up on a tray. I thanked her and gave her a kiss and she said she was right glad I was staying.

I slept until lunchtime the following day and went for a walk in the afternoon. When the neighbours shouted to me out of their windows to know how I was getting on in t'caff, I shouted back that I was getting on fine, and why didn't they drop in some time. That evening I went to a film and got to bed early and read for a while before going to sleep. The next day I went back to the café.

It went on being hard work, but there was never another week like the first, chiefly because I didn't mind it any more. I learned a lot, specially the week the cook was off with her sinus. I'd never cooked before beyond heating things up out of tins, but now I learned how to make batter that fried golden, and how to mix welsh rarebits with dry mustard and grill them eight at a time, and how to make an omelette such as the customers had never tasted before because I used a French recipe out of a book I borrowed from the library. From this I also learned how to make baked beans taste special by adding chopped onion and brown sugar and some garlic salt, which had to be ordered from York by our local grocer. Not everybody liked it at first, but I didn't tell them what the funny taste was, and after a bit people were coming specially, not to look at me, but to eat.

I got on very well with the proprietor. I used to think up rich new insults to make him laugh. He thought I was a proper caution, but he said I was a good worker too. The week I was doing the cooking he got worried by the unusual smells that came out of the kitchen, but when custom increased and regulars came in asking for this or that 'cooked the new way', he raised my wages to £6 and let me help with the cooking even after the cook came back. She didn't care for the arrangement much, but when she complained he told her she could like it or lump it.

I wrote to my father every week and told him what play was being put on, and I invented other things to tell him and hoped he wouldn't notice that I'd stopped sending cuttings from the local paper. I didn't read the reviews and I didn't go near the theatre.

One night the actor came into the café. He was leaving the company and going back to London, he said. There was something rotten about the feeling in the company that he couldn't stand any more. The new girl had fallen in love with Malcolm. The actor had tried to tell her it was no use, but she wouldn't believe him. The actor told me the interesting thing was that Malcolm found it disgusting that a woman should want him, and he was quite vicious to her, screaming insults one minute and sneering with sarcasm the next. The girl kept having hysterics and threatening to kill herself. The actor said the whole atmosphere was unbearable; in fact he was fed up with the theatre generally and was going to try to get a job in journalism. He asked if I was all right and I said I was. He said would I have dinner with him when I got back to town, if he had any money by then. I said I'd see. There didn't seem anything else to say and there were customers waiting, so he got up to go.

'Good-bye,' he said. 'You're not missing much. The houses are dropping off and we're doing one Aldwych farce after another.'

'I know,' I said.

He hesitated, then kissed my cheek. Not the scratched one, the other.

'What was she like as Christina?' I asked.

'Ghastly. She played her like a games mistress.'

My spirits rose suddenly and I laughed. 'Good-bye,' I said. 'Good luck. I really would like to have dinner with you.'

But I never did. By the time I got back to London, he was engaged to be married.

Chapter 2

I WAS sitting in Frank's in Fulham, sipping coffee and remembering all this, for two reasons; one I didn't admit to myself, but it was to do with the actor. The other was because Frank's reminded me of this other place. I'd stayed on there for two months, till it was time to go back to London. I could have gone three weeks earlier because the company ended its season before it had meant to. But the proprietor offered me £6 10s. a week for as long as I'd stay on. £6 10s. wasn't bad pay for a waitress in those days; for the first time in my life I was saving money. So I went on for another three weeks, laying tables, cooking the specials, carrying food and cups of tea to the tables; and I went on writing lies to my father.

When I finally left, the proprietor gave me a present of £2 which brought my savings up to £15. I was filled with confidence. I remembered coming home in the train and listening to the wheels saying 'I can do anything – I can do anything – ' Sitting with Frank's coffee fighting the cold inner emptiness, I thought of that feeling of triumph and excitement, trying to recreate it, but it was like being stone cold and trying to get warm by remembering what being warm was like. I picked up a teaspoon and let it drum on the table to the rhythm of those six-year-old wheels and whispered to myself, 'I can do anything . . . I can do anything . . .'

'Do you mind?'

Two girls in overalls at the next table turned round, twisting their mouths and rolling their eyes at each other. I stopped drumming. It wasn't doing any good anyway. But there was one thing – I could work as a waitress in a place like this, if I had to. And do it well enough so that I needn't be too ashamed of it. I wondered how much they paid waitresses now. Or perhaps it would be better to be a cook, in the kitchen where nobody would see me. I picked up the menu and saw that Frank only did sandwiches and snacks. It wasn't important. I didn't have to start worrying about a job yet. I had one that I wanted to keep for as long as I could.

I left Frank's and walked back to the house. As I walked, I thought about my job. It was a good one. I'd had it for two years. I was assistant to the public relations officer at Drummonds Hotel, which is not so big as Grosvenor House but more expensive. Because it's so small it's considered exclusive and a lot of big wheels who used to go to the Savoy and the Dorchester were now fighting for the privilege of paying a few extra guineas a day for a suite at Drummonds. My job was to arrange Press receptions for the ones who wanted publicity, and fight the Press off for those who didn't. There were a lot of sidelines to the job too, but that was most of it. It was largely a matter of keeping people happy. I had a small office to myself next to the large plushy one my boss had on the ground floor of the hotel. My salary was twelve hundred a year and expenses. There were a lot of perks, too – quite legitimate ones. And it was great fun and very interesting. Not the way acting had been, of course. But I couldn't have earned twelve hundred a year on the stage if I'd hung on for the rest of my life.

Sooner or later I'd have to tell my boss. I couldn't predict how he would feel about it. Perhaps he would make me leave at once. On the other hand, he might let me stay on until the last moment. That seemed more likely, in view of the sort of man he was; but even the most broadminded men are apt to be funny about things like this.

I wondered how long it took to be really obvious. Three months? Four? I could save quite a bit in four months, living as I was going to live. That was the reason I gave myself for choosing such a scruffy place to live in; there was another reason, but I hadn't explained that to myself yet. On the other hand, some women begin to show almost at once. I was no sylph, but I was flat across the front. As I walked, I put my hand through the slit in my trenchcoat pocket and felt my stomach. It didn't feel any different. It seemed incredible that there was the beginning of a baby in there.

I wondered, too, when you start being sick in the mornings. That would make it more difficult to keep on working. Perhaps morning sickness was a mental thing, like travel sickness. Some women went through pregnancy without being sick at all. I decided it was necessary for me to be like that. I had to keep on working as long as possible at the job in the hotel. Whatever job I got after that, it couldn't pay anything like the same money.

But then there was afterwards. I hadn't let myself think too much about that. It was hard enough to imagine how I was going to get through the next eight months. I'd thought through every minute of it when I first began to worry – before I knew for certain. I didn't sleep for five nights; just lay awake until four or five o'clock, thinking, imagining. The days weren't so bad because I had plenty to do, but the nights were very bad. Each one was worse than the one before, because at first I could tell myself it would be all right in the morning. When in the morning nothing had happened I'd tell myself it would come during the day. Then another night would arrive and it would be that much more difficult to sleep than it had been the night before, because my doubts seemed that much nearer to becoming certainties.

On the fifth night I began to think about afterwards and I panicked. I began to cry aloud and I couldn't stop myself. My father slept in the next room. Both our doors were open and as my sobs rose I knew he must hear. I knew he would come and ask what was the matter, and I knew I would tell him. It was stupid because, although I felt sure, I couldn't be completely sure, and what was the point of telling him before it was necessary? I knew how he would feel about it. But in that moment I felt as if I were alone in a trap. Nothing mattered if only I could tell someone. If only I didn't have to be alone with it.

That was how it seemed before I heard him call from his room, 'Is that you, Jane? What's the matter?' And when I didn't answer, 'What are you crying like that for?' Then I heard him getting out of bed and grunting and fumbling for his slippers and my sobs stopped. I lay without moving and felt the ice of real fear freeze the artificial panic which had made me want to tell him. I lay still, with my face in my pillow. I didn't move or breathe. I felt him standing over me. He had never hit me in his life. I wasn't afraid of him that way. I was afraid of his disgust. I would have preferred anything now, anything at all, to telling him what I had so much wanted to tell him two minutes before.

'What were you crying about?' His voice was gruff and sleepy, and sounded kind. But I lay, motionless, frozen, willing him to go back to bed.

He put his hand on my shoulder and shook me a little.

'Come on,' he said. 'If you didn't want me to come in, what did you cry so loudly for? What's the matter, lost your job?' He squeezed my shoulder with his fingers. 'Mm? Is that it?' I was trembling and he could feel it. He sat down beside me on the bed. I thought, *Let me just die* . . . I dug my face deeper into the pillow. I felt as if I were suffocating.

'Come on,' he said again. 'That damned shyster sack you? If it's that, don't worry. I've kept a roof over your head before when you were out of a job.' *Yes*, I thought, *yes, you've done that. For months on end you've kept me, and every day of those months I've been aware of it. I felt you were wondering if I had no self-respect: not that you grudged the cost exactly, but I knew you were asking yourself what sort of person could live on her father when she was over twenty-one, rather than give up calling herself an actress. Which it seemed nobody else did . . . When I'd come back from an audition you would say, 'Don't contact us, we'll contact you'– an old theatrical joke I foolishly told you once, which stopped being a joke when you had said it a few dozen times. And when at last I gave in and started going to secretarial school, do you think I wasn't conscious all the time that this was the second career you'd paid to train me for? The day I took my first secretarial job you told me I'd never stick it, that any girl who could be content to sit behind a typewriter all day must be a cretin . . . What do you want of me, Father?* I thought fiercely. *What have you ever wanted?*

Not this, anyway. Not a scandal, not a bastard grandchild. This won't go far to make up for my shortcomings, like not being a son and like killing my mother by getting born.

I turned on my back and looked up at my father through the half-darkness. His big square head with the strong hair sprouting unbrushed above his forehead was outlined against my window. His ears were big and stood out. Mine do that too. I have to wear my hair in a special way to hide them. I thought if my baby had ears like that I would stick them back while it was little and malleable. My father could have saved me a lot of misery if he'd done that with mine, but he hadn't bothered because he'd lost his chance of having a son. I had a sudden feeling about my baby, not just as something terrible that was going to happen to me, but as a potential person with feelings of its own. It was the ears that made me think of it – lying there looking at the silhouette of my father's big ugly ears.

'Well?'

He wasn't sleepy any more, and his voice was more querulous than kind. I lay on my back and said clearly, 'No, I haven't lost my job, Father.' *I know you keep expecting me to lose it because it's such a much better one than you ever thought I'd get, but the fact is that I'm good at it and I don't think I'll ever lose it through inefficiency.*

But I only said the first sentence aloud. That was how it always was when I talked to my father.

'Then what was all the noise about?'

It occurred to me he was disappointed with my answer. It always galled him, I believed, in some subtle way when I actually succeeded in anything. It gave me an odd sense of advantage to be reminded of this.

'I'm unhappy about something. It's something private.'

'Not so private you'd be bothered to get up and close your door before you wake me up with your weeping,' he said. He stood up and pulled his dressing-gown round him. 'You seem to forget that my job lacks the advantage of frequent mornings in bed.' He said that because sometimes I work over the week-ends when someone important arrives at the hotel, and I'm given mornings off in lieu. My father has been at work at nine o'clock every week-day morning for thirty-two years. He's a civil servant. The only time he stayed away from work was when my mother died. Even then he worked on the day of the funeral, in the afternoon; he went straight from the crematorium to his office. He told me that himself; he was very proud of it, for some reason.

So the moment was put off. I fell asleep with a sense of overpowering relief; but it was gone in the morning.

I decided I must go and see a doctor. I was still only five days overdue, but I couldn't wait any longer. I'd never been ill in my life, so I hadn't got a regular doctor. There was a man whose name I had heard; I couldn't remember in what connexion, but it stuck in my mind because it was the same as mine, Graham. I looked him up in the phone book and was relieved to find his surgery was in Wimpole Street. I didn't know why I should feel relieved about that. Perhaps there was something about the way I'd heard of him in the first place, which I didn't actually remember, but which made me suspect there was something wrong about him. But if he practised in Wimpole Street, I thought, he must be all right.

I rang him up. His secretary, or perhaps it was his wife, answered the phone and when I said I wanted to come at lunch-time I could hear the superior smile in her voice.

'The doctor can't make any new appointments for three weeks,' she said. I knew it would be better to wait three weeks, then he could tell me at once; but I couldn't wait three more days. I had to know, so that I could start thinking properly and stop praying for something that wasn't going to happen. I said, 'Please, it's very urgent.'

The woman said, 'Are you at work?' and when I said yes, she said, 'It can't be as urgent as all that, then, can it?' I felt myself begin to loathe her unreasonably. I thought, *He's not the only doctor in London. I'll find one who isn't so busy, and who hasn't got a wife like this.* I said, 'All right then, never mind,' and was surprised that my voice sounded so strange, as if I were crying.

I was just going to hang up when the woman said, in a completely different voice: 'Just a moment. Are you married?'

'No.'

There was a pause, and then she said, almost affectionately, 'Why not pop along at about one-fifteen? I expect the doctor could squeeze you in.'

I got there at one. It was a tall, sober house with black double doors and brass name-plates, the names worn illegible with polishing. A smart white-haired woman let me in, and showed me into the waiting-room. It had a high ceiling and deep leather chairs; there was a big round table in the middle of a red Persian carpet, covered with magazines, the society type, neatly stacked. On the Adam mantelpiece was a single tasteful ornament, reflected austerely in a huge mirror. My eyes kept going back to the mirror. It was wrong in that room with its elaborate gilt frame and fat-bellied cupids. It was more the sort of thing you'd expect to find in a brothel.

I sat on the arm of one of the leather chairs. I almost never smoke, but now suddenly I wished I had a cigarette. I was very nervous, wondering what to say to the doctor. I hadn't really worked it out, and now it was too late to. I couldn't even think of a false name. All the names there are in the world, and the only one

I could think of was my own. I tried to concentrate, but my mind wouldn't work properly. I was terribly nervous. I was even sweating a little. That made me think that he would want to examine me. I hadn't thought of any of that. I stood up suddenly and almost ran to the door; but it opened in my face, and the white-haired woman stood there smiling.

'What name?' she asked pleasantly.

'Jane Graham.'

'How odd – the doctor's name is John Graham.'

'Yes,' I said, 'I know.'

She led me up the curved staircase and knocked on a white door. Everything was carpeted into silence. Even her knock hardly made a sound. There was a faint, unpleasant smell of hospitals. I was very frightened.

The doctor was very ordinary-looking, like a stage doctor. Small and comfortable, rather bald, with pudgy hands. He was sitting behind his desk making out a prescription. The woman smilingly showed me into a chair and went out. The doctor said, 'Won't – be – a – minute – ' in a slow voice, and went on writing. His fountain pen was gold and he had a big gold signet ring on his little finger with a moonstone set in it. The leather on his desk – the blotter corners, the ink-stand, the appointments book – were all green Florentine leather. There was a gold cigarette box.

I looked at the doctor. His bald patch gleamed domestically. The signet ring gleamed too, on his little fat hand. I hadn't seen his face, and I couldn't understand why I didn't like him.

At last he finished writing and put the cap on his pen. He looked up, already smiling. He was pink and jolly-looking, with small eyes behind glasses.

'You haven't been to see me before, have you, Miss – er – '

'Graham. No.'

'Graham? Really? Fancy that – no relation, I suppose?' His smile spread into a laugh, but my face felt frozen. 'Well, now. You look healthy enough. What seems to be the trouble?'

'My period's late.'

'How late?'

'Five days.'

He smiled again. 'Well, you know, that's nothing. Nothing at all. Are you usually regular?'

'Yes, I think so, fairly.'

'Five days, you know – it doesn't have to mean anything's wrong with you. Could be caused by anything – change of air – change of diet – emotional upset – cold in the head . . .' He was watching me closely; at least I felt he was. With the light on his glasses I couldn't really tell. But I felt he was trying to drive me out into the open.

I said nothing. His smile was as steady as ever.

'Unless, of course,' he said, in the same cosy voice, 'you've got any reason to worry . . . ?'

I wanted to shout at him that of course I had reason to worry, or what would I be doing here? Instead I said awkwardly, 'Yes,' praying he would understand, or rather stop pretending not to understand.

He took off his glasses and wiped them, exactly like an actor playing a doctor, and said, 'Oh dear oh dear oh dear.' Then he looked up at me reproachfully. I stared back at him, feeling suddenly angry. I hadn't come to him to be looked at like that. He wasn't my father, it was nothing to him. But I couldn't think of any stinging words to say; I just sat there, feeling angry and humiliated. I thought he was trying to make me drop my eyes, and I wouldn't. I was ashamed to my very soul, but I was damned if I was going to let him see it. I stared back at him and finally he sighed heavily and put his glasses on again.

'When did it happen?'

'On the twenty-third of last month.'

'And you were due five days ago? My dear child – !' He leaned forward, wearing a tolerant smile now. 'Don't you know anything about your own body? Don't you know you could not have picked a worse day – or rather, night?'

I felt a wave of disgust, as if he'd made a dirty joke about it.

'Took no precautions at all, I suppose?'

'No.'

'Oh dear me no. "It couldn't happen to me"– that's what they all think. "Don't let's bother with all that nasty nonsense – it would spoil the wonder of it all." ' He twitched one eyebrow and slumped back disdainfully.

'I didn't think anything of the sort!'

'I'm not deaf, Miss Graham, so please don't shout.' He ran his fingers along the shaft of his fountain pen, watching me. I looked at his banana fingers and dreaded the moment when he would tell me to undress.

'Well now,' he said, his voice abruptly cheerful and cosy again. 'What's the young man – the proud father-to-be – going to do about this, eh?'

It was like watching a film in which there is suddenly a large, clumsy cut, and you're left not knowing what has been missed out, not quite understanding what's happening now. I said bewilderedly, 'What's that got to do with it?'

The doctor said blandly, 'Well, it's a not unimportant aspect of the situation, is it?'

I said, 'I don't see that it's an aspect which concerns you.'

He swayed forward sharply and landed with his elbows halfway across the desk. There was no smile now, and he held the gold pen pointed at me like a pistol.

'Now let's just get ourselves tidied up about this,' he said hardly. 'You've come to me for help. There's no need to be on the defensive. You're not the first, and you won't be the last. But you must clearly understand that it's not as simple as buying a pound of sugar. I have my own position to protect.'

I couldn't understand what he was talking about. I shook my head, and then, when he stiffened angrily, I quickly nodded instead, hoping vaguely that that would please him. It seemed to, because he lowered the pen and sank back again, his face softening. 'You really must trust me,' he said. 'I'm not just a nosy old man, you know. If the young man could be persuaded to marry you, obviously that would be a better solution, wouldn't it?'

I wanted to ask, better than what? Instead I said, 'There's no question of that.'

'He's married already?'

'It isn't that.' I couldn't go on talking about it. 'Please. All I want to know is if I'm going to have a baby.'

He smiled patiently. 'I think we can take that as read,' he said. He looked at me dreamily for a moment, and then abruptly became brisk and businesslike. 'Now then,' he said, 'don't look so worried. It's not as bad as all that, you know. When have you got a free afternoon?'

I frowned, trying to follow. 'On Wednesday . . .'

'That might do. You'll have to see my colleague, and he's rather busy.' He picked up his telephone and spoke a number, smiling at me all the time while the light flashed on and off his glasses like a danger signal. He spoke briskly to somebody, making an appointment for me for Wednesday afternoon. He was still smiling as he hung up.

'Why do I have to go to another doctor?'

'Because that's the only way these things can be arranged. My colleague will countersign a certificate to say you're psychologically unfit to have the child. After that's done, I'll arrange for you to go into my clinic for the operation. You'll be home again as good as new in a couple of hours, but it's just as well to stay in bed for a day or so if you can. Most girls choose Saturdays, but if you could make it a week-day I'd be grateful, because the week-ends are such a rush.'

I sat quite still, looking at the green Florentine leather on the gold-topped inkwell. I'd seen such things for sale in Bond Street. They were very expensive. All the tooling was hand-done, and the gold for it was real.

The doctor was still talking. 'I hope you won't think it indelicate of me to mention the fee at this stage. Whoever told you to come to me probably warned you that the charge is high – in the nature of things, it has to be. You'd be asked the same sort of price by some back-street merchant in Paddington, and he hasn't any of my overheads. And at least I can promise you the thing will be done conclusively and under conditions of hygiene . . .'

I was watching him now, really looking at him carefully. He was so clean and bland and well-fed. Outside, beyond the lace curtains, I could hear the genteel traffic purring along Wimpole Street. It seemed impossible, and yet it was real, it was actually happening.

'How much is the fee?' I asked. I was suddenly so interested I could hardly wait to know.

Dr Graham took off his glasses again and looked at me with his small short-sighted eyes.

'A hundred guineas,' he said.

Then he took out a cream silk handkerchief to polish the lenses. I could see his monogram on the corner, J.G., the same initials as mine.

I stood up and the room rocked for a moment. I felt a bubble of nausea come up into my throat. I closed my eyes, and swallowed, and felt better. I picked up my coat which was over the back of the chair.

'Where are you going?' the doctor asked sharply.

I held on to the back of the chair and looked at him. There was so much to say that I couldn't find words for any of it.

'Well now, look here,' he said in an altered voice. 'I can quite see it might be difficult for you to get hold of a lump-sum like that, especially if you can't turn to the man for help. I'm always so afraid of what you silly little girls will rush off and do to yourselves . . . You must realize I have certain basic costs to meet, but in the special circumstances I can waive my own fee, and my colleague would do the same, I'm sure. Let's say sixty guineas all-in. There, what could be fairer than that?'

My mind was suddenly as cold and clear as ice-water. I said, 'One thing could be.'

'What's that?'

'You could make some effort to find out whether I'm really pregnant before you charge me sixty guineas for an operation that might not even be necessary.'

His face didn't change, but his hands paused about the business of polishing his lenses.

'You might even stop to ask me if I want to get rid of my baby, if there is a baby.' I clutched the back of the chair with both hands. I could feel a fever of shaking beginning in my wrists and knees.

'But I suppose when all those guineas are at stake, nothing else seems very important.'

My indignation burned me like a purifying fire. I stared at the doctor with triumph. My accusation, I thought, was magnificent, unanswerable. I forgot my own guilt in the enormity of his.

He put his glasses back on slowly and tucked his handkerchief away in his breast pocket. Then he leaned on his elbows and looked up at me.

'You want to have your baby?' he asked curiously.

'I wouldn't have chosen to have one this way. But if it's happened, yes, I want it. Anything's better than your cheating way out.'

He looked at the snowy blotter between his elbows.

'Don't, please, misunderstand what I'm going to say. I'm not trying to persuade you to change your mind. In fact, I couldn't have you in my clinic after what you've just said – the risk would be too great. But I wonder how much thought you've given to the child. A lot of the women who come to me aren't just panic-stricken cowards trying to escape their just deserts, you know. They have the sense to realize they're incapable of being mother *and* father, breadwinner *and* nursemaid, all at once. A lot of them have thought what the alternative means, of handing the child over to strangers who may or may not love it. And don't make the mistake of imagining the word bastard doesn't carry a sting any more. There aren't many illegitimate children in this world who haven't, some time or other, thought unkindly of their mothers.'

'How many of them do you suppose honestly wish they'd never been born?'

He looked at me for a long time, and then shrugged. He seemed tired, suddenly: 'I don't know,' he said. 'Life is precious, once you have the realization of it; even the vilest sort of existence can seem better than nothing. But I think a woman, when she finds she's going to bring a human being into the world, has the right to judge in advance.'

'Well, I don't. That's sheer sophistry. Those women are rationalizing their own fear. They're judging for themselves, not for the child.'

'Possibly, in some cases. It's not for me to say.'

'Yours not to reason why, yours but to do – and collect a hundred guineas.'

He smiled wryly. 'There really are overheads involved in doing the thing properly, you know,' he said without anger. 'For me, too, it's a question of considering the alternatives. If there weren't men like me to come to, I wonder how many more deaths there would be following abortions . . .'

'That's a rationalization, too.'

'Tell me something,' said the doctor gently. 'How did you rationalize your acts of fornication?'

'There was only one,' I said.

I sat down again on the chair because my knees wouldn't hold me any longer. My coat slipped off my arm on to the floor. Without warning the tears came, and ran down my face in streams. I couldn't stop them. There was a great weakness in my whole body; nothing seemed to matter except the enormous sadness of the fact that one raw, mismanaged, unhappy night could result in this, this misery, this huge frightening vista opening in front of me, this mountain of responsibility. That so little – a wrong decision, and two inept, unsatisfactory performances of the sexual act, which gave so little pleasure – could result in a changed world. As I wept I wondered, foolishly and pointlessly, which of the acts had conceived the child – the first with its bungling and pain and apologies, or the second with its cold frantic struggle to achieve or give the pleasure which might have begun to justify either of them . . .

I felt the doctor's banana hands on my shoulders, and the cream silk handkerchief was put into my hand. 'Don't get so upset,' he said. 'I know it seems bad now, and unfair and all the rest of it, and there'll be moments when you'll wish you'd done what I thought you'd come here for, but there are compensations too. How old are you – twenty-six, twenty-seven? It's time you had a baby. You're old enough to appreciate it. If you've got the courage to enjoy some of it, it'll do you good.'

When I stopped crying he gave me a drink of sherry and some addresses. It was all suddenly matter-of-fact again, as if he were an employment agency giving me addresses of jobs, but actually they were for an ante-natal clinic, the Society for Unmarried Mothers, and a general practitioner in Hammersmith. He told me the names of books to get out of the library. I wrote everything down carefully on a sheet of paper he gave me. It had his name and degrees printed at the top in small, discreet lettering. When I offered to pay him he wouldn't accept anything. I came away feeling that we had had a battle, and that he'd won.

That had been four days ago. A lot had happened since. I'd been to the general practitioner, a tall, bluff man called Maxwell, and been given a special test which had cost a surprising amount of money because the doctor said it was unnecessary – I only had to wait a few weeks and he could tell without it. But I had to be sure. And after it, I was.

Then there was no point in putting off telling my father.

When I know something terrible is inevitable, I don't want to go on putting it off, I want to precipitate it, because thinking about it and dreading it seems so much worse than the thing itself could possibly be. So it wasn't courage that made me go straight to my father's office from the doctor's without even waiting for him to come home. I wanted to get it over, to get started on the changed world. As I sat waiting for the woman to tell him I was there, I felt a bit the way I felt before I went to my first bull-fight.

I didn't want to see the bull killed; I just wanted to know what it would do to me to see it.

I hated going to my father's office at any time. I didn't go often, although he was always suggesting I drop in. Often I felt dislike for my father, but never more than in his office. It was a very ordinary, dull one in a block in Shepherd's Bush, something to do with death duties; the usual thing, long lino'd corridors with thick ageless girls in grey flannel skirts and cardigans walking along them, and doors leading into outer offices with names scratchily painted in black on their pimply glass panels. The outer offices were too small to turn round in and littered with very tattered copies of government handouts. And the inner offices, which led in and out of one another like a rabbit warren, weren't much better.

My father often said he didn't know where all my 'acting nonsense' came from. If he could have seen himself putting on his head-of-an-industrial-empire act in that shabby, poky office, he'd have known it came straight from him. The way he glanced up from his work, looked at me for a second as if trying to place me, then slowly let a tired smile play round his lips – it was a perfect performance of the weary tycoon smiling tolerantly at the carefree daughter who knows no better than to interrupt his Atlasian labours.

'Well dear, what is it? I'm very, very busy, as you can see.' He spread his hands to indicate his desk, cluttered with unimportant-looking papers. 'The new Bill means a complete reshuffle . . . I sometimes wonder if H.M.G. dreams them up specially so none of its servants can ever be accused of wasting public money by having a minute to themselves . . .' He droned on like that for a few moments. I sat quite still with my hands folded. In some strange way I was almost looking forward to telling him now. I was glad I'd decided to do it at his office. I wasn't afraid of him here. I saw him here, not as my father, perpetually demanding strengths and achievements of me, but as a supremely unimportant cog trying to pretend it was the whole dull wheel.

At last he stopped talking about his problems and turned to me again. 'Would you like a cup of something?'

'No, Father, thank you. I've got something to tell you.'

'Yes, well, so I imagined. It's not your habit to pop in and visit me, exactly, is it? Still, you're always welcome, you know that, I hope.' He spread his hands out, palms down, and shifted the papers on his desk with swimming motions. He couldn't relax. I never could either, until I had to learn to for the stage. It struck me now as ironic that he, with nothing to worry about, yet, was twitching and fidgeting nervously while I was able to sit perfectly still, waiting, like a schoolteacher, for undivided attention.

At last he gave it to me, by taking off his glasses – an infallible sign that he was going to listen because he couldn't see to work without them.

'Well, come on,' he said jovially, 'out with it.' From the joviality I could tell he knew it was something fairly serious.

I had meant to tell him straight out, but when it came to the point I found I had to hedge a little. And the way I hedged surprised me. It may have had something to do with the blind way he turned his eyes to me when he'd taken off his glasses. He had a sudden look of helplessness which defeated my intention not to spare him.

'What's the worst thing I could do to you, Father?'

For a long moment he sat absolutely still, with those naked-looking eyes fixed on me frowningly as if peering through a mist. I didn't expect a direct answer; I expected some jocular evasion. But suddenly he said decisively:

'Take to drink.'

I almost laughed. I don't know why; perhaps it was partly relief.

'Well, it isn't that.'

'No? Oh, good!' He smiled indulgently.

'Don't smile, Father. I think you'll think what I've got to tell you is just as bad, or worse.' He kept on smiling, though, almost patronizingly, as if to say he was sure it couldn't be as bad as all that. I didn't regard this as a compliment to me. It was just that he thought me as incapable of excesses, admirable or otherwise, as himself.

'I'm pregnant,' I said.

Those two words shocked even me with their crudeness. I instantly wished I'd said the softer 'I'm going to have a baby', or even something fatuous and euphemistic. The blunt statement of the biological fact had the same after-echoes as a slap across his face, a thing I'd abruptly lost all desire to give him, even figuratively.

Numbly I watched the tolerant smile slip off his face as his cheek-muscles sagged. I waited almost impatiently for them to stiffen again in anger and outrage. They didn't, and the tableau seemed to be held and held until I could feel my eyelids beginning to smart from being held rigidly open. At last, with a huge effort, I made myself move, and choked out, 'Do say something, for God's sake!' My voice held all the anger I'd expected in his face.

But he still didn't speak. He just kept numbly staring. It was as if he'd just had a bullet in the stomach and knew it was going to start hurting like hell at any minute. Finally he blinked rather stupidly and rubbed his eyes as if he'd been asleep. 'I can't seem to take it in,' he mumbled. Then he put his elbows on the desk and covered his face with his hands like a tired old man.

Suddenly I was appalled. At one stroke I had punished him for all the nameless agonies he had put me through, and I regretted it. I regretted it so deeply that in that moment I felt this was the worst part of the whole thing. Looking at the dark, disordered top of his head, with the sturdy blunt fingers pressed into the hair, I thought that all the rest of my life would be easy, compared to seeing this.

Chapter 3

WELL, that had been at noon. When he'd recovered a little, he'd turned to me with a sort of shaky, fumbling anger and told me to clear out of his house, that I was no better than a street-woman; and I'd been glad, because I couldn't have stood it if he'd turned round and been sympathetic and helpful.

Walking back now to the house in Fulham, I let myself wonder why I'd instinctively chosen an ugly, degraded district in which to find myself a room. There was the practical aspect of cheapness; I'd never been any good at saving money and the need to do so now was acute. But there was something more to it than that. In some obscure way I wanted to punish myself, I wanted to put myself in the setting that seemed proper to my situation. It was odd that I wouldn't have felt the backstreets of Fulham to be the most fitting place for me before what had happened in Father's office.

It was raining properly now, with a spiteful drubbing persistence. My hair clung to my head and the water ran down my sleeves and hands and made little puddles in the pockets of my trenchcoat, transforming the dust there to a consistency like the sediment at the bottom of a bottle of cheap wine. A bottle of cheap wine suddenly seemed like a good idea. Half-way back along the sloppy grey streets I turned into an off-licence and bought some port-type, that sickly, syrupy muck that you can get three bottles of and have change from a pound. I'm no connoisseur of wines, but I know what's bad. I chose this not only because it was cheap but because I could get an effect from it without enjoying it. The way I was feeling, it would be quite dangerous to buy liquor I might enjoy drinking.

It was nearly dark when I reached the house. I let myself in and felt my way along the passage, bumping my hip against the hall table as I groped for the banister. I swore viciously at the table; I swore again as I tripped over the bottom step of the staircase.

'Why not switch on the light, instead of using words which have no possible application to a static object?'

'I didn't know there was a light,' I said sullenly.

It came on. It wasn't much of a light, a 40-watt bulb dangling nakedly from the hall ceiling, but it was enough to show me the table, the stairs and the man who'd spoken to me.

He was small and dark and thin like a fledgling blackbird. He had maroon-coloured shadows round his eyes and didn't look very clean.

'The switch is just here, inside the door,' he said. 'You have to run like hell to the next landing before it goes out.'

'Thanks,' I said, turning to go.

He followed me up and showed me where the next switch was. I thanked him again, rather shortly. I wasn't sure whether the faint sour smell was the house or him.

'Where's your billet?'

'Right at the top.'

'Front or back?'

'Front.'

'Oh. Oh of course, it would be. I've never been in there.' He was lounging against the wall at the first landing, one foot on the next flight of stairs. 'Know who had it before you?'

'No.' I didn't care either, and didn't pretend to, but that didn't stop him.

'An old girl called Mrs Williams. Decayed gentry. Well, no, not gentry really, sort of next drawer down. Originally. Needless to say she wasn't even bottom drawer when she was here – she'd fallen through the whole lot on to the floor, poor old duck. None of us ever quite knew what she was living on, I mean for food and so on – she never paid any rent. I gathered she'd done something for Doris once, so she had that room as a sort of grace-and-favour.'

'Who's Doris? The landlady?'

'She's no lady, ma'am, land or otherwise.' I noticed he'd dropped his voice. 'I don't know what it was she owed Mrs W., she must have bailed her out of jail or something once, because I can't imagine anything else that would make her waive the –'

There was a faint pop, and the light went out, plunging us into irritating blackness. Immediately the sour smell seemed stronger. It was partly stale cooking, I realized, as well as mustiness and dirt. I didn't think it could be coming from the young man, after all.

He pressed the switch again and reappeared. 'Look, can I come and look at that room? I've often wondered what it was like – the old girl used to behave as if it was full of heads she'd shrunk.'

'It's just an ordinary room.' I started up the next flight, pushing past him. He followed, taking what I'd intended to be a refusal as an invitation. I felt uneasy but too tired to do anything about it.

'My name's Toby Coleman,' he said. I privately thought it was probably Cohen and chalked it up against him that he should have changed it. I felt annoyed at this intrusion. I didn't want to meet or get on any sort of friendly footing with any of the other people in the house. I wanted to bury myself in this alien world; I'd chosen it with the vague idea that here nobody would bother me or interfere with me; coming from such a different life I had had some dim snobbish feeling that I and the other inhabitants of this house would scarcely speak the same language, and that they would all remain unknown to me except as closed doors to pass, or occasional footsteps or voices through walls, or names on envelopes on the hall table. I hadn't thought of them in terms of faces and curious eyes and minds beset by their own problems and driven by the inane need to communicate.

We climbed to the top. It was only the third time I'd done the climb, and the first time I'd stopped to think how it would be to do it six months from now. We were both panting as I unlocked the scabrous door and switched on another 40-watt dangling bulb.

I hadn't seen the room at night before. It was infinitely depressing. The bulb threw a mean, chilly light on the shoddy, shabby furniture and by its plentiful shadows increased the day-time impression of dirty walls and dark, unloved corners.

Toby Coleman went ahead of me and stood with his hands in his pockets, looking round. 'Gawd,' he said, 'it's bloody well worse than mine.'

This was exactly what I'd wanted to avoid, though I didn't realize it clearly until then. It was all right so long as nobody else saw it, or saw me in it. As soon as this damn boy walked into it and started passing opinions, I felt instantly ashamed, and to my fury I heard myself saying defensively:

'Well, I only moved in two hours ago. I haven't fixed it up yet.' I had had no intention of fixing it up; I remembered how I'd even decided not to bother cleaning the window. I glared at Toby angrily, but he was impervious.

'Well, I don't know what even the Editor of *Homes and Gardens* could make of a dump like this, but jolly good luck to you. I say, is that a bottle of wine? You couldn't spare a glass, could you? I'll pay you back. I haven't even any coffee left and it's too damn' wet to go out.'

'Look,' I said, 'don't think me rude or anything, but I want to be by myself.'

'Oh hell, do you?' He sounded genuinely disappointed. 'What, the whole evening? Couldn't I come back later?'

'Is it the drink you want, or just company?'

'Well, neither really. Or you could say both. You see, I write. I mean, I'm a writer. Have you ever tried to write? It's the most bloody business. Any excuse is good enough to get away from the typewriter.' He settled down with a look of cosy permanence in the arm-chair. 'Did you ever hear the story about the man who was commissioned to do a piece for the *Saturday Evening Post*? I don't know why it was the *S.E.P.* except that they pay so well, and this chap was as broke as the rest of us. Well, he needed the money, he wanted to do the piece, he had a deadline to meet, but he kept putting it off. Any excuse not to get started. He missed two deadlines, and the third and last was set for 1 January. On the last night of December the Editor rang him up and said was it ready? No, not quite, said this character, he was just going to start it but first he had to clean his tennis shoes.' He stared at me solemnly. 'My God, I understand that bloke! If I had any tennis shoes, I'd probably be cleaning them this minute instead of talking to you when you obviously wish me in hell.'

He picked up the bottle and looked at the light through it.

His face was very thin and quite plain, with its big, beaky nose and starveling eyes, but it was an interesting face. I found myself studying it against my will.

'If you won't share your wine with me, which you've every right not to do of course, do you know what I'll do? I shall go down to my room and sit at my table for five minutes, getting maybe three sentences typed before convincing myself that my need for coffee is strong enough to drive me out into the rain. That'll take half an hour and on the way back I'll detour past a cinema which will be showing some piece of rubbish that I've no real wish to see, but I'll tell myself that I've got to study every market, and in I'll go. On the way home I'll have such a dry throat from guilt at wasting the evening that I'll nip into a pub for a beer. Then when I get chucked out of there it'll be after eleven, and Doris won't let me type beyond half past so it won't be worth starting . . .' He smiled at me with his head on one side. It was a funny, wry smile. 'That's actually how I make my living. So now you don't have to ask me why I'm living in this bug-house, you should pardon the expression. It doesn't explain why you are.'

I felt myself growing angrier and angrier while he was talking. I didn't want to know. I didn't want to listen. I knew very well if he went on talking like that much longer I should get interested in him, I might even get to like him, with his funny alert face and absurd, useless fund of self-knowledge. He wasn't even the sort of person you could enjoy being rude to. But, I thought, if I'm thoroughly unfriendly and unpleasant right from the start, not only to him but to any of the others who might try to turn themselves from anonymities into individuals for my benefit, then they'll leave me alone and I can start being whatever this business is going to turn me into.

'I'm sorry,' I said curtly. 'It's none of your affair why I've come here, and it's none of mine what you do with your time. So long as you don't use it to waste mine.' It's funny how, when you really want to say something bitchy and cutting to someone who's been bitchy to you, you can't think of anything till afterwards. When there's no real call for it, you come suddenly out with a piece of 9-carat bitchery that shakes even you.

He looked at me for a minute and his eyebrows went up. Then he remarked, in his very nice cultured accent, 'Okay, bugger you mate,' but without any particular malice, and went out, leaving the door open. I could hear him thudding down the stairs and a door closed on the landing below.

I was left in the solitude I'd so pointedly asked for, in the middle of the room that I had no intention of fixing up.

I closed the door and stood with my back to it, looking. Now that other eyes had seen it and identified it as mine, I couldn't regard the room with the same calculated indifference as before, when I'd deliberately refused to notice any of its squalor or inconveniences. There were two rooms under the sloping roof, which had once been one biggish square one. It had been divided by the simple process of putting up two partitional walls set at right-angles. This resulted in a small square room and a small L-shaped room along two sides of it, which was mine. The square room which had been stolen, as it were, from the main area, had a little window up near the ceiling in the short partition. The partitions didn't look very thick. I leaned over and knocked on the nearest one, to test it, and immediately someone on the other side knocked back.

I snatched my knuckles away as if the wall had been red hot. But I'd found out what I wanted to know. The partitions were somewhat thicker than ordinary hardboard.

Feeling my sense of security dwindling, I instinctively bolted my door. Then I continued my examination.

I couldn't see the whole room from where I stood at the end of the short arm of the L. This was as narrow as a corridor. One wall – the partition – was bare; along the other ran some rudimentary cooking facilities, consisting of a wash-basin-cum-sink with a tin draining-board and a small cupboard with a top just large enough to hold a gas-stove, about a foot square, with a grill and two small elements. Under the window, with its dirty-looking brown curtains, was a small kitchen table scarred with ancient cigarette burns.

Moving to the elbow of the room, I considered the longer, wider arm of the L. It contained a camp bed covered with the remains of a wartime afghan, made up of lopsided squares, ill-knitted from scraps of clashing wool and full of dropped stitches; there was the chest of drawers, leaning drunkenly over its missing leg; a kitchen chair and an arm-chair with the thin brown cloth of its seat rent by the hernial pressure of escaping springs and the arms worn shiny by many grimy hands. There was also a small gas-fire beneath the mantelpiece, on which stood a pair of hideous plaster Alsatians standing guard each side of an embroidered picture of a crinoline lady in a cottage garden. The walls were covered with the regulation nicotine-coloured paper splashed with dead flowers, peeling in many places. The floor was lino'd; it looked as if it had had football played on it in cleated boots. There was a Hallowe'en coloured rag rug in front of the fire. Lying on this was a metal ashtray, which had evidently slipped off the chest of drawers. I picked it up. It had CINZANO printed across it in patriotic colours. I looked round for a waste-paper basket to throw it into, but of course there wasn't one.

I put it between the grinning Alsatians, and turned my back to them to survey the room from the opposite direction. The outlook was equally uninspiring. From here I could see the miniature stove head-on; its rusty gas-taps snarled at me like bared teeth. In a small fly-spotted mirror over the sink I could see my own face; not a pretty sight at present.

I felt a wave of depression swell round me suffocatingly, and hastily tore the paper off the bottle of port-type. I tried to open the drawer in the table, which I supposed held cutlery and other utensils including a corkscrew; it stuck, and I was cursing freely by the time it jerked open. Inside were two bent forks, a tin-handled table knife and a bread knife, one ordinary spoon and two teaspoons almost black with age and egg, a fish-slice with a burnt handle, and one of those cutters that enables you to make wavy chips. That appeared at first to be all, though later I did find two knitting-needles of different gauges, a rusty skewer, two corks and an empty thermometer case right at the back.

I wanted a drink so badly that I was quite prepared to rush downstairs to Doris and demand a corkscrew, with menaces. Then I stopped to consider that there were probably other, more important battles to be fought over more essential items Doris would prove not to have provided; a cursory glance into the china cupboard revealed a very sparse and motley collection. In the meantime I had the wine but not the means to get at it, which seemed an intolerable situation.

I sat down on the bed, which, like all its kind, had a hard wooden rim backed up by a deep sag. I would have to borrow a corkscrew from someone, and the only possible person would be Toby. It seemed very humiliating, but there it was.

Just as I was wondering if I could possibly face it, the knocking which had answered mine on the partition started again. I sat frozen, staring at the wall, half-expecting someone to burst through it like a circus lion through a paper hoop. There were three knocks, then an expectant pause, then three more knocks. I didn't move. After a moment, the knocks were repeated, but this time on the other wall of the partition.

Drawn irresistibly, I moved round the angle. I felt a shiver of nervousness as the clear, hollow sound emphasized the thinness of the barrier. Suddenly the knocking changed. It was on glass this time, near the ceiling. I looked up and saw, in the little window, a huge black face.

I gasped with fright and ran back round the angle again where I couldn't be seen. I felt my heart slamming and caught sight of my own face in the mirror, as deathly white as the other had been black. I blundered about for a few seconds in a blind panic, then my knees buckled and I flopped on to the cold lino by the bed with a thump. I caught up handfuls of the friendly afghan and hung on to them with my eyes screwed shut.

After a little while I opened them and listened. Apart from my heart, which was still making a distinctly audible noise, there had been no more knocking; I took a deep breath and forced myself to relax. After all, why in God's name should a black face be more alarming than a white one? So, I was next door to a negro. I should have expected something like that from what the old newsagent had said. I didn't know what atavistic terror had caused me to behave so stupidly; I felt very silly, crouched there on my knees, and I told myself to get up and stop being an idiot. At that moment there was a knock on the door.

Once again I froze into paralysed stillness. Then I forced myself to call out 'Who's that?' My voice was a croak, and I held the afghan like a talisman.

'It's me, Toby.'

I scrambled to my feet and went to the door unsteadily, edging along the wall beneath the little window. I slipped back the bolt and let Toby in, bolting it again after him.

'What's the idea of that? Frightened of burglars? They'd never make it up all those stairs.'

Ignoring this, I said, 'What made you come up?'

'I thought I heard you knock on the floor.'

I remembered the thump my knees made as I fell on them, and shook my head. 'Oh,' he said. 'Sorry, I thought you wanted something.' He started to go.

'As a matter of fact, I did, I mean I do,' I said, and found I'd caught hold of his arm to stop him leaving. 'I haven't got a corkscrew,' I finished lamely.

He grinned. 'Doris's methods of distribution are a bit eccentric,' he said. 'I've got three. I'll give you one. You haven't by any chance been given two bread knives? No? I just wondered. I'll pop down and get the corkscrew. Be right back.' He hurried away, leaving the door open. I quickly closed it and stood against it until I heard Toby returning.

He opened the bottle while I looked for glasses. I found one big tumbler with 'Stella Artois' across it in gold, and a bakelite toothmug. Both looked filthy and I tried to turn on the Ascot to wash them in hot water, but although the pilot was alight nothing further happened when I turned on the tap.

'It's the diaphragm, I expect,' Toby said philosophically. 'Perished. Mine's been like that for weeks. I keep meaning to ask Doris about it – not that she'd do anything. You're lucky to have running water at all, Mavis hasn't.'

The words *Who's Mavis* trembled on my tongue and were forced back.

'I haven't found a kettle yet,' I said instead.

'That seems odd, even for Doris; she's a tea-maniac. Oh wait a minute. I remember she burnt the bottom out of hers recently – she probably pinched the one from here to replace it rather than shell out for a new one. She's a mean old cow,' he added without rancour.

'What would happen if I asked her for one?'

'Bugger-all, I should think, judging by my own results. Since I got here I've had to buy – ' ticking them off on his fingers – 'cup and saucer, hers being so cracked they fell to pieces, a dish-towel, a coffee-pot, a cruet (I pinched that from the ABC actually), a shaving mirror and God knows what else. Oh, and sheets, of course, the old hag doesn't supply those.' Before this had had time to register he went on: 'All that, apart from basic things like new lightbulbs so you won't go blind, and a few quarts of disinfectant. Have you looked at your bed yet? For your sake I hope it's better than mine was. I'm not too fussy, you get over that in the army, but bugs I don't care for.' I was sitting on the bed with my glass in my hand; I stood up sharply and started to withdraw the afghan, but he stopped me.

'No, no. Not now. Drink first, it's better that way, believe me.' He made me sit in the chocolate arm-chair; the springs weren't as uncomfortable as they looked. Toby sat on the floor. 'Mind if I light the gas? It's a bit more cheerful with it on, though if it's anything like mine half the elements will be defective - ' He patted his pockets absently. 'Got any matches?'

'No,' I said.

'What, none at all?' With sudden suspicion, he added, 'Don't you smoke?'

'No,' I said again.

'Oh hell,' he said dejectedly. 'I was counting on you for a cigarette. I'm completely skint. I'll have to try John.' He finished his glass of wine in three enormous swallows, and then bounced to his feet and disappeared round the corner. After a moment, I heard his voice through the partition, and a deeper one answering him. He came back almost at once with a box of matches and two cigarettes loose in his hand.

'Good old John, he never fails me,' he said contentedly, settling down again. I watched while he twisted the tap and heard the faint hiss of gas trickling out of the pipes. Toby applied a match, but all that happened was that five small blue bubbles appeared at the base of the elements. 'Out of juice,' he said. I got my wallet out of my mac and found three pennies in it. At last we got the fire going.

'Not bad – better than mine,' was Toby's comment when we found that only one element was broken. He lit a cigarette and drew on it with relish.

I swallowed a mouthful of wine and then pointed to the partition. 'Who lives in there?' I asked casually.

'That's John,' he said, as if that told me everything.

'Yes, I know, but he's – what's he like?'

'Good bloke.' He dragged at his cigarette again and added with a grin, 'A *very* good bloke.'

'He was knocking on my wall before you came up.'

'Well, it's his wall too,' he said reasonably.

'Yes, but what was he knocking for?'

'I don't know. Why not ask him?'

'He was peering in through the window.' I was keeping my voice very low, but Toby kept his at a normal level.

'Probably wanted to see what you looked like.'

'It gave me a hell of a fright.'

'Why? Oh, I see what you mean!' He threw back his head and laughed heartily. 'Hearing knocks, then looking up and seeing those white eyes rolling at you . . .'

'It wasn't the white eyes so much as the black face round them.'

'You mustn't mind old John. He's just naturally inquisitive. Like a chimp, you know, he can't help it. He could no more resist having a look at you than a monkey could resist picking up anything new and giving it the once-over.'

'Yes, and then when he's picked it up he'll probably try to eat it.'

Toby laughed again. He had a very infectious laugh. My own mouth started twitching a bit. It was an unfamiliar feeling, after a whole week, the feeling of a laugh starting.

'You've got him all wrong. He wouldn't hurt a fly, old John. He's got those great brutal-looking hands that you'd think could snap your backbone like a twig, and then when he shakes hands with you and you feel them, damn me, they're like a baby's bottom. And you see him handling anything delicate – well, like an egg, for instance. He's a first-class cook, old John, you must get him to make you an omelette one day, and just watch him break those eggs. He takes them between his finger and thumb – massive bloody great thumb just about as big as the egg – and the other fingers spread themselves out like a duchess holding a Dresden teacup and he just taps the egg against the edge of the bowl, so lightly you can hardly hear it; then he lifts the two halves apart – I tell you, it may not sound like much, but it's bloody marvellous.' He shook his head wonderingly, grinning to himself. 'He does needlework too,' he added as an afterthought.

'I don't believe you!'

'So help me!' He swivelled round on the floor excitedly, as if to try and convince me, and then suddenly changed his mind and raised his voice. 'Hey, John!' he shouted.

Instinctively I made a gesture to silence him, but from next door came a prompt, baying shout of reply.

'Isn't that right, you do needlework?' Toby yelled.

'That's right boy!'

'You see?' said Toby to me in his ordinary voice, and craned backwards to get the wine bottle. 'My God, this is filthy stuff! What do you drink this for?' He poured another glass each for us.

It didn't seem so bad to me; I thought it was going down rather nicely.

I said, 'Look, you don't have to drink it.'

'Oh, it won't kill me,' he said tolerantly, topping up. 'It's a bit sticky, that's all. I like a dry wine, myself. Preferably with a thick steak. A bloke once told me, an old Frenchman actually, that what you should do is get a hunk of underdone steak in your mouth, then pour in some wine and sort of suck it through the meat. It gets mixed up with the blood, he said; it's supposed to improve it somehow. All that happens when I try it is that I make disgusting noises and suck half the steak down my windpipe.'

'Maybe it was a Gallic joke.'

'Could be; I've never been sure. Another tip he gave me that never works is to fill the bottom of your mouth with a kind of lake of wine and bring your tongue smacking down on it like a beaver's tail, so that wine squirts between your teeth. You can imagine what happens when I try *that*.' He drank ruminatively. 'The nose-trick. Are you some kind of an artist?'

'No,' I said.

'I can see you're revelling in your mystery-woman act. Never mind; I'll prise it out of you eventually.' He sighed heavily. 'I suppose I ought to get back to work. As a matter of fact I'd just begun to get steam up when I heard your knock. Now it'll take me hours to get into it again.' He looked at me aggrievedly as if it were all my fault.

I was on the point of asking him about his writing, but then I remembered my determination not to get interested. He was squatting on his heels, bouncing gently and staring at me. 'You're quite pretty, aren't you,' he said at length. 'What's your name?'

'Jane,' I said.

'That's funny. One of the tarts is called Jane.'

Two tarts in one house called Jane, I thought.

'The other one's called Sonia. She's Czech or something. Did Doris tell you about them?'

'She mentioned them.'

'Must say that for old Doris. She's nice and frank about things like that. I mean, if I were a landlady, I'd boast about having artists and musicians in my house and keep quiet about the tarts. Wouldn't you? But actually, you know, in some crazy way I think Doris is rather proud of having them here. Shows what a great big all-embracing tolerance she's got. Not that we ever see them, or practically never. They've got a separate entrance.'

'How do you know their names then?'

'Men ring up for them on the party phone, and we have to buzz them. And then of course one listens to their conversations. At least I do, and I expect everyone else does.'

'How do you justify that?'

'Hell, I don't try to justify it! I just couldn't possibly stop myself. I can barely stop myself reading other people's letters. It's an occupational disease. Of writers. Curiosity, I mean. Will *you* be having any intriguing phone calls?'

'I'll take good care not to.'

'Look out, you're smiling,' he said suddenly.

He continued to bounce and stare for a moment, then with an extra vigorous bounce stood upright.

'Thanks for the excuse,' he said. 'I'm being terribly strong-minded, leaving now and not waiting to be thrown out.' He crushed out his cigarette in the Cinzano ashtray and drained the last of his wine. 'You must come and visit *my* room sometime. Don't worry, no etchings. No nothing very much. Still, what's mine is yours, and don't get too grateful till you see what it amounts to. Well, good night. Don't drink too much more of that, it's pretty vomit-making, especially on an empty stomach. Whee – ' He lurched down the room in a parody of drunkenness, swinging on the angle as if it were a lamp-post, and left me alone.

I picked up the bottle. His advice was kindly meant, I expect, but unnecessary, as it was empty. I was a little startled to realize we'd put away a whole bottle in what seemed like a few minutes. I thought Toby must have had the lion's share, because apart from a rather tight feeling across my forehead I felt perfectly normal.

I sat on in the arm-chair, thinking about John breaking eggs with gestures like a conductor, and giggled a little. I wished I had something to eat, but it didn't seem very important. Then, idly, I began thinking that there must be something I could do to make the room look a bit better.

The first thing to get would be another lamp; a table lamp would do, with a long flex and a 100-watt bulb. I began to examine the skirting-board for a plug, and when I found one beside the crockery cupboard my spirits gave a little lift. I'd get two 100-watt bulbs while I was at it, and put one in overhead. Even if the dirt and flaws did show up more under a brighter light, it would be less depressing than this, and anyway, some of the dirt I could remove. I gave a tentative tug to a raw edge of the offensive wallpaper and felt how easy it would be to rip it all off. Underneath was firm white plaster which would gratefully accept a coat of some light-coloured emulsion paint – pale green, perhaps. All the walls at home were pale green; it was Father's favourite colour. Against my will I heard Father's shaky voice again, telling me to go; as clearly as if he'd been with me now, I knew that he was already regretting it. For no apparent reason I remembered a photograph of him in his first-war sergeant's uniform . . .

No, well, not pale green, then. I passed rather quickly on to the pock-marked floor. How much would it cost to put down some of that cheap matting stuff? It couldn't be much, the area was so small. I looked again at the arm-chair, with its greasy chocolate-coloured cover. I wasn't much good at sewing, but with a generous remnant of cretonne I could probably manage something . . . I couldn't make it look worse, that was one sure thing. And curtains – hell, any fool could make those. Perhaps John would help! I found myself giggling.

I still had my key from home. Father couldn't object to my going back while he was out and picking up some of my things. My French print, that'd go well over the mantelpiece; some books; my bits of green glass from Majorca with which to replace the foredoomed Alsatians. I might even pinch that white mesh firescreen with the plant-stands, to mask the gas-meter? Father never liked it. Get some pots of ivy to trail round, disguising things . . .

I began to feel elated. Already I could see the room as it would be when I'd finished with it. It needed me. My transformation of it would be a work of creation, like making a garden. I began to sing, and then to dance. My head was light. I felt wonderfully alive and capable, as I had felt on the train coming home that time, with fifteen hard-earned pounds in my pocket. 'I can do anything! I can do anything!' I fitted the exultant words to my tune.

The bright colours of the afghan kept spinning past me as I whirled round and round. No, I thought suddenly, whatever I changed, the afghan I would keep. It was a friend; vivid, tattered, rakish, with its torn black wool fringe, I loved it! I would keep it forever and have it buried with me. As I danced past, I snatched a corner of it, meaning to wrap it round me as a bizarre cloak. Then I stopped.

The pillow on the bed had no cover except its own soiled mattress-ticking and there were no sheets, only a pair of dingy grey army blankets. The mattress was also soiled. As I lifted the blankets aside to look closer, something moved.

When the blackness cleared I was leaning against the partition wall, fighting back an ocean of dismay. My excitement of a moment earlier had disappeared like a pricked bubble. I stood looking at the room, not as it could be, but as it was, feeling the beginnings of a horrible sick lonely fear. Suddenly I was in the middle of a nightmare – the more so because I couldn't remember what the point of my being here was. Where was my own room at home, and safety, and familiarity, and where was my father? I began to cry like a baby, blubberingly. Why had I run away, and if I had to run, if I had to be alone, why hadn't I found myself somewhere bright and clean to live? I remembered it had had something to do with pride, but that seemed crazy. Surely if one had one's self-respect to keep up, one needed light and sheets and hot water ... This place was horrible, a pigsty – what had Toby called it? A bug-house. I was living – I'd chosen, of my own free will – to come and live in a bug-house. There was a black man watching me and things crawling in my bed. And it was too late to back out, too late to change my mind. There was something at the bottom of it all, some prime cause, some terror I couldn't even bring myself to remember. I only knew that somehow I was irretrievably, inescapably trapped.

I slipped down on to the floor in front of the fire and lay there sobbing, the afghan cradled in my arms for consolation, like a child's teddy-bear.

Chapter 4

WHEN I woke up in the morning I was so stiff with the hardness of the floor – and cold, the fire having gone out hours ago – that I could hardly move. I levered myself up with the help of the arm-chair. The overhead light was still on, supplemented by grey daylight filtering dismally through the thin curtains. I sat down heavily in the chair, and began to shiver. I wrapped the afghan round myself, but I was cold to the bone. My teeth were rattling uncontrollably. I thought I must get myself something hot to drink, even if it was only hot water. I stood up, and suddenly saliva rushed into my mouth. On aching legs I staggered to the wash-basin and threw up violently, only there wasn't much to throw up and the result was what seemed like hours of empty convulsive retching that left me feeling half-dead.

Forgetting my discovery of the night before I fumbled my way to the bed and lay down on it. The folded blankets made uncomfortable lumps underneath me, but I was beyond caring. I lay there, groaning with misery.

After a long time came a knock on the door. I scarcely heard it, submerged as I was in the backwash of nausea. The next thing I knew, someone was standing over me.

'Hey, miss,' said a soft voice. 'You like a cup of tea?'

I looked up. Beside the bed stood a huge bulky figure in a plaid shirt, surmounted by a broad black head split like a ripe chestnut on a crescent of snowy teeth. Dwarfed by the enormous black paw which held it was a steaming cup.

Sluggishly I struggled into a half-sitting position, too exhausted to feel anything but grateful that I wasn't going to be left to die all by myself. The welcome cup was put into my hands.

'You sick, miss?'

'I was,' I said faintly. 'Better now.'

'Better still when you drink hot tea. See how you hands shakin'! Here, John hold it. You spill it all down youself, you not careful.'

As he bent over me I was assailed by an almost overpowering warm, animal smell. It was not quite like sweat or blood, or anything I'd ever smelt before; but though rather unpleasant in itself, I found it oddly comforting and reassuring. It was such an alive sort of smell; in my pale, stale, cold, sick state I breathed it in with the perfume of the tea and was glad of them both.

He held the cup and helped me to drink. The tea was hot and strong and very sweet, and I drank it all greedily. John dipped a teaspoon into the syrupy sugar at the bottom of the cup, and fed me that too. 'Sugar is good for you, you see,' he insisted earnestly. 'Give you energy. You got to go work today?'

'Oh God,' I said. 'Yes. What time is it? What day is it?' My mind was still not functioning properly.

'It half past eight, Tuesday morning, October sometime. What exact date, I don't remember.' He grinned. 'You like more tea?'

'No, thank you.'

'Got a whole pot . . .'

'No, really, I must get up.' I pushed my legs over the edge of the bed.

'You well enough?'

'Yes, I'm fine. Your tea's done the trick.' But my head was spinning ominously.

'You shiverin'. I light the fire.'

'I've got some pennies –'

'Never mind, I got some here. You sit a minute.' He jabbed the pennies in and lit the gas, striking a match on his thumbnail. 'You don't look good. Try puttin' you head down 'tween you knees.' I did as he told me. I could sense him watching me in concern. 'You sure you well enough go to work this mornin'? You best ring up you boss, tell him you don't feel so good.'

I longed to do just that. It would be wonderful to crawl into bed and get warm and stay there all day. Then I remembered what I'd seen under the blankets the night before.

'No,' I said. 'I can't do that. I'll be all right.' I stood up slowly, a little at a time. John hovered anxiously, his big hands ready to steady me. But oddly enough, I did feel a lot better. My head was clear and the nausea gone. Only the deep-down chill remained.

I went to the basin and bathed my face in the icy running water. John was looking at me curiously.

'You don't take you clothes off to sleep?'

'I didn't go to bed last night.'

'Where you sleep then?'

'On the floor.'

I heard him suck in his breath. 'No wonder you sick!' I started groping for a towel, remembered I hadn't one, and swore rather feebly. John gave me his handkerchief. It was unironed, but spotlessly clean. 'What you sleep on the floor for?'

'My bed's lousy,' I said shortly.

He gave a deep, sing-song laugh. 'That's bad, that's real bad!' he said, chuckling.

'I'm going to kick up hell with Doris about it.' I went to the chest of drawers and started fumbling about looking for make-up among the clutter I had dumped in there when I arrived.

'That won't do no good.'

'Why not?'

'She heard it all before. She pretend not to believe you. She say it's all lies, say you insult her house. She kick up more hell than you can.'

'I'll show her, then!' I went to the bed and stripped off the blankets. To my amazement, there was nothing to be seen on the stained mattress. John laughed again.

'Them bugs too smart to let you catch 'em twice. They crawl away in the daytime, only come out at night.'

'Then I'll show them to her tonight!'

'She smarter than the bugs. She come in making big noise. She get to the bed before you, and she say, loud-like so that bugs can hear: "This is best, cleanest bed in the house," and she pat, pat, like this – when you pull back the blanket, bugs all gone. That woman has them bugs trained up real good. They in league, to make a fool of you.'

'What can I do then? I can't sleep on it while it's like that.'

'You got some soap?'

'Soap?'

'Yeh, you got a cake of soap? Never mind, I got one. When you come home tonight, you knock on my door – before you come in here and scare them bugs away. Then I show you how to catch them little devils.'

'What, catch them all?'

'No, no! Not all. Never catch 'em *all*. Just catch enough to show Doris.'

'What'll happen then?'

'I dunno. Be fun to see.'

'Did you do that, when you first came?'

He laughed again, throwing back his enormous head with such vigour it seemed it must tip him right over backwards. 'No, ma'am! I more scared of Doris than I is of them bugs! I used to them now, and they used to me. They tired of my taste, they don't bite me no more 'cept when they's real hungry. And then they's welcome.'

When he'd gone I tried to make myself presentable for work. I was beginning to realize just how ill-managed was the move I'd so precipitously made. I'd brought a few clothes, my sponge-bag, my make-up – and nothing else. No food, no linen, no clothes-hangers even. I changed my night-crumpled clothes for others, almost equally drawer-crumpled, as I'd hung nothing away – indeed, there was nowhere to hang anything.

I knew I'd have to go home for the rest of my things. I shrank from the thought of it. I knew now how close I'd been, last night, to crawling back to the security of Father's protection and – well, I wasn't ready to call it love, but whatever it was which made him cuddle me sometimes and say I wasn't such a bad old thing. I only had to beg – not even that, perhaps – and he'd give in. He'd help, as he'd helped before – and, as before, I would be constantly aware of an ever-increasing debt to a man I didn't want to have to respect because he wasn't my sort of person. But even that seemed preferable to months of coming back to this room every night, with its tribes of bogies, real and imagined.

The best thing to do, I reflected as I felt my way down the stairs, dangerously dark even by day – the obvious thing was to go somewhere else, somewhere clean and pretty, even if it did cost more. It was worth extra money to stay reasonably sane, not to say unbitten. I bought a copy of *The Times* at the tube station and read the Personal Column on the way to work, thinking, *From the ridiculous to the sublime.* Half-way down was an advertisement put in by three girls wanting a fourth to share their flat. Own bedroom, share bathroom and kitchen, £3 10s. It was in Kensington, and there was a phone number. I decided to ring them as soon as I got to work. It would do for a few months, anyway.

The hall-porter said a pleasant good morning to me as I went in the main door of Drummonds, and so did one of the page-boys who was lounging about. The difference was, the boy, who was a cheeky little devil, noticed the creases in my dress and the fact that my hair hadn't been pinned up the night before, and smirked suggestively.

'Nice night out, Miss Graham?'

'One of these days, my lad,' I said equably, 'you'll go too far.'

'Never, miss! Not me, don't you worry.'

'I'm not worried,' I retorted. 'I can't say I'd miss you.'

'Drummonds would, though, that's where I'm safe. They'd never find anyone to fit my uniform.' This was a reference to his size, which was small, even for his calling.

'Don't count on it. They're growing miniatures nowadays, you know.'

I was surprised at being able to carry on this sort of light-hearted badinage, as if everything were just as usual. It might be just a fluke, a habit of mind held over from before; but on the other hand, perhaps I would be able to keep it up, keep my mind functioning, as it were, on two separate levels. It would be a great help if I could. If I behaved as I felt, everyone I knew would very soon guess something was wrong, and equipped as all my colleagues were with minds like sinks, their first more specific guess would inevitably be the right one.

My boss, a gentle-hearted giant called James Paige, was already in his office, though it was only just after 9.30. He was talking on one of his four telephones, the red one, which meant an internal call. He winked at me in greeting as I passed, and I heard him say: 'Well, tell the silly bitch that if she doesn't think she can find her own way to the Beatrice Room, I'll send someone up to collect her. Actually, she should have no trouble. Half Fleet Street'll be howling for her blood in there by twelve-thirty. Or tell her to follow her nose, if she can see round it.'

I went into my own office and shut the door behind me. As always, a feeling of secret peace descended on me as soon as I was safely inside. It was a nice little room, and it was all mine; no one except James ever came in without knocking. It was quietly but attractively furnished with a desk and a telephone – two, actually – a typewriter, a filing cabinet that locked, a very comfortable chair for me and a less comfortable one for visitors, and various of my personal bits. It also had fresh flowers every three days, and a view of the park. It was my little kingdom.

Today it was more precious to me than usual because I knew I would have to lose it. I even went around touching things, as if I were saying an immediate good-bye. My desk was in a mess as usual – James was always nagging at me with homilies about untidiness being a symptom of mental chaos; yesterday there had been some excuse, but today and henceforth, there was none. I sorted the scattered letters into trays and collected the various semi-legible (and frequently libellous) notes of instruction from James about current or incipient visitors to the hotel, and docketed them on a row of clips hanging on hooks down the side of my desk. Those hooks were my own unpatented device. They were labelled in code, for example 'FOP' stood for 'Fend off Press' and 'NCH' meant 'Needs Careful Handling'. There was one hook with the initials 'MFP' which was always thick with slips bearing famous names. It stood for 'Mad For Publicity'. It was a simple scheme, but James and I had a lot of fun with it.

James and I had a lot of fun altogether. He was a very good sort. He'd taught me all I knew about my job, which still wasn't a quarter of what he knew, and when I put my foot in it with some big wheel, or made a nonsense, as I sometimes did, especially at the beginning, he always got me out of it, even if it meant storming into the Manager's office and skating aggressively over the thin ice of a lot of bare-faced lies. Being such a big man gave him an advantage over the manager, to whom he often referred amiably as a 'ferret-faced little runt', and he never hesitated to use it.

My position with Drummonds was a piece of incredible good luck and a constant source of satisfaction. It couldn't help comparing favourably with the memories I had of previous offices I'd passed through – usually the glassed-in 'typists' pool' variety in the City, or North Kensington, where you clocked in and out and were 'rung for'. My recollections of these hell-holes were blurred by there having been so many of them. I could never stand any of them for longer than two weeks; the secretarial agents often got tired of my caprices and advised me severely to settle down and join a good pension scheme somewhere.

'I hate being in a pool,' I would say rebelliously. 'It's so anonymous.'

'Ah, but we all have to start at the bottom,' would be the arch reply. 'Sooner or later, if you'd just stay on a little and apply yourself, you'd become somebody's *secretary*. Then the job becomes *personal*.'

But there was never anybody whose secretary I wanted to be; so I continued going to a new office every Monday morning, and usually giving notice every Monday evening, until the agency sent me to Drummonds to be James's secretary for a week while his regular girl was on holiday. ('You won't have to give notice this time,' said the agency woman acidly.)

James, on my first morning, in response to some mistake I made, took occasion to inform me at the top of his voice that I was a silly stupid ignorant cow and that all women of my stamp should be lined up against a wall and mown down with flame-throwers. He went on to say that while this was going on he would be laughing and dancing with glee and warming his hands at the merry blaze. All this was such a pleasant change from my previous mealy-mouthed employers that I merely blinked mildly and remarked, 'Jolly good, why not toast some bangers while you're at it?' Whereupon he yelled with laughter and said thank God I understood him, and he'd better offer me a little liquid to put the fire out.

At the end of the week we learned that James's regular secretary was ill, and likely to be away for some time, and James asked me to stay on. Of course, I was delighted.

'How much do those vinegary-voiced crones at the agency give you?' he asked. I told him. 'Christ Almighty!' he bellowed, 'we pay three pounds on top of that! Lousy blood-sucking parasites! Sitting there on their fat backsides living off your sweat! Right, we'll soon fix them.' He telephoned the agency and in a very polite voice informed them that he was highly satisfied with me and wished to take me on permanently. I could hear high, excited squeaks from the other end. I could imagine their relief – £3 a week for doing nothing further about me. The squeaks subsided, though, when James went on to explain that he would in due course send them a cheque for £3 for the current week, and made it clear that that was the last they could expect. There was a shocked pause, followed by a long and voluble protest. James made attentive sounds, meanwhile pulling horrible faces and making busmen's signs for my benefit. When the protest ran out, James said in exactly the same polite tone as before, 'Madam, you may get stuffed.' He hung up, we shook hands, and so the bond between us was formed.

That was two years ago. My promotion to being James's assistant had come about six months later. It resulted indirectly from one of James's infrequent drinking-bouts. He had been boozing with some buddy the night before, and arrived in the morning two hours late with pink borders round his eyes and bevelled edges round his nerves. It so happened that there was a Press reception fixed for noon that day on behalf of a millionaire art dealer who'd come over from New York to sell some pictures at Christie's. I had laid this on the night before in James's absence, notifying by phone all the columnists I could think of who might be interested, booking one of the larger Heroine rooms (Drummonds for reasons of intellectual snobbery calls all its salons after Shakespeare's heroines) and ordering drinks and canapes with a lavish hand, in keeping with the art dealer's millionaire status. I felt rather satisfied with this, my first solo laying-on of a full-scale Press party, and was dismayed to learn from James, who was shambling round the room bumping into things and impartially heaping curses on his hangover, me and the art dealer, that the latter's name should have been put, not only on the MFP and NCH hooks, but on another one which was labelled 'MAH'– Mean as Hell. The trouble was, it was now 11.30 and too late to modify the caterers' order.

I had a stiff drink and we settled down to await the explosion which would surely follow the art dealer's realization that champagne-cocktails and scampi-on-toothpicks for thirty-five ravening journalists would set him back a goodly percentage of what Christie's was likely to get for his pictures.

There might well have been an explosion, had it not been for the absolutely splendid publicity the man received, before it was time to give him his bill. Christie's the following evening was packed to capacity with the cream of Society, who had all read in their *Daily Expresses* what a hell of a good fellow the art dealer was. Many of them, while probably having no intention of buying, spent a happy evening pushing up the bidding, as a result of which the pictures were sold for a record figure. Another result was that James called me a bloody genius and made me his assistant.

Well, so there I was – and there I wouldn't be for long. Looking out across the still-lovely autumn park, with its skeletal trees rising through the faint mist like a Chinese water-colour, I thought that at this moment my greatest regret was that the act, the cause of all this, had not been beautiful. The whole disproportionate aftermath would be a thousand times easier to bear if I could only have felt it was a payment for something I'd truly wanted and enjoyed.

But I wasn't ready to think about that yet. I sat at my newly-neatened desk and unfolded my copy of *The Times*. My hand was on the telephone to call the flat of the three girls when suddenly I thought of something. While my stomach was turning itself inside out that morning, I'd dimly supposed it was the wine which had upset me. It now occurred to me that the undignified heaving of my soul up over a basin might well be a regular feature of my morning routine from now on. Obviously if that was going to happen in a shared bathroom it wouldn't be too long before my flat-mates would begin to run their prying little female eyes over my silhouette. I took my hand off the phone and dropped *The Times* into the wastepaper basket.

All right, so a room by myself, in a nice clean house and district. But where? And how much? And how long before the nice clean people in the nice clean house started to watch me out of the corner of their eyes and think nasty dirty thoughts? Not long. Three months, at most. At least Toby and Co. wouldn't turn a hair, and if I had to go on having contact with human beings (which after John's Good Samaritan act earlier I now saw might have some advantages) I felt it must be with those who wouldn't raise their eyebrows at me. My own were pitched so near my hairline in shock at myself that I knew I couldn't endure too much of other people's opprobrium. After all, I reasoned rather fiercely, it was nothing to do with them. Only Father had any real right to be shocked . . .

James came bursting in. He was in his shirt-sleeves, and his glasses were slipping down his short, pugnacious nose.

'You're late!' he scolded. 'And you look awful! What the hell do you look so awful for? Can't you have a home-perm or whatever other women do with straight hair? You look like Medusa. Look, you know we've got this opera-singer woman throwing a lunch for a few hundred of her more intimate enemies – just go along and see that nobody slips cyanide into her grapefruit, will you – are you listening?'

'Yes, James. I want to ask you a favour.'

'No, in advance. You've had one off already this week. What do you do with all these afternoons off all of a sudden? Why can't you have your sex-life at night, like everyone else?' I stared out of the window. 'Nothing's wrong, is it?'

'No, just may I be off this afternoon, James please, because I'm moving.'

'What do you mean, moving, for God's sake? You've got a nice comfortable home, haven't you?'

'Yes.'

'Then what are you moving for? Why don't you stay at home with your father? That's what I'd do if I were a single woman, and Christ, don't I wish I were, sometimes! No responsibilities, somebody else to worry about slates falling off the roof and the lousy pipes freezing . . . you must be insane, wanting to move. What do you want to move for?'

'I want to try living on my own.'

'Oh, balls! Who wants to live on their own? – well, I wouldn't mind it sometimes, nice bachelor life, no worries, not that marriage isn't okay most of the time; but you! You'll hate it. Stay with your father and don't be silly. You'll think it over, won't you?' he coaxed.

'I must move, James. As a matter of fact, I have already.'

'What? When?'

'Yesterday.'

'Where to?'

'A – a flat in Chelsea.'

'Oh well, if it's done, it's done; I suppose you're old enough to know your own business. Don't forget to let me have your phone number.' He went back to his own office and I followed him.

'All right about this afternoon, then?'

'Oh God, do you still want that? I thought you said you'd already moved? Oh, all right, all right. You're a good girl, you do work late when I insist and don't grumble too much. I wish you weren't such a fool, though, leaving home like that. You'll soon want to beg back, I'll bet.'

He didn't know how right he was. When I stealthily let myself into my father's house that afternoon and found it all waiting for me, as it had been countless times before when I'd been away somewhere – all the dear or irritating familiarities meeting my eyes in regular and anticipated progression as I walked through it, each object and colour and smell fitting with clockwork precision into the grooves of my memory – it was as if strong hands of habit took hold of me. The feeling the wine had induced in me the previous night – a feeling of the senselessness, the pointlessness of leaving all this at the very moment of life when I most needed it – recurred now, stronger than ever, because here it all was, all the most powerful attachments of my world, the place where I belonged.

Forgetting the taxi ticking away outside, I wandered about the quiet house, looking yearningly at everything, and asking myself how it was that I'd been able to leave it yesterday without a backward glance. Partly because it had all happened so fast; and partly because I hadn't really stopped to think what it would be like somewhere else ... I seemed to have done about six months' living in twenty-four hours. The house embraced me now with the slightly reproachful, but forgiving, arms of a mother. Compared to it, the room in Fulham seemed about as feasible a place to live in as the set of a rather sordid play.

It was ridiculous to think of going back there. Every instinct I had rebelled at the idea. And yet – I can't explain why, perhaps it was the forces of inertia – I started slowly gathering together the things I had come to collect. The picture, some coat-hangers, books, and ornaments from my bedroom; some towels and bed-linen from the linen cupboard . . . I plodded numbly from room to room, picking things up without any real intention of actually taking them away, just doing it stubbornly because it was what I'd planned.

Suddenly I remembered the taxi outside, and began, inexplicably, to hurry. I found an old cardboard box that groceries had come in, and piled my loot into it. When it was stowed in the taxi, I rushed through into the garden – Father's garden, his pride and joy – where I hastily picked a bunch of late chrysanthemums. On my way back through the house I stole, with only slight hesitation, first a nice heavy glass ashtray, then two wine glasses, then the fire-screen, and then, as I warmed to my felonious work, a waste-paper basket, a spare pair of curtains just back from the cleaners, and last and best (or worst) a large Persian rug which had lain in the hall since before I was born. I didn't mean to take that, but I thought of the pock-marked lino, so cold to the feet and the eye, and somehow I found myself rolling the rug up and carrying it off.

The figure on the taximeter was astronomical by now, but I had to leave Father a note to let him know who had taken the things. I scribbled it hastily on the hall pad.

'Dear Father – I came back while you were out, so you wouldn't have to see me. I've taken some things for my new room, which is rather poorly equipped; I hope you don't mind, but most of the things are mine anyway, except the rug and the curtains and one or two small things you won't miss. If you're angry and want them back, and/or in case you want to contact me for any reason, here's my address.'

I re-read it and crossed out, very heavily, the last sentence. Then I wrote it in again over the top, cursing myself for my pusillanimousness. It was like a plea for pity to leave it in, but I couldn't bear to cut myself off from him completely. I yanked my mind away from the realization that I had been hoping he'd arrive home, miraculously early for once, while I was there, so we could make it up.

As I climbed into the taxi, my spirits bounced up again ludicrously in the knowledge that I'd eluded the clinging hands of security and comfort. I wondered for the first time about my friends. I had quite a few, chiefly the nice sort who don't need constant attention to keep them warm. It was only to be expected that periodically one of them would phone up at home, and soon they would begin asking themselves, and each other, what had become of me. I thought it would have been only fair to give Father some hint as to what I wanted done in such cases. But again I turned my mind away. Reverting to my former hurt at being turfed out, I thought, *It's his fault I'm not at home. Let him cope.* But I shivered a little at the thought that he might tell everyone.

On the way back to Fulham I stopped off to pick up some groceries and the light-bulbs. This taxi would be my last extravagance before a routine of total austerity set in. Still my heart was light from my victory, and I relished the thought of the poor little room, bedizened as it would shortly be in stolen finery. It wasn't until we pulled up in front of the dead-eyed, peeling house and the taxi-man said uncertainly 'Is *this* the place, miss?' that the floor fell out of my jerry-built high-spirits.

Chapter 5

FOR years I've been struggling to base my life on the supposition that it doesn't matter what other people think, so long as you know what *you* think. But some stubbornly suburban piece of social conditioning has impeded my efforts to the extent that I couldn't even bring myself to let the taxi-man help me carry my things into the house. He had to stand uneasily beside his cab watching me stagger up the steps sagging under three separate loads; his repeated offers of aid were met by gasps of 'No, really, it's perfectly all right, I can manage!' until he subsided into baffled silence.

When I completed my final sortie, I found Doris's formidable figure parked beside my pile of boxes and bundles.

'What's all this, then?' she asked suspiciously.

She had the landladies' asset of being able to make you feel in the wrong long before you'd done anything. From the way she said it, you'd have thought I was running guns into the house.

'Just a few things from home,' I said defensively.

She bent and fingered the curtains, which were soft and thick with a rather elegant regency stripe. 'What are these?'

'Curtains,' I said, sounding, in spite of myself, as if I were making a clean breast of it.

'I thought so!' she said with some triumph. 'There's curtains in that room already, every room in my house has curtains!' She was very indignant. 'What do you want to bring more curtains for, great heavy things like that? Catch all the dirt, they will.'

I forbore to say I'd be grateful if they would, and merely mumbled something about keeping the heat in. She grunted, obviously unmollified, and started picking over the other things. She let the sheets pass, though not without a sniff, but when she lifted one of the wine glasses out of the box my heart sank.

'What do you want these for?'

'To drink out of,' I said with restraint.

'Liqueur glasses, ain't they?' she said, in the same nasty tone as she might have said, 'Opium pipes, eh?'

'Wine, actually.'

She sniffed again, louder, and commented that she didn't like tenants drinking in the rooms, and anyway what did I want two for? She didn't like tenants to-ing and fro-ing. She seemed to have forgotten all about the advantage the presence of the tarts in the basement was supposed to confer, that of no-questions-asked, or perhaps it was that she as landlady was exempt from this convenient house-rule. She peered into the carton of groceries and said she hoped I wouldn't be doing too much cooking as it made the place smell and added that the reason she never supplied frying-pans was that she didn't like her walls getting splashed with fat.

Then she spotted the rug.

'What's that dirty-looking thing, then?'

'It's a rug.'

This was too much. 'What's wrong with the one that's up there? My sister made that rug with her own hands, it's a lovely rug that is, nothing wrong with that rug! I really can't have you bringing a whole lot of junk into the house, you know. What would happen if everyone filled the place with their own blooming furniture? You wouldn't be able to get in and out. If you're not satisfied with the room as it is, well you don't have to live in it, I'm sure, if it's not what you've been accustomed to. It was always good enough for Mrs Williams, the lady as had it before you; lived there ten years, she did, with never a complaint. Loved that room, never touched a thing in it. A lady in all senses of the word, Mrs Williams was, not just la-di-da like some.' She glared at me.

I would have liked to have a row then and there, but I remembered the bed-bugs and decided to hold my fire. Mildly I said, 'I'm sorry you object to my bringing in a few of my own things; I did it because it makes me feel more at home. As for your sister's rug, I think it's lovely, and I've no wish to move it, it's just that I'd like another one as well.' While she was still digesting this choke-sized piece of the other cheek, I quickly gathered up as many of the offending objects as I could carry at once and started up the stairs with them.

'Mind the paint!' she shouted after me as a parting shot. I looked round for some paint that I might possibly damage but could see none, so presumably she just said the first thing that came into her head.

On the first landing I met Toby, finger to lip, grinning from ear to ear. He'd obviously been eavesdropping. Motioning for silence, he took my load away from me and we tiptoed conspiratorially up the next four flights of stairs.

When we were out of earshot, Toby whispered: 'She always starts something with a new tenant, just to establish her authority. With me it was the typewriter. With John it was his guitar. Mavis – have you met Mavis yet? – she used to sing in her bath. Innocent enough, you'd think, but Doris used to come and bang on the door and yell that she was waking the house up – this at eight o'clock at night, mark you. Why didn't you tell her where to get off? Don't worry, she won't throw you out, she's a fearful snob in a Bolshie sort of way – she likes tenants with posh accents, (a) because she thinks they lend tone to the place, only that's subconscious; the reason she gives herself for liking them is (b) that it gives her a sense of power over the broken-down remnants of the so-called ruling classes. I've made a deep study of Doris's psychology; she's easier to bear if you know what makes that half-cocked brain of hers tick.'

We reached the top of the stairs, out of breath. I said, leaning on the banister rail, 'Is she very nosy?'

'You mean all that stuff about to-ing and fro-ing? No, she doesn't give a damn really. She just likes to put the wind up people. Good God, if she gave a hoot in hell about morals, the population of this house'd be more fluid than it is, by a long chalk. Any time she starts anything along those lines, you've only got to mutter "Jane and Sonia to you" and she's stymied. Why, do you fancy a bit of to-ing and fro-ing?' He gave his eyebrows a deft double-twitch upwards. 'I'll to if you'll fro,' he offered with a lecherous but gallant leer.

'I'd rather you went down for the rest of my chattels,' I said.

'Okay,' he said readily. 'As I told you, any excuse not to work.' He went rattling down the stairs.

I tapped somewhat apprehensively on John's door. He opened it at once, and I had a glimpse of glorious disorder behind him. A surge of the powerful negro odour preceded him.

'Hullo, how are you feeling?'

'Much better, thank you. I hope I'm not disturbing you?'

'No, miss, not disturb me, never. I'm not working in daytim now, you see. I sleep a lot in day, but any noise wake me up quick.'

'Were you sleeping now?'

'No. I hear you coming up and I wait for you to knock. Now just wait a minute, I get the soap to catch the bugs.'

He turned back into the dark tousled cavern of the little room and returned with a huge cake of washing soap. 'I soak the bottom, you see, make it all soft and sticky. What time is it?'

'Five o'clock, about.'

'Maybe be too early for them. In the day, they hide, then come out at night for bite you when you's asleep. Still, we try.' He took my key and, opening the door, tiptoed with exaggerated caution into my room. 'Now,' he whispered, 'when I say, you turn light on quick. Okay?' I heard Toby crashing up the stairs, and shushed him with a gesture.

'Having a bug-hunt?'

'Sh! Quiet, now!' hissed John.

I could see him groping his way to the bed, the tablet of soap in his right hand. 'Now!' John ordered. I switched on the light, and at the same moment he hitched back the covers from the bed and made several lightning dabs with the soap, moving it from place to place on the mattress as if making a feverish move in draughts. I watched, fascinated and horrified, while Toby stood at my elbow, holding the rug in his arms. John straightened up and examined the under surface of the soap. Then he showed it to us. It had four small black corpses embedded in it. John was delighted with himself, and crowed like a child.

'We got 'em! We got 'em! Now you take and show Doris.'

I looked at Toby. He grinned laconically. 'What will she say?' I asked doubtfully.

'It doesn't matter what she *says*,' he replied, 'it's what she *does*, if anything, that counts. Actually, you know, the house isn't what you might call infested with them. My room's practically clear of them now, since I fumigated it. Most of them were in the mattress, and I just burned that, in the back yard, one day when Doris was out. No doubt she found the remains of it, but she never said anything.'

'Why didn't you say something to her?'

For the first time I saw Toby look uncomfortable. He shrugged. 'Dunno, really. She's a bit of an old termagant when you really tackle her, at least I should think so.'

'In other words, you're scared of her, for all your big talk about her mental processes.'

He didn't deny it. 'Well, she *is* a bit of an old witch. She's got a tongue like an asp.'

So – there they were, both egging me on to do something they wanted done but dared not do themselves.

I tried to decide in advance what the outcome might be. I was completely in the right, and my proof was unanswerable; but of course she could say if I didn't like it I could go elsewhere. And indeed I could, and why the hell didn't I? Could I face a bug or two, could I undertake constant counter-attacks with a DDT spray, for the sake of a room at 30s. a week and no raised eyebrows?

I looked at it once again. It was pretty awful, there was no doubt about that. But I'm a fool about places. They talk to me. The park in the mist that morning had reproached me subtly for my situation. My little office said 'Shalom' (I didn't know why it said 'Shalom'– perhaps because it's a Jewish-owned hotel) every morning. Now this dismal little hovel of a room, with its repulsive inhabitants, looked at me piteously, like a mangy mongrel covered with fleas, and said 'Love me'.

But pride had to be satisfied. 'All right,' I said at last, with a heavy sigh of reluctance. 'If I get kicked out, I hope you'll both be bloody well ashamed of yourselves.'

I took the soap gingerly and went downstairs. The men followed at a respectful distance.

I didn't quite know where to look for Doris, but I turned sharp left at the foot of the stairs and knocked on the first door I found. I could hear voices on the other side, and a shuffling of loosely-slippered feet. The door opened a crack, and a small strip of Doris appeared in it.

'Yers?' she said, with off-putting sharpness.

'I'd like to speak to you for a moment,' I said, clutching my proof and trying to feel brave.

Without opening the door another inch, she said, 'What about?'

'Bugs,' I said clearly, taking the bull by the horns.

I thought I heard a stifled snort from the next landing. The door was flung wide open to allow me to see the whole of Doris's outraged breadth. Over her shoulder I could see another woman sitting in front of the fire looking interestedly in our direction. It was so obviously either Jane or Sonia that my eyes popped. Doris instantly stepped outside and closed the door after her. In doing this she forced me to give ground and I found myself with my back literally to the wall.

'I – beg – your – pardon?' she said slowly and ominously.

'I couldn't go to bed last night,' I said, 'because there are bed-bugs in the mattress.'

For a moment, it seemed Doris was going to explode. She puffed out her already enormous chest still further and grew dangerously red in the face. Her eyes actually went glassy and her shoulders shook with internal pressure. Then she lowered her head like a bull and advanced it towards my face on the end of a surprisingly long and mobile neck, and said in a voice low and trembling with conviction: 'That is a dirty lie.'

She sounded so sure of herself that for a moment my confidence wavered. But after all, I'd seen them with my own eyes, so I found the courage to retort: 'And this is a dirty house. I can prove it,' I added, as she withdrew her head like a tortoise with a hiss of rage.

'I don't want to see your proof!' she cried. 'How dare you! That I should stand here in my own house and have such a thing said to me! Dirty, indeed! MY house!' It was a marvellous act; she seemed more pained and aghast than angry at my attack. She went on for a long time about how hard she worked, how hard she'd worked all her life, to keep a decent home; how particular she was, ask anyone, all her friends and relatives kept telling her she was too pernickety in caring for the well-being of her tenants; how she'd cleaned the room out specially, from top to bottom, after Mrs Williams went, just like she always did, and what did I want for thirty bob – Windsor Castle? She kept wanting to know how I dared. I was gravelled, not for lack of matter of my own, but due to a superabundance of hers.

But at least her filibuster gave me a chance to decide on my next speech, should I ever get a chance to make it. And when at last she paused for breath I was able to say, quite tersely I felt, 'Nevertheless, there are bugs in my mattress and I want a new one.'

That stopped her cold, but only for a moment. Then she came back with the answer I'd been expecting all along.

'If you don't like it,' she said shrilly, 'you can get out, and the quicker the better. And you can take all your rubbish with you.'

'All right,' I said agreeably. 'But of course I shall stop my cheque at the bank first thing tomorrow.' I had paid her a month's rent in advance, at her insistence.

'What do you mean, stop it?' It was plain Doris wasn't used to cheques.

'I mean I shall phone my bank and tell them not to meet it.' When she went on looking blank, I made my point a little clearer adding, 'You won't be able to cash it.'

A crafty look came into her eyes. 'I cashed it today,' she said with sly triumph, and then ruined it by adding, 'at the grocer's.'

'Oh no you didn't,' I retorted, 'because it's a crossed cheque, and those can only be cashed through a bank.' Although nothing was settled, I felt instinctively this was such a good exit-line that I couldn't waste it. I turned and started up the stairs, hoping she'd stop me. But she didn't.

At the landing I was seized from either side and bundled up two more flights to a safe distance away from Doris.

'So what?'

'What happen now?'

'I don't know.'

'You going?'

'It looks like it.'

They looked at each other in dismay.

'This is our fault!' moaned Toby. 'We made you do it! God, I *never* thought the old bitch'd throw you out! You were *terrific*,' he remembered to mention.

'Where you go to?' asked John.

'God knows.'

'That wicked, lying old cow! Oh Jesus, I am sorry, I feel terrible!'

'So do I,' I said. 'Come on, you'd better help me get my things down.' We trailed up to the top of the house.

'Are you positive she can't have cashed your cheque?' asked Toby.

'No. The grocer might have cashed it for her, if he knows her well enough.'

'If he doesn't know her well enough, you mean. Anyone who knew her wouldn't trust her for sixpence.' I packed my clothes in glum silence while the others watched guiltily.

'If only there was something we could do,' said Toby weakly.

I said, without looking at him, 'How easy is it for her to find people to rent these rooms?'

'Bloody difficult, at least to find people who won't actually break the place up. She's not too fussy, as you gather, but she's got a thing about noise.' There was a pause, and then he said, 'Oh. I think I see what you mean.'

I said nothing.

'It'd be pure bluff. Do you really think she'd wear it?'

'I don't know.'

'We could try,' he said, not very willingly.

John looked from one to the other of us. 'Try what? What we try?'

'Jane thinks if *we* both threatened to leave, too, she'd have to give way.' He really sounded so unhappy about the idea that I said, 'Look, on second thoughts, don't. She isn't in a very bluffable mood, and it wouldn't improve things for all three of us to find ourselves on the street.'

But John said, 'I think this is good idea, you know. She can't throw us all out, can she?'

'Can't she?' muttered Toby; but he led the way down the stairs. I followed with mixed feelings. How on earth had I got myself into this position in twenty-four hours? I, who wasn't going to get involved with anyone? For what they were doing I would be everlastingly in their debt, and I hardly knew them.

At the first floor I caught up with them and grabbed their arms. 'Please,' I said, 'do stop and think! Supposing she says get out? That'd be infinitely worse than now! Oh, please don't do it! I'd much rather you didn't, honestly!'

Toby hesitated, but John plodded on down the stairs. 'She bad woman,' he said. 'If she say go, we leave, find something better.' Toby looked after him, looked despairingly at me, swallowed, and fell in behind John's massive back. They looked so funny from behind, like a tanker and a tug; I sat down on the top step and began to giggle weakly.

They went out of sight round the bottom of the stairs, and I heard whisperings and scufflings outside Doris's door before one of them knocked. Then there was a deathly silence; the house seemed to ring with it. I clenched my fists in suspense.

I heard the door open, but neither of the boys spoke. Instead I heard a grunting noise and then Doris's voice saying, quite affably, 'Come for her mattress, have you? Here it is, then, brand new, I bought it for meself, tell her. Tell her to let me have the other and I'll get rid of it. Well, you can understand it, really,' she went on confidentially. 'Didn't like the idea of sleeping on a mattress somebody'd died on. I told her Mrs Williams didn't have nothing catching, but she just didn't fancy it, somehow. You can understand it, really.'

When the boys came up, with the new mattress between them and stunned looks on their faces, I was lying on the stairs almost helpless with laughter. On top of everything else, I'd just remembered I'd never shown Doris the soap.

Chapter 6

We spent that evening fiddling about with my room. I was determined to strip the wallpaper off and paint the walls sometime, and the boys, though not quite sharing my view that this was imperative, expressed themselves willing to help with the work. John also said he'd fix me up something to serve as a wardrobe. But for the time being we contented ourselves with putting in the new bulb, exchanging the embroidered teacosy-like cottage picture for my French print (Toby went into ecstasies over this), and putting down the rug, on which John, for some reason, immediately lay and rolled about, laughing exuberantly.

We hid the Alsatians in my suitcase under the bed and replaced them with my green glass. Toby stood on the table, which, though lacking grace, was sturdy, and changed the curtains, while I arranged the flowers, stepping periodically over John who lay on the rug, tracing its patterns with the flat of his hand and crooning lovingly to himself.

Then Toby suggested that John should make us a meal, something quickly cookable so that he, Toby, could not do any writing while it was being prepared. John disappeared into his own room with some of the food I'd brought while Toby and I made up the bed. We pulled it right away from the wall and shook out the blankets carefully, dislodging a few more intruders. I killed them tolerantly and without horror; I felt my battle with them was morally won. Toby lent me his Flit-gun and a king-size bottle of Dettol with which we liberally sprayed and swabbed everything, including, to some inevitable extent, each other.

I looked dubiously at the coming-away strips of wallpaper and asked if Doris had a spare key to the room. Toby said she had, but avoided climbing the stairs except to silence some intrusive clamour, so I obeyed my impulse and tore off all the loose strips. Toby pumped Flit at the plaster beneath hissing gleefully, 'Die, blast you die!'– although there was nothing to be seen. 'Eggs,' he explained meaningly, filling the air with fumes.

By the time John came back with a strange concoction, the room really looked quite a lot better. Scarcely elegant, but better. You couldn't see details for the fumes of disinfectant and the clouds of smoke from Toby's perpetual cigarettes, which probably helped; the general impression was of a blur of colour (I'd hung my dresses and suits on the picture-rail) and some nice bright light. John gazed round approvingly and pronounced judgement: 'Smell bad, but look good.' The exact opposite could have been said of the meal, but with the important addendum that it tasted delicious.

Most of my share went down the drain early next morning.

I was very alarmed, apart altogether from the physical unpleasantness. Even after I'd recovered to some extent, I felt awful and looked worse. There could be no question this time of wine having caused it. I tried to convince myself that my stomach had rebelled at something John had introduced into the hash; but having proved in the past that I can eat anything that isn't actually poisonous or rotting, I grimly told myself to come to terms with this morning horror.

I forced myself to go to work, disconcerted by the way people stared at me in the train and unable to read my paper without the print swirling before my eyes and an omninous white ache starting in my jaws.

James looked at me as I walked into his office and did a genuine double-take.

'Sweet God, what's wrong with you?' he demanded indignantly. He always regarded signs of illness or emotional instability in those close to him as a personal affront.

'Nothing,' I said faintly. 'I just don't feel very well, temporarily. Leave me alone, I'll be all right.' I retreated to my own office, which said 'Shalom' to me in a far-away voice. I sat down at my desk and put my head on my arms. Reality swam away from me. My desk was as soft as a floating rubber cushion. Sounds came and went faintly and insignificantly. I dozed.

I came to with an unpleasant start to find James skulking furtively nearby with a cup of tea in his hand. For a second I thought he was a bleached version of John.

'I brought this,' he muttered, uncomfortable at being caught out in an act of kindness. He put it down in front of me and stood watching me warily as I slowly picked up the spoon and stirred, wondering whether it was safe to drink. 'You look worse, not better,' he said accusingly at last. 'You'd better have a brandy.'

'No, James, please, I couldn't drink it.'

'What's the *matter*, Jane?'

I was touched by the impatience in his tone, which I well knew masked anxiety and affection.

'I don't know,' I lied. 'I must have eaten something.'

'It's now you're cooking for yourself, of course,' he upbraided me. 'I knew no good would come of you moving.'

'I've cooked for myself for years, and Father too,' I said uselessly.

I took a sip of the tea and it seemed to stay down all right, so I drank the rest slowly. James stood by shifting about in embarrassment. Sick people put him out of countenance in some obscure way. There was a longish pause while I sat with my eyes closed.

'I suppose you'd better go off home,' he said finally.

I snapped awake again and said, 'Well, if I go on feeling like this I might just as well. I'll be about as much use to you as an ingrowing toe-nail.' But it seemed so inexcusable, to have his veiled sympathy and let him do all my work thinking I was just ordinarily ill. 'I tell you what, give me something to do and maybe I'll forget to think about it.'

James brightened at once; this was the sort of positive thinking he understood. 'That's the ticket,' he said briskly. 'You'll soon be okay.' As though hoping by sheer weight of work to crush my disquieting illness out of existence, he heaped tasks on me, pausing once in a while to say gruffly, 'You're sure you'll be able to manage,' but without a question mark in case I might answer 'No'. And by about eleven, my colour was back, my queasiness had magically vanished, and James was able to say triumphantly, 'There, you see? It's all mental, all illness is a symptom of neurosis, that's why I'm never ill. I should be a Christian Scientist, they've got all the right ideas, if only they weren't so bloody stupid about broken bones and thinking it's all mixed up with God . . .' He was as pleased as Punch with me for being all right again. 'Go on off and have a damn' good lunch on expenses,' he said, as if he were rewarding me for some piece of cleverness.

The next morning I was sick again, and the morning after that. I put on thick make-up with lashings of foundation under my eyes, and rubbed a little lipstick mixed with cold cream on my cheeks instead of rouge, which I never wear. I looked positively bizarre, like a cross between a clown and a tart, but if James saw the difference he didn't let himself notice it and about mid-morning each day I scrubbed it all off with Quickies and put on my normal make-up. At first I thought I would die each time I woke up, knowing that as soon as I tried to get out of bed the ghastly inner tumult would begin again; but one gets used to anything, and by the end of the week, although it was still ghastly while it was going on, I could take my mind away from the heavings of my stomach to some extent by thinking firmly, *It's quite natural and at eleven o'clock it'll all be gone.*

Unfortunately it didn't follow quite as regular a course as I'd have liked. On one occasion, although I felt like death as usual on rising, it didn't actually come to anything before it was time to leave the house. But I was under no illusions about having a morning off; on the contrary, as I neared the station I had reason for growing apprehension, to such an extent that I nearly turned back. But the sinister oncoming signs died down and I was encouraged to think I might hold out until I got to the hotel ladies' room. No such luck, however, either for me or for my fellow-passengers.

During one free lunch hour I walked down Charing Cross Road and surreptitiously consulted some of the latest and most enlightened books on pregnancy, to find out how long I was going to have to submit to this misery. They seemed vague and discordant on the subject. One said that if it hadn't stopped by the end of the third month (dear God!) the attendant GP should be called upon to Take Action as being too sick for too long was liable to cause miscarriage. Another, written by a man of course, suggested that morning sickness was a matter which a strong-minded woman could easily bring under control. I almost threw that one aside, and proceeded to a third, which said that a certain amount of sickness was inevitable in some women, who, at its onset, should recline full-length and be ministered to by their husbands, until all traces of nausea had passed.

Fate appeared bent on pushing its moral home to me around that time. It seemed that not a day passed without my picking up some magazine, or listening to some radio programme (Toby had lent me his radio to rid himself forcibly of one distraction) which had a bearing on the behaviour of husbands during their wives' pregnancies. Stories about blooming young brides developing cravings for crushed pineapple or mango chutney, which their devoted spouses combed the town to obtain for them in the dead of night; or articles urging masculine Patience and Understanding during this Difficult Time (even if it referred to the change of life, it still reminded me); or radio plays in which married couples sat *tête-à-tête* holding coy conversations about names and schools and first words . . . Well, maybe it wasn't quite as bad as that, in fact it can't have been or I'd have laughed instead of crying, which I seemed to be doing with monotonous regularity each time I was alone – even without any external moralizing reminders.

My plans for redecorating my room stood in abeyance. I simply didn't feel up to it. During the afternoons at the hotel I'd think about it, as an alternative to thinking about being pregnant, and plan to buy some paint next lunch-time and get down to it at the week-end. But somehow the week-end came and went and the remainder of the tobacco-coloured wallpaper stayed more or less in place.

Toby kept nagging at me to be more social. He was determined that I must meet this Mavis who shared the house with us. I tried to discourage Toby's social enthusiasm, because the more people I got to know, the more would have to be told, sooner or later, about the baby. This was something I used to lie awake at nights thinking about. How would I break it to people like James, Toby and John – and of course, other friends?

These were beginning to be a problem. One day my erstwhile closest friend, a girl called Dottie Cooper, telephoned me at the office, and as soon as I said 'Hallo?' she exclaimed in a tone of mingled triumph and reproach 'So!'

'What do you mean, "So!"?' I asked uncomfortably.

'You haven't gone abroad! I thought it sounded fishy.'

'Abroad? Who said I had? What are you talking about?'

'Your papa said so, that's who.'

'*Father* said I'd gone – ' My mind burst through its bonds of bewilderment and found itself face to face with unwilling gratitude. So he hadn't been abusing and accusing me to all my friends. Grudgingly I had to admit to myself that he was hardly the sort to, however he might feel about me. So that was what he'd decided on, and for a basically unimaginative man it wasn't bad. Now nobody would pester me. 'Why was I supposed to have gone abroad?' I asked her.

'Some sort of exchange with another hotel owned by the same people,' Dottie said. My respect for Father's strategy grew. 'He said you'd be gone about a year. I don't know why I didn't quite believe it – vanity, I suppose. Couldn't credit you'd go off without letting me know. So. What gives?'

I thought of telling her, but rejected the idea without knowing quite why. 'Dottie, I can't tell you anything at the moment.'

'You mean, over the phone, or at all?'

After another pause I said, 'At all. Not yet.'

She didn't say anything for a minute, then said, 'Okay, sweetie. I'm no dumpkopf, I know when I'm not wanted. No, don't be a goon,' she said as I started to speak. 'I'm not a bit hurt, but I *would* be if I thought you were rotating on the horns of some dilemma that I could help with and you didn't come running.

Look, I won't get in touch again till I hear from you, but make it soon, eh? You've got me a bit worried now.'

Several times later I was tempted to go round to Dottie's flat and ease my heart with a thoroughgoing girl-chat. But I didn't go, principally because she would naturally want to Know All, and All was something I couldn't talk about, even to myself. I'd shut that part of my mind off as completely as I could, and I didn't want to risk any conversation which might open it up again.

Well, so I was trying hard to avoid enlarging my acquaintance. I told Toby again and again that I didn't want to meet anyone else, that while I was happy to have him and John as my friends, even they exceeded my original intention, and that what I really wanted was to be left alone. But I said it without conviction, because it was no longer strictly true. I had come to depend rather heavily on the small comforts arising out of my friendship with this oddly-assorted pair. Our relationship was undemanding, yet rewarding and warm. John made me tea in the mornings to help combat my pre-noon death-wish; I did some sewing and ironing for both of them, and sometimes we all had an evening meal together, prepared either by John or me according to who felt like it, which meant it was more often John. Toby's material contributions to our companionable threesome fluctuated, in fact they were generally limited to his own presence whenever a meal or a cup of tea or a cigarette was in the offing; but without him, there would have been no conversation. He was the adrenalin in our corporate body. I grew very fond of him as I had known I would, and although I couldn't get rid of the shadows on his face I did put a little flesh on his bones by a course of more or less regular evening meals. I scolded him about his hair, which was never brushed, and his shirts, which were seldom washed, and although it only showed spasmodic results at least he didn't mind; our affectionate interchange of teasing and insults, in contrast to John's solid, easy-going calm, broken occasionally by unexpected outbursts of singing or wild, toothy laughter, soon built up a relationship that was more necessary to me than I cared to admit. I often wondered how long I would have lasted with no one to talk to or take an interest in, or be cared for by.

But I never talked about myself, though Toby fished and fished. So long as nobody knew about the baby, it didn't seem, even to me, quite real. I could sometimes forget it almost completely.

One Saturday I was blundering about in my dressing-gown at

around noon (having successfully foiled the inner demon by staying in bed until past the witching hour) when Toby came banging on my door to announce that Mavis was making coffee as only Mavis could, and I was to come down and partake. I made various excuses, but none of them washed, and eventually, more because I could now smell the coffee than out of any desire to meet its maker, I pulled on some slacks and went down to the third floor, where Mavis's room was.

I don't know quite what I had expected her to be like, but I know I was surprised to be greeted by an elderly and upright spinster, powdery-skinned and grey-bunned, in a well-worn cardigan and skirt, but with brightly painted lips and a touch of mascara and exuding a strong but pleasant odour of Chanel No. 9 toilet water.

When you're living with an assortment of people who have little or no money, it's very interesting to notice that they all permit themselves some luxury to which, in their straitened circumstances, they probably have no real right, but for which they'll do without so-called necessities. With Toby it was – as often as he could manage it, and he'd go without food for it cheerfully – good-quality typing-paper and a new ribbon for his machine as soon as the old one started to get faint. John, who made what passed for his living playing the guitar in a club in Soho, spent a ridiculous proportion of his income on long-playing jazz records. This baffled me completely at first because of course he had nothing to play them on; but it seemed he just like to have them, and their purchase gave him the right to spend many mornings in a local record shop just listening to one record after another. So long as he occasionally bought one, nobody minded.

Well, Mavis's little weakness was perfume, and in that house I could well understand it. Despite her age and circumstances she was a very robust and cheerful woman. Her small room (one of the ones without running water) was pin-neat, which was a marvel considering how many knick-knacks she'd managed to cram into it. Every available surface was jagged with them, tiny coloured boxes, statuettes, minute vases that wouldn't hold a daisy, balding velvet pin-cushions, countless little dishes and ashtrays with place-names on them (she seemed to have souvenirs from almost every seaside town in England) and a great many photographs of all sizes. The walls, too, were smothered in pictures, embroideries, beaded purses, plaques and tiles in a variety of colours and to suit a variety of tastes. Evidently all was fish that fell into her collector's net. The bedcover was patchwork, done in tiny hexagons about the size of sovereigns; her cushion-covers were thickly embroidered. There was a bookshelf, garnished with a bobbled fringe, on which stood a row of second-hand paperbacks, mainly detective and love stories.

She had obviously lived in the room for years, and had everything organized. There was a large bucket under the basin in which she kept her current water supply. Her cooking facilities were limited to a single gas-ring, but she had a trivet in front of the fire (on which the coffee-pot now rested) with the help of which she was able, as I later discovered, to prepare quite complicated meals and serve everything hot. She had no bedside light, only the central one, but I noticed a cord had been run from this to enable her to control it without getting out of her bed, under which, as another example of her trouble-saving devices, reposed a large and gaily-flowered pot.

After Toby had introduced us, I was urged to sit down and make myself at home. I found a small, precise-looking cat in possession of the arm-chair, so I sat on the floor near the fire, a deference which Mavis evidently regarded as quite proper. She poured the coffee, which was so strong it practically snarled as it came out of the pot, and then sat down herself, taking the small cat on to her knee.

'Well duckie,' she said brightly, 'and what do you do with yourself?' Her Cockney accent, although not of the strongest, jarred somehow in the same way as the lipstick and the perfume – it seemed unrelated to the rest of her. So did the coffee, if it came to that. Looking at the room, I'd have expected that nothing but tea, rather weak tea, would be drunk here.

'I work in town,' I said.

'Oh, in *town*, do you?' she repeated, as if this were the most fascinating information. 'What sort of work?'

'In an office.'

'Really? In an *office*? Well! Do you like it?'

'Yes, very much.'

'Whereabouts is your office, then?'

'In the West End.'

'Really?' she said again. She seemed very surprised. 'I thought they always paid very well in these West End offices?'

I saw that she was leading me on to dangerous ground. Toby's ears were so pricked they almost met on top. 'Not always,' I qualified.

'In my day, if a girl worked in a West End office, she could afford to live rather well – only of course they all lived at home then, until they got married.' She gave me a sharp little look. 'Mind you, I approve of this getting out on your own. It's the only way to learn, really, isn't it? Someone like me, now, I lived with my mother till she died, and by that time I was thirty, and aside from running a house and sewing, there wasn't one blooming thing I could do. Nasty business, starting to try and earn your living at thirty, especially in those days. There was only a few alternatives, of which the theatre was the least respectable but one; but I had a go at it because it was a touring opera company and I wanted to travel.'

'Were you an actress?'

'Gawd help us, me? Never. I was wardrobe mistress. Went all over England, I did – loved it. Stayed with the same company for twenty-five years, saving the war, and I'd be with it still if it hadn't broken up. Didn't have the heart to start again with a new lot after that; and anyhow, my eyesight's not what it was, so I thought I'd just settle down somewhere and have a bit of a rest.' She sipped her coffee and glanced round the room, letting her gaze rest affectionately on this and that. 'Do you like the way I've done the room?' she asked contentedly. 'Nice, isn't it? Every trinket tells a story. Got enough to start a junk-shop but I love them all, they all mean something special to me. See this?' She picked up a round thing made of china, prettily painted, with holes in the top like a salt-cellar. 'Know what it is? It's a pomander. Smell.' She held it out and I breathed in the musty, spicy smell of old herbs. 'Manager of the company give me that for my fortieth birthday. He guessed me thirty-one. That was a lie, of course, but if I do say it I didn't look more than thirty-five. I always had the feelin' if he hadn't been such a snob he'd have asked me to marry him.'

'And would you have done?' I couldn't help asking.

'What, marry him? Not likely!' She laughed. 'Oh, he was all right, but not for life. That's always the trouble with picking a husband. However much you like a man, it's never enough to last for life.'

'But have you never been in love, Mavis?' asked Toby seriously.

'In love! Get away with you!' she retorted as if the notion were preposterous. But the topic was obviously not displeasing to her. She ruminated.

'Well, of course I've been in love,' she said. 'I suppose. I mean, I must've been, mustn't I? Everybody is, sometime or other. If I wasn't in love that time in Eastbourne, I'm sure I don't know what I thought I was up to . . .' She hummed reminiscently to herself, and her hands, with their long seamstress's fingers, strayed about among the oddments nearest to her and rested on a little ivory box. 'Brought that back from India, he did,' she mentioned vaguely. 'Well, now, I don't know what we're talking about me for, I'm sure. How are you getting on, Toby? Let's have some more coffee.'

Toby did the honours. This was obviously established routine between them. A dish of coffee and milk was respectfully submitted to the cat, who drank it contemptuously and then retired to her box of shavings with an air of having sustained an insult. Meanwhile Toby, who needed little encouragement to talk about himself, was in full spate.

'I've mentally committed myself to two thousand words a day,' he explained. 'I know it's not much, but all the writers' biogs I've been reading lately say it's absolutely essential to set a schedule for yourself and stick to it. Even if it's not a very demanding schedule. Well, of course, *they* didn't say that – I say that. Because I always find, with good resolutions of any kind, if you ask too much of yourself you might just as well give up in advance; your subconscious sort of boggles right from the start.'

'What are you writing two thousand words a day *of*, dear?'

'Oh, the same old book.'

'Let me see – is that the one about the French Revolution?'

'Mavis, no! That was years ago. Anyway, it was a short story, and I gave it up after ten pages. What do I know about the French Revolution? Only what I've found out from other writers.' He brooded with his chin in his hand, a lock of black hair falling in his eye. He looked like a Jewish leprechaun.

'Well, what's this one about, then?'

'It's a bit difficult to explain in a few words. There's this man you see. He's a cameraman for a newsreel company, and it's a good job financially, but he's not satisfied with it; he wants to be a film producer, a great one. And his wife – '

'She doesn't understand him?' suggested Mavis.

'But she does, you see, that's the whole point!' Toby got to his knees, his beaky blackbird's face lighting with excitement. 'She *does* understand, she'd be glad for him to chuck in the good job and have a go at the thing he wants to do, but the thing is, he never puts it to her, because he thinks it wouldn't be fair to her to ask her to decide. They've got two kids, you see. He thinks he hasn't the right to risk the kids' future. But what he's really afraid of, though he won't admit it to himself, is that if he ever did try, he'd fail; so he goes on *not* trying and kidding himself he's sacrificing his dream for his family's security.' He paused and looked from one to the other of us. 'That's as far as I've got so far,' he said, adding, with concealed anxiety, 'What do you you think of the idea?'

I thought it was a very good idea indeed, but before I could say so Mavis remarked, 'Well, I don't know, dear, I like a bit more of a story, myself. Why couldn't you have the wife not understand him, and drive him into the arms of another girl – a film star, say? I like it being to do with the films,' she added encouragingly.

Toby looked at her uncomprehendingly, as if she'd suddenly started speaking in a foreign language. There was a pause, and then, presumably because he liked her and wanted her to understand, he tried again. 'But Mavis, it's nothing really to do with films, as such. I mean, he could just as well have been a –'

He stopped in the middle of his sentence, chilled by her look of simple disappointment. 'It doesn't matter,' he said, giving it up. He swallowed the last of his coffee quickly. 'I'm off,' he said. He stood up and gave Mavis a quick kiss. 'Coming, Jane?'

I thanked Mavis for the coffee and followed Toby up to his room. I'd never been into it before, as Toby, after his first invitation, had seemed to lose his nerve about my reaction to it and had said several times that he must 'tidy it up' before I saw it. Now, however, he made no protest. He went directly to his table by the window and, tearing the latest sheet out of his small, battered typewriter, began to read it frowningly, as if it had in some way betrayed him.

I stood in the doorway, ankle-deep in crumpled-up pieces of quarto which littered the room. The bed was unmade, obviously chronically, and everything was thick with dust; but the room had an air of male austerity which surprised me. I had thought it would be full of symbolic distractions like pictures, magazines, trimmings of various sorts to match the frivolous side of Toby's personality. There were none. The walls were bare; the surfaces of furniture had the basic minimum of functional objects on them. There were a few books, mostly the sort you can pick up at bookstalls for a bob or two, plus Penguin classics. For the first time I began to realize Toby's writing might really be a force to be reckoned with.

'Here, why not sit down somewhere?' He shifted a pile of papers off a chair. He was still re-reading his recent output, obviously with new eyes. Eventually he put the pages down with a deep sigh. 'What do you think of Mavis?' he asked.

'Well, I thought she was a nice enough old thing. But I could have hit her for being so crass about your book.'

His whole face changed, as if someone had switched on a light behind it. 'Do you really think that – that she was crass? I thought I was going nuts – what she said had absolutely no relevance to the idea of the book at all. But then I wondered if perhaps that meant that there wasn't any real idea. I mean, as all she could see in it was the film angle. I couldn't wait to get back here and look at it again, to make sure there was some point to it.'

'Haven't you any confidence in yourself at all?'

He drew back, as if I'd attacked him physically. 'Of course I have! What do you mean?'

'Well, I mean, how can it matter a damn to you what Mavis says? Why do you even bother to tell her about it? One minute with her should tell you she'd never understand. Did you look at the books she reads herself? Mysteries and romances. You might just as well describe your plot to a shop-girl in Woolworth's and hope she'd see its possibilities.'

He stared at me, looking from one of my eyes to the other, his mouth slightly open. At last he began stammeringly, 'Well, I – I – I mean, she's part of the public, isn't she?'

'Not part of your public,' I said firmly.

He sat down and stared blankly at the pages in his hand. 'Why did you say haven't I any self-confidence?'

'Having to rely on somebody like Mavis to keep your morale up – your belief in your work – '

'But no, you're wrong!' He jumped up and began to pace about excitedly. 'It's just the opposite! When I get an idea, I'm so certain it's good that I believe everyone – everyone, even people like Mavis – will see it the way I do. I've got too much self-confidence, if anything, not too little!'

I said, 'I don't believe there's ever been an idea that *everyone* thought was good.'

He stopped. 'What are you saying, then?'

'It's none of my business –' I remembered belatedly.

'No, go on, go on!'

'Just that you shouldn't need to submit your ideas to anyone for approval. If you do, you'll get as many reactions as there are people. In the end, if you're stupid enough to try and please all of them, you'll tinker and adapt and mess about until there's nothing of your original idea left – it'll be just a disgusting hotch-potch product of a lot of people's brains where it should be the pure product of one. Whether the finished result is good, bad or indifferent, the very least it should be is *yours*.'

He opened his mouth to speak, and then shut it again. 'Damn it,' he said. 'Now I can't ask you what *you* think about my plot.'

I was so dying to tell him that I said jokingly, 'If you must ask somebody, at least choose a person whose judgement you respect.' But I got what was coming to me because he said thoughtfully, 'Yes, you're right'– and proceeded *not* to ask my opinion.

Interludes like this became, as the days passed, more and more like short patches of calm water on a storm-and-fear-ridden ocean voyage. I, who had wanted, or thought I wanted, above all to be alone, soon grew afraid to be left alone for five minutes. Because as soon as I was, with nothing to keep my mind busy, the bogies came – as surely as they must come to a criminal with a guilty conscience, or an alcoholic fighting temptation. My bogies were chiefly questions. How am I going to keep it? Should I keep it at all – wouldn't it be better to have it adopted? What will it think of me when it's old enough to realize it hasn't a father? Or more immediate ones like: How am I going to tell people? What will James say? What shall I do, when I have to leave the hotel? Shall I wear a ring and pretend to be a widow? Have I the courage not to tell any lies? How will it feel to be the only woman in the maternity ward whose husband never comes to see her? And over and over again: why did this have to happen?

One bogey was not a question, but a statement, always for some reason in the third person: *You'll never be free again.*

I never thought about the baby as a person in its own right, or wondered what it would look like, or speculated about its sex, or thought of names for it. I tried to turn my thoughts that way sometimes, but the only face that came into my mind was a face blackened by my own dark rebellious anger against it, and the only name spread a cold, slow poison through me. So my thoughts were always heavy with bitterness, and a responsibility I didn't want and wasn't ready for.

Sometimes I longed to have someone to talk to. I thought if I could talk about it to some other woman, the back-breaking seriousness of it might lift a little and reveal some exciting or entertaining aspects of the situation squashed underneath. Dottie was the obvious choice, but when I imagined her probable reaction it didn't entice me. It wasn't that I was afraid she'd be shocked or censorious, but that I felt she would regard the whole thing in the light of her own situation. She was twenty-eight and getting a bit worried for fear she'd never find anyone to marry. I imagined her attitude to my predicament would be along the lines of: How marvellous to have a baby, at least you'll have *that*, and: Of *course* nobody frowns on illegitimacy these days; what fun, I do think you're wonderful, can I be godmother? In a way this sort of light-hearted approach was just what I wanted; in another way it was utterly out of keeping with my own feeling of the terrible importance of the thing. Somehow I felt that what I really needed was an older woman, someone who understood all the implications, who could see the thing in the perspective of wisdom and experience. It took me some months to realize that these dim yearnings of mine must be for my mother.

I often thought of Father. The raw edge of my dislike for him was already blunted by separation. I remembered many cheering, comfortable and endearing qualities in him. Very often, sitting in the office with those two telephones so temptingly close, I nearly phoned him; but in the end I always decided against it.

I'd made up my mind that if the sickness didn't stop by the end of the next week, I'd have to leave work. I couldn't keep it up. Although I fed myself religiously with all the right, digestible, nourishing foods I could think of whenever I felt they'd stay where I put them, the constant repetition of throwing up every morning, followed by the titanic effort involved in getting myself to work afterwards, was telling on me. I felt perpetually feeble and weepy.

I went back to Dr Maxwell, the GP Graham had sent me to, and he told me I should try and rest as much as possible. I explained the situation to him and he said well, he couldn't help that, morning sickness was morning sickness; if you had it you'd had it, ha-ha, and why didn't I take a holiday? I told him I'd already had my holiday for the year, and I couldn't get another one without saying why. 'Why can't you just be ill?' he said. 'I'll give you a certificate. You'll get fagged out if you go on like this.' I said I'd think it over and let him know, and he gave me various things to take including some pills which he said might do some good.

They didn't seem to. After two days of dosing myself with the stupid things I looked so terrible that even James, who'd been studiously closing his eyes to my increasingly haggard mien in order to give me a chance to ignore it myself, couldn't avoid noticing it. He kept giving me fractious sideways glances, and popping into my office at odd times for no special reason; the impression he gave was that he was watching out to see I didn't pull a fast one on him and he found several opportunities to slip a homily on mind-over-matter into our conversations.

However, just as I was ready to take the doctor's advice, the sickness stopped. I was all right all over the week-end, most of which, it's fair to say, I spent in bed; but when on Monday morning I crawled gingerly up, taking it slowly and keeping my head well down so that I must have looked like a giant turtle scrabbling about, nothing happened. Nothing felt as if it might be going to happen. I hurried to the hotel, fearing a repetition of the ghastly episode in the train, but all was well. When I strode, bright-eyed with relief, into James's office, he gave himself completely away by breaking into a great soppy grin and saying, 'Gosh, you look marvellous! Hell, I'm glad to see you looking so much better, I thought you were going to croak on me!'

Chapter 7

THERE followed a period of physical well-being in which I learned what pleasure can be gained from absolutely negative sources. Getting up in the mornings, something I had loathed and dreaded all my life, now became a positively jolly part of the day's routine. I used to sing about my toilet out of sheer relief, and sometimes

John would join in next door and we would produce a creditable duet. If I'd applied myself during this patch, I think I could have had moments of real happiness about the impending event; I felt well and strong and my heart tended to be light; but instead of using this sound bodily basis as the jumping-off point for a little constructive thinking, I used it as the foundation for straight escapism.

In other words, just as often as possible I pushed the thought of 'it' completely aside. 'It' had stopped being anything as concrete as a baby I was due to have in roughly seven months, and become an almost unidentified problem that I would think about some time in the future when it became more pressing. My figure, so far as I could judge – which wasn't far as I had no long mirror in my room, but I occasionally gave it a passing glance in the hotel ladies' room – was exactly as always. The whole thing was surprisingly easy just not to fret about any more. I slept soundly; my brain was clear and full of ideas; my step was light, and James looked as if he'd recently exchanged a hair-shirt for a rather expensive silk one from Simpsons.

I did more to the room. While I was being ill, I not only hadn't felt any interest in improving my surroundings, but the perpetual consciousness of the need to save money had prevented me from buying anything non-essential. Now with my new to-hell-with-it outlook, every shop window with a relevance to house interiors drew me like a magnet, and I began to bring little parcels back to the house – or rather, sneak them back; I didn't feel like trying my luck with Doris too far. I started moderately with small, necessary items like a potato peeler and a kettle; then I branched out a little and acquired a small casserole dish and three coffee mugs; and finally I got really reckless and bought material for re-covering the chair, a three-layer vegetable rack, two cushions, a burgeoning pot of ivy and a totally unessential object called a sink-tidy which I fell for in a bargain basement.

John and Toby were the worst possible influence. They rejoiced at everything, exclaiming like children over each purchase and generally encouraging my improvidence.

'The next thing you must get,' Toby egged me on, 'is a table-lamp. You can't imagine what a difference it would make.'

I could, all too well, but I did make a feeble protest. 'I can't afford it,' I said weakly.

'All right then, if you can't afford a new one – why don't you get this thing turned into one?'– indicating a sea-blue vase of singular shape which I had brought back from a holiday in Italy. 'It looks like a blue urinal at the moment.'

'It does not!'

'It'd soon stop if you put a lampshade on top of it.'

So I had the blue urinal-vase turned into a lamp, which in the end cost a lot more than a lamp would have done, but it looked lovely and imparted a much more friendly, cosy aspect to the room in the evenings.

'When you goin' to do the walls?' John would ask.

'I'll get around to it sometime – it means such an upheaval.'

But John did make me a wardrobe. One day I left the Yale on the latch accidentally, and when I came back I found a brand-new shelf, with a brass rod below it, high up in the shallow recess beside the fireplace. It was solid as a rock, and just the right height to hang my things on; all it needed was a curtain, and I felt nothing but the best was good enough to grace John's generous handiwork; so during the following day's lunch-hour I went to Debenham's and bought a length of beautiful yellow curtaining, with some red in it to pick up the colours in the rug which John loved. I made it up myself, with Mavis's help – she was doing the chair-cover for me, and I spent quite a few evenings sitting in front of her fire chatting away and trying to master the eccentricities of her ancient sewing-machine.

'You have to love it, like,' she explained as she tenderly coaxed the contrary brute into operation. The net result was she had to do most of the work; the finished products were, as one might expect, completely professional, but she flatly refused a fee, though I did everything except stuff the money into one of the daisy-vases.

'If you want to do something for me, dear,' she said, 'just thread me up a few needles in different colours – can't see the blooming eyes any more.' I did this, of course, and after careful thought I also bought her a splendid pink cineraria in a pot. Round the rim of this I got one of the sign-painters at the hotel, who did our notices and door-names and things, to write 'A present from Park Lane'. I was a bit doubtful about this last touch; I was afraid she might think I was making fun of her. But she was thrilled to pieces, and nearly watered the poor thing to death until I managed to convince her it didn't need it.

I was settling into a routine of nest-making which was as much of an opiate as a new toy is to a child. I understood for the first time how Father felt about his garden. I wondered how often and how obviously I'd shown my lack of sympathy at his enthusiasm for it. Oddly enough, I was thinking this one morning when I was leaving the house, and there on the hall table was a letter from him.

I went all the way back upstairs so that I could shut myself up in my room and read it.

'Dear Jane,' it began. 'As you can imagine, I find this letter hard to write. We haven't been very close these last years, which may have been my fault, I suppose, though I don't quite see where we went wrong; I've always done my best, but that seldom seems to be enough in this world. This isn't an apology, however, as I think any parent would have felt as I did, being told a thing like that without any preparation. You almost seemed to enjoy telling me, or that's how it seemed to me. But I am still your Father and I don't enjoy thinking about you alone somewhere. Your home is here and if you want to come back to it you should feel free to. It's not right for you to be among strangers. You are still my reponsibility in a way, though legally you're old enough to live your own life.'

He'd signed it just 'Father'. There was a P.S.: 'I'm telling anyone who telephones that you've gone abroad. You didn't say what you wanted done and that seemed the best thing.'

I felt cold shiver after cold shiver pass through me as I read this letter. It wasn't until it came that I realized how badly I had wanted him to try and make contact with me; and now he had, my disappointment was so acute at the cold formality of his manner that all my past dislike of him, my resentment of his patronage, returned full-force. 'My responsibility.' Yes, that was just what he would say. Not a word of warmth or welcome or affection, or even forgiveness. Anger would have been easier to bear than this stiffly-extended hand of duty, held out grudgingly under the banner of 'Blood is Thicker than Water'.

I screwed the letter up and shed hot, angry tears on it. Go back! I would see him in hell first. But my bitterly-phrased thoughts brought no relief, only renewed tears of guilt for which I refused to seek a cause. I threw the letter into the waste-paper basket. But that night when I came home from work I recovered it. I smoothed it out, and without re-reading it put it into my suitcase with the Alsatians and told myself to forget it.

It hurt for a while, then stopped. I thought how quickly and easily all the ties of one life could be broken and those of a new one built up ... It was sad to reflect that the new friends were probably just as transitory, and the links with them just as fragile. This thought was, at that time, the nearest I let myself get to the monstrous pit of insecurity which I could sense lurking just under the surface of the fool's paradise of respite I was letting myself bask in.

Stupendous days – turning-point days – come without warning, and start as innocently as if butter wouldn't melt in their mouths.

One Saturday when Toby and John were having tea in my room John suddenly said: 'Why you and Toby don't come hear us playin' at the club some night?'

Toby said nothing, but looked at me inquiringly. Feeling rather at a loss, I said, 'I don't know, why don't we?'

'Because you've never asked us,' said Toby.

'I ask you now.'

'Would you like to?' Toby asked me, and added tactlessly, 'You never seem to have an evening out,' which made me suddenly suspect that he and John might have cooked this up between them.

'Yes, I would,' I said, without giving myself time to think. It was true, I hadn't been anywhere in the evening for weeks; in moments of self-pity I'd wept for that, as well as for other things. It's funny what petty things can push you over the border of tears when something enormous keeps you perpetually at the brink.

Toby, in one of his lightning spasms of enthusiasm, jumped to his feet, kicking his tea all over my-sister-made-that-rug. 'Oh sod it,' he said happily. 'Look, let's go tonight! Why not? It's Saturday, we'll see all the fun. Is it nice and noisy and sordid, Johnny?'

John grinned right across his wide black face. Do negroes have more teeth than other people? I'll swear they do.

'Sure, it good and sordid, you'll like it. All the time police comin' in, we is all runnin' like the bugs.' He held his feet, which were crossed beneath his thighs, and rocked backwards, laughing his stupendous black laugh.

'Really, police, Johnny?'

'No, I jokin'. Only when girls strip-tease and do dance under the bar, like in Jamaica. Then police come. Not strip-tease for a long time now – very good club, nothing wicked, you see. You come tonight, you'll like it.'

So we went.

I felt strange, getting ready. It was the first time I'd gone out with a man since – *Stop.* My mind obeyed me perfectly now. But just the same, it was strange. More particularly because it was Toby; somehow I'd never foreseen going out with Toby. He was just a nice boy to have around, but not one to get dressed up to go out with. For one thing, he was so small – I've always liked tall men, and Toby was shorter than I was. Still, what did that matter? It wasn't an evening of mystery and romance, for heaven's sake. I put on flat heels and a short-sleeved sweater, in case the place should be very hot, and then I dug out a straight skirt I sometimes used to wear for dancing. It was a bit creased and I pressed it carefully through a damp cloth on the table, and then tried to get into it. I struggled with the zip for about two minutes before I realized why it wouldn't do up.

I went quite cold, and had to sit down on the bed. It seems silly to say I'd forgotten, it was just that I hadn't let myself think about it for so long I'd stopped looking for symptoms. This one came as a frightful shock. My mouth was dry. I just sat there with the skirt open round my hips and my heart thumping away in my throat, seeing all that I'd pushed on ahead of me now irrevocably piled up and waiting, too big to be pushed any further.

After a long time, Toby knocked on my door.

'Are you ready, Janie?'

He sounded gay and excited. I remembered, idiotically, that he'd done today's two thousand words this morning, so he could go out with a clear conscience.

The old trapped feeling came racing back. I can't, I thought, I can't face it! Then I thought, If I don't go, what will I do? Sit here all the evening, with *It* – and *It* suddenly once more personal, explicit and terrifying. 'Just a minute,' I called back, my voice croaking out of a dry throat. I put the tight skirt back in my drawer with a sense of burying an enemy, and put on another, a full one. Even this didn't button comfortably, but it was too late to start changing my whole outfit now.

When I opened the door, there was a strange new Toby I scarcely recognized. He did, it seemed, have one decent suit, one clean white shirt, and one rather smart tie, all of which, together with polished shoes and a neatly-shaved face, transformed him utterly. Absurdly, I wasn't sure I altogether liked the result; I think it was the hair that worried me most; all those wild shaggy locks were slicked back behind his ears and off his forehead. It made him look like a baby seal emerging from the sea.

'Good heavens,' I exclaimed with tempered admiration.

His face fell a little. 'What don't you like?'

'It's marvellous – you look so different – '

'Yes, but what don't you like? Do you think it looks too dressed-up?'

'No, no! It's terribly smart – it's just – ' My fingers itched.

'What? Well, say it, will you?'

'The hair,' I said tentatively. 'It's a bit – well, it's just not you, that's all.'

'Let's face it, none of it's exactly the me we all know and love.'

He came past me and stared at himself in the mirror. 'I do look a bit of a spiv,' he admitted. He turned to me. 'Go on, do whatever you're dying to do to it – I'll submit myself.' He closed his eyes tightly as if waiting for a blow, and I felt an unexplained pang as I reached up very diffidently and ruffled it gently free of its watery bonds. His head bent and pushed up under my hand a like a cat being stroked. He purred.

I took my hand away, but he said, 'No, go on,' still with his eyes closed, and put his forehead unexpectedly against my shoulder so that his hair was tickling my cheek. The back of his neck had a shallow channel down it, lined with commas of dark hair. I put my hand on the big bump that was the back of his head and ran it lightly down to his collar. While it was still resting there he raised his head and looked at me. He had a little pleased grin on his face. His eyes, which were very bright and dark, were only slightly lower than mine.

There was a moment during which my hand stayed on his neck. His grin suddenly widened and he said impishly, 'So, what would you do if I did?'

Then it was quite easy to reply in the same tone, 'You'll never know. Come on, we'd better be off.'

The club was called The Rum Punch, and was situated, incongruously enough, in the crypt of a church. Actually the church had been bombed almost out of existence so it wasn't hallowed ground or anything, but it seemed odd, trooping through the remains of a cemetery and across the quiet paving-stones under the ruined arch, which all retained an air of desolated sanctity, and then going down the steps and instantly finding oneself in the heat and frenzy of a jazz-club. The change from the holy to the hell-like was too abrupt to be anything but faintly shocking.

It was such a crazy jumble of noise and colour and smoke and bodies that for a moment I held back instinctively from launching myself into the midst of that mindless crush; but Toby took my hand and said, 'Keep behind me – I'll fight a way through,' and then I was in the thick of it and it was too late to back out.

It was a long time since I'd been to a place like this, and it seemed to be a lot wilder than anything I'd remembered. When one was pushing through the crowd it was impossible to get bearings or even be sure what direction one was heading in – whether towards the small bar with its bamboo and fishing-net, or towards the dance-floor. This was just a small circular piece of the floor somewhere lost in the welter, whose demarcation lines seemed to be a matter of indifference to the dozens of dancing couples, most of whom couldn't possibly have heard a note the band was playing for the roar of voices, and who went right on dancing even when there was no music. If you could call it dancing; many of the couples just leaned against each other and went to sleep, as far as I could see.

Toby found the band, and John, by the simple expedient of heading into the deepest concentration of people and noise. It was an amiable crowd and nobody seemed to mind how much you pushed, and eventually, sweating and exhausted, we forced our way to the front of the mob standing and jiving round the band. There were five of them, all coloured, though four seemed to be West Indian and their relatively lighter skins made John look blacker than ever.

When he saw us he grinned broadly and waved. They were having a break between numbers and he motioned us to go and have a drink at the bar, mouthing 'On the house!' As we struggled through I saw him catch the eye of the bartender.

There were no seats at the bar; we just about managed to get a place against one end of it, near the coffee machine. Toby stood behind me to ward off inadvertent pushers, and when the barman came up he ordered two glasses of wine.

'You Johnny's guests?'

'Yes –'

'He said to give you rum punches.'

'No, thank you –' I began.

'He paid already. Speciality of the house.'

When they came they were enormous, hot and spicy, with slices of lemon floating among the bubbles of melted butter. We sipped them cautiously at first, but they were delicious and went down as innocently as hot milk, so we raised our mugs to John and then downed them.

'What a drink!' said Toby. 'Boy! Let's have another.'

'I couldn't.'

'I could – but okay, let's dance first and then have one.'

The band had struck up again, something fairly lively from the look of them though we couldn't hear much. Beginning three inches away from us, the whole cavernous room was a jigging, hopping, seething mass of dancers. The problem was, how to get oneself absorbed into a space which had already reached saturation-point.

I felt strangely reluctant anyway. The same feeling of unease which had assailed me as we first entered now returned. I didn't feel like getting jostled and bumped and pushed. But Toby had his arm round me and was firmly backing into the mass to establish a small beach-head for us away from the bar. Quite suddenly we were a part of that bouncing, pulsating entity; like single cells in a living organism, we seemed to be no longer individuals in the sense of having a separate identity; on every side we were hemmed in by other cells, as helplessly conformist as we were.

Like many small men, Toby was a good dancer, or he could have been under more favourable circumstances. As it was we did what the others did – stayed more or less on our own little spot and moved to a rhythm we could sense in the movements of the others round us, rather than hear. Toby started off by holding me in the conventional way, with only one arm round me, but before long it was obvious that our other arms, stuck out as they were, were in imminent danger of being torn away; so he put both arms round my waist and I tucked my elbows in and rested my hands on his chest. In this position I felt in some way protected from the buffetings of the crowd. Before long our cheeks came together, but it was too hot to be comfortable; they stuck, and when the number ended they came apart with a peeling sound.

'The heat in here's frightful,' I gasped as the coagulation broke up a little round us, restoring our right of individual movement.

'You need another of those rum things.'

'You must be mad! I want something iced.'

'You just think you do. A hot drink's much better for you. Like curry in India,' he explained seriously.

We were back at the bar. My eyes were smarting from the smoke and the top of my head felt as if someone were gently unscrewing it. 'Anyway, you can't afford it,' I said, which was fatal, of course.

'Who says I can't? I sold an article a week ago, didn't I?' He ordered the rums, and when they came we fought our way into one of the dark corners of the room where there were a few tables and benches. There we sat down in the shadows, feeling aloof from the whirlpool centre of activity; from here we could stand aside, observe, and comment. We drank our drinks and watched curiously the goings-on in nearby shadows.

'That one looks about thirteen,' whispered Toby, indicating a girl in a cheap cottony sweater which showed her under-developed pointy little figure. A gangly boy of about the same age was leaning over her, touching the points with what appeared to be simple fascination. The girl wasn't paying much attention; she was smoking a cigarette and occasionally brushed his hand away like a bothersome fly.

'God, that's terrible,' said Toby under his breath.

'Well, don't keep looking at them, then,' I said rather irritably. Something about the pair made me want to cry, and the sight of them gave me a physical pain too, in my breasts, a sort of sympathetic sensitiveness. I finished my drink and stood up. 'Let's go and see if John's ready for a drink,' I said, rather too loudly. Toby followed me willingly enough, but he seemed subdued.

'A couple of babies like that,' he said. 'That girl – just bored with the whole thing, long before she knows what it's supposed to be about.' He was really shocked. He nodded his head towards another, much older, couple running their hands all over each other and laughing without pleasure into each other's faces. 'That sort of thing doesn't bother me, somehow,' he said. 'It's disgusting, but then so are lots of things; those two'd be pretty disgusting even if they weren't touching each other. But that back there – that's not disgusting – it's sad. It's tragic. She just doesn't know what it's *about*,' he said again. He shook his head, frowning, as if bewildered.

I had a frightened feeling that he mustn't go on talking about them. In some oblique way, without knowing it, he was talking about me, he was telling me something about myself that I'd never allowed myself to know. There was a direct parallel somewhere; I wasn't quite clear about it yet, but it was close; one step further in his thoughts, and he'd put it into words, words I didn't want to hear . . .

'Do let's find John, he'll think we've run out on him,' I said urgently; but it was too late.

'One of these days,' Toby said, 'that poor half-baked little bitch is going to have a baby, without ever having understood what love really means.'

There it was; he'd said it, and I'd heard it, and it couldn't be unsaid. It was true, and it was my truth; I understood it for the first time.

I must have stopped moving, because he turned and came back to me and his face showed a sudden anxiety. 'Jane, what is it? Aren't you well, love? You've gone awfully pale . . .' I couldn't speak, nothing seemed worth saying or doing. I was right in the middle of a moment of truth, and it was still and quiet and empty in there, as it is supposed to be in the heart of a tornado.

Then John came forcing his big flame-coloured chest through the crowd and said, 'Hallo, there! I thought I never find you!' And I came out at the other side of the moment; the truth was still there, and still just as terrible, but after all it was something I'd known before, really, only I'd never let myself look at it. The trouble was that now I'd been made to look at it I couldn't seem to stop, the enormity of it kept shoving everything else out of my mind until I thought if I didn't get rid of it for a while I'd start shouting and banging my head against a wall to drive it away. So I drank the new drink someone had given me and asked for another. After that I started to feel better in one way, but not altogether, because now I was getting drunk and I knew I was, and for the first time in my life I made myself go on drinking when I reached the stage of wanting to stop.

I danced with Toby again and this time I didn't notice the crowds; I seemed to be cushioned against everything around me, and in Toby's arms I felt safely insulated. I rocked and floated gently and the pain was like the crowd, near and all round but unable to touch me.

I don't remember leaving the club, but I remember being in a taxi and saying to Toby, 'I'll pay for this,' and him saying 'This is my party, and I'm not sure this isn't the best part of it.' He put his arm round my shoulder and feeling it behind my neck I relaxed against it and I think I went to sleep, because the next thing was he was helping me up the stairs at the house; there were hundreds of flights, we kept finding more and more, and I kept going to sleep, and then the lights would come on again, and I was giggling because there were so many stairs and it kept being black and then light and then black again, like a checker board. Then at last we reached the top, and while Toby was fiddling with the key I thought I wouldn't wait for him to open the door but would just lie down there and go to sleep, because I'd never in my whole life felt so tired.

At last we got safely inside. Toby lit the table-lamp and the gas-fire, while I stood at the angle of the room looking at it. It looked better than it had ever looked, and I said to Toby, 'It's pleased to see us.'

'What do you mean? What is?'

'The room,' I said. 'It's happy we're home. It's saying "Shalom".'

He stared at me. 'How do you know that word?'

I shook my head. 'I don't know,' I said. 'But it means "peace".'

'I know what it means,' he said.

Then I started to cry. It was because the little room was wishing me peace, and there wasn't any peace, any more, ever. And because of the truth, too, the ugly truth about the sin I'd committed, the blasphemy of creating a life by accident, without understanding the true pleasure and beauty of love. Toby sat me on the bed and held my hands and said to me, 'What is it, darling? Don't cry, love, please, don't, what is it, can't you tell me?'– wiping my face with his handkerchief. And then he was taking the tears with his lips, he was kissing them away; he was kissing my eyes and my mouth and our arms were round each other, and somehow my crying changed, I wasn't crying in despair and wretchedness any more, but with a kind of luxury. My tears weren't coming out of pain now, but out of a new feeling, a feeling his lips were rousing, and his hands, and there was no part of my mind or body that wished to resist it, or had the strength to: without reasoning or doubting, all of me wanted what he wanted. But apart from that, there was a reason, a dark reason somewhere at the back of my mind that was urging me, that came from something I'd once heard or read that had lodged itself in my memory and rose up now and said that this might solve everything. But whatever wickedness in me added that vile motive to the other clean ones, was foiled and deluded; because if he had been my husband, and known I had his child in me, he couldn't have been more gentle. And the thought that wasn't really a thought fled before the pleasure I didn't deserve, but which came anyway, swelling and overtaking, in a generous wild exploding splendour that I had thought I would never know.

I hardly knew when it was over because that part was so wonderful too that I thought the magic would last forever. And when at last it began to fade, when I could begin to think again, his lips were still against my face and his arms warmly round me, and his voice murmuring to keep the frightened thoughts away.

After a long time he lifted his face and it was a new face to me, as if I'd never seen it before. Then he grinned, and that was the same, a left-over from before, and said, 'These idiotic beds aren't big enough for one person, let alone two,' and he rolled off and stood up. I clung on to his hand, in terror lest it should all become ordinary and awful with our physical separation; but he understood and bent towards me, whispering, 'Don't worry, darling, I'm not going. We can't both sleep on that bed, but I'm going to pull up this chair and sit beside you all night.' He reached out and caught the chair by the arm, and dragged it over one-handed so that he need not let my hand go. Then he sat down in it as close to me as he could get. He helped me to get between the sheets, and turned out the light, and I could still see him beside me in the half-darkness, and feel his hand holding mine.

'You'll be so tired . . .' I began.

'I'll sleep, don't you worry. And so will you. Go to sleep and don't be unhappy about *any*thing, and in the morning the first thing you'll hear will be me telling you that I love you.'

I slept because he had told me to. I dreamt no dreams, and in the morning the first thing I knew about was his hand, still in mine; I opened my eyes and there was his face, with the shadows deep on it, but awake and smiling; and before I had even moved he leaned over me and said, 'Jane, I love you.'

I closed my eyes and said to myself, Oh God, now what have I done?

Chapter 8

As with drinking, so with love – it's the morning after that counts, often more than the night before. And on this morning, of all mornings, James phoned at the crack of dawn and asked me to preside over a ridiculous Press party. Shivering at the landing extension, I heard his brisk boisterous voice rattling on about the historic meeting of a famous comic and a famous bust who were going to make a film together. 'The whole thing's a farce, of course, they've known and loathed each other for years, but the official version of this world-shaking meeting of titans has to take place in public where it can be duly recorded – and one of us must be there, and why should it be me on a Sunday morning when I've got an angelic assistant? You don't mind, do you, Jane dear, dear Jane?' I said no, I didn't mind, feeling nothing but numbness and coldness.

Toby stood at my elbow, and when I'd hung up and told him said, with a strange urgency, almost like despair: 'No, *no*, not *this* Sunday, for Christ's sake, can't you get out of it?' And I said no, I simply couldn't, banishing the thought that I probably could, quite easily, just by ringing James back and sounding a bit pathetic. I got ready with ludicrous haste (why? I kept thinking. There's no real hurry, it's not till 11.30) chatting brightly to hide the hollow empty absence of anything at all in the way of feeling, and kept my eyes off Toby's face which had a look on it as if someone were dragging his insides out.

When I was ready I went and stood beside him and touched his shadow-stained tired face and said, 'You look dead, Toby. Go to bed and get some sleep. Please. I'll be back before you wake up.'

He pushed his face awkwardly into my hand, nuzzling it like a puppy, and then suddenly grabbed it in both his and kissed it. 'I wish you weren't going out now,' he mumbled into the palm.

'I wish not too,' I said, not knowing what I wished.

He came down to the front door with me. There was no one about and he kissed my cheek and looked at me speechlessly.

'Don't look like that,' I said, trying to laugh. 'I'll be back in a couple of hours!' I started off, but he stopped me.

'You're not sorry?'

I had so hoped he wouldn't ask that. But as he had, I could only give him the answer he needed, without knowing for sure whether it was true or not. 'Of course not, darling!' The endearment eased the expression of pain on his face a little, but still he held me and still he searched my eyes for something I knew wasn't there.

'You haven't said you love me,' he said in a low voice.

My heart almost stopped with its own heaviness. I closed my eyes.

Quite suddenly, he let me go and his voice changed. 'I'm sorry,' he said, sounding as he might have sounded yesterday. 'I am an idiot. How could you say that yet?' I looked at him, surprised at his quick recovery, but then I saw he hadn't really recovered, he was just pretending in order not to hurt me. 'Go on,' he said lightly, 'quick, or you'll get the sack. And when you've done your duty, come 'ome, Jim Edwards.' He kissed me again, a different, unanguished sort of kiss which was somehow much more difficult to bear than the other.

Sitting in the train, with a Sunday paper which I'd automatically bought lying unopened on my knee, I felt a sense of relief at being away from him, at being surrounded by a lot of impersonal uncaring strangers who could see nothing different about me because they'd never seen me before last night. I was sure I must look a different person, that my guilt and radiance must have transfigured me.

I struggled to make some sense of this new and appalling complication. This time yesterday I would have said that what had happened last night was a laughable impossibility. I had done nothing to precipitate it; on that score at least my conscience was clear. Until the very last minute I had had no idea it could happen. But it had happened, and happened in a way that changed me, changed Toby, changed everything. Everything except the one thing that needed changing; that alone remained unspeakably the same.

Why, why hadn't I told Toby about it long ago? Then this would never have happened, or if it had (I couldn't bring myself to unwish an experience which still washed over me with waves of delight when I remembered it) at least Toby would have known what he was doing, his eyes would have been open. He wouldn't be suffering now, and he wouldn't have to suffer more, oh, how much more, later, when I told him . . . To think of telling him, now, made me feel sick with horror.

I was almost afraid to examine my feelings for him. It seemed dreadful that I didn't know whether I loved him or not, that I had never even thought of it in those terms. Everything had happened in the wrong order, and now I had to try to bring my feelings up to counter-balance the overpowering weight of this physical attraction which had sprung up out of nowhere and knocked me sideways. I closed my eyes and tried to think of Toby – just his face. What came was a sort of double-image – the boy I had known up to yesterday, young, grubby, entertaining, kind, lively, with his impish, monkey-plainness; and the face I had seen last night for the first time, a face wiped clean of everything but rapture and tenderness and astonishment, a different face, a face to love and find beautiful. They were the faces of two entirely separate people, and try as I would to superimpose them they wouldn't focus into a single man for whom I had a single, straightforward feeling.

As I came into the hotel I tried to project myself back into a time when I'd have been thinking – 'Sunday press party, rather fun. Wonder if old so-and-so will turn up?' Now my mind was so burdened with problems I couldn't even remember what James had said the party was about. I had to ask the man at the desk which room the reception was in; he mentioned the two famous names, and then I remembered, *Oh yes, the phoney meeting*. Several of the photographers and columnists were already drifting in in the hope of an early drink (they'd be unlucky – we couldn't serve drinks before twelve). I nodded to them, but when they looked at me I turned away quickly, for fear I should see them exchange puzzled glances.

I hurried into my own office, locked the door and stood before the mirror. Apart from the fact that I'd put my make-up on badly in my haste, I looked fairly normal – a bit flushed, maybe, and my eyes seemed unusually bright, but perhaps they only looked that way to me. I sat down behind my desk and tried to pull myself together; I was trembling suddenly, and I felt the hollowness inside me growing into a pain. I remembered I'd had nothing to eat or drink before leaving the house, and thought how awful that I hadn't even made Toby a cup of tea before obeying my impulse to run.

There would be hot coffee in the reception. That was what I needed – strong hot coffee. But something kept me sitting at the desk. I hated the idea of going in there among all those cheerful, back-slapping journalists with their good-natured vulgarity and genial earthy humour. I felt naked and horribly vulnerable, like a snail with its shell off; every nerve was close to the surface; I thought if anyone so much as touched me, I'd scream. Suddenly I wanted Toby, very much; I knew now how he felt when I left him. In a sense we were still in the aftermath of being one person. I realized suddenly that that was why lovers always feel the need to sleep together after making love, and to rest and be together the next day. They've been joined and need time to separate again into two complete people; if they're torn apart too soon there's a spiritual bleeding. I was beginning to understand a lot I'd never known about before, and for the first time that day Toby's fatal unthinking words came back to me: 'One day she'll have a baby without ever having understood what love really means.' Perhaps that wasn't completely true of me any longer. Certainly the sting had gone out of the words; I could think of them without being quite so ashamed.

I picked up the phone and gave the switchboard the Fulham number. Just to talk to him for a few minutes . . . I could say some of the things I hadn't been able to say when I left him, because I hadn't shared his feelings then. But I remembered I'd told him to go to bed; he'd be asleep by now. Well, it served me right. He'd had to go through that wrench of premature separation alone; now I had to. It was only fair.

I clicked the receiver-rest. 'Don't bother,' I said to the girl.

I went into the Juliet Room, where the reception was being held. The coffee cups were all laid out on long white-napped tables, and waiters hovered over the silver urn, dispensing coffee to a few early arrivals. I went round commiserating with the ones I knew, pointing out that if the lady with the bosom was as late as she normally was, the reception would undoubtedly extend into licensing hours. More people came. They were nearly all men, show-business or gossip columnists, old hands at the game and professional cynics, which well they might be on an occasion like this. Promptly at 11.30 the little comic arrived. He was a very nice man and popular with the journalists, who gave him a ragged but friendly cheer for turning up on time. Then we all settled down to wait for Madam.

Quarter to twelve came – twelve o'clock. I caught a waiter's eye and before long the drinks arrived; they were greeted with anything-but-ragged cheers, in which the comic wholeheartedly joined. I got a drink for him and he grinned gratefully at me.

'I'm awfully sorry about the delay,' I said.

'Don't you be sorry, lass,' he said. 'She's always "all behind", in more senses than one.' He winked good-naturedly over the rim of his glass.

I went from group to group apologizing, and then telephoned up to the lady's room. Her PRO answered the phone. He sounded as if he were distracted, but having to control it. 'We're not *quite* ready yet,' he cooed, if one can coo while grinding one's teeth. 'We want to look our very best – which shouldn't be a real problem as we're *so* gorgeous – but we've just had to change our clothes a couple of times. How are you getting on, Angel?' he called sweetly to Madam, and then hissed into the phone in a totally altered voice, 'She's in the loo, top-heavy cow that she is, I hope she falls in. What am I saying? – Could I pull the chain on my bread-and-butter?' He raised his voice and shouted, through the loo door, presumably, 'YES DARLING, OF COURSE I'M WAITING!' – and then to me, in a tormented undertone: 'And so are the Press, I know, I know – they must be ready to eat me for lunch. Stall them another five minutes, Janie, please, I'm trying to hurry her up – it's like pushing a ten-ton truck with its brakes on – YES MY PET, THAT LOOKS DIVINE – (dear kind God, wait till you see this) – well!' – brightly – 'Looks like we're on our way. 'Bye for now, Janie!'

He hung up and I went back to the salon. The crowd had just started to thin out, and there was a disgruntled note in the talk of those who were sticking it out. 'One more minute,' I told them. There was another onslaught on the drinks trays.

She came at last, swathed in mink, ushered in by the perspiring PRO. The photographers reluctantly put their glasses down and picked up their cameras as the PRO, his hands daintily plucking at the collar of the mink, prepared to unveil the famous figure. When every camera was in place, he whisked the coat away.

It really was the most extraordinary outfit I've ever seen. The red hair flowed over bare white shoulders. The celebrated bust, looking like two dunces' caps applied to her chest, was encased in a puce halter-necked sweater which left all but essentials bare. Her sizeable bottom and not-too-marvellous legs were thinly coated with bright yellow silk jeans ending just below the knee; her bare feet were thrust into pink mules with diamond spike-heels. She also wore a diamond brooch at her waist, the size of a buckler.

For a second there was an unbelieving silence – then a chorus of whistles and concerted pops and tinkles as every flashbulb in the room went off.

'Eeh, booger me,' murmured the little comic, who was standing near me. 'Have I got to 'ave me picture taken alongside of that? I'll feel like a seaside postcard.'

While all the posed pictures were being taken I was edging round among the columnists saying, 'Please, give us a break, don't put in that it happened at Drummonds. This is supposed to be a respectable hotel.' This was what I knew James would have done; the boys laughed wryly. 'Don't blame you. Don't worry. Thanks for the drinks, Janie.'

It was nearly over. I had a small breather in which to feel pleased that there was this part of me that could take over, like an automatic pilot, and carry on as usual. I knew that not one person had guessed there was anything wrong.

At this moment, Madam, who knew me, shrieked to me over the heads of the crowd: 'You – there – please! I'm simply *dying* of thirst. Could you do you think possibly find me a small drink?' The waiters were all busy at that moment so I picked up a full glass from the table and fought my way to where she was holding court in the middle of the mass – standing up, of course. She couldn't sit down; the yellow pants were too tight. I handed her the drink and she smiled at me with all her splendid teeth and said, 'Thank you. The men are all being *so* unkind, they're making fun of my relaxing clothes. Don't you think they're divinely chic?'

At this moment, at this precise moment, a feeling came over me that I hadn't had for nearly a month. My face went deathly cold and saliva rushed into my mouth. There'd been no warning. I clutched my throat and gasped. Madam's smile froze on her lips. 'What's the matter?' asked someone. 'I'm going to be sick,' I replied hollowly. A passage was cleared through the crowd like magic, and although they were all kindly men, a great shout of irrepressible laughter went up as I fled. As I left the room I heard the little comic bellow, 'That's what she thinks o' thy relaxing clothes, ducks, and I must say I see what she means!'

It should have been just one of those stories one dines out on afterwards, only the wretched woman thought I was being deliberately insulting and complained to the Management. And this time James wasn't around to cushion the blow.

I was sitting in my office smoking one of James's cigarettes – not the best thing, perhaps, for the queasiness I was still feeling, but I hoped it might calm my juddering nerves – when a pop-eyed page-boy knocked on my door and said the Old Man wanted to see me in his suite. I guessed what had happened, and despite a clear conscience began shaking in my boots. I lit another cigarette from the stub of the first (unheard-of for me) – not because I wanted it but because I felt it might give an illusion of poise to walk into the Presence with a cigarette dangling carelessly from my lips.

The Management was waiting for me in the lounge of his magnificent suite. He wore a Paisley dressing-gown which was a reminder of his good taste – not that one was necessary; the whole room, in fact the whole hotel, was a monument to it. I admired this man, though it was unfashionable to say so in conversation with the rest of the staff. He'd built the hotel himself, on a bombsite, and developed goodwill from scratch in competition with the best and oldest hotels in London by applying a maxim which, according to him, has fallen into disrepute – namely that quality pays. Every article and member of the staff, from the fire-buckets to the boot-blacks, had to be the best available. Compromises with his few but firmly held prejudices were only made when to hold out meant risking something irreplaceable. James, for all his vagaries, was the best PRO in the hotel business, which explained why I, a non-Jew and a woman, had obtained my present job. I knew he'd fought James on it tooth and nail, and though in all honesty I felt I'd won him round to some extent since, the prejudices remained beneath the surface of benignity, waiting only for some unwary blunder on my part to crack the surface and let them burst through.

Such a blunder I'd now committed. As I entered the room I wished I'd thought of phoning a desperate SOS to James. I wasn't sure what he could have done from Purley, where he lived, but I had very great confidence in his championship. Standing small and shaky before that vast desk, surrounded by all the trappings of success and power, I felt very helpless and the cigarette seemed about as much of a morale-builder as a pocket-handkerchief is a protection against a firing-squad.

He sat at his desk writing, and I almost groaned aloud as I thought: *Oh God, no, not another one!* The junctures of my life seemed to be marked off monotonously by men at desks, as if Fate had adopted this as a regulation traffic-signal meaning 'Sharp turning'.

He didn't keep me waiting, however; he was not the sort of man who needed gimmicks to make his effects. Smiling at me politely he said, in his still slightly-accented voice, 'Sit down, Miss Graham. Cigarette? Oh, you have one. Well now, I had a complaint about you this morning. You know who from?'

I sighed to combat the hollowness of nerves. 'I can guess.'

'Would you like to tell me your version?'

I told him simply that I had felt ill at a very unfortunate moment.

'No offence meant, eh?' I shook my head wearily. 'Now Miss Graham, as you know, I think, I am not a fool, and I am always on the side of my staff – if it is possible to be so without alienating a client. I know that she is a silly woman, a vain woman – I speak now in confidence, of course. I knew that what she told me couldn't be the whole story. I defended you.'

'Thank you.'

'In such a way that she felt I was in sympathy with her, of course.'

'Of course.'

'What caused you to be ill?'

'I don't really know. It could have been a number of things.'

'Something you ate, perhaps? Only not in my hotel.' He smiled, and I smiled back rather pallidly.

'Have you been to see a doctor?'

I was confused by all these solicitous questions, and found myself telling more lies than I had to. 'No, I haven't bothered.'

'But this is not the first time you have been unwell, is it?'

I was startled. It was true what was said of him – he knew everything, but everything that happened in the hotel, even, it seemed, what took place in the ladies' lavatories.

'I'm sure it'll pass off.'

'One hopes so. In the meantime . . .' The lines of his face tilted downwards and he shrugged. 'Episodes like this morning are very unfortunate. They create such a bad impression, cause so much needless ill-feeling. A hotel such as this, with a reputation for perfection, cannot afford such incidents. You understand?'

I sat there silent for a moment while he went on looking at me sympathetically as if I'd been telling him a hard-luck story. I shifted in my seat and said, 'No, I'm afraid I don't quite. Are you sacking me because I was taken ill?'

He smiled a little, without altering the sad expression. 'No, Miss Graham, that would not be fair. I am only suggesting that you take a little time off, shall we say, until you are quite well again?' He had his chin resting on his hand, and one finger was against his long nose in a curious gesture that suggested that he was saying one thing and meaning another. Something in his eyes, too, gave the impression of a deeper meaning underlying the conversation. He had a formidable reputation as a hard, cryptic, ruthless man whose god was perfection and whose greatest intolerance was for any weakness or sentiment which undermined it; but there was something in his face as he looked at me which was very like kindness. I thought I must be wrong, because kindness didn't go with what he was doing.

The moment ended, and he grew sharp and brisk again. 'I shall speak to Paige about it,' he said. 'In the meantime, you go off home.' His tone was dismissive, and I got up to go. At the door he stopped me. 'You like Paige, don't you?' he asked unexpectedly.

'Yes, very much.'

'He's a good fellow, and a good friend of yours. Perhaps you wish he were here now, eh?' If I hadn't detected the kindness before, I'd have thought he was sneering; now I wasn't sure. I wanted to hate him for doing this to me, so much earlier than I had thought it would be done, but it was difficult to hate a man I had such respect for.

I smiled, rather ruefully.

'Good, you are smiling. I hope you do not feel bitterly towards me. You understand, my hotel comes before everything.' I nodded. 'But about Paige. It would have made no difference, had he been here. And to be quite truthful with you, this morning did not make much difference either. I had heard you were not well; I was going to speak to you anyway. My staff must be, as you say, one hundred per cent.' He looked at me with his head cocked on one side like a bright-eyed bird. 'Thank you for the very good work you have done here,' he said.

'I've enjoyed working for you very much.'

'Good. You know you would not have been engaged if Paige

had not insisted. I cannot approve of women in key positions. But Paige is a man of very good judgement, like most Jews.'

He knew, and he knew that I knew, that James was no more Jewish than I was. But it hurt him in some way to admit that one of his key men came from the wrong end of the Bible, so to speak.

I went back to my office and shut myself into it for the last time. I tried to recapitulate all the rude names James had ever called the Management. I raged inwardly against his injustice and vindictiveness; I told myself he was a pro-Jewish fanatic, and anti-feminist to the point of misogynism; that he was a bigot, a bully and a nepotist (this last was more than unfair, as the extent of his nepotism was his sister's husband's niece who was a chambermaid).

But in fact all I was doing was putting off the moment of reckoning. When I had stopped kicking against the pricks I began to ask myself how much longer I could have gone on without somebody noticing the change in my figure. Had I proposed to keep working until the hotel was a hotbed of gossip, and leave only when I'd made myself the centre of a tasty little scandal? Wouldn't my dismissal, inevitable eventually, have been a whole lot more unpleasant at that stage? In a way, without knowing it of course, the Old Man had done me a favour.

But all the same, leaving was hard. I sorted my few things out slowly, and splashed them with valedictory tears. It was James I wanted at this moment, more than Toby, who couldn't have been expected to understand this.

But as soon as I had left the building, James and the Old Man and all the ties and affections of my ex-job began to blur. My life lay away from them now, and the problems I had brought to work with me that morning reclaimed me with redoubled urgency. A great longing for Toby seized me. The thought of the complicated journey back by London Transport seemed unbearable. I called a taxi.

Chapter 9

OUTSIDE Toby's door, I hesitated. People asleep are so vulnerable; I didn't want to disturb him too suddenly. Holding the door handle, I savoured in advance the small luxury of waking him. I wondered if he would see at once that something had happened to make my need of him as great as his had been of me when he last saw me.

I turned the handle gently and opened the door. There was no one in the room.

The sense of disappointment was as sharp as a blow, painful out of all proportion, so much so that for a moment I was almost angry with him for not being there. I stood in the doorway, feeling quite dazed with loneliness, looking at the bed where he should have been lying.

Then I realized how absurd I was being. Obviously he'd gone out for cigarettes, or lunch – or perhaps – it was a sudden exciting hope – he was upstairs in John's room, waiting for me there.

For the first time, a thought occurred to me. We had left John last night at the club, and I wondered with a quailing sensation when he had got home. It seemed incredible I hadn't thought of that before – normally I was constantly aware of his proximity through the thin dividing wall.

I went upstairs uneasily and knocked on his door. Instead of opening it, he called out after a moment: 'Who there?' and when I answered, there was a long silence which alarmed me.

'Go away,' he said at last. He seemed to be standing just inside the door.

'What's the matter?' I asked, sharply because of my nervous embarrassment. Then, as he didn't answer, I said, 'I want to ask you something.'

After another pause the door opened. Any doubts I had had were dispelled by the look of contemptuous hostility on his face. I felt myself turning hot and cold.

'What you want?' he growled like a hurt child.

'What's the matter?'

He turned his back on me and walked into the room. I followed, tentatively. I'd never been in there before; it was dark and stuffy and full of bloody, primitive colours. John pulled a chair forward with a violent, angry gesture and sat down on it facing away from me with his arms along its back.

I went up behind him and put my hand on his shoulder. I suppose I must have touched him many times before, but not consciously or deliberately. It seemed a rather difficult thing to do, somehow, which surprised me, as I hadn't realized I still had some atavistic buried fear of him because he was black.

John twitched his great shoulders as if a wasp had landed on them.

'Why you don't go away,' he muttered without looking round. His voice was muffled and I thought he was trembling.

Without touching him again, I said, 'John, have I done something to offend you?'

He put his face down on his arms and his voice was muffled. 'Yes, you done somethin' to offend me. You done somethin' offend any decent person.'

Well, there it was, you couldn't ask for anything plainer than that. My armpits pricked with embarrassment. But I couldn't leave it at that.

'John, listen. What happens between two people only concerns them. If you hadn't been next door here, you'd never have known.'

'You think that make it all right – if no one know?'

'But why should it upset you so much? Toby and I are the same two people we were yesterday – we're still your friends –'

'Not the same. I don't know you from yesterday.' He lifted his head, but still without looking at me; his huge hands were clenched into fists. 'How you think I feel, lyin' here listenin'? My friends. My friends.' He was crying.

'How do you think I feel, knowing you heard? But John, it's not – a crime or anything. People . . .' I faltered and stopped. I felt he wasn't listening. I leaned over him and said in a different tone, 'Do you know where Toby is?'

John shot me a look, and then looked away again. Without knowing why, I felt the advantage had suddenly shifted. He shrugged uneasily. 'I don' know. Maybe he downstairs in the basement.'

A dull presentiment of hurt came over me. 'What do you mean – the basement?'

He turned to me slowly, and I saw his face, expressionless in its blackness, with his yellow eyes fixed on me coldly, like an animal's. 'With the other whores,' he said distinctly.

I got out quickly. My own room was no good; it was too close. I thought I could feel his disgust penetrating the thin wall. I went downstairs into Toby's room and locked the door. I was panting and trembling and icy cold. After a minute or two I was sick again. I felt no better after it. I sat numbly by the open window, with my legs pressed together, my arms hugging my sides and my hands gripping each other, to combat the sensation that I was going to shake myself to pieces. *He said that without knowing*, I thought. *If he knew about the baby, what would he call me then?*

I must have sat there for about half an hour or more. My brain was scarcely working at all. Odd words and phrases came up occasionally into my mind, like obscenities on a blank wall. Whore was the main one.

Suddenly I got up and went downstairs. I went out of the front door and down the area steps to the basement entrance. I don't know what I thought I was doing. I had some dim idea that I should see what sort of creatures these whores were, so that I might find out what *I* was.

I knocked on the door. I had to wait a long time for an answer, and just before the door opened I nearly came sufficiently to my senses to run away, but sanity came too late.

'Yes? What do you want?'

She wasn't a young woman, by any means. She didn't look much like my idea of a prostitute either, but that was because she hadn't any make-up on. She had a longish, plain face with a straight nose and almost no eyebrows; she must have plucked them away in order to repaint them in higher up. Her hair was in rollers in the front, and had a dull reddish look like old rust. She was wearing an old woollen dressing-gown and smoking a cigarette.

I stood staring at her. She was a good twelve years older than me, but allowing for that, I'd seen myself look not much better some mornings in the last few months, my skin blotchy, my eyes shadowed and swollen, my lips pale and dry-looking, my hair lifeless and uncombed.

The woman was frowning at me. 'I've seen you before,' she said. 'You came to see Doris about bed-bugs.'

'Yes, that's right,' I said.

She smiled. Her teeth were a better shape than mine, only tobacco-stained. 'Old Doris!' she said with a snort. 'My God, she was fit to be skinned! Never seen her in such a state. Laugh! I nearly fell out of my chair. You know, you've got me to thank she didn't chuck you out. I told her straight, the kid's right, I said. You should've seen this place when *we* moved in.' She gestured over her shoulder into the gloomy flat. 'She's a dirty old faggot, but she's got a good heart when you know where to look for it.'

She took a long draw on her cigarette, looking at me curiously. 'Want to come in for a minute?'

'Thank you.'

I followed her in and she closed the door. There was a smell inside that made all my senses rear up like a horse that smells blood. It was dirt, and stale perfume, and something else. I breathed through my mouth, but I still got the feeling of it.

'It's all in a bit of a state, I'm afraid. We don't get around to much cleaning.'

She led me into a bed-sitting-room. I was very surprised by how cosy it was. The colours all yelled at each other; most of the furniture was cheap and shabby and it was in a clutter of smelly untidiness, but the general effect was of a room somebody had made the best of according to their taste, and enjoyed living in. Like mine.

She scooped some underwear off a chair and said, 'Sit down, dear. Sorry it's such a mess. I don't often have a woman's eye over it; men don't notice these things much.' She spoke quite casually. 'As a matter of fact, you got me up. Oh, it's all right, I was awake anyway. I'm not sleeping too well just lately. Do you ever get that? Not being able to sleep? I've tried everything for it – nothing's any good. Call themselves doctors! Like a cup of tea?'

I said I'd love a cup of tea, which was surprisingly true. 'But don't go to any trouble,' I said.

'No trouble, I'm just going to make some. Son'll be wanting one when she wakes up – she's the girl I share the flat with. Nice kid – Hungarian, she is. Come over with the refugees, right after the revolution. You hear about that?' I nodded. 'Well, you know how it is, things that don't concern you, in the papers and that – you don't always read 'em, do you? But with Son being here, talking about it once in a while when she gets a bit down, and don't we all – well, I feel like it all happened last week, and what's more as if I was in the middle of it. Fair makes your hair stand up, the way she tells it. Kids making their own bombs and chucking 'em into the tanks, getting theirselves blown up... those lousy Russians, sound worse than the Jerries, if you ask me. Not that I've got anything against them personally. But Son! You know, she's sworn to me she wouldn't have a Russian if he offered her a thousand quid. She says she can smell 'em. I sometimes think she half-hopes one'll come up to her one night, just so she can spit in his eye.'

She was wandering about the room, pulling the covers up on the bed and tidying up half-heartedly, waiting for the kettle on the gas-ring to boil. While she chatted I could feel the hard knots inside me untying themselves, the way tensed muscles relax in a warm bath.

'I used to tease her about it,' she went on. ' "Meet any Russians today?" I'd ask her. But she didn't like it. Can't blame her, really. There's some things you just can't see the joke in. Like, with me, it's – ' She stopped. 'Gawd, listen to me, going on! Oh good, there's the kettle.' She got the things out of a cupboard crammed full of everything, and made the tea, rambling on as she did it. 'You probably came about something, and here I never even asked what it is! It's having someone to talk to, I'm not used to it. Like Son, she's a good girl, but she doesn't understand English too well, even now. Speaks it okay, but doesn't understand it. Hungarian's a funny language – sounds like a mouthful of peanuts. Listen to this.' She stood with the teapot in her hand and recited carefully: 'Ha-yoke-lesteck-cop-toke-chock. Know what that means? "If you're a good boy, I'll give you a kiss." Isn't that a scream? Son taught it to me, in case I ever got a Hungarian. I never have, though. Bet it doesn't mean that at all, bet it's something terrible, like calling an Indian a son of a pig. How do you like yours, weak or strong?' When she'd poured the tea she said she must go out soon – 'It gets dark so early this time of year' – and started to potter about the room getting dressed. I noticed that she was very modest in front of me, going through mild contortions putting on her undies beneath her dressing-gown, and once when it fell off, revealing her shabbily but quite decently clad in a mauve rayon slip, she snatched it up with a quick 'Sorry dear'.

Sitting in front of a small baby-frilled dressing-table to put on her make-up – a fascinating procedure – she remembered again to ask what I'd come for. As I wasn't very clear about it myself, it was naturally difficult to think what to tell her; but I managed to falter something unconvincing about borrowing something. She laughed.

'Don't give me that!' she said kindly. 'You'd have asked at the door if it had been that. Come on, tell the truth and shame the devil – what are you, one of these writers? Or an actress, going to play a prossie or something, is that it? I've met your sort before.' But she didn't seem at all angry, just amused.

'I'm sorry – ' I began awkwardly.

'Chuck it, ducky, I don't mind, why should I? Just seems a bit silly, that's all. I mean, how can you really know what it's like without trying it? Still, it's nothing to me. What do you want to know?'

'How did you start?' I asked, fiery with embarrassment, and yet intensely curious at the same time.

'I thought you'd ask that first. They all do. Believe me, starting's the easy part – it's keeping going that's hard. Still – how did I start? Well, it was in the war. Younger than you I was then, but no chicken. Let's see. First of all there was an American. I thought a lot of him. He was killed somewhere or other.' She was applying her eyeshadow, thick and purple on the tip of her little finger, and gave me a quick sideways look in the glass. 'Oh don't get the wrong idea – I wasn't driven on to the streets through grief, or nothing like that. Tell you the truth, there was two or three others after the first one went overseas, before I knew about him being dead. I suppose the truth was, in those days anyway, I just plain liked it. Seems funny to think of that now.'

'You don't like it any more?'

'What, f—ing? Doesn't mean a thing, ducks, one way or the other. Lumme, you'd go mad if it did. Have another cup?'

I had another cup and watched her take the rollers out of her hair and comb it carefully into a high, curly pompadour. She was turning into a tart before my eyes.

'Have you never wanted to be married?' I asked.

'No-o-o! Well – ' she hesitated. 'Perhaps I did once. But after a few years of this, you can't really see any attraction in it, except the security, of course. Fancy promising to love, honour and obey – some *man*. That's what'd stick in my throat.' She picked up her eyebrow pencil and looked at me shrewdly. 'Now you're going to ask if I hate all men. Well, I don't. You can't hate what you don't respect. I'm sorry for them – I don't suppose you believe that, but it's true. Even the queer ones, the ones that want a bit off the other side of the cake, well, you can't help but be sorry for 'em. And some you can only laugh at – only you mustn't let 'em see it, of course. They expect you to take 'em seriously, no matter how pitiful they are – in fact, the more pitiful they are, the more their wives at home probably laugh at 'em, the more they expect you to behave as if they was some Eastern potentate or something. That's really what they pay you for, those sort, and if you do your job right, off they go looking six inches taller. How they can fool themselves you mean it, when you tell 'em they're wonderful, I don't know, but there you are. Men can always fool themselves, that's what they're best at. It's a pity they can't make a living at it then they'd all be millionaires and prices'd be better.'

Her eyebrows were on now, thin grotesque parodies above the purple lids. There was a long narrow mirror by the window and she went over to it and examined herself, full-length but in sections.

'You probably think my life's some kind of tragedy, but I'll tell you – one of the hardest parts of it's keeping a straight face. I mean, if you're not enjoying it yourself, you can't help but think how funny men are when they're doing it. Puffing and blowing, their bottoms stuck in the air – well, I mean, it's *funny* – like, undignified.' She started going through her bag, making sure she had everything, like a woman going out for an ordinary evening. 'Girl I knew – Holy Roman she was, Irish – she used to say God thought it up as a joke, and when he found people taking it serious instead of laughing, he was so put out he made it a sin. Ever so religious she was, though, underneath. Used to cry her eyes out sometimes when she'd had a few, and say she'd be in purgatory for about a million years. Can't be worse than this, I'd tell her to cheer her up, but she said oh yes it can. Fancy believing in a God like that!'

She snapped her bag shut and groped under the bed for her shoes. They were light beige with high heels. 'Do you like these?' she asked. 'They're Italian – ever so smart. Soft, too. I spend a lot on shoes; it's worth it when you're on your feet so much.' She slipped them on. I noticed she had slightly knotted veins in her calves. 'That's another nasty thing about this job – all the standing about. What I'd like is just a few regulars, that'd come by appointment, like, so I could stay at home. I'd keep the place a bit tidier, too. Had a nice place once, you know – in the West End. That was when I just had the one fellow. He was a real gent. You should have seen the place I had then – carpets and pictures, lovely it was, I kept it a treat. I could've had the Queen Mum to tea there and not been ashamed. Oh well, it was nice while it lasted.' She had a quick look round the room and shoved a few things out of sight in the glory-hole cupboard. 'Look at the time!' she said. 'I wonder what's happened to Son – still, better not wake her, she worked till all hours last night, she deserves a bit of a lay-in. You don't mind if

I throw you out now, do you, dear? I'm ever so sorry, but you know how it is.'

I followed the clack of her high heels down the dark corridor to the front door. The smell wasn't half so bad now, because I was following a newly-laid trail of fresh scent. I felt quite calm again, as divorced from my own immediate problems as if I were coming out after seeing a particularly absorbing film. Standing outside in the gloom of the area she said, quite naturally, 'You go ahead, dear, and I'll follow you after a minute or two. You don't want to be seen with me.' And before I could protest, she went on: 'I hope you found out all you wanted to know. I'm apt to chatter on about nothing, and I must say it was nice to have someone to talk to, like I said.'

'I've enjoyed meeting you,' I said.

She looked at me for a moment, measuringly, as if wondering whether I meant it. 'Have you?' she said at last, curiously. Then, briskly: 'What a lousy night! I hate this bloody mist, it gets into everything and makes your hair straight.' It was the first time she'd sworn, except the one perfectly correct use of a word more generally used in any but its proper context. My language was considerably worse than hers.

'Good-bye,' I said, and shook hands with her. I went up the stone steps into the street, and let myself into the house. I didn't quite close the door, and after a few moments I could hear her footsteps walking briskly past. Looking after her, I saw her reach up and tuck a strand of hair into place before the dark mist swallowed her up. I suddenly remembered her name was Jane.

Chapter 10

TOBY didn't come back that night, or all the next day. It was a very long twenty-four hours for me, long and full of worry. With no work to go to and nothing to do except sit in my room and think, I got through a fair number of mental scenarios by the time the next damp grey evening arrived.

In the meantime, James phoned. At half past nine in the morning, to be exact. I'd hardly got the receiver to my ear before he launched into a blistering tirade.

'How the hell did it happen? Why didn't you phone me? How dare that little bastard do a thing like this without a word of warning? That slimy, devious little kyke, I'd like to break his scrawny Yiddish neck! Don't get me wrong, Jane, I've nothing against the Jews, I like them; I haven't got a single Jew for a friend, but they're a fine race. But that rotten yellow-gutted two-timing little toad – ' I let him go on like that a while, to get it out of his system. I knew perfectly well that he respected the Manager and even liked him though it was against his nature to admit it; the thing that maddened him was that this had happened behind his back, and for a reason which he obviously found as inadequate as I did.

Eventually when he'd exhausted his immediately available epithets and had to pause to think up a few more off-beat ones, I interrupted.

'Listen, James, thanks for the fireworks, but it's not worth it. I mean, don't get yourself into a state over it, or issue any rash ultimatums or anything.' I couldn't explain that I would have had to leave in a month or so anyway – but I pointed out that in fact I wasn't well, hadn't been for quite a while whatever he chose to think, and that a rest would do me good. 'If you want to do me any favours,' I said, 'maybe you could get me reinstated later, when I'm better. The Old Man said something that suggested it might only be a temporary suspension. What do you think? Do you think it was just an excuse to get me out?'

'I don't know what the hell to think. A more utterly feeble excuse for sacking anyone I've never heard – it's just not *like* the Old Man,' he said, doing a volte-face. 'He knows when he's on to something good, and he's loyal to his staff, I'll give him that, whatever he may have to say to anyone behind closed doors.'

'Have you seen him?'

'SEEN him? Little pieces of him are quivering all over his deep-pile carpet right now, but it didn't seem to make the slightest impression. He just smiled and wouldn't even fight back. I just can't understand what the bloody hell's going on in his mind – his crafty crooked little beetle-brain, I mean,' he added to keep his end up.

'Well listen, don't worry about it, James. I've got two years' superannuation to come, and I've saved a bit since I left home . . .'

'Balls to that, we'll see you get another job. I know everybody in this lousy shyster business – I'll ring – '

'No, look, don't do that just yet. I really do need a rest, James. Honestly.'

There was a baffled pause, and then James said, in a worried voice, 'Jane dear, you're not really ill, are you? I mean, it's not anything serious or anything, is it? I mean, if I'd thought there was something really wrong, I'd have seen that you stayed at home – this makes me feel I've been driving a sick horse or something –'

I couldn't help laughing. 'Well, thanks very much, but don't feel like that. I thought I was perfectly all right, and then it chose yesterday to catch up with me again suddenly . . . you've been quite right to ignore it; it's helped, truly.'

He grunted, obviously unpacified. 'Well, anyway, you'll go home now, won't you – I mean, to your father's? You can't possibly be ill in digs, you might die and nobody'd know anything about it –'

I said I thought it better to stay where I was. 'I've got friends here,' I said, my cheerful voice belying a heavy heart. 'Anyway, I'm not going to retire to bed or anything, I'm just going to laze around. Please don't worry, James.'

'I think I'll come round and make sure you're all right,' he said suddenly.

'No, don't, don't do that!' I said, too urgently.

'Why not?' he asked suspiciously. 'Is there something wrong with the place? It's a nice flat, isn't it? You told me it was.'

I was getting in deeper and deeper with my lies. Never having foreseen James would suddenly develop a sense of extra-office responsibility for me, I had rather let myself go describing the flat of a rich friend which allayed James's earlier mild concern about where I was living.

Now I protested that it wasn't properly decorated yet and that I'd rather he came when I had it looking its best. So far I'd managed to avoid giving him the exact address, but now he asked for it with a determined note in his voice – 'Just in case I'm down that way' – and I was forced to invent one, praying that he'd never check up on it. 'I'll invite you one of these days soon, James, and a thousand thanks for everything.'

'Keep in touch,' he ordered sternly. 'I shall ring you every few days anyway, to make sure you're okay.' I knew the chances were he wouldn't remember to do this, and said good-bye with a lightness which was a piece of very good acting. In fact, I felt it was pretty sure to be a final good-bye. I knew I would never have the courage to go and ask for my job back after the baby was born, even if circumstances allowed it; it would soon be filled again, and it's always horrible to go back to a place where you've been happy in your own little niche and find somebody else in it.

I put the phone down, wondering how many people had been listening in on the extensions, and went back into my room. It was looking a mess because I hadn't had the heart to tidy it; the sky outside had a yellow-grey sameness, without a hint of where the sun might be, and in that light the flowers on the dirty brown wallpaper looked sadder than ever. It struck me suddenly we were within two weeks of Christmas. It was a depressing thought. There's nothing more depressing than facing Christmas without having anyone to buy presents for.

But that was morbid. Toby would come back – of course. I went down again to his room to make sure he hadn't returned in the night. Everything was the same as it had been when he left it to go to the club the night before last. I picked up a towel off the floor – it was still damp – and his ordinary clothes, the creaseless grey flannels and aged corduroy jacket which he wore day in, day out, were slung across the bed. Only the table where he worked was orderly, the piles of flimsy and top-copy paper lined up neatly, the newly-typed draft face-down beside the covered machine.

I put my hand on the last page, and hesitated. Toby had never offered to read me any of his work; but now I had a sudden longing to know whether or not he could really write. I turned the page over.

It was not clean and tidy as if the thoughts had flowed easily; it was double-spaced, and the spaces were larded with corrections in type and pencil, crossings-out, insertions, changed words . . . it was very hard to make it out. It seemed to be about a young woman, thinking aloud as she went about her home doing her chores. Her children were both obviously too little to understand more than the tone of her voice, and as she dressed them to go out with her to the shops she was saying '. . . and when Daddy comes home, we'll show him, shall we? We'll show him we're happy, and comfortable, and safe, and we'll pretend our happiness is enough for all four of us. Because that's all he's got, his knowledge that we're happy; it's got to make up for hating what he does every day to keep us safe.

And wouldn't it be awful if he ever realized that it's not very important to us, that we'd rather *not* be safe if only he had the courage to take our safety away . . .'

I remembered what he'd told Mavis and me about the book and more than ever I thought it sounded like a good idea – the story of a man rationalizing his own lack of self-belief . . . Mavis! I thought suddenly. She might know . . .

I ran down the next flight of stairs and knocked on Mavis's door. I found her bustling about with a feather duster looking as if she'd been up for hours.

'Hullo, dear, not at the office today?' she said.

'No,' I said. 'As a matter of fact, I've lost that job.' I tried to sound as matter-of-fact about it as possible, and she picked up my tone.

'Oh dear, well you'll have to get another then, won't you?' She was tenderly dusting all the objects on the mantelpiece. 'Clever girl like you, I don't expect you'll have any difficulty,' she added comfortably.

I knew it would be wiser to settle down and chat for a while, and drop my question casually into the conversation, but I couldn't wait. 'Mavis, have you any idea where Toby is?'

'Toby? Isn't he in his room?'

'He hasn't been home all night,' I said, trying to keep the anxiety out of my voice.

'Now I come to think of it, I haven't heard him moving about. Well now, fancy that, I wonder where he could have got to? Perhaps he's gone to visit one of his friends – he does that sometimes.'

'Does he stay away overnight?'

'Well, he *has* done. Not very often, though. Still, you're not worried, are you, dear? He's all right. He couldn't get into any trouble, he's not the sort that attracts it. Some sorts do and others don't. Now, you, for instance,' she said, her vague look suddenly sharpening into pinpointed attention, 'you, I should think, do. Draw it like a magnet, your type does. If you were missing from the house overnight, I *would* be worried. Almost anything could happen. But Toby, no.' She resumed her vague look and her dusting. I excused myself and went back to my room, not feeling very reassured.

I sat there, restlessly, until late afternoon. I forgot about lunch.

John was next door. I was unhappily aware of him all day, moving about his room, occasionally muttering to himself. When it began to grow dark I noticed through the little connecting window that he didn't put his light on; this alarmed me, somehow. It didn't seem natural to be sitting there in the dark. What could he be doing?

Round about four o'clock he did a thing I'd never known him do since I got there – he started to play his guitar. He beat out ten minutes of pain-filled, throbbing rhythm, sometimes accompanied by low, anguished singing, before Doris came stamping and puffing up the stairs and banged on his door and told him to stop it at once. I expected him to answer her back – there was such a passion in his music, he didn't sound like himself at all, any more than he had looked like himself yesterday – but he just struck the wires of his guitar into a tortured discord and after that there was a beaten silence, and Doris stamped off downstairs again, talking all the way about her poor legs and her poor head.

We sat on the opposite sides of the partition and sensed each other's misery.

After a long time I heard him get up and come over to the long wall, near to where I was sitting listlessly in the arm-chair. Then there came a knock, very light and tentative, the sort of knock one might make accidentally, brushing against the wall. I reached out and knocked back.

We met outside on the landing. The tears were streaming down his face; I could see them in the light from my room. For a second something stopped dead in me, as if paralysed by feeling his pain on top of my own; then we groped forward in one mutual movement and fell into each other's arms.

Even in that very emotional moment, I felt a little twinge of uneasiness at being embraced by this huge, odd-smelling, odd-coloured man. It was a very strange feeling, and the strangeness didn't come entirely from his being of a different, a 'forbidden' race. It came from there not being even that trace of sexuality which there always is between men and women, even those who are just friends. I tried to remember when I'd been held like that before, and by whom. Then I did remember – it was Malcolm, the little queer who had scratched my face all those years ago. But the contrast was so ludicrous that the thought flashed straight across my mind and was gone.

We went into my room and sat down on the floor together, and dried each other's tears; then I began to laugh a bit, ruefully, because I suddenly imagined how we must look, a hulking great coloured man and a girl sitting snivelling in front of a gas-fire mopping up the tears with dozens of paper hankies. John's tears were so enormous it was like trying to stem a leak in the plumbing.

'Please do stop,' I begged at last. 'We can't go on like this, I'm running out of Kleenex.'

'I sorry, I very sorry,' he kept on saying.

'I know. It doesn't matter.'

'Please forgive me.'

'I forgive you.'

He stared at me tragically, the yellow whites of his eyes bloodshot. 'But I call you a whore!'

'Yes. Well, there are worse things you could have called me.'

'Worse name than whore?' he said incredulously.

'Whores aren't so bad,' I said. 'Anyway, I'm not one, and you know it and I know it, which is all that matters.'

He hadn't quite understood this, and hastened to assure me, 'You not a whore! I was angry when I say that.'

'I know. I know I'm not a whore,' I said. That at least I knew now. I might still get called one, but it would never hurt again.

'And you forgive me?' he repeated, just like a child.

'Yes. Now let's have something to eat. I haven't eaten all day.'

While I got us some bread and butter and milk he sat on the floor with his great head bent, staring at the carpet and tracing its patterns with his forefinger. When I brought him the food he pushed it away and suddenly burst into tears all over again.

'John, for heaven's sake! What's the matter now? It's all forgotten and over!'

'Not over!' he blubbered. 'I haven't told you – you will be angry and this time not forgive me!'

A sudden fear gripped me. 'Toby – '

He turned to me, grabbing both my wrists and shaking them beseechingly. 'Say you forgive me now!'

'Tell me what you've done.'

'Forgive first!'

'All right, I forgive you. Now tell me.'

He dropped my wrists and began picking at the bread, rolling bits of it into little grey balls.

'He come to my room when you go,' he said. 'He say he don't want to be alone. Play to me, he say, Doris don't hear nothing, please play. I don't play for him. I don't speak, even. I am sick, sick in my head like you see me yesterday, for what I hear in the night. He say, like you, what's the matter, what's the matter.' He stopped, squeezing two balls of bread into a pancake between his giant fingers. 'I tell him you a whore,' he whispered.

'What did he say?'

'He call me liar. He say you no whore. He say because you let him stay with you, that don't make you whore. He very angry.'

'And then what?'

'I get angry too, angry he call me liar. So I tell him.'

'Tell him what?' I said, utterly bewildered.

He shook the bread into the broad palm of his hand and closed his fingers over it gently, as if it were alive. 'Tell him about the baby,' he said softly.

I seemed to shrink into myself. I could hear the gas-fire hissing away in the silence. John and the rest of the room seemed to be miles away – even my own voice, when I produced it finally, sounded as if it were coming down a long-distance telephone.

'How did you know – about that?'

'I know a long time. Each morning you sick. I think all the time you going to have a baby. Then you begin to get big; after that, I know for certain.'

I sat stupefied. I couldn't think of anything to say.

'At first,' John went on, obviously bent on making a clean breast of everything, 'at first when I tell him you a whore, he don't believe me, so I got to make him believe. I say to him, why do you think she come here, a girl like her, to a house like this? You think she like to live here? And I see he beginning to believe, and so I go on, I say, what work do you think she do? He say, she work in an office. Funny time she work, I say. This is Sunday, office not open on a Sunday. So where she go to? He say, I stand beside her, hear her talking on the telephone; her boss call her, say come to work. He say, I listen other times when her boss call her. I say, how you know that her boss? Does he talk like a boss? Then I see, in his eyes, he got a doubt now, a big doubt. Then, when I see there is the doubt, that when I tell him about the baby. And this time, you see, he believe.'

'And then he went away.'

'Yes . . .' After a long pause, he said pleadingly, 'You think he come back?'

'I don't know,' I said dully. Why hadn't I told him myself? Why hadn't I?

'But you forgive me?'

'What? – Oh, yes.'

We sat in heavy silence for a long time. The gas-fire ran out of money and dropped abruptly into the five little blue blisters; then it died altogether. The room chilled quickly. I couldn't seem to be bothered to move. I sat in the arm-chair, gazing at the bed, wondering drearily why it was that you couldn't crawl away anywhere and hide, why there were always people wherever you went, new people to get involved with and to create new meshes of unhappiness and responsibility.

John was very gradually edging along the floor towards me, and at last he was near enough to put his head down on my knee, like a penitent dog creeping to its angry master when it thinks he's had time to forget its offence. Poor John. I knew he loved Toby. I stroked his big woolly head, and after a while it got very heavy and I suspected he'd dropped off to sleep.

Chapter 11

WITHOUT another mind ticking away in the room, I was able to think more clearly. So, Toby knew about the baby. He'd got it all wrong, thanks to John – he had some mad idea James was my lover. Could he honestly believe that when I went off to work at nine o'clock each morning I was really heading for some regular-as-clockwork day-long love-nest? Probably not. But in a way, even that wouldn't be more difficult to credit, perhaps, than the truth.

For the first time I saw clearly that it would be impossible to go through the rest of my life with a barrier in my mind between the baby and its conception. The child itself would want to know who its father was, and the fact that *I* could get no comfort from the circumstances would be no excuse for hiding them from – him, her? (It was a painful effort to personalize *It* even to the extent of apportioning sex.) And however much I hated the idea, sooner or later I would have to tell somebody about it – Toby, perhaps – either the truth or a lie I would have to tell, because I couldn't any longer pretend it was nobody's business but mine.

With the weight of John's head slowly reducing one leg to numbness, I decided to try and explain it to myself. Truthfully, of course; I'd see how it sounded, and if it were too reprehensible, well, I'd just have to think up a good lie, that was all, right now at the outset, and stick to it until perhaps I'd begin to believe it myself. I'd never been very good at big lies, and the thought of living one terrified me, but it was important that not only I, but the baby, should have some self-respect about its origins. However, a lie might not be necessary. After all, *something* must have made me do it, pointless and unjustified as it seemed now; perhaps if I went over it all again carefully, I could find out that the truth didn't condemn me out of hand. I might find *some* excuse for myself, however inadequate.

Where to begin? In fairness to myself, eight years ago, when I was twenty and in love with the actor, in that repertory up North. We weren't really in love, but it seemed a very great deal like it at the time, before we spoiled it; we both thought we were, and how can you tell for sure when it's the first time and you've nothing to compare it with? Anyway it was very strong and we longed and longed to go to bed together. There was every possible opportunity and we discussed it; he was keen but not importunate, which naturally made me love him more and be more inclined to give him what he was so sweetly not insisting on, but something held me back. Part of it was my upbringing, of course, but I could easily have had a violent reaction away from that if it hadn't been for the inhibiting atmosphere in the company itself. Three separate couples were sleeping together in the most overt and sordid way, one pair on a mattress in the theatre itself (we called it 'the bed of Sin'). Another girl, who looked wretchedly unhappy and as if she might be going to fade away at any moment, practically had a miscarriage on stage one night as a result of some pills she'd been made to take by her awful lout of a lover. Then there was the complication of Malcolm, and one way and another it wasn't the most ideal setting for the consummation of young love.

Afterwards I was very glad that we hadn't, still being at an age to believe that there is something intrinsically precious in virginity, and I decided to carry mine intact to the altar. But I didn't go to the altar; to be honest it wasn't for lack of offers, but because they always seemed to come from people I wouldn't have been caught dead at an altar with. I wasn't completely heart-free during those years; sometimes I allowed myself to be fooled that I loved someone, but when it came to the point of saying 'yes' to anything final there was always the small honest inner voice which jeered 'For *life*? Are you mad?' or 'Bed with *him*? Is that the best you can do, after you've waited so long?' – and sometimes to this the voice would add irritatingly – 'and after saying No to that darling actor?' The truth was, I never again experienced that warm, urgent magic I had felt with the actor – I never again saw an ordinary, or even ugly face change and become Apollo-like through the intervention of love. If they were plain, I might get fond of them and no longer notice, but they stayed inescapably plain and I, despite my best efforts, stayed stubbornly unenchanted.

So the years went by, and such involvements as came along never satisfied me as being quite right enough either for one thing or the other. And one day, with jarring abruptness, I was twenty-seven, and the little inner voice stopped jeering and sneering at every man I met and began to whimper and bleat. 'Is it going on forever, this lonely-nights policy? So supposing you never marry, and if you go on being so fussy you probably never will – are there to be no cakes and ale?' And I began to be conscious of my unnatural state, and cry in the night sometimes for no real reason except that I wanted a man beside me – any man at all, I sometimes thought, and the little voice which had been so snooty before, now held its peace on the subject.

I kept thinking about the actor. I hadn't seen him for seven years, though I'd heard about him now and then – he had graduated through minor journalism to publishing, and was now (I learned by well-placed casual questions) a leading light in a go-ahead new publishing house specializing in novels by Angry Young Men. He had married; the marriage had gone wrong. He lived alone now, in a small house in Highgate which he'd shared with his wife before she left him. There had been no children.

Once, in an idle afternoon when the feeling of uselessness which had lately beset me was particularly strong, I went out to Highgate and walked past the house. It was very ordinary, one of a row; the garden was a mess. The front door was painted bright yellow. It was the colour of a skirt I once had that he had specially liked. I didn't really imagine he'd chosen the paint for the front door on that basis, but I liked the door being that colour, though it hurt stupidly by making me remember a lot of things. I came home quite convinced that I'd never met anyone since that I had had the same feeling for.

While I was being so damned honest all of a sudden, there was no use pretending any longer that I had chosen the obscure fishing village of Collioure for a holiday for any other reason than because I had heard he usually went there. Nor was it mere coincidence that I arranged my holiday for a special part of September. Jane-downstairs had remarked on men's capacity for self-deception; women aren't bad at it either.

At the time I told myself that I would take a train to Perpignan and from there explore the more accessible small seaside places just because they sounded nice and quiet and I hadn't seen them before. Perpignan, had I expected anything of it, would have been a disappointment. It was hot and dry and there was a thin layer of grey dust over everything, including the famous plane-trees which languished ungreenly in the heat. Even the river was only a trickle among the parched white boulders. I wasn't inclined to linger anyway; the day I arrived I caught a bus in the square which just happened to have Collioure on the front.

At Collioure there was a great castle built right on the sea, and little boats, and placid fat women in black stockings. There were widely-spreading nets forever in need of mending, and small rough cafés where you could choose your own dishes in the kitchen, and many painters. The swimming wasn't very good; the whole place stank of sardines, and the noble castle turned out to be a youth hostel; also there was a forty-mile-an-hour gale blowing much of the time. But somehow I had no desire to move on. I drank Banyuls and went for walks round the dusty countryside, and lay in the sun, and waited.

And of course, he came.

We met one evening as I was coming out of my favourite café after supper. He was strolling down the steep narrow street towards the sea, his hands deep in his pockets and his shirt open at the throat, very pale and Londonish, looking about him with the fond, proprietorial air of an Englishman returning to a favourite spot abroad. In the purply warm twilight the tiny traces of time didn't show; he looked exactly as always.

I felt my pulses beating with excitement as he came closer. If I had specially ordered the moment, it couldn't have been more to my liking. I had had a week in this quiet place in which to relax and order my thoughts – a week of peace to sustain me for this encounter, not to mention a good meal and a half-bottle of wine just consumed. My skin was brown and my hair streaked with nature's own blond from the salt and sun: my very bones seemed to have absorbed the heat and now gave it back in the form of a glowing sense of confidence and well-being.

He saw me standing there waiting in the warm light from the café and hesitated a second, then walked on a few paces, then stopped and looked back. It was delicious to watch; I could scarcely keep from giggling with delight. We stood looking at each other for a long moment; then he walked slowly up to me.

'Well,' he said. 'Well!' The pleasure was rich in his voice. I looked anxiously at him, partly to make sure the pleasure was really genuine (it would have been unbearable if he had thought me an intruder) and partly to see whether any of the magic was left. It seemed that there was some, because his face, which I knew was not handsome, with its thin nose and high, bony forehead and small mouth, had still some special quality for me which an unbiased analysis of the features couldn't explain. I saw that he was examining my face during the same silence. We had discussed this business of how people's appearance literally alters in the eyes of their lovers, and suddenly I blushed, for it seemed to me he must be remembering this too, and that we must be looking for the same thing, as one might take down an old book in a moment of hungry nostalgia and start to re-read, hoping it may provide the same remembered enchantment as before.

He saw my blush and put his hands on my shoulders. 'Did you know I was going to be here?' he asked.

I had about four separate answers ready for this one, but they all failed me. I dropped my eyes and nodded sheepishly.

He began to laugh. It was a laugh of happiness and male conceit, and I was so pleased by the first that I didn't mind the second too much. 'Oh, good, darling! Good, good, good. You're just the same! I could see you getting ready to lie, and then you just couldn't. You always were the honestest woman I ever knew.' He lifted my chin up and looked into my eyes with a funny, half-actorish solemnity, and said quietly, 'I am so glad to see you again.' Then he kissed me, and for a moment I remembered a play we were in together, when we'd done the same sort of kiss, starting with his hand under my chin and just our lips lightly together, and then developing into a full clinch; but by the time we were deeply embraced I had forgotten the play and could think only that this was like coming home.

I hadn't come to this place with the conscious intention of divesting myself of my now cumbersome virginity; but from the moment I saw the actor again – certainly from the moment his arms went round me and I felt the sense of fond familiarity, of affection rediscovered – I knew it was inevitable that we should, sooner or later, make love. But there was no hurry. I was happy to let the pleasant sunny days go by. Now I had a companion to share everything with, someone I knew of old and with whom there were no constraints, and seven years' news to keep the conversation flowing. Life was a slow, blissful progress towards an unnamed but predecided climax which we both realized was there, only waiting for us to reach it. We took our time.

We went sailing and swimming, and once we went out at night with the fishing-boats; we ate every meal together, and lay prone on the stone piers, reaching shoulder-deep into the water to catch the scarlet starfish, which petrified with fury when we lifted them out. We talked endlessly – there was so much to catch up on. And often we would lie together in the sun after a bathe, and kiss and caress each other, and it was a dear, familiar pleasure, associated in my mind and body with safety and mutual delight and no demands made; his hands were wondering and tender, and his face when I opened my eyes to look at it had the extraordinary beauty it used to have when I had given him even this limited sensual happiness. It pleased me immeasurably to know that he could sense the difference now, the promise of fulfilment, which would be the sweeter, it seemed to me, for having been so long deferred.

I was very happy; and if sometimes the familiarities in our relationship were of an irritating nature (like the way he teased me, as he had always teased me, about my sticking-out ears, for instance) I pushed them aside and refused to acknowledge them – even when they were quite important, the sort of things on which the nagging small voice was once wont to pounce as reasons against any positive commitment. The voice was silent now; I was on my own. 'And about time, too!' I thought to myself. 'This is right, at last; I feel it. I know this man. I'm taking no chances. He'll look after me.' I was thinking more of my mental welfare than any physical repercussions.

And so the end of my holiday drew near. In the last few days, our conversation ran out; we were often silent in each other's company, and I took this to be a good sign. It put my mind at rest on one point – often in the last weeks we had seemed more like friends than incipient lovers; the silences now seemed to betoken a quiet awareness of the new status that would soon envelop us. I refused to consider that the silences lacked something – the quality that the silences between lovers have, of being full of unspoken thoughts. Ours were different; sometimes they seemed almost – empty. It was like waiting for something important to happen which has got to happen before life can go on. And I grew almost impatient, thinking, when is it going to begin? I knew the first time was seldom ideal and I wanted to get past it to the second and third times, and all the times after that, when our love could go forward and mature and develop.

Our last evening came. I was going back to London the next day; the actor was staying on for another week. It occurred to me this was not an ideal arrangement; I had a funny, cold feeling in the middle of dinner that perhaps we had been wrong to delay matters until this last moment, where there could be no immediate follow-up, when I must leave him the next day. But there was no going back now. Without a word having been spoken about it, it was settled between us, I knew; it had been from the beginning. It had seemed right and touching that verbal arrangements had not been necessary; but now I couldn't help wishing we had spoken about it, and he had said, 'Dearest, it shall be the climax of our wonderful holiday, and when I come home . . .' That was really the reassurance I most wanted, the knowledge that what was going to happen was only a beginning and not just – an incident. But he hadn't given it, and I began to wonder why he hadn't. I began to want to run away.

I could hardly eat. My throat just wouldn't swallow food, and my mouth was dry with an unexpected onset of acute nervousness. For once I drank no wine with my meal; it would have helped considerably, if I had but known, but it seemed wrong that one should need artificial stimulus. Always before he had only had to touch me for me to be ready for the final act which we'd always denied ourselves; there was no reason to suppose that wouldn't happen again.

But it didn't. Nothing happened at all. I lay on his bed later and strove to want him, strove to feel even a faint shadow of the sensations that had always engulfed me before, when I had known they must be frustrated. He did his best to rouse me; I listened to his tender words and felt his hands on my body, all in a cold agony of indifference. It was quite unbelievably terrible. And remembering it now, with the child of that night growing towards a life of its own in my body, I was appalled again by the memory of a frustration worse than any self-denial, which ended at dawn with us lying apart from each other, both pretending to be asleep but both staring with dry wide-awake eyes into a bottomless pit of dismay. I don't know what he thought about, but what I thought about was how in God's name we were going to be able to face each other in the morning.

Well, we did it somehow, of course. He tried to be nice about it, but it was fairly obvious he didn't want me any more; and truthfully, I didn't want him any more either, except in so far that I couldn't bear that it should all have been for nothing – worse than nothing. I felt the most awful failure, and thought that perhaps if we could try again – since the thing was done, the point of no return passed – we might arrange things better, somehow recapture the basis of feeling we had had, which should have been a perfect foundation for a love-affair, but which we had somehow bungled and thrown away. It was like having jumped up and down on a beautiful springboard, relishing the thrill of the plunge into the deep roaring water, and then diving at last into an empty pool.

He saw me off on the bus. Up to the day before I had hoped he would come with me at least as far as Perpignan, to see me on my way; now there was no question of that, and indeed I could hardly wait to get away from him. We didn't look at each other as he kissed me perfunctorily good-bye.

'I'll give you a ring when I get back,' he said distantly.

'Yes, do,' I said. It was unbelievable; it was as if we were barely acquainted.

The long journey home was a nightmare of hot sticky carriages and not enough to drink (my thirst was terrible all day). I knew that soon I would have to come to grips with what had happened, to wring some meaning out of it to make it endurable; but for the moment I simply couldn't bear to think about it.

When I got home I picked up the threads of my ordinary life again very quickly – you might say I snatched them up, and plunged into a round of work and social life deliberately intended to give me as few idle moments as possible. I grabbed at every invitation, no matter how uninteresting, that would occupy my evenings, and if I had one free I would fill it myself by visiting friends or, in the last resort, going to a movie alone. I carried a book with me everywhere, and read it desperately, over meals, in buses, even in the street. I wouldn't think. I wouldn't.

But at the end of the week, when I knew the actor was due back, I couldn't prevent myself waiting for his call. Because I hadn't sorted myself out about the whole thing properly, my feelings while waiting were a complete tangle – although I didn't want to see him, I did desperately want him to want to see me. I didn't see how I was going to live with the memory of him as it was; I thought there must be something we could do, just something; even one friendly lunch together might help.

He didn't phone. My heart grew sick and I couldn't eat, a phenomenon so strange that even Father noticed and asked what was wrong. I told him I was on a diet, which he believed. As the days passed I might have been telling him the truth, for I lost weight far more successfully than on any diet I have ever attempted. And then his note came.

Dear Jane,

Sorry I haven't rung you, things really have been pretty frantic for me since I got back. I've got a brand-new job in Paris, leaving almost at once. Marvellous, eh? It's a step up, too, I'll practically be in charge there.

I wish I could suggest a meeting before I go, but it's all happened so suddenly I just can't see how I could fit it in. But I'll be back one of these days, and we'll have a slap-up meal together (NOT on the old X's, I promise!)

Cheers,
Terry

Terry was his name, by the way. Not that it matters. I'd never call any child of mine Terry. It sounds too bloody weak-kneed.

Chapter 12

QUITE soon after the note, I began to suspect – what I had never even thought about, for some naïve reason – that I might be pregnant. Then it became doubly important not to think back, and so I never had, not until this moment. I had only known, positively though without details, that there was no help and no comfort forthcoming from the source, and that being so I shied away from any mental flashbacks which could only make me more unhappy and ashamed.

And now that I'd forced myself to take it all out of its cobwebby cupboard and look at it remorselessly from start to finish, I knew I had been instinctively wise not to do it before. If I had done it before, before my visit to Dr Graham, for instance, I'd now be sixty guineas the poorer and no longer pregnant. Sitting in my L-shaped room, stone-cold to my very marrow, with John still sleeping as peacefully as a child at my feet, I faced that fact, too, while I was at it; and also a few others.

For instance, that there were quite definitely no mitigating circumstances. I was not in love with Terry, never had been; I went after him, deliberately, because I was ripe for an affair and I thought with him I could have one and enjoy it and still feel like the nice clean girl-next-door afterwards. I saw now what I'd known all the time, only I'd hidden it craftily from myself because it didn't fit in with what I wanted to do, that Terry and I had *no* basis for a love-affair; we were friends who happened to be attracted to each other physically, which was far from enough, and by thinking it was enough we'd gone against the very nature of our relationship. I also recognized that it was more my fault than his. That didn't stop me from thinking bitterly that he'd got away scot-free.

I also had a look at the fact that Toby might well be – or have been – the man I'd been waiting for, though God knows I'd never have recognized him in a million years if we hadn't happened, entirely by accident, to stumble into each other's arms. The pool that had been so jarringly empty when I took my premeditated dive into it with Terry, I fell into with Toby and found it full of champagne.

But it was too late, that was the terrible thing. It had happened at a time when all I had to offer him was absolute misery for both of us.

Now I was thinking clearly and coldly. The doctor had been right. Who did I think I was imagining glibly that I could bring up a child all by myself? I had no money. I had no home. I had no job. And most important, I had no moral courage. I didn't want the child, I wasn't at all sure I was going to love it, even – certainly I'd had no hints up to now that mother-love hadn't been completely left out of my make-up. Wasn't it plain, common-or-garden cowardice, not the sturdy self-righteousness I'd credited myself with, which prevented me from ending the whole business? If only I'd gone along with the doctor's proposals, it would have been over by now – completely and painlessly over, and any feelings of guilt I might have had as a result I would surely have dealt with ages ago. After all, as he had said – and now every word of our conversation came back to me as clearly as if played back on a tape – a woman has a right to decide, on the basis of her own capacity to cope with the situation, whether she is justified in going on with it. Justified – that was the word. It was the *child* that had to have first consideration, and what had I got to offer it that *justified* my bringing it into the world? Nothing.

And besides, I couldn't face it. I'd suffered enough for my mistake. One little mistake! What horrible injustice, to impose a life-sentence for that! What moral law can compel anyone to stay in prison if they can get out?

I looked at the time. It was, to my astonishment, only a quarter to six. I felt as if I'd been sitting there half the night. But that was good – not six o'clock yet – Dr Graham might still be at his office. And suddenly I had to act quickly. My pulses were hammering in panic, as if I were really behind bars and spied an escape route that would close forever in a matter of seconds . . . I'd heard somewhere that you can't stop it after the end of the third month.

I lifted John's head carefully with both hands and slipped out from beneath it. He grunted a little as I rested it against the arm of the chair, but didn't wake. My leg had gone completely to sleep and I couldn't feel it at all, but I managed to hobble to the door, collecting fourpence out of my wallet, and down the stairs to the first landing where the telephone was. It struck me as I fumblingly dialled the number that it would be better to go out to a kiosk, where I would be more sure of privacy, but having come to this decision

I only wanted to hurry, hurry – every minute's delay seemed dangerous.

It rang a long time before a woman's voice answered – the same woman.

'This is Miss Graham,' I said, surprising myself by the furtive urgency in my own voice. 'I came to see Dr Graham two months ago. May I – is he there now? Could I have a word with him?'

The voice was chilly and formal. 'I'm sorry, the doctor's off duty from five-thirty. Is there anything I could do?'

'I want to make an appointment to come and see him again – tomorrow.'

'*Tomorrow?*' The voice held the same polite incredulity as it had the first time. 'I'm afraid that's quite impossible. His appointments book is full until – '

'Please,' I said, 'please.' It was exactly like the first time. Only now I knew all the facts, and I knew what I wanted. 'I can't wait. It's most urgent. I'm sure if you tell him, he'll remember me.'

'Well . . . I could give him a message. Miss – who, did you say?'

'Graham, Jane Graham. He'll remember me because our names are the same. Tell him – tell him I've changed my mind. Please.'

'Very well.'

'May I come round tomorrow? I don't mind waiting until he's got a moment free between patients.'

'I think it would be better if you gave me your phone number. I'll telephone you in the morning and tell you if the doctor can see you.'

I gave her the number and hung up feeling baulked of my escape, almost as if I'd expected that the thing could be done now, tonight. But at least I'd taken the first step, and not an easy step, considering what I'd said to the doctor at our last meeting. It proved to me that I was in earnest, that I was truly resolved. Three months was not too late – it mustn't be. I had sixty guineas, I had a hundred if he asked for it. That was about all I did have, but it wasn't much to pay for peace and a future of freedom. And it was for Toby, too, and for the baby itself. I stood by the phone prodding away at my mind with the unanswerable rationalizations, wondering why I didn't feel happier and better now I'd decided.

I climbed the stairs slowly. On the next landing up, there was a faint suggestion of Chanel No. 9 and a small, tell-tale movement of a door swiftly closing the last two inches. I remembered now another give-away sound which at the time I hadn't noticed – a click on the line at the beginning of my conversation with the woman. So, Mavis at least had been getting a good earful. Had I said anything revealing? I thought not.

John was awake. He'd put some more money in the meter and was warming himself by the newly-lit fire. He jumped to his feet as I came in.

'I go to sleep,' he said accusingly. 'Why you don't wake me? Let the room get cold . . .'

'It doesn't matter,' I said. I stood by the window staring out into the foggy darkness, taking deep breaths to try and stifle some hollow feeling of new dis-ease.

He stood awkwardly. 'You forgive me?' he asked.

'Yes, yes,' I said, a little impatiently.

'You think Toby come back?'

'I expect so. I hope so.' Then I thought of something cheering. 'He'll have to, all his things are still here – his writing – '

John's face broke into a grin; I could see it reflected in the windowpane. 'That's right!' he exclaimed. 'Then I tell him – I tell him – ' he broke off, the grin fading uncertainly.

'You can tell him,' I said, turning and looking him in the face, 'that you were entirely mistaken; that my boss really is my boss, and that I'm not going to have a baby.' There. That meant I had to do it. That meant it was as good as done.

He put his big head on one side and looked at me, puzzled. 'Not going to have a baby?' he repeated.

'No,' I said, trying to sound convincing but daunted by the simple bewilderment in his face. 'You were quite wrong about it.'

He took it in slowly but uncomprehendingly, and shook his head. '*Honestly*, Johnny. Now, please don't worry any more. Go on off to the club, and don't worry. He'll come back, and we'll all be friends again. All right?'

He shook his head again, not in denial, but just in unbelief. 'I sorry,' he said once again, in a hopeless voice that told me I hadn't convinced him. He went to the door, and then turned round and said simply, 'You know, I like you. Even when I sick in the head, I still like you. I like to help you, any way I can.' His face lit up again. 'I'm good carpenter. Make you wardrobe shelf, remember? Make you something else – very good cradle, like I see here sometime. You like that?'

I stared at him helplessly. I thought of several things to say to him, but nothing sounded right. At last I said, 'Let's talk about it tomorrow,' and he nodded happily and went padding off to work.

It was very early, but I was suddenly feeling horribly tired, and I thought bed would be a good idea. I got undressed and, after my usual battle with the crumbling Ascot in the bathroom, forced it to yield enough hot water for a miserly bath. On my way back to my room I had another look into Toby's. It was dark and empty. I thought then that, much as I longed to see him, it might be as well to start hoping he wouldn't come back until I could truthfully tell him there would be no baby. I wondered uneasily whether he would be able to see from my face that though it might be the truth, it was not the whole truth.

I got into bed, turned the light off and lay with just the fire lighting the room. I lay on my back thinking deliberately how lovely it would be when it was over and I didn't have to worry any more. I wondered where Toby was – he'd been gone for over thirty-six hours now. I thought of his sweetness in sitting beside me all night, and of the shadows on his face in the morning, and how I had gone off without telling him I loved him. Did I love him? I wasn't sure. It wasn't like anything I'd ever felt before. All I knew was that I felt married to him.

My hands were folded over my stomach like a sedate effigy, and now, against my will, they started to explore, pressing gently into the flesh. There was no definable shape to the bulge yet – in fact, I could make the bulge non-existent by drawing in my muscles. Surely a being so undeveloped – no, not even a being, an appendage, a little lifeless nubbin of my own flesh – had no claim on me, no claim on life when it couldn't even sustain an existence of its own. There couldn't be any wrong in disposing of it. It wasn't a baby yet, just a potential; not much more than a seed. The chief reason I'd always been against abortion was that it seemed like tearing up a bill instead of paying it. What a piece of high-flown theorizing that seemed now! Why should one pay a bill that was out of all proportion to the goods received? It was absurd.

(Even if you knew in advance what the bill might be?)

Why should I pay it all alone? Anyway, I paid at the time.

(And since when was living a matter of straightforward cash-and-carry transactions? How do you know you're not paying now for something you'll get later?)

So you're back, are you? I snarled at the inner voice. *A fine time you picked to wake up! Where were you in my hour of need?* I was still arguing childishly against myself when I heard a little noise at the door.

It wasn't a knock, really – more like a dog scratching to be let in. I lay frozen for a moment, and then I called out, 'Who is it?'

There was no answer, but after a moment the scratching was repeated. I got out of bed and put on my dressing-gown with shaky haste. Could it be Toby? I ran round the corner to the door and opened it.

It was Mavis.

I was completely taken aback. She had never come up to my room before, in fact I'd never seen her outside her own. She had a shawl-thing round her shoulders, and a knitting bag in her hand, which seemed oddly heavy. She smiled at me shyly, as if uncertain of her welcome.

'Hallo, dear,' she said brightly. 'I hope you don't mind me coming up – I thought I'd just come and see how you were, and perhaps sit and chat with you for a while.'

I said of course I didn't mind, and stood aside to let her in.

'Oh, but you've been in bed!' she exclaimed as soon as she went round the angle. 'I'm disturbing you!' But she made no move to leave, so I had to say not at all, I'd gone to bed because it seemed the warmest place.

'Quite right,' she said approvingly. 'Now, you just jump back under the covers, and I'll sit myself here. I don't want to be a nuisance.' I did as she suggested, keeping my dressing-gown on, and watched her settle herself in the arm-chair and get her knitting out. She looked very homely and comfortable, but I had a feeling of misgiving. It was so unusual for her to move out of her own domain. I wondered suddenly whether her unexpected visit could have anything to do with my phone call. And almost at once, she confirmed it.

'Well now, how are you feeling?' she asked. 'I've been quite worried about you – you haven't been looking well lately, I noticed it this evening particularly when you dropped in.'

She had nothing at all to go on, I thought, except that phone call, and she naturally wouldn't admit to having listened to that. I decided to bluff it out.

'I don't know where you got the idea I was ill,' I said as heartily as I could. 'I'm fine – I just felt a bit sleepy and chilly, that was why I went to bed so early.'

'Oh come now, dear, you can't fool an old hand like me.' She smiled complacently down at her swiftly-flashing knitting needles.

'What do you mean?' I asked, with an edge in my voice.

'Just that I *know*, dear – that's all.'

I felt myself turn pale with the sort of impotent fury a goldfish in a bowl might feel. Was there nobody who didn't know? Did I look so obviously the sort to get into trouble that I couldn't go about with circles under my eyes, or telephone a doctor, or throw up once in a while, without everyone immediately jumping to a single conclusion? Tears of futile anger and chagrin stung my eyes. 'I don't know what you're talking about!' I almost shouted.

Mavis laid her knitting aside and came over to the bed, where, to my redoubled annoyance, she sat down and took my hands.

'Now listen, dear,' she said kindly. 'Don't get upset. I know how you feel because I've seen other girls go through it. You may think it's none of my business – '

'I do!' I interrupted rudely, enraged now more by the tears streaming down my face than by her.

' – And I wouldn't have said a word, ducky, if I hadn't heard you phoning that doctor.' My nose was starting to run and she released one of my hands and put a Chanel-smelling handkerchief into it. 'Now, Jane, you must be sensible. Don't go to that awful man and spend all that money.'

I stared at her, aghast.

'Yes, dear, I know all about him. One of the girls in the company, ever such a nice little thing she was, she thought she'd got into trouble; well, I could've told her she would, the way she was going on – actors – you wouldn't believe! They say the stage is a respectable profession nowadays, well maybe it is, but I can't think it's changed all that much in the five years since I left. There was one – the same one this little girl was carrying on with – tall handsome brute, not my type I'm glad to say, too florid like, but he was a regular *goat*. You couldn't walk into his dressing-room five minutes after the curtain came down for fear of what you might find him doing. Where he found the energy – ! Anyway, this poor child, only nineteen she was (he should've been ashamed of himself and him a man of forty) – if she'd only come to me at the start! But no, she let *him* tell her what to do – him that was the cause of it all – and what does he do but fix up for her to go and see this Dr Graham? Mind you, *he* paid, I'll say that for him, but it might just as well have been her – the money was thrown down the drain all the same!'

In spite of myself I was forced to ask, 'What do you mean? Didn't the operation – didn't it work?'

'Work?' she said. 'Work? There was nothing for it to work *on*. When she came round after the anaesthetic the first thing she says to the nurse is, Well, was I or wasn't I? Because I'd told her it was funny this doctor never even touched her before he sent her in there. Nothing of the sort, says the nurse, wherever did you get that idea? It was some little blockage or something, not a baby at all. All that money! She could've had the same thing free on the National Health! And then of course, silly girl, she went and told *him* – he was so livid he wouldn't have nothing more to do with her.'

'But – ' I struggled to digest all this. 'In my case, it's different. There's no doubt – '

'Oh, I dare say,' she said with a sniff. 'What I'm trying to tell you is, the man's a crook. He's not to be trusted. And why should you give him all your money for doing something – '

She stopped. She looked at me slyly.

'How far along are you, dear?'

'Three months,' I mumbled.

She sucked in her breath and shook her head. 'Pity you let it go so long,' she said. 'Have you tried anything at all? No? Well, you know, you'd be silly to spend all that money, now wouldn't you? If you didn't have to?'

I was staring at her as if she were turning into a witch in front of my eyes. I felt faintly hypnotized.

'What are you suggesting?'

'Oh, nothing *wrong*, dear,' she said, giving me a clear-eyed look of total innocence. 'Don't think that. But you know, there are ways, without any sort of tinkering about. Now, look here.' She picked up her heavy knitting-bag and took out of it a half-bottle of gin and a small tin of Nescafé – only it wasn't Nescafé, because it rattled. I had a good idea what was in that. It was the gin that surprised me. It was a good brand. Did Mavis drink? Where did she get the money? Again as if she read my thoughts, she said: 'After I heard you talking on the phone, I nipped out and bought this – you can pay me back, if you like. Mother's ruin. Now you know why they call it that – one reason, anyway. Of course, you have to drink lots of it – "lots and lots, no tiny tots", as they say.' She tittered genteelly. The double meaning, when it struck me, forced a gasp of half-hysterical laughter out of me before I could control myself; I clamped a hand over my mouth. I felt I must keep a very firm hold on myself if I were not to lose control altogether. The whole situation was so grotesque, so funny and so preposterous. 'Nothing *wrong*, dear!' Oh no, nothing at all wrong. It was all just like being given a new recipe or a knitting pattern. I put my other hand up to my face too, and put my head down on my knees, trying to keep myself from going to pieces.

Mavis thought I was crying, and indeed I wasn't far from that either. She patted my shoulder with her dry, spinsterish little hand. 'Now, don't upset yourself, there's a good girl. I'll stay with you, if you like, and by the morning it'll probably all be over.'

I didn't answer. I was wondering how often she did this ministering-angel act, and what she got out of it. Not money? Surely not. Not when she wouldn't take any for making chair-covers. Perhaps she just did it out of the goodness of her heart – or perhaps (and this thought provoked a fresh spurt of giggles in my throat) half the little souvenirs that littered her room were tokens of gratitude – from Torquay, Margate and Llandrindod Wells – I pulled myself together with a great effort, and took my hands from my face. I couldn't bring myself to look at Mavis, with her neat grey bun and demure brooch linking the lapels of her Peter Pan collar.

I said, 'That's very kind of you, Mavis, and of course I'll pay you for the gin, but if you don't mind I'd rather be alone. If I need any help, I'll call you.'

'Oh – all right, then,' she said, concealing her disappointment. She got up and gathered her knitting together. 'Now, you know what to do? Just take two of these every two hours, and drink plenty of gin. If you feel you're going to be sick, just try not to be, and don't drink any more till it passes off, otherwise it'll all be wasted, won't it? Mind you,' she said quickly, 'I'm not making any promises. Three months is rather late.' It was as if she were giving me some hyacinth bulbs and saying December was a bit late to plant them. I said seriously that I quite understood, and that I wouldn't hold her responsible if nothing happened.

She started to go, and then turned back, saying cheerily, 'Just think how nice it will be when it's all finished with,' and then she actually added, 'Well, I must go and feed my puss-puss now, or she'll be ever so cross.' She waved to me encouragingly. 'Good luck, ducky. Don't forget to call if you need anything.' And off she trotted, shawl, knitting-bag and all.

After she'd left the room I sat still in bed for a while, thinking it really wasn't so funny after all. Then I picked up the Nescafé tin and prised the lid off. There were about ten pills inside. I remembered them from when Alice – the wraith-like girl in the rep – had showed me similar ones. I remembered other things, too, things she'd insisted upon telling me later – all sorts of unlovely details. I shook out a couple of tablets, rolled them about in my hand, and then put them back, cursing Alice heartily. I'm afraid I cursed Mavis too. Why couldn't she mind her own business? Throwing in this unbalancing element of bizarre comedy just when I'd got everything settled. I thought about the gin, but that was tarred with the same brush. 'No tiny tots' . . . The wretched woman had well-meaningly reduced the whole thing to the level of bar-room farce.

Damn it all, you couldn't just . . .

No, I thought, none of that. That way madness lies. If I start thinking of It as a person, entitled to a dignified end, the next thing will be of course that I have no right to end It at all. But all the same – not that way. And not, by the same token, all on my own. Was I respecting the life within me, or pandering to my own healthy terror or going through what Alice went through? I wasn't at all sure. But anyway, I put the pills and the gin firmly aside, turned out the light again, and tried to go to sleep.

I lay wide-eyed and wakeful. I didn't have to wonder why. I was missing Toby. I discovered it's a very different matter, lying awake thinking it would be nice to have a man beside you, and lying awake longing for one particular man. In one case it's a feeling of vague discontent. In the other . . . you might just as well try to go to sleep when your feet are cold or you want to spend a penny, or you're hungry for a special kind of food you haven't got. As a matter of fact, all three now applied, I realized, as well as the other. Almost every part of my infuriating body seemed to be nagging at me for some sort of attention. I even had a tickle between my shoulder-blades that I couldn't reach.

At last, exasperated beyond bearing, I switched on the light again. It was *still* only eight o'clock. This seemed to be the last straw – somebody was really gunning for me: slowing the whole bloody earth down now. All right, I thought furiously. I know when I'm beaten. Grinding my teeth with rage at everything, I got up and dressed in slacks and my old trenchcoat. A glance outside told me it was still foggy – getting worse, if anything. Naturally. I knotted a headscarf round my throat so savagely I nearly choked myself, and crept – I had to creep, because of Mavis – downstairs and out into the fog.

The special food I fancied was – of all things – curry. As I strode along, glaring at the ground, hating everything, I thought: I'm not dealing with this matter a moment too soon. Cravings in the middle of the night? And where am I to find curry, in God's name, in this benighted neighbourhood? Hammersmith? Hardly. Putney? Loathsome place. Chelsea? Yes, at a price. Oh, God damn and blast, why curry? Why not fish and chips?

But the vision, complete with mango chutney and mounds of yellow rice, persisted. I got on a bus and grudgingly paid my fare to the King's Road. There was an Indian restaurant I'd seen there, near Sloane Square. It would probably, I reflected bitterly, be shut when I got there – some Hindu feastday, or something. Probably the only day in the whole year. Almost certainly there would be no curry to be had in the whole of London. I was actually weeping with advance self-pity before I got there.

The restaurant was, to my surprise (and, in some perverse way, disappointment) open. In fact they were quite busy. Everyone, including the Indians, seemed to be happy and laughing, and in my surly mood I unkindly wished them all in hell – chiefly because no one was in any hurry to serve me and I had to sit and watch a party at the next table consume a feast that looked to me as if it had issued straight from Nirvana, before I was even shown a menu.

I ordered so recklessly that the waiter looked first surprised, then delighted, then alarmed. 'Are you sure you can eat all that?' he asked solicitously. I was, quite sure; even when it began to arrive, dish after khaki-coloured dish, covering the whole surface of the table, I was not daunted. 'Thank you,' I said confidently, and glared at the man when he discreetly placed a huge jug of iced water at my elbow.

The first dish was wonderful. I ladled the curried object,

whatever it was, on to a heap of saffron rice, smothered it with sauce, rolled up a chipathi and set to. I demolished it without difficulty, though it was extremely hot and I had recourse to the water when no one was looking. Then I tackled the next dish, which had succulent fat prawns nestling in it. After that the jug of water was empty and I was full, but the waiter was smirking in an enigmatic Eastern way, so I toyed with the final concoction, just to prove I could if I wanted to, and that any I happened to leave was just for manners. I was rewarded by several admiring looks as I paid my sizeable bill and blundered out, sweating, into the fog.

It had got considerably thicker while I'd been eating. I was beginning to feel sleepy, and very cold; the temperature seemed to have gone down, and I was shivering even while I sweated from the furnace-like emanations of the curry.

At last I got on a bus, which trundled quite briskly to the far end of the King's Road, but after World's End, where the streets were darker, the fog seemed to close in and the bus was forced to nose its way cautiously along in first gear. The journey went on and on – before long we were travelling at a walking pace, and I and the few other passengers were anxiously clearing the condensation from the windows and peering into the murk in an effort to see where we were. Passing a street-light came to seem quite an event; one watched their brave little sulphurous smudges receding with a feeling akin to despair, as if we might never find another.

I asked the conductor to tell me when we came to my stop, and he said, 'Lady, you think I got X-ray eyes or something? I can't see the stops, no better'n what you can.' He sounded irritable, and whenever the bus stopped (which it did frequently) he went round to the front to talk to his mate. A bus had been rammed in the fog two nights before, when it wasn't nearly as thick as this, and I wondered if he was scared.

At last I judged it time to get off and start walking. The district was sinister enough at any time; now, with the feeling that any and every form of menace, from a cut-throat to a coal-hole, might be within inches for all I could tell, my small remaining resources of courage were exhausted within minutes. I felt my way along, a few steps at a time, and every time I heard a voice or a footstep I stopped dead, clinging to whatever bit of masonry was under my hand and almost cowering with fright.

After a while, though, when I'd turned down the side-street

where the house was (I hoped), there were no more sounds to frighten me, and as a result of course I grew much more afraid of the stuffed, dripping silence. Far, far away I could hear the slow, grinding sounds of traffic – but muffled, as if I were wearing ear-plugs. The house was right down at the bottom of the street, and I moved like a ghost from lamp to lamp, tiptoeing for some reason, as if I were in a jungle in dread of attracting the attention of wild animals prowling near me. I couldn't decide whether I felt safer near the lamps, or in the dark stretches between. The thick patches of light seemed to be focal-points, somehow . . . I was beginning not to feel very well. The mixture of inner heat and outer cold was making my head light. The lamp-smudges seemed to swim towards me, dipping and swaying off-centre as I approached them. My legs were trembling and when I put my hand against my face it was burning, and yet clammy. The next time I reached a lamp-post I clung to it. It was wet and cold, but it held steady, which was more than anything else seemed to. I put my forehead against it and hung on with both hands. Then I felt the post begin to slide upwards through my hands, as if more of it were coming out of the ground. It slid up faster and faster, though I tried to hold it down. Then I felt something hard strike my knees, and I smelt a very strong smell of dog.

'. . . Come on, dearie, help me a bit – put your head forward – that's it. Are you feeling better? Say something, there's a love – come on, you can't sit there all night . . .'

The fog had solidified into a strong pressure on the back of my neck. When I opened my eyes reluctantly, I was staring at a small piece of pavement miles below, between two sloping hills. Then I saw that the hills were my legs, and that my head was being pushed between them. In the process my middle was doubled up and it felt roughly as if somebody were squashing it between two metal plates studded with nails.

'Oh God – ' I gasped, trying to straighten up, trying to relieve the intolerable pressure in my inside. 'Let me up – '

The weight on my neck instantly lifted, and I straightened my back. Crouched beside me looking anxiously into my face was Jane, the other Jane. The fog had made her eye-black run and it lay in ridges in the lines under her eyes; her hair was hanging in strands from under her hat. I could smell her scent, very sharp and close, through the fog and dog smells at the foot of the lamp-post where I was sitting on the ground.

'You must've fainted!' she exclaimed in awe. 'Lucky I come along when I did! Whatever happened, then? Did you have a drop too much to drink?'

I couldn't answer. Sitting up had done nothing to relieve the cramping agony inside me. I clasped my forearms over the pain and bit my lips.

'You look bad!' she said suddenly. 'Come on, you can't stay there. I'll help you – it's not far. On your feet, then – there's a good girl.' Coaxing and hauling, she managed to get me upright. I clung to her and tried to keep my nails from digging into her arm. With my other hand I pressed my stomach. It made the pain worse, but I kept hugging it, holding it. With the woman urging me, I put one foot ahead of the other and we started to move.

The pain died down for a moment, and I relaxed my hold. Then it came again like a whiplash.

'No!' I felt like shouting. 'No! I didn't mean it!'

I wouldn't let her take me beyond the door. I waited until a break came in the pain, and then pinned a healthy smile on my face and told her I felt perfectly well.

'Are you sure, dear? Because I could easily take you upstairs . . .'

'No, really, I'm fine now. I do thank you for finding me – '

'But whatever do you think made you faint? Do you do it often?'

I could feel the pain beginning again, and my smile was turning into a grimace.

'I don't know . . .' I said vaguely. I couldn't think up a lie, despite all my recent practice. My mind was fastened on this new and fearful thing that was happening. 'I think I'll just go and lie down for a while . . .' I managed to get my key in the door and immediately forgot about my rescuer. I must have just left her standing on the steps. I stumbled to the first landing before the recurring cramp forced me to sit down on the floor. I felt the world beginning to drift into the distance again, but I knew what was happening this time and got my head down quickly. With my cheek resting on the worn linoleum things came back into focus almost at once. I was learning. The pain faded, and I pulled myself up immediately with the help of the banisters and gained the second floor in the lull.

I was probably more afraid than I'd ever been in my life but I was too busy to notice it. If I could just get to my room... I thought of it as a sanctuary, and something more – as if there were some magic property in the room itself that would stop this happening, if only I could reach it.

The effort of getting up the third and fourth flights, which I tried to manage in one go, muddled me somehow. I hadn't bothered with landing lights and I wasn't sure, any longer, where I was – I only knew I had to keep climbing and that somewhere at the top was relief and safety. Then I saw a strip of light. It was more or less at eye level, because I was on the floor at the time, and I crawled towards it with a muffled sensation of triumph. Whatever it was I was trying to do, which was now unclear, I'd done – that line of light was the goal. When I got as far as the door I dragged myself upright again, turned the handle, and lurched in.

Toby was sorting papers at the table; there was an open suitcase on the chair. Everything became bitingly clear to me as soon as I saw him turn round sharply and stare at me.

'Oh, you're leaving!' I said brightly. 'I wondered when you'd be coming back for your things. Well, I'll just leave you to pack.' I turned round to go, but things were blurring again and I misjudged the turn and banged my head against the edge of the door. I closed my eyes tightly because this silly new pain was going to make me cry. Toby's voice came from somewhere very close. It was loud and harsh.

'What's the matter with you? Are you drunk?'

'Everyone keeps asking that,' I said conversationally. 'No, as a matter of fact I'm having a miscarriage.' Why had I said that, in God's name? That was the last thing I had wanted to say, especially in that silly, off-hand tone. Then the words rebounded back to my ears and I heard their sound and their meaning, and the pain came back at that moment, too, and it all made sense, the way a policeman's knock on the door must make sense when you've committed a crime. I groped for Toby in the dark and found his hands, and they held on to me, and I shouted again to an unknown listener as I had wanted to in the street: 'I don't want this! I didn't mean it, truly! Stop it, please make it stop!'

Toby picked me up bodily and carried me to his bed. I wasn't being good about it any more; it was as if the effort of getting upstairs had used up the last of my good behaviour. I was sobbing and pleading; the tears ran down the side of my face into my hair.

When the pain came I twisted away from it and clutched at anything I could get hold of, and swore. But I didn't shout any more. In the back of my mind I recognized the need to avoid attracting a lot of people.

In the first lull I opened my eyes and saw Toby's frightened face hanging over me. He looked more than ever like a baby blackbird, rakish, half-strangled and very dear to me. I tried to smile at him through my tears, but I realized it hadn't turned out very well, so I squeezed his hand which I was holding.

'I'll get a doctor,' he said; his voice was breathy and distorted with shock.

'No – ' I said, shaking my head violently. But I wanted one. He saw it in my eyes. 'Don't be frightened,' he said, trying not to sound on the edge of panic himself. 'It'll be all right.'

He drew his hand with difficulty out of my rigid grip.

'Don't leave me!' I implored him, seeing the pain coming towards me like a shadow.

'Only to phone – '

I was torn between wanting him to get a doctor, and wanting him with me. 'In a minute – ' I gasped. 'After this one – '

It overtook me, but it wasn't quite as bad as before. I clenched Toby's hand and he clenched back, and I could see his face all the time in the middle of the surrounding blackness. When it withdrew I licked my salty upper lip and said, 'That wasn't so bad . . . do you think it might not be that?'

'Did you make this happen?'

The tears started coming again. 'Not on purpose,' I sobbed childishly.

He saw my eyes begin to widen and his voice changed immediately to anxious concern. 'It's all right, darling – hold on – I'll get someone to help you.'

'Dr Maxwell!' I got out, feeling alone and rootless now that he had let go of my hand. By a miracle I remembered his number, which was an easy one, and by another Toby had four pennies. I, who had protested I didn't want a doctor, now called after him, 'Tell him to hurry!'

I lay alone under the glaring light. I thought no deep thoughts about the justice of it, or the punishment fitting the crime, or the irony of fate. I thought how the baby would look if it were born now, just a red dead morsel to be wrapped up quickly and thrown away, something disgusting and of no significance, not even fit to be buried as a human being. It didn't have a chance; not even a tiny chance of living. I hadn't given it houseroom for long enough. Another pain came. I sobbed again, not because it hurt, which it did, but because I was so helpless against what was happening, and because the small voice was saying blandly, 'Well? Isn't this what you wanted?' and I was answering, 'It's not what I want any more! It's my baby and I want it to live!'

Toby seemed to be gone a long time, but I wasn't measuring time very accurately. It felt like an hour, but it was probably only a few minutes. When he came back, his face was so strained with worry that I felt the sting of another guilt, and I smiled properly (having just finished with a not-too-terrible pain) and put out my hand to him to show him I was better.

'Did you get him?' I asked, trying not to sound as if it were a matter of life and death.

He nodded and sat down beside me. 'How's it going?'

'Better. Much.'

'You look a bit better.' He sounded relieved.

We sat in silence for a while, waiting for the next pain. It was less bad than the one before, but I couldn't tell if they were dying down for good or if this were the prelude to something else.

'What did he say?' I asked presently.

'He said he'd be along in ten minutes.'

'You were gone ages.'

'I went to the box at the corner.'

This was something so endearing I couldn't speak for a moment. 'In the fog!'

'It isn't so bad now.'

'But you went out . . . instead of – '

'You don't want the whole house knowing.'

I love you, I thought distinctly. But nothing gave me the right to say it now. So instead I said, 'Mavis knows already.'

'She would. How?'

'I don't know,' I said wearily. 'It seems people only have to look at me to know. Everybody seems to have known, all the time.'

'I didn't,' Toby said, with despair.

I'd been so preoccupied with the physical results of my condition for the last hour that I'd forgotten its other effects. Something tightened in my chest as I remembered the two days since I saw Toby last. 'Where did you go?' I asked.

'To Mike's. He's a friend of mine. I stay there sometimes.'

'Did you tell him?'

'No. It's your thing.'

'But he doesn't know me. It would have helped you to tell him.'

'Well . . . anyway, I didn't.'

I love you.

'Thank you.'

He held on to me through another pain, and wiped my face. Then he said, 'He should be arriving soon – the doctor. I'll go down and wait for him, so he won't have to ring.'

'Thank you,' I said again, inadequately. At the door I stopped him. 'Toby.'

'What?'

'The other part isn't true – about James.'

He hesitated and frowned. 'Oh,' he said non-committally. 'I won't be long.'

I closed my eyes while he was gone. In the dark it was easier not to think.

Quite soon I heard them coming up the stairs. Toby had evidently asked the doctor to be quiet. He stayed outside and Dr Maxwell came tramping and booming in alone. A subdued boom is almost more formidable than a boom that's allowed full bent.

'Now then, what's all this?' he boomed in a hearty whisper.

'Please – ' I tried to formulate some plea in the middle of a pain, but it came out as a whimper.

He examined me and then straightened up, shaking his head.

'You naughty girl,' he said severely.

'Doctor, I didn't!' I exclaimed, looking, sounding, and in fact feeling as if the idea had never crossed my mind.

'Come, come,' he said sceptically. 'Then what brought this on? A normal, healthy young woman like you – '

'I ate some hot curry and then got lost in the fog and fell down . . .'

'And I suppose your conscience is perfectly clear?' he said, good-humouredly. 'There are more ways than one of ending an unwanted pregnancy, you know. Indigestion, for one. Or am I meant to believe you didn't realize that?'

'I didn't think – I wanted – '

'Is that young man the father?' he asked unexpectedly.

'No.'

'Not? Pity. Well now, look here, I think we'd better pop you into hospital for a few days, where we can keep an eye on you.'

'Am I going to lose the baby?'

'Possibly. I don't know. You've done your best to see that you do – now we'll have to do ours to see that you don't.'

'I don't want to lose it.'

He looked at me for a moment, halted in the act of folding his stethoscope. 'Well,' he said equably, 'if that's true, it'll help. Is there a phone here that I can use to call an ambulance?'

'Two floors down,' I said. 'You'll need fourpence.'

'I'll charge it to the National Health,' he said.

Chapter 13

THEY kept me in hospital for a week, even though after the first day they were able to tell me that my violent indigestion following my curry debauch had not dislodged – or even seriously inconvenienced – my small passenger. But they decided to keep me under observation until I was safely out of the third month.

I was in a large ward full of ailing women, many of them, so far as I could judge, suffering from senile decay. I'd never been in hospital before, and after the first day I felt well enough to notice things like the faint smell, which I thought was of death, but which was disinfectant, and to be mildly infuriated by hospital routine. But it was pleasant to feel safe and looked-after, and another nice thing was that nobody remarked on, or even appeared to notice my absence of rings – except the Matron, who was inclined to toss her head a bit as she passed me, but perhaps she just had a tic.

I didn't know whether it was fair to expect Toby to come and visit me. When he didn't come, I told myself I'd been foolish even to hope. Stupidly, I kept on hoping, day after day. But he didn't come. In fact, nobody did, which was only to be expected since nobody except Toby (and possibly John) knew where I was. Nevertheless, visiting hours were an ordeal far more to be dreaded than the occasional unattractive things the doctors or nurses came and did to me. I longed for company and felt unreasonably deserted. When the appointed hour approached and we could see the visitors massing outside the glass doors at the end of the ward, waiting for opening-time, I would bury myself in a book to hide my pink eyes; but they would none the less be drawn irresistibly to watch the passage of each visitor along the aisle while I thought babyishly, '*Somebody* might think to come.' I wished I could have screens put round my bed like the really sick people had, so that instead of giving me sidelong glances of pity because I had no visitors, people would drop their voices and whisper sepulchrally to interested outsiders, 'Poor little thing – she's *dying*, you know.'

All in all it was with a feeling of indescribable joy that on the sixth day I saw a familiar figure coming towards me among the prompt arrivals. It was Dottie, looking very smart in a new scarlet coat and a little matching hat, fairly exuding personality and with a huge bunch of daffodils in one hand and a bulging hold-all in the other. She was a being apart from the visitors belonging to everybody else, and there were admiring stares and not a few tut-tuts of disapproval from some of the senile-decays for her vivid make-up and briskly clacking high heels, all of which sent my morale skyrocketing.

'Well, rat-girl,' she greeted me, pulling off her hat and throwing down the flowers on the bed. 'You've led me a merry dance, I must say.' She kissed me and then glared into my face. 'How are you? You look marvellous. I expected to find a tiny shrunken corpse. I brought some bits for you that I thought would probably be redundant, but they're obviously not. What a ghastly place! Like a morgue. Here, I brought some American magazines – trash, but gorgeous – and some blissful eau-de-Cologne to bathe your pallid brow and drown out the Dettol – some grapes – corny, I know, but if you turn your nose up at them, I'll eat them, in fact I probably will anyway. And look!' From the depths of the hold-all she lifted a heavenly blue bed-jacket, all loops and fronds and frivolity. She wrapped it round my shoulders at once, ignoring my protests, splashed the nice smell around, propped up a couple of magazines to combat the gloom, and divided the grapes into two bunches. Then she sat down beside me and said, 'Now.'

'How did you find me?' I said, not caring a damn so long as she was here.

'It wasn't easy,' she said grimly. 'First I waited patiently for you to contact me. Then I waited *im*patiently, etcetera. Then I phoned your office, and spoke to that nice James man, and he said you'd left there too! But he had an address for you, and he gave it to me...'

'Oh no!' I groaned.

'Oh but oh yes. You may well hang your head. If you had to give a phoney address, couldn't you at least have picked something that didn't have a remote basis in reality? There are about fourteen roads, streets, crescents, avenues, walks, and squares all called whatever it was you told James, and I visited number fifteen in all of them before I realized I'd been had. Then I got on to James again.'

'You didn't tell him –'

'Well, no, I didn't. I was utterly baffled, but I gave you the benefit of every doubt, which by this time added up to a couple of thousand. I pretended to be another friend, and asked for your phone number.'

'Clever girl.'

'Yes, I thought so. Well, you can guess the rest. I found out the matching address from Directory Inquiry and went round there.' She was silent for a moment and just looked at me. '*What* have you got to say to explain that place, I should like to know? Well, never mind. Egalitarianism's never been my strong suit, but I overcame my natural snobbery and banged on the door. Some fat old hag in a dirty apron came and said so far as she knew you were in hospital. You can imagine how that brightened my day. I croaked out, which hospital, but she hadn't a clue and sent me up to ask somebody called Coleman.' She ate a grape and looked at me shrewdly. 'Who *is* he? He's interesting. First of all I thought he was just some little fledgling that had fallen out of its nest, but I very soon realized there was more to him than that.'

I wasn't able to hide my eagerness as I asked, 'What did he say?'

She grinned malevolently. 'Ah ha!' she cackled, witch-like. 'Oh-ho! I thought as much! Goings-on! He had exactly the same expression on his face when I mentioned your name as you've got now. Then he covered it up quickly with a look of studied indifference (very unconvincing) and mumbled some nonsense about you being in hospital for a few days for a check-up. Naturally I didn't take much notice of *that*. But I couldn't shake him on it, so then I concentrated on finding out which hospital you were in. He hummed and hawed for quite a while about it, but in the end I asked him if you were getting any visitors, and if not, I said, mustn't you be feeling pretty lonely, and that did it. He told me – and here I am. At last, and no thanks to you.'

'But many thanks *from* me, Dottie. I am glad you came – really – and bless you for the things – I so needed to see you. I didn't realize how much, or I'd have written to you. Honestly.'

'Great. Well, now that I've tracked you down, perhaps you wouldn't mind letting me in on the key to all this mystery. Mind you, I have my own theories, but I think I've earned the right to know if they're correct.'

'I expect they are,' I said.

She sat quite still and her eyes were fixed on me with a curious, dark look of sympathy mixed with something else. Wryness? Envy? Could it be envy? I wasn't sure.

'A baby?'

I nodded, and she closed her eyes and I saw her shoulders slump a little. 'A baby,' she repeated softly, to herself. Then she opened her eyes. 'Well love, that's no joke for you, is it? Poor honey, has it been awful?'

'Fairly, at times.'

She held my hand tightly. 'I wish I'd known – surely I could have helped somehow – you didn't think I'd be shocked or anything, did you?'

'No, I didn't think that. I just couldn't seem to tell anyone.'

'But your father knows?'

'Oh, yes – that's why – '

'You can't mean he threw you out! But that's incredible! It's like a Victorian melodrama – '

'He doesn't like me very much,' I explained, and it was the first time I'd ever realized that. It was a very sad thing not to be liked by your own father, and obviously it must be just as sad not to like your only daughter. So I must have failed him in some way, to make him not like me, as well as him failing me.

Dottie couldn't think of anything to say to that. She pretty well knew how things had stood between Father and me in the last few years.

'But why move into a dump like that?'

I tried to explain, and she was more understanding than I had expected. 'Oh, I see! You felt you weren't good enough to be anywhere nice! Well, do you know, I've felt just like that. When I flopped at my first job, I was so fed up with myself I thought I wasn't worth any decent firm's money, so I went off and got a frightful job working in a dirty old canteen, just to punish myself, sort of. Then when I'd proved I could do that really well, horrible and moronic as it was, I let myself off and got a better job nearer my heart's desire.' I could have burst into tears when she said that. It meant I didn't have any kind of mental kink or a leper-complex or anything strange. I squeezed her hand gratefully. It was such a tonic to see her. I'd forgotten what a joy it is to have a girl-friend.

Almost before we'd begun to really talk, visiting time was over and they were ringing the bell for everyone to leave.

'Don't worry, I'll be hot-footing back tomorrow for the next instalment – that is, if you want me to.'

'Oh, please! Do come!'

'Is there anything you need? Anything I can do?'

'No, nothing. At least – '

'What? Say the word!'

'Do you think – is there any way of – of letting Toby know that I'm all right?'

'Is Toby the fledgling? Because if so, there's no need to tell him. He knows exactly how you are.'

'How? How could he?'

'Who's that other old girl, the common-prim one with the cat?'

'Mavis?'

'Well, she waylaid me as I was leaving after seeing your Toby, and asked me to give you a message. I forgot it till now, to tell you the truth. She said to tell you she was glad it worked all right, and not to worry about paying her back until you were quite better. What are you smirking at?'

'Nothing. Go on, what else did she say?'

'That was all there was to the message, but then she got chatting. She's quite a chatterer, isn't she? She told me she takes an interest in everything that goes on in the house, and that the party line was a great help to her. I rather liked her unabashed frankness. Anyway, she cited as an example the fact that it warmed her heart to hear the fledgling ringing the hospital every day to find out how you were.' She smiled at the look on my face. 'I needn't ask if that's what you wanted to hear. Well, I'm off. Take care of yourself.' Before I could reply, she'd whisked off, running up the aisle after the last leaver, waving her little red hat at me from the doorway like a rallying signal.

Despite the fact that so many people seemed to have so many wrong impressions, I slept very soundly that night. When Dottie came again the next day, bearing chocolates and, of all things, a pomegranate, the first thing she said to me was: 'You know it's Christmas in a week, God forbid? Where are you going to spend it?'

'At home, if they let me out of here in time,' I said.

'What do you call home?'

I realized I was calling the L-shaped room home for the first time, and thinking of it as such. I was longing to get back to it, or perhaps its associations with Toby were what lent it this sudden magnetism.

'The dump,' I answered sheepishly.

'You can't be serious?'

'I think I am –'

'*Christmas* – in that place? Have you thought?'

I hadn't, but it would do no good to think, since everything depended on Toby. If he were not there, it would be terrible. But then, so would anywhere else.

'Because I've been thinking,' said Dottie, 'what a good idea it would be for you to spend Christmas at my place.' Dottie had a very nice flat in Earls Court.

'It's sweet of you to ask me,' I said, 'but I'd better not.'

'But why? You'll die of depression in that bug-run . . .'

That hit home. I felt an unwonted defensiveness rising. 'It's not all that bad,' I protested.

Dottie stopped short, frowning. 'Do you love it?'

'Well, I do in a way. It's seen me through a lot.'

'You and your places!' she said, mildly exasperated. 'But it'll still be there waiting for you after the Christmas festivities are over. It's not a time to be on your own, truly . . . Please come.'

I nearly said, 'You don't want a pregnant woman on your hands, even during the season of good will,' but something prevented me. A new set of feelings about the baby had begun to emerge since I had nearly lost it, and I wanted to be sure that they were going to take root before I risked dispersing them with talk.

I got out of it anyway. Dottie's feelings were seldom bruised by honesty – I simply said I'd rather not and she said that in her opinion I was crazy, and that was that. We talked about other things, and I told for the first time the story of how I lost the job at Drummonds, which made us both laugh so much the nurses came running with shocked looks to shut us up.

When time was up Dottie said, 'You seem indecently healthy to me – I bet they'll send you home tomorrow. I'll ring here and check before I come. And if you do go back there, at least phone me occasionally and ask me over for a meal – I'll bring a bottle of vino. I'll force a bit of Christmas spirit on you, whether you like it or not.'

She didn't ask what my plans were, or press me for details of any other potentially embarrassing subject. It's odd how wrongly you can judge people's reactions.

She was right about them letting me out. They came and prodded me and conferred, and then Dr Maxwell said I could go home. But he was evidently even less happy than Dottie about my going back to what he referred to with thinly veiled distaste as 'that place'.

'Haven't you any family?' he boomed.

I explained the position very briefly and in a pointed undertone.

'Well, I'd like a word with your father,' he shouted, louder than ever. 'Damn it, we're not living in the Middle Ages. And there are one or two other things, while we're on the subject.'

'Doctor, please don't shout,' I importuned vainly.

'What? Who's shouting?'

'Couldn't we talk about it another time?'

He seemed to realize what I was getting at at last, and glanced round the ward at all the aged but fascinated faces turned in our direction. 'Oh. I see what you mean. Nosy old harpies, eh? Well, let 'em look. If a few more of them had had children, legitimate or otherwise, they wouldn't look like a lot of dried-up old lemons. I'll send you home in an ambulance, and come and see you tomorrow. You don't have to stay in bed all the time, but take it easy – and, er . . . watch your diet.' He pulled a fierce face at me.

I was due to leave at five-thirty in the afternoon. At five o'clock I was dressed and ready. I'd put on weight while I'd been in bed, and the zip on my slacks wouldn't do up more than half-way. I felt a tremor that was partly apprehension and partly excitement. Still in there, safe and growing! I wrapped my trenchcoat over the bulge and asked if I could telephone.

Doris answered. 'It's Jane Graham,' I said, very uncertain how much she knew and what sort of reception I could expect.

'Oh, hullo dear,' she said without any detectable emotion.

'I'm coming home today,' I said.

'Oh, yes? That's nice.'

I waited for her to say something else, but she didn't, so I asked to speak to Toby. I heard the buzzer go four times. My heart was behaving as if I were going before a judge. He was a long time answering.

'Hallo?' he said at last.

'Hallo. It's Jane.' My voice would hardly come out.

There was a pause, and I heard him take a deep breath.

'Hallo,' he said. His voice was cool, but not cold.

'I'm coming home today, in about half an hour. I thought I'd ring you up and tell you.'

'Well, thanks.' There was another long pause. I was breathing heavily and so was he. It was awful.

'Will you be there?' I asked at last. My hand holding the receiver was shaking; I pressed it against the corner of a door to stabilize it.

'Well, I don't know, I might be going out this evening,' he said casually. Then he said in a slightly different voice, 'Are you all right?' Before I could reply he took himself up quickly, as if angry with himself for asking. 'Silly question, of course you must be or they wouldn't have let you out.'

'Yes, I'm fine,' I said. It occurred to me for the first time that he might not know whether or not I'd lost the baby. I gathered my courage. 'Toby, please don't go out. I want you to be there.'

There was another long pause and then he said unsteadily, 'All right.' He sounded far away, as if he had partially covered the mouthpiece with his hand.

I couldn't think of anything to say. I thought this phone call had been going on for hours. I wondered suddenly how many of the household were listening, and as if he read my thoughts Toby said, 'Mavis is out for the evening.'

'That's good,' I said, 'How's John?'

'He's fine.'

There was another throat-drying pause, and at last I said, 'Well – I'll see you.'

'Yes,' he said, and then added carelessly, 'How are you getting back?'

'Ambulance.'

'Get you!' he said dryly, and a little hope trickled back.

We said good-bye, and I went and waited in the hall, which was ablaze with the Matisse colours of Christmas decorations. Two enormous red paper bells hung from the centre of the ceiling, and from these radiated countless paper-chain ellipses dripping with silver icicles. It was all overdone, like the decorations in the ward, but even while I was having a superior little mental scoff, they were making me feel obscurely uneasy and near to tears. The hospital and all that went with it had been such an oasis in the alarming wilderness of doing everything for, and chiefly by, myself; now it came to the point of leaving it, I was scared. I blamed Christmas. Why, of all times of the year, did it have to be Christmas? It just wasn't a thing you could ignore, and being alone at it was to combine the worst elements of being alone at any other time, and multiply them by two hundred and fifty.

The ambulance came. It was the sort you sit up in, and there were two other people being taken home at the same time, so we didn't go straight to Fulham but did a detour through Kensington. The other two had evidently been in hospital longer than I had, and they were like children let out of school, peering through the unblacked-out part of the window at the bright lights in the shops and rejoicing that they would be home for Christmas. I sat in a corner and the uneasiness grew. Why hadn't I taken Dottie at her word? Christmas in her nice, cheerful flat, with her gay company and no empty hours to fill, no guilty feeling about letting Christmas pass without recognition . . . I realized I was getting extremely slushy, and tried firmly to pull myself together. If a week of being looked after had gone such a fair way to turning me into a drivelling weakling, it was just as well I hadn't let Dottie tempt me to any more of it.

Because there were very serious considerations ahead. Now that I'd definitely decided to welcome the baby, I'd have to start planning with a bit more efficiency than in the past, when, so far as one could see, I had been working vaguely on the basis that God would provide; and why the hell He should in a case like this was probably more than even the most devout believer could have told me.

Dr Maxwell had assured me that I shouldn't be troubled by any more sickness. So now I needed a job that I could do for approximately four months – something well-paid, light, congenial, preferably among colleagues with a physical inability to drop their eyes below shoulder level.

The trouble was, I didn't feel like working. I felt like sitting about with my feet up, knitting. I astonished myself with this realization. I must have accepted the prospect of this baby with a vengeance, if I were seriously thinking of knitting as a desirable occupation. Anyway, it was out of the question. Work I must, and for money. A hundred-odd pounds wouldn't take me very far.

We dropped the others off, and now the big shops would be left behind as we waded through the gloomy streets of Fulham. I looked out. Not so gloomy; even here, the small shops were gay with holly and fairy-lights, and once we passed the end of a market street which was as bright and rowdy as a fairground. In the windows of some of the dark, staid villas, usually so depressingly uniform, were the marks of individualism – small trees speckled with colour, or a silver ball with streamers, or a holly wreath, or nothing. Even the absence of a Christmas token seemed like a personal statement and stirred the imagination to wonder why.

We drew up at the house at last, and the man came round to help me down. He treated all his passengers with the same cheerful courtesy; if you had VD or had lost an ear in a knife-fight, it would all be the same to him. He said, just as he had to both his other passengers: 'Home for Christmas, eh ducks? Manage all right? Bon Noël, as they say in Jamaica.'

He saw me up the steps and then bounded down them and drove away. My last link with the false security of the hospital was broken. Now I had to start 'facing up to things' again. I grimaced at the phrase. What a grisly expression, like chins-up and stiff-upper-lips. But then it was a pretty grisly necessity. I put my chin up and tried to stiffen my upper lip, but found I didn't seem to have any muscles in it. So I put my key in the door and went in more or less as I was.

The house was as quiet as a tomb, and twice as dark. The first thing I was conscious of was the smell; I'd ceased to notice it when I was in and out all the time, but after a week away from it, it hit me in the face. Then I switched the dim hall light on, and experienced again the initial impact of the tobacco wallpaper and chocolate paint, the threadbare linoleum, the high gloomy ceilings that you were reluctant to look at for fear you should see bats hanging there. I groaned inwardly as I climbed the narrow stairs and was plunged in darkness when only half-way up. I thought hungrily of the scarlet-and-white cleanness of Dottie's self-decorated flat, with all mod cons and an atmosphere of spanking modernity. I really must have been insane. Perhaps even now it wasn't too late to change my so-called mind . . .

Then I came to the fourth floor landing and Toby's door opened and there he was.

I put my small but suddenly very heavy suitcase down for a rest, and we stood looking at each other. His hair was untidy; his long thin hands hung below the leather-bound sleeves of the green corduroy jacket, dangling awkwardly as if he didn't know what to do with them. The main light was behind him, but I could still see the shadows on his face; they were more marked than ever, and I had the foolish illusion that I could remove them by stroking them with the tips of my fingers. At the same time I felt so inordinately tired that all I wanted was to lean my face against that corduroy and shut out the world.

Then the light on the landing went out and he was in silhouette. I couldn't see his face any more with its closed, guarded expression which had kept me from going towards him; now he was just a figure in a doorway, a symbol of home-coming. I shut my mind to the facts and thought, idiotically: 'I'll put my trust in love.' Afterwards I thought that that, after all, is what religion is – the pinning-up of faith across the ugly vista of logic and reality, to fulfil a need. Maybe it works in the case of God; I've always been so afraid it wouldn't that I've never tried it. But Toby wasn't God, except to me for just that second, and he'd been hurt. So when I stumbled against him and threw my arms round his neck he just stood there, unmoving except for a slight step backwards to keep his balance – though I thought I felt his hands touch my waist for just an instant as if they had made an automatic move to hold me which he had cancelled.

I drew back immediately and gasped, 'I'm sorry – '

He said, 'I'm sorry, too,' in a quiet, dead voice.

I was so hurt it was like a serious wound, it would start being painful soon but in the meantime there was just an apprehensive numbness.

Toby put the light on again, and his face was set. He picked up my suitcase and carried it up the last flight, putting it down outside my door and turning to me. I couldn't look at him.

'John's done some work on the room,' he said. 'He got the key from Doris. He's worked on it every day you've been gone. He wanted it to be a surprise for you, and I'm only telling you in advance in case – in case you should think it might have been me.'

I wished I could have felt any sort of advance enthusiasm, but I couldn't have cared less if John had spent the week transforming the room into the Crystal Palace, or even if he'd been laying everything waste with a meat-axe.

'Toby,' I said.

'No,' he said. 'I can't talk about it.'

'Supposing it had been your baby. Supposing all this had happened three months from now.'

We were still standing on the landing. I had my eyes closed to do this, but I heard him catch his breath.

'Would you have thought I was a whore then?'

'Shut up,' he said in a queer, strangled voice.

'You must have known that you weren't the first. That didn't seem to make any difference to you. Were you able to pretend to yourself then that it wasn't true, and now you're not? Is that it?'

'Why can't we leave it?'

'Because I love you,' I said. 'And this isn't fair!' Before either of us could react to this confession, unexpected even to me, I ploughed on. 'I'm twenty-seven years old. Did you think I was a virgin? If it could happen like that with you, why should you think it couldn't happen with someone else? And if you accept that, why does a baby make it so much worse? A baby doesn't have to mean a girl's been whoring – it can come from a single night. It could have come from what happened with us, even if we'd never seen each other again!' I stopped, out of breath and out of specious logic.

Toby said quietly, 'I can't help it if it's not fair. I know it isn't. It's not a matter of fairness, it's a matter of feeling. You've got another man's child in you. That's all I can seem to think of. You say you love me. Well, I love you too. How would you feel if I told you there was a girl going to have a child of mine – some other girl, some stranger? You're probably quite prepared to stomach the fact that I've slept with girls before you, you'd think it odd if I hadn't, but if you can't see that a baby makes a difference to how much other affairs matter, I can't explain it to you.'

He tried to walk past me down the stairs, but I stopped him.

'Toby, please wait!' The hurt was beginning from when he had stood unmoving when I put my arms round him, but I drove myself through it. 'If we love each other, surely something can be done!'

'Like what? Do you want me to marry you?'

He had been driven to bitterness through pain, but I didn't see that then. I only died a small death at his words and the way he said them. I shrank away from him, feeling a coldness run out all over me as if I really had died.

He stood there for a moment and then said, in a gentler voice, 'I didn't mean that the way it sounded...'

'You did!' I cried accusingly, lost in misery.

'All right,' he said quietly, 'I did. But only for a moment. Forgive me.'

'No!' I shouted from the depths of my hurt. 'What's the good of forgiving each other! If I forgive you for being male and cruel and unreasonable, you must forgive me for being female and for carrying another man's child and wanting you at the same time. The whole thing's unfair, life's unjust and people are continually hurting and hating each other, and forgiving doesn't help – why should I forgive you anyway, when you'll never forgive me?' I was crying outright now, and he made a move towards me which I sensed in the darkness, but I lashed out with my hand and knocked his arm down, and cried, 'Leave me alone, that's what you want to do!'

'I don't,' he said painfully. 'I don't want to leave you. Why do you think I'm still here?' He reached out slowly, as if with a conscious effort, and took hold of both my arms. I was stiff and shaking and I had my face in my hands, crying unrestrainedly. But the touch of his hands released something in me and the crying began to ease. 'Don't,' he kept saying. 'Don't. It's bad for you to cry like that.' Very gradually he drew me closer until our bodies were touching. His was trembling too. My arms ached to go round him, but I kept them rigidly at my sides for a long time, punishing him for what he'd done to me earlier. But now he was cuddling me and whispering in my ear with helpless pleading, 'Hold me – hold me–' Suddenly I was hugging him with all my strength; our bodies were strung tight together and we were kissing each other's cheeks with little frantic kisses – we couldn't bear to draw apart even enough to find each other's lips.

We went into my room at last, with our arms round each other, and in the doorway I stopped dead because I'd forgotten what

Toby had said about John and for a second I thought I was in the wrong room. There was no more ugly brown wallpaper; it had all been stripped off, and the walls were white-washed. It made the room look bigger and lighter and altogether different. He'd tidied everything up and put back all my things, even the picture. Over the picture was a spray of holly. It made the room bright and welcoming and almost beautiful.

I turned to Toby to exclaim about it, but he was standing there staring round with a look of desolation. 'What's the matter?' I said. 'Don't you think it looks wonderful?'

'Yes, I do,' he said. 'I just wish to God I'd had something to do with it. I heard him working away up here alone, and he kept coming down all eager and excited and asking me to come and look, and I wouldn't . . . of all the ridiculous, petty . . . I could kick myself.'

I understood perfectly. 'It doesn't matter. Truly it doesn't.'

He sighed and moved into the room. He couldn't stop torturing himself by examining the room's new look from every angle. He even switched on the blue urinal lamp to see how its light looked against the clean walls. I could see he was going to be unhappy about it for a long time, and that there was nothing I could do about it.

I drew back the curtains and stood looking out. After a moment Toby came up behind me and rested his chin on my shoulder. In an upstairs window across the street was a small Christmas tree. It had no lights of its own, but the lights from the room behind glinted on its bits of tinsel.

I put my hand up and rested it against Toby's cheek. 'Do you realize it's nearly Christmas?' I said.

'I've been dreading it,' he said.

'Do you still?'

He turned his head and kissed my wrist quickly, almost shyly. 'No.'

'Couldn't we make some concessions to it?'

'Do you mean, get a tree?'

'Perhaps that'd be going too far,' but I must have sounded wistful, because he said, 'I don't see why. We could go out to-morrow and get one in the market.'

'What would we put on it?'

'We could pick up some cheap stuff at Woolworth's.'

'Woolworth's! That's about the most expensive place you can go!'

'Well, or perhaps we could make some. I've always thought it would be fun – We never celebrated Christmas at home.'

I realized I knew almost nothing about his background. It would be fun to find out all that, slowly and at leisure. But first there was the other thing, which we seemed to be glossing over and which couldn't be glossed over. I turned to him and said deliberately, 'There are other things I'll have to start making.'

The flinch was only in his eyes, and he didn't turn away. He just said, 'You've faced it, haven't you? Completely, I mean.'

'Yes, I think so,' I said.

'And I'll have to, too, won't I?'

'It would help.'

He walked away to the fireplace and stood with his head bent, thinking. After a while he said, 'There's such a lot I don't know.'

'I'll tell you – '

'No, I don't think I want you to. I only want to know one thing; I know it shouldn't be all-important, but deep down it's the thing I've thought about most.' He looked up and his eyes were dark, and we were both embarrassed in a way that we wouldn't have been if we'd been close together, but it was better that we should stand on our own for this.

'What is it?'

'You said just now – if it could happen like that with us, why should I think it couldn't happen between you and somebody else? But I can't – I mean, I don't want to believe it could happen – with anyone else – the way it was with us. It's the same act – basically – but it's so different each time, and I've *never* felt with any other woman what I felt with you. I'm getting tied up in what I'm trying to ask – it's simply this – was it – the same – no, that's not the word. Was it – '

'Oh darling – '

' – as perfect, as – '

'No, Toby, please stop! There's no comparison, none! You don't know, it's like asking me how hell compares with heaven, it's just absurd! If that's all – '

'Is that really true?'

'Yes, I promise! Oh, if only I could tell you – '

'Never? With anybody?'

That stopped me short. I stood helplessly, staring at him. 'There's only ever been one other person,' I said, stumbling over the words so that they sounded false even to me. I couldn't add to them. I just willed him with all my mind to believe me.

He came to me and put his arms round me and said, 'I'm terribly glad,' and from the simple way he said it I knew that against all the evidence he had believed me, perhaps because he wanted to. He kissed me; it was intended to be a sealing sort of kiss to show me that he believed me and that things were going to start being all right, but the kiss altered in the middle and suddenly he pulled himself away. His face was drawn and I could feel the tension in his hands holding my wrists. 'Oh God,' he said harshly. 'I want you. I've wanted you all the time, that's what's been half the trouble, thinking I was never going to have you again.'

'I want you too,' I said – which was the simple truth.

Something flared up in his face, and then was quenched. 'We can't,' he said flatly.

'Why not?'

'But – it might – '

'It won't. I'm sure it won't.

'I'd be so gentle – '

'I know. That's why it's all right.'

This time there were no rum punches and no tears to act as aphrodisiacs, and it was not quite as before. But there are, I was learning, different landscapes in the country of love. If the one we crossed this time was a steep climb and then a pleasant sweep into a warm green valley, and not the mountains of the moon, I was the better pleased, because although it was different it was also wonderful, and because I felt instinctively that the heights must be earned.

The first words Toby spoke to me afterwards were, 'I thought that was never going to happen to me again.' And then a minute later, he said, 'We must get a double bed immediately.' He was lying with his head in the hollow of my neck and shoulder, breathing quietly; his voice had a languorous, far-away sound, as if he were rocking slowly in a hammock on a hot summer day. I held him with one arm and the other lay between him and the small bump that was the baby. I was comfortable and very happy. I had nearly dropped off to sleep when he said:

'Am I too heavy?'

He started to move, but I drew him back. 'No, stay there. You're like a rather overstuffed eiderdown.'

He relaxed with a happy grunt, and we lay peacefully for a bit longer. It couldn't last, though. It was only comfortable with the afterglow of love-making. He stood up, and I said, 'Put something over me.'

'Why, darling? Are you cold?'

'No, but I feel silly, half-undressed. If I were completely, it wouldn't matter.'

He laughed and said, 'We'll soon fix that.'

I'd always thought it would be embarrassing to have a man undress you, especially the suspenders which are so ugly and comic, but I helped, and except for the girdle which must be the most resistant, unromantic garment since the chastity belt, it was all easy and delightful.

When I had nothing on at all he sat on the floor beside the bed with his cheek resting on one arm and watched my face while he caressed me. Whenever I smiled, he smiled back happily as if I'd given him something. Once his hand stopped over my stomach and lay there. I covered it with mine and we looked at each other and he said, 'How is he?'

'He's not complaining,' I said. It was the first time I'd ever thought of the baby as 'he'.

His gentle stroking went on. In a way it was more exciting than the act itself, and I was so physically enraptured that I said: 'We should have done this before.'

'Before what?' he said lazily.

'Before making love.'

He smiled into my eyes.

'I've got news for you,' he said. 'We are.'

Chapter 14

THE next day, walking hand in hand through the festive market, we saw a sandwich-board man pushing through the crowds. He had a cheerful red face which he hadn't succeeded in making entirely solemn and gloomy, though he was trying hard. On the board over his head was written, in white letters on black: 'THE

LORD COMETH'. The one down his front said, 'ARE YOU READY TO MEET YOUR MAKER??'

'Frankly, yes,' Toby answered it. 'Never more so. Let's see what it says on the back.'

We hurried past the sandwich man and looked over our shoulders. On the back board was written: THE WAGES OF SIN IS DEATH'.

We glanced at each other, and I pulled a long, apprehensive face.

'Doomed,' said Toby mournfully.

But we didn't feel doomed. We felt, or at least I did, intensely happy, and I found myself looking straight into people's faces and smiling at them. It wasn't just being in love, or having made love – it was the feeling of being two against the world.

Doris stopped us in the hall when we came in, loaded down under a small tree and a carrier-bag full of bits and pieces we'd seen and liked, and, inevitably in our mood of reckless gaiety, bought. She looked a bit different, somehow, old Doris – for one thing, she had a clean apron on, and her hair had been home-permed. I found out later Sonia had done it for her. The girls got on better with her than any of the rest of us did.

Still, she was in a very good mood that day. She greeted us with a cheerful smile, and whereas we had been anxious to avoid her for fear she should forbid us to bring our tree into the house, she astonished us by saying: 'Hullo, dearies. Well! Bought a tree, have you? That's nice. Like a pot to put it in?' We gazed at her blankly for a moment before recovering and saying we would, please. She got one out of the cupboard under the stairs.

'This is what we always used to have our tree in, when Fred was alive. Great one for a bit of Christmas cheer, old Fred was. Used to tie a bit of red crêpe paper round it, make it look more festive. Put it on the table in front of your window, I should. No harm in sharing your blessings, I always say.'

I felt stunned by this affability, and stammered my thanks.

'All better now, are you?' she inquired kindly.

'Yes, oh yes, thank you.'

'That's right.' She glanced downwards, just exactly as she had on the day I'd come for the room. Her eyes literally bulged. I was happy enough for this to be more funny than embarrassing. I started to shrink inwardly, and then I thought, well, she had to spot it sometime.

However, she made no comment. Instead, she said meditatively, 'You know, I haven't taken much notice of Christmas, since Fred went. I mean, you don't really feel like it, do you? But this year it's a bit different, like.' She didn't say why, but went on: 'Seeing you two with that bit of a tree's made me feel like celebrating. After all, why not?' She seemed to be convincing herself. 'Who knows where we'll all be this time next year? Who knows but what them politicians won't have us all blown to kingdom come? It's a poor heart that never rejoices.' This seemed a bit of a *non sequitur* and Toby smothered a giggle in a cough. 'Why don't you come down and have a bit of a drink with me on Christmas Eve, if you've nothing else to do? I'll invite the lot, that's what I'll do, and the girls too. You don't mind, do you, dear?' she said to me, glancing downwards again pointedly. 'It'll be good for a giggle, as Charlie says,' she concluded, with a look which on a lesser woman could have been called coy.

'Who's Charlie?' asked Toby. He evidently knew all about Fred.

'You'll see,' she said, with a roguish smile. 'Christmas Eve, then. Bring a bottle,' she added as we mounted the stairs.

We collapsed round the first bend. 'I knew damn' well there was a catch in it,' snorted Toby.

'Still, she did give us Fred's pot. Who is Fred, anyway, or rather who was he? Her husband?'

'Yes, good old Fred. They fought like tigers for twenty years; he drank – talk about liking a spot of Christmas cheer, he liked it all the year round – used to come home and beat her – '

'I can't imagine anyone beating Doris!'

'Well, of course she beat him back. It was entirely mutual. Apparently they were black and blue, the pair of them, every Sunday morning. Mavis has told me about it. Doris was always coming weeping and shrieking to Mavis in those days, saying he'd be the death of her, and meanwhile Fred would reel down the cellar steps and visit the tarts for consolation. Then the next morning when he was still sleeping it off, Doris'd go off to the pub herself and have a few, and bring back a quart of mild, and they'd get drunk again together. Then they'd usually sing. Yes, things haven't been the same since Fred fell down the cellar steps and broke his neck – '

'He didn't!'

'Well, no, he didn't actually, that would have been too good a story. He just quietly died one day – about three years ago. Poor old Doris was inconsolable. She'd no one left to fight with, and Fred, on whom she'd always called down curses, turned into a sainted memory. That's when Doris developed her thing about noise. She seemed to feel that if it couldn't be her and Fred bashing about and howling and singing, nobody else was bloody well going to. And the funny thing was, how friendly she got with Jane – the other Jane. She just had to have someone to talk about Fred to, and Jane, who'd been through exactly the same cycle of experiences with him as Doris had, only one floor below, was the ideal person.' We were trying to make the tree stand erect in Fred's pot and not seeing quite how it was to be done. 'We'll have to ask John to fix it.'

I hadn't seen John at all since before going to hospital. I hadn't thanked him for doing the walls. Now I thought about him, and thought about all the unsolved mysteries of his behaviour. I asked Toby why he thought John had reacted as violently as he had to the whole business of our falling in love.

Toby seemed oddly uncommunicative on the subject. 'They're apt to be funny that way,' he said vaguely.

'Who are? Negroes?'

'No, of course not, not Negroes,' he said. Then he changed the subject rather clumsily. 'Well, are we going to Doris's do?'

'Could you resist? I'm dying to know who Charlie is.'

'I can hazard a guess.'

'Could anyone replace Fred?'

'People are always replacing other people,' he said with unlooked-for soberness. He looked at me searchingly across the horizontal tree, and I said instantly, 'I love you.'

'Let's leave this tree for the moment, I want to talk to you.' We sat down, I on the arm-chair, he on the floor at my feet. He held one of my hands and played with the fingers.

'Jane, about this baby. Look, I don't know much about it, but shouldn't you be going to – hell, I don't know, classes or something?'

'What, on child-care, do you mean? I certainly have plenty to learn on that subject. I don't know a bottle from a safety-pin.'

'No, I meant – this other business, this relaxing thing. I've read about it, you do exercises and train yourself, and then when the time comes you pop behind a bush and reappear with the baby slung on your hip, and go on toiling in the paddy-fields as if nothing had happened.'

'There are no bushes in paddy-fields.'

'Well, behind a rice-stook, then – don't quibble. The point is, it doesn't hurt.' He looked up at me with a little grin operating on half his mouth only. 'If it's all the same to you, darling, I'd a whole lot rather it didn't hurt.'

'I'll get a book from the library,' I conceded. The idea of its hurting or not hurting hadn't occurred to me before, but now he mentioned it, it did seem preferable that it shouldn't.

When Dr Maxwell came along a little later, I asked him about it, and although he pooh-poohed it a bit and said it was all a lot of nonsense, I did get him to admit it couldn't do me any actual harm to go to the classes and do exercises. 'Keep you from getting too fat,' he said bluffly. 'And why aren't you in bed? I thought I told you to go straight to bed when I sent you home last night.'

'I did, doctor,' I said demurely, not elaborating on what happened when I got there.

'Well, I suppose it's a good sign you're not lazy,' he said. 'Now take plenty of fruit and milk. Are you short of money? Because there's an organization . . .'

'I know about it. I don't much want to be a charge on charity if I can avoid it.'

'Quite right,' he said. 'You want to get a job, something quiet of course. Put a ring on your finger, call yourself Mrs. Now don't look like that, it just simplifies life, that's all. What does it matter if it implies something that isn't quite true? None of their business,' he said vaguely. 'Where's the father, by the way?'

'My father?' He'd shot the question at me so unexpectedly I had to have time to recover.

'No, no, not your father. Don't tell me where *he* is, or I'll go and tell him what I think of him. *The* father.' He prodded my middle to make his meaning unmistakable.

'He's in Paris.'

'Done a bunk?' he asked with gruff sympathy.

'Not exactly. He doesn't know.'

He looked exasperated. 'Well *tell* him, girl, write to him and *tell* him!' he exclaimed, his moustache bristling. 'Doesn't know, indeed. He's got some responsibility in the matter, hasn't he? Not exclusively your doing. I suppose? Good God, give the blighter a chance to do the right thing!'

'I'd rather not.'

'You'd rather not,' he mimicked, and shook his head impatiently. 'And what are you going to use for money to begin with, eh? Tell me that. Or perhaps you're going to wash your hands of the whole business? Have it adopted, is that the plan? Because if that's it, you'll have to warn them at the hospital, you know. I've booked you in there, by the way – twentieth of June, or thereabouts. The point is, if you're going to give it away, you have to let 'em know so they don't let you see it. Once you've seen it, you'll want to change your mind, they always do, and that causes a lot of extra bother.'

'I'm keeping him.' I wasn't going to call him It any more.

'On what, I ask again? Forgive an old man's natural curiosity. On what?'

'I don't know yet.'

'Well,' said Maxwell wearily, 'I've done my best. Come to see me in a fortnight. Plenty of fruit and milk. Oh, I said that before.' And he stumped out.

It was too close to Christmas to bother about embarking on any sort of adult education before it, so I pacified Toby by saying I'd got plenty of time and would look into it after the New Year, and we settled down to wallow in being together and getting into the Christmas spirit.

We were dyeing popcorn, of all things, in two bowls of red and yellow Dolly-dye in my sink the next morning when I heard John moving about. I'd been fast asleep when he'd come in from work the night before. I knocked on the wall and then opened the door and waited for him. He came shambling shyly out of his room, his black face almost coy in the embarrassing anticipation of being thanked. I kissed him. 'It's the nicest present I've ever had,' I said.

'I done it all right for you?'

'I can't imagine it possibly looking better.'

'I wasn't sure for the right colour; I think in the end, white is safest.'

'It's perfect. You must have worked like a black.'

It was one of those unspeakable moments. But to my overwhelming relief, John threw back his head in one of his gargantuan laughs. 'Like nothin' else!' he roared. Then he saw my yellow hands. 'What you doin' here?'

'We're dyeing popcorn,' Toby said grandly.

John was fascinated. He moved between us and looked at the bowls of deep colour, and little puffs of red and yellow dotted about the draining-board to dry. 'But what you do this for?'

'We're going to string them together and hang them on our Christmas tree.'

John looked at the tree, and touched it. He said nothing.

'We were going to ask you to fix it in the pot so it'll stand up,' I said quickly.

He grinned slowly. 'I make a bargain,' he offered. 'I make the tree stand up, if you let me make some of them little colour things.'

We had such fun with the tree. I don't know which of the three of us was the more childishly involved in its decoration. John sat cross-legged on the floor with a big needle and some coloured wool threading the popcorn in bright strings – not at random but with meticulous counting, to make regular patterns. He loved it because of the colours and because it needed his nimble fingers. He looked like a mammoth black Tailor of Gloucester, delicately plying his needle. Toby was more reserved at first. I thought he was only joining in to please me, but before long I saw that he was enjoying it too, chiefly I think because to him it was a novelty. I remembered his words: 'We never celebrated Christmas at home.' No, I thought. Jewish homes don't. It was a subject he had never raised.

As for me, I enjoyed it because it was companionable and because Christmas is a sore on the conscience unless you minister to it. We always had a tree at home, and the family congregated – my two uncles and their wives and their one-son-apiece, and Addy my father's unmarried aunt, darling strict Addy, who had helped to bring me up. She cooked the turkey and booted the uncles' wives out of her way when they came cluttering into the kitchen trying to help, i.e. interfere, which they did unfailingly each year. Then they'd come bleating to my father and their husbands and complain that Addy was autocratic and impossible, and the men would say, 'Why can't you leave her alone?' The aunts would reply indignantly that they only wanted to help, whereupon Addy would shout from the kitchen that if either of them could cook worth a damn perhaps they could be something other than a bloody nuisance. The uncles would hide rueful grins, because they knew better than most what sort of cooks the aunts were, and there would follow the inevitable patch of family 'atmosphere' before Addy would relent and appoint them to do some menial task like laying the table. The strained atmosphere never survived beyond the first trickling bouquet from the roasting bird, stuffed pot-bellied with chestnuts.

I found the uncles and their wives, and the cousins, too, who were respectively scruffy and stuffy, trying and used to dread the annual get-together – though now I thought back to it it seemed I'd always enjoyed it in the event. I had to laugh at myself for thinking rather longingly now that I should miss it this year, and especially I would miss Addy, whom I loved. Would they all meet at Father's as usual? Would Father tell them about me, or had he already circulated the news? Probably they all knew by now; my uncle Michael was a great gossip, and he and my father often met for lunch at week-ends. I felt a little ashamed that I had never cared enough for any of my father's relatives to give even a thought to their reactions to the prospect of an irregular addition to the family. I could predict them with reasonable assurance in each case, except Addy. You could never be sure what she was going to feel, do or say about anything.

The day after we'd decorated the tree and stood it in my window, I left Toby writing and went out alone. I had a vague idea of sounding the newsagent boards for a job, but it was a fine, bright day and I found myself walking, just walking, enjoying the feeling of not being afraid any more. I stopped at a stationer's and ordered two reams of Devon Valley Thin, two black ribbons to fit Toby's portable, and a box of the best carbon papers. I looked at the Christmas cards. Normally I bought fifty, this year I bought six though basically I only needed one. But there was Dottie and James and Addy and I'd be sure to think of some others. I thought, *I really must stop spending money. Anyone would think this was just any Christmas.* But being happy always makes me want to buy things.

I told the stationer I'd be back for my parcel, and wandered on through the cold sunny streets. When I realized I was walking towards my father's house I quickly changed my direction. It gave me quite a shock. It was as if I were a mindless pin, being drawn through a magnetic field. To distract myself, I went into a draper's and bought a pair of knitting needles, a large supply of soft yellow wool and some nice simple patterns. While I was looking through them, the woman, who was a friendly, cosy old body, noticed my bare hand and laughed at herself.

'I thought for a while it was for a baby of your own,' she said.

I wanted to say 'It is', but something stopped me. When I got out of the shop I felt angry with myself, and a little alarmed. If I wasn't able to admit it to some old woman I'd never see again and who didn't matter a scrap to me, how was I going to face it out for the rest of my life? I decided it was just *because* she hadn't mattered that it hadn't been worth shocking her. It didn't exactly lend weight to my decision to realize, when I'd finished making it, that I was standing outside a second-hand jeweller's looking at a selection of gold rings.

At a junk-shop a little further along I saw a china snuff-box painted with ribbons in lover's-knots, and an M on the lid, which I bought for Mavis. It was only 2s. 6d. and rather her sort of thing, I thought. The problem of John remained. How I wished I could buy him a record-player for all those useless records, but there was no point in thinking along those lines, so in the end I got him a belt, made of different coloured woven leathers, very gay and rather spivvy, only of course it wouldn't look spivvy on him. Then I picked up my things at the stationer's and walked home, ignoring the distressing tugs of the magnetic field, which made me feel I'd wasted my morning by not doing the thing I'd set out to do. I couldn't understand why I should want to leave the relative safety of the house in Fulham to walk into a hornets' nest of horrified disapproval and rejection.

The first thing Toby said to me when I got in was, 'Somebody's been here to see you.'

My heart froze for a second, as if I had put on an elaborate disguise and suddenly been addressed by name – I didn't feel safe any more. I'd been discovered.

'Who?'

'A man. Big, tough-looking character. Wouldn't give his name.'

James, I thought dully.

'Is he coming back?'

'Yes, this evening, he said.' Toby looked at me inquiringly.

'It's my old boss. You know, the one John said was my lover,' I said. 'Oh, damn, I never thought he'd look for me.'

'He seemed in an awful state about something.'

'The house, probably,' I said. 'I didn't exactly describe it accurately. Also, he may have had quite a job finding it.'

I felt very tired suddenly, and Toby saw it.

'You've overdone it rather, haven't you?' he asked. 'Why don't you pop upstairs and lie down for a bit? I'll fix you some tea later.'

'No, that's my job,' I said. I looked at the sheet of paper in the typewriter. 'How have you been getting on?'

'Not too well,' he said shortly, and then added an odd thing: 'I hope being happy isn't going to stop me writing.'

'Why should it?'

'I don't know. I can't seem to concentrate. I keep floating about in the thought of you, like wallowing in a hot bath and not wanting to get out.'

He was sitting at his desk and I went and put my arms round him from behind, and nuzzled his ear. 'I've got a confession to make,' I said. 'When you went away I came down here and read – '

'What!' He jerked away from me.

'Only one page,' I said soothingly. 'I thought it was terribly good.'

He stared at me for a moment, and I thought he was going to be angry. Then he said, 'If you thought it was so bloody good, why did you only read one page?' We laughed, and then he grew serious again and said, 'But don't praise me. It dries things up somehow.'

'A lot of things seem to dry you up,' I teased.

'It's the truth,' he said gloomily.

I went away and made tea and then sent off my Christmas cards, only not James's. I dreaded seeing him, and thought I'd go out for the evening, but then I realized there was no point in that, it was only putting off the inevitable. Perhaps he won't come, I thought. But I knew he would. Then I began to wonder whether, by wearing a loose jacket and sitting down all the time, I could keep him from noticing. Men aren't very observant about these things. What on earth had prompted him to come hunting for me? I sighed uneasily and began to cast on stitches for the back of a matinee jacket . . .

Knitting was a painful business for me, but it was absorbing, and I'd lost track of the time when I heard crashing footsteps approaching and a determined bang on the door. I hid the inch of yellow knitting, which represented two hours' work, under my chair, tipped the lampshade to a more discreet angle, and called, 'Come in.'

The door was flung open, and there was a baffled pause, like that of a charging bull who's lost sight of its target. 'Well, where the hell are you? Oh, here!' he exclaimed, bursting into sight round the corner. 'Ah, so I've found you at last!'

He sounded exactly like an outraged father, but the expression on his face was contradictory. He had the anxious, wary look he always wore around women who were indulging in any essentially feminine pursuit – like crying, being coy, spending money on fripperies, or gossiping. Or being in some way fragile and in need of protection. I knew that look too well to mistake or ignore it. With a sigh of resignation I untipped the lampshade and raked out my knitting from beneath the chair.

'Sit down, James,' I said wearily, and when he had done so, his big hands dangling between his knees, I asked, 'How did you find out?'

'How did you know I knew?' he mumbled, incoherent with surprise.

'That look,' I said grimly.

'Look? But I didn't – not at – I mean – '

'Never mind James. How are you?'

'How are *you?*' he asked accusingly.

'As you see me.'

'God, if I'd known! If only you'd told me! Living here – in this place – '

'Now, James, it's quite all right. Keep calm. I like it here.'

'I admit this room's like a daffodil in a crap-heap,' he conceded.

'How did you find out?' I asked again.

'Well, you'll never guess,' he said. 'The Old Man told me.'

'WHAT!'

'He's known all along. He knew when he fired you.'

I sat with my mouth open.

'Well, you can imagine, I felt the way you look. The bloody old hawk, talk about X-ray eyes! Heard about you being sick and put two and two together – though what the other two was, I'm damned if I know. These old Jews, they've got such a feeling for kids, they can spot 'em almost before they're conceived. It floored me.'

It had floored me too. I'd dropped three stitches. But it explained a few things – the kindness I'd thought I'd detected, his seemingly unreasonable act of firing me . . .

'So – why on earth did he tell you now?'

'Got the wind up about you. Christmas and all that. Those Yids, they set far more stock by this Christmas nonsense than most of us – damn' nuisance – God, I've missed having you to do my shopping for me this year. What do you think Audrey'd like, damned if I know – and Joan's getting to the stage where she looks at toys and says politely, "Yes, but what does it *do*?" Anyway, the Old Man – well, he called me into the Sanctum this morning and said, had I heard anything from you, and I said no, and he said silly bitch, or words to that effect – with which I agree – said he'd told you you should keep in touch with me. Then he said, he'd heard you'd moved away from home. Is there anything he doesn't hear, I ask myself? I said, yes you had. Did I know where you were living now? Yes, I said, you had a nice place in Chelsea. Check on it, said he. Why? I asked. Never mind why, he said, just do it. So I rang here, didn't ask for you, just asked the address. When we found out you'd pulled a fast one, the Old Man said I was to get round and find out if you were all right. Why shouldn't she be all right? I asked him. I was beginning to think he'd gone off his chump. He gave me a sort of world-weary look – and then he told me. Seemed to think I should have known it for myself. Jesus, Jane,' he finished peevishly, 'why didn't you tell me, dear? When I think I kept you working . . .'

'Thank God you did, or I'd have cracked up and had even less money saved than I have now.'

James coughed. 'That's really what the Old Man wanted me to find out – how are you off for money?'

'I've got about £87 10s.,' I said.

James ran his fingers through his hair distractedly.

'Jane – I don't want to interfere – I mean it's none of my business, but – '

'Who's the father?'

'Well – yes – no – '

'He's an ex-actor. I've known him for seven years. We went to bed once. He's in Paris. He doesn't know anything about the baby, and I never want to see him again. Okay?'

'Sorry, dear,' James muttered, rigid with embarrassment.

'I'm sorry, too,' I said penitently. 'It's just that it's all very well to talk about his responsibility and all that – nobody thinks how awful it would be for me to go crawling to him wailing, "I'm in trou-uble? I'm going to have a ba-aby?" I couldn't, James. I'd rather manage alone. If I can.'

'Ah, but that's the whole point. Can you?'

'Well, that remains to be seen.'

James watched me prodding away at the knitting for a while, and I sensed his helplessness.

'The Old Man said – if fifty quid'd help –'

I stopped knitting again and stared at him.

'Are you telling me that – he wants to *give* me –'

'Well, not really give. A sort of advance on salary.'

I took this in.

'You mean, he'd be willing to take me back, afterwards?'

'It's fair to say I've never stopped griping since you left. And you know how I can gripe.'

'Thank you, James,' I said, feeling humble.

'So what about the fifty?'

I sat and thought about it.

'I can't get over him doing this for me – a shiksa.'

'A what?'

'A non-Jew.'

'Well, you've worked for him. That practically gives you a hook-nose in his eyes. He mentally circumcised me the day he signed my first pay-cheque.'

'What do you think? Ought I to take it?'

James sat back on the bed and shouted, 'Take it! Of course you should take it! Good God, are you crazy? You might just as well say to a publisher, should you take his advance royalties!'

'Yes, but I might not be able to come back – it's all so uncertain ...'

He grimaced in exasperation. 'You flaming women, you're so stuffed with bloody honesty it's a wonder you don't choke on it. So you don't come back. So the book doesn't sell a single copy. So what? You can pay it back sometime –'

'Oh, sure!'

'Well, or if you don't, he can afford it. Better you than some club for Jewish juvenile delinquents. Take it and buy a pram, and if your conscience bothers you, paint "Down with the Arabs" on one side and "I like Kykes" on the other. That way you'll be doing him a favour.'

I laughed and said, 'All right. I could do with it.'

He got out a cheque-book and wrote a cheque.

'I suppose you wouldn't accept an extra bit from me?' he asked.

'You're damn' right I wouldn't.'

'Never mind, Audrey and I will give you a pile of disposable nappies or something when the time comes.' He gave me the cheque.

'I must write and thank him,' I said, gloating over it.

'No,' said James quickly, 'don't do that. I'll thank him for you. Hell, it's chicken-feed to him.'

'Shiksa-feed,' I corrected. 'But I must write, all the same. It really is darling of him.'

'Well – ' he said, 'I tell you what, write the letter now and I'll take it in. Why waste a stamp?' Then I looked at him and he looked quickly away, James who was incapable of telling the simplest lie without making a hash of it. Silently, I handed the cheque back.

'Well tried,' was all I said, but very tenderly.

He blustered and turned scarlet as if caught out in a crime, and tried to bluff it out, but I knew him too well.

Then he tried to force me to take the damn' thing, and I had to call attention to my delicate condition. At last he sat back, tousled and infuriated, crumpled the cheque and hurled it across the room.

'I won't cash it,' I warned him.

'I know you won't, blast you.' We sat in stubborn silence for a minute. Then he said, 'In fairness to the Old Man, all the rest of it's true; I mean he did say you could come back to Drummonds later, and it was through him that I found out . . . he'd probably be glad for you to have fifty out of petty cash – which was where I was going to get it from to pay myself back – '

'A likely story.'

He sat quiet for another moment, and then began raging. 'Bloody, stupid, stubborn, neurotic – '

'Yes, James. I love you.'

He stood up, shaking his head, and picked up his coat.

'I'll be back,' he threatened. 'Oh – here. You can't bloody well refuse this.' He took a half-bottle of Glen Mist out of his pocket. 'Shut your trap,' he said, as I opened it to protest. He plonked the bottle on the table, and shambled muttering round the corner. Then he put his head back into sight.

'And I still think you should write to Paris!' he yelled as a parting shot.

Toby came up when James had gone. I told him what had happened and we sipped the Glen Mist out of egg-cups.

'This is one bottle we won't be taking to Doris's come-all-ye,' he said.

I said nothing. I was thinking of all I could have bought for the baby with fifty pounds. I picked up the crumpled cheque and spread it out, looking at it with the sort of hopeless hunger with which one admires things in the window of Fortnum & Mason. Toby watched me.

'I think I'll have a cigarette,' I said suddenly.

He looked as if he were going to object, then didn't. He gave me one, and I folded the cheque carefully into a spill and lit the cigarette with the flame I had obtained from the gas-fire.

'God,' said Toby violently, 'I wish to Christ –'

'What, darling?'

'Nothing,' he said miserably, staring at the charred remains of the cheque, burning away in the Cinzano ashtray.

Chapter 15

We were late getting to Doris's party on Christmas Eve, because Toby and I had a sort of row.

I hadn't been feeling too well all day, but after opening-time when Toby'd gone out to get the wine I started to feel better and began to dress. But nothing I had looked right on me. My skirts wouldn't fasten and my loose-fitting dresses weren't loose any more. I thought it wasn't fair that I should begin to show when I was barely into my fourth month, and I got angry with my clothes, as if it were their fault that I pulled them out of shape. Also, my hair wouldn't go right. For no apparent reason it was hanging on my head like lank seaweed; I couldn't make it puff out in a way that hid my ears properly. It was just that bit too long. I got hot and sticky trying to fix it, and my arms ached with holding them up. I thought, *I must get it cut* – and then I remembered that I had no money to waste on that sort of thing any more; it would just have to grow, or I'd have to cut it myself. In the end I completely lost my temper with it. I got a pair of rather blunt scissors out of my sewing-kit and, swearing out loud, began to chop.

Of course, after I'd cut off one bit, my temper cooled down like a hot poker dipped in a rain barrel. I stood in front of the mirror, aghast at what I'd done. There was one raw edge, straight from my left cheek to my ear-lobe, then a drop of about two inches, and all the rest hung down unhappily, like a dropped skirt-hem.

At that moment, Toby knocked. He was a bit subdued that day anyway; the work wasn't coming right. He'd got about half-way through the book, and stuck. He'd added nothing since the night James came. I knew well enough what the trouble was. *He* wanted to be able to give me fifty pounds, and he was suffering from a deep sense of inadequacy because he couldn't have given me five. As I knew this, there was no excuse for the way I behaved. I think I'd have been more sensitive, but for my hair, and my clothes not fitting.

When he came in he saw I was on the verge of tears and said, 'What's wrong?'

'My hair!' I wailed. 'Look at it!'

I held the curtailed lock out to him. He looked, and laughed.

'What's funny?' I snapped.

'That is. You ass, what did you want to start hacking at it for? It looked lovely as it was.'

'Now's a fine time to tell me!' I fumed unreasonably.

'Well, I'd have told you earlier if you'd asked me.' He walked round me, judiciously. 'You'll have to cut it all now, I suppose.'

'I can't,' I retorted. 'You'll have to do it.'

He looked alarmed. 'Hell, darling, what do I know about cutting women's hair? Can't you do it?'

'No. Here, Figaro.' I handed him the scissors, put a towel round my shoulders, and sat down on a chair. He stood, non-plussed, the scissors dangling.

'How?'

'Just cut,' I said grimly.

He cut. He did the only thing he could, which was to chop it straight all the way round. There was a tense silence as he moved slowly round behind me, breathing heavily.

'There,' he said at last, when he'd travelled in a half-circle. He got out a handkerchief and wiped his hands.

'How does it look?' I asked tremulously.

He looked at me, glumly. 'Do you want the truth?'

'No,' I said. I stood up and looked at myself in the mirror.

After a short, ugly pause, Toby came up behind me and hung

his handkerchief over the mirror with a mortician's gesture. I was experiencing something very like despair, which was not altogether relieved when he turned me towards him and said, 'I'd love you if you were as bald as a coot. No, now don't cry, it doesn't look as bad as you think. You look like a little Dutch girl. Come on now, we're going to be late, the others are all in there, I could hear the revelry as I came through the hall.'

'I don't want to go,' I said childishly, looking at the sad bits of cut-off hair lying like a dead bird's feathers on the floor.

'Well, I do,' he said cheerfully, trying to snap me out of it, 'and I've bought the wine and everything. Come on, Janie, we must go now. It'll be fun, you'll see.' He took my arm, but I pulled it away. It was such an odd feeling, as if I'd lost twenty years somewhere. I didn't seem to have an ounce of grown-up character to draw on. I felt helpless in the face of my own infantile bad temper and sulkiness; I could remember exactly how I'd felt when I was six, and somebody was trying to cajole me into doing something I didn't want to do . . . in a minute, I thought in some recess of my mind, I'll be stamping and shouting, 'Won't!'

'What's the matter, darling?' Toby asked gently.

I knew I didn't deserve his patience; I had to think up some justification of my silliness, so I said, 'They'll all notice,' which was something that hadn't been worrying me up to then.

'Well, so what if they do?' he said robustly.

There was no answer to that, so I sighed heavily, and said, 'Oh, *all* right,' as if he'd bullied me into it. All might still have been well, if he hadn't, in a desire to make me happier stood away from me and said, 'You look lovely.'

'I know how I look!' I barked. 'I look bloody awful!'

'You don't,' he said mildly.

'I do!' I retorted, not mildly at all. 'I look as if I were going to give birth to an elephant at any minute!'

He looked astonished, as well he might, and glanced downwards instinctively to verify this.

I turned my back on him. 'Don't look at me!'

'Darling – honestly – are you mad? You can hardly see a thing.'

'I can't do my skirts up!'

'Well, that was inevitable, eventually.'

'If I go on blowing out at this rate, I won't have a thing to wear by January!'

'Janie, you'll have to get maternity clothes sooner or later. With you it's a bit sooner, that's all.'

I turned on him. 'So you admit I'm enormous?'

'Dear God,' he said, beginning to get rattled. 'No, of course not! All I said was – look, darling, let's go to the party. Please.'

Something pleading in his voice reached me through whatever senseless barricade of childish rage I'd thrown up, and I relaxed a bit, and managed to smile and say I was sorry to have been so silly. He looked relieved, kissed me, and picked up the bottle. 'Look, I got a nice Beaujolais,' he said, showing it to me.

'How much?' I asked.

His normally open, boyish face closed for a moment, and then he said warily, 'Why do you ask?'

'Because we're going halves, of course.'

'We're not,' he said in a rigid voice that should have warned me.

'But Toby, we are, of course we are! That's only fair!'

'What's fairness got to do with it? Please shut up about it. I'm paying for the lousy thing, and that's the end of that.'

'But you can't afford –'

'I know I can't!' he shouted suddenly. 'I can't afford any of the bloody decencies of life! I can't afford to take you out properly or buy you a proper Christmas present, or be able to tell you not to worry – I'm twenty-eight years old and I'm still living from hand to mouth like a bloody tramp. Since I was eighteen I've been writing, ten years already, and so what? I've written two novels and five plays and God knows how many short stories, and what keeps me alive, even? A couple of lousy articles a month, stuff I mug up and toss off and get no feeling from doing, just a feeling of disgust because it seems to be all I'm fit for!' He turned away, his shoulders slumping suddenly. 'Why don't I shut up,' he said, the anger gone from his voice and only bitterness left.

Shaken, we stood at opposite sides of the room, in separate silences. But I couldn't bear to see him standing there so desolately, face to face with his own failure. I knew how it felt, and it must be worse for a man. I went over, tentatively, and touched him.

He turned round to me abruptly and his face had a new hard look. 'Jane,' he said, 'will you tell me the truth if I ask you something?'

'What is it?'

'Do you think I'm a failure as a writer?'

'Failure's a thing you measure at the end of a life,' I said. 'You haven't failed yet – not till you give it up, or die.'

'But I've failed up to now?'

'You haven't succeeded. It's not the same thing.'

He paused, and I thought, *What he's going to ask me now is very important*. 'Do you love me in spite of the fact that I haven't succeeded, or because of it?'

'In spite of it,' I said, fearing that this was not the answer he wanted. But his face gave me no clue, and he went on: 'Would you love me more if I did succeed?'

'Yes,' I replied promptly, 'if by succeeding you mean in your own eyes, not necessarily the world's.'

'Why would you?'

I had to think about it to get it clear in my mind. 'Because,' I said slowly, 'because success is important; it's as important as self-respect – it's *part* of self-respect. Without self-respect and a sense of satisfaction in his work, a man's nothing, and if he's nothing, he's not worth loving.'

In the pause that followed I had to stifle a feeling of panic. *And wasn't that the completely wrong thing to say?* I thought. If he doesn't understand – if he's one of the people who says 'If-you-really-loved-me-you'd-love-my-failure-too' – this could be the finish of us.

He didn't relax suddenly, or smile, or kiss me – it wasn't that simple. But from the way he reached out slowly to pick up the bottle and said, 'In the meantime – my treat?' I thought that at least part of what I'd said had satisfied him. At least he knew I told him the truth. I nodded, feeling a sense of relief, as if we'd cleared some giant obstacle in a fog.

But still he didn't smile, and later I wondered if perhaps we'd hit it without knowing it.

'Let's go,' he said.

It always seems odd, looking back on a turning-point in life, that bells did not ring and warning hooters go. The party seemed to be just a party – quite an entertaining one, but nothing world-shaking. I mean, of course, *my* world.

Everyone who lived in the house was there, and so were a number of other friends and neighbours of Doris's. They were a mixed bag, which became a lot more mixed after sampling Doris's noxious black punch, to which every liquid contribution, no matter how incompatible, was swiftly added. There was a lot of dancing to the radio and, later, to John's guitar; a lot of Christmas cards were repeatedly sent toppling; a lot of seasonal goings-on went on under the veritable forest of mistletoe that hung from the centre light. And Mavis told fortunes.

I hadn't known she did, but apparently she could only be persuaded when she was in her cups, which was a rare occurrence. The first person so honoured was Charlie, an elderly retired spiv with the face of a well-meaning gorilla who came approximately (and frequently) up to Doris's ear. Mavis informed him archly that when she looked into his horny palm she could hear wedding-bells. Charlie, undismayed, threw out his incredibly long arm like a lariat and encircled Doris's ample waist with it. He winked at Toby and me, standing together in the audience which had gathered round.

'Cupid ain't fussy,' he said. 'Look what he done to me, at my age!' Doris was so overcome with girlishness she actually giggled.

Then it was Toby's turn. I was surprised at his eagerness.

'Come on, Mavis, while you're in the vein.'

'Oh you!' Mavis said, giving his hand an almost flirtatious slap. 'You never believe a word I tell you.'

'On the contrary, I believe every word, specially when it's depressing. Then it's sure to be true. Come on, tell me something nice for a change.'

She examined his hand.

'Unsettled,' she said peevishly. 'Everything's always muzzy with you. No clear pattern at all. A bit of this, a fiddle with that – never really put your whole self into anything, do you?' I saw Toby's face change. 'And your work-line – look at it. Little branches wandering off it every whichway. Blurred. That's what you are, my lad. Blurred.'

'That's enough, thank you,' said Toby, quite sharply for him. I'd rather not hear any more, if you don't mind.' He stepped back out of the circle and stood frowning into his drink. I touched his arm, but apart from deepening his frown for a second he didn't pay any attention.

We had some hot bangers and the room got thicker and thicker with smoke and noise and people. Charlie had his eye on Sonia. She was a dark, broad-faced girl with Slavic eyes; under her thick make-up she was probably little more than twenty. Whenever Doris wasn't looking, Charlie would play peek-a-boo with her and she would stare at him stonily for a minute and then turn her head pointedly away. Jane had evidently told her they were both off-duty for the evening.

Toby didn't ask me to dance. He spent most of the evening sitting by himself. It wasn't hard to see he was unhappy about what Mavis had said. I felt a stifled anger against her. I tried to cheer him up but he only grunted and wouldn't respond. I felt further away from him than I had ever felt, even when I came back from the hospital. It seemed such a childish thing he'd allowed to upset him; a silly woman telling fortunes . . . but silly or not, she had brushed the truth, and hit him where it hurt.

I found myself sitting with Jane and Sonia. John was near by, playing his guitar. People were getting tired, and everyone was sitting about. There came one of those breaks in the conversation, and in the middle of it Jane suddenly asked: 'Are you all better again now, dear? I was quite worried about you, after you fainted that time.'

Naturally everyone listened. I couldn't see many people; most of the lights had been turned off, and we happened to be sitting in the patch of light thrown by one small lamp. All round were people in the gloom – an audience of attentive and potentially malignant strangers.

I thought: *These are just the first hundred, for the rest of my life – strangers who'll know, who'll find out, who'll try not to react but who will react.* Their attention was idle, impersonal; Jane's question was rhetorical. But abruptly it seemed to me that the moment should have meaning, even if it were to my discredit. I felt a rush of impulsive courage to the head and said pleasantly 'Yes, thank you. Luckily I didn't lose the baby, so of course I'm very happy about that.'

I heard Mavis gasp, and Jane looked puzzled and surprised. I thought, *I've misjudged Doris. She hasn't told anyone.*

'You having a baby, dear? I didn't know that.'

Mavis found her voice. 'But dear – I thought – '

I located her in the gloom and shook my head, smiling. She was obviously very put out. 'Well I never!' she said crossly. 'It never dawned on me.'

There was what seemed like an age of silence before the general hubbub mercifully resumed. In that age I learned that 'confession' doesn't ease the soul, but challenges it. My rash courage ebbed and I wanted to run. But instead I sat quite still and thought, *If I can say it here I can say it anywhere. And anyway it's none of their business.*

Mavis drew me aside as soon as she saw an opportunity.

'Jane, you couldn't have done what I told you – '

'Never mind it now, Mavis.'

'But I've never known it to fail – '

'Will you read my hand for me?'

It was rather a haphazard reading, as Mavis was now well away and the light was almost non-existent. I wasn't really listening. I'd only suggested it to distract her. My attention was fixed on Toby, still sitting by the window. He'd drawn the curtain back a little and was hunched up over his glass, staring into the street.

'Toby,' I called softly. He looked round. The frown was still there, out of place on that blackbird's face. 'Come and sit here for a bit. Mavis is going to read my hand.' I thought if he heard her nonsense directed at someone else he would get back a sense of proportion about it.

He came slowly and sat beside us.

'I can see a number of roads up ahead for you,' Mavis was saying. 'Whichever you take will be rough and rocky. But there's always a silver lining, isn't there, dear?'

'To the rocks?' murmured Toby, and I thought *It's working.*

'You be quiet,' said Mavis. 'She knows what I mean. It won't all be hard; there'll be, like, compensations. They do say they're a great comfort,' she added vaguely. 'Often thought I'd like one myself. Thought I'd call it Violet – or Myrtle, I always liked nice smells – '

'Then why not Eucalyptus?' suggested Toby. I reached out with my free hand and put it in his. His fingers closed round it and I felt the emptiness of fear fill solidly with relief. I stopped listening to Mavis and sat staring at Toby. He flicked a wry, sheepish little look at me, and I pushed my head against his shoulder and put my other hand tightly over our clasped ones.

'Oh, now you've spoilt it!' Mavis exclaimed. 'Just as I was getting into it, too. Did you hear what I said about the tall fair man, dear?' But I wasn't listening. Toby had come back for the moment. He put his arm round me and I closed my eyes. We sat quietly together, our breathing synchronized. I felt rather sleepy, and very safe and unworried. I'd told, and Toby hadn't minded, and soon we'd be alone together.

The thing that made the turning point happened just as we were leaving. The numbers were thinning; there'd been a small brawl when Doris caught Charlie sitting at Sonia's feet; Jane had told Sonia off in no uncertain terms and dragged her off downstairs; one neighbour had passed rather noisily out and been lugged home; somebody had announced an engagement. In other words, the party was a success; honour was satisfied. Toby and I went to say thank you to Doris and she shouted jocularly after us as we went up the stairs, 'When are you two going to get married? The double room on the first floor's vacant!'

I could actually feel Toby's hand stiffen in mine as he withdrew himself. He said nothing as we climbed the stairs, but he didn't switch the lights on as we passed them on the landing. I felt my breathing quicken with uneasiness.

The frown was back between his eyes as I put on the light in my room. He sat broodingly beside the fire while I made some coffee.

'I suppose she thinks I arranged for you to come here,' he said at last.

I thought it better to pretend I had forgotten the incident, as if it were of no importance. 'Who?'

He glanced at me sharply. 'Doris. I suppose that's what they all thought. No doubt the whole neighbourhood's waiting for me to make an honest woman of you.'

'Does it matter what they think?' I asked, forcing a light tone.

'I guess not.'

We drank our coffee in silence. My heart was thumping with disquiet. The atmosphere was unnatural. We should have been holding hands, post-morteming the party.

'This coffee's disgusting, I'm sorry,' I said at last, to break the silence.

'It's all right,' Toby said absently. He put his cup down and added, 'It's not too terribly late. I might try and get a bit of work done before I turn in.' He grinned a bit, not looking directly at me. 'Mavis put the wind up me, talking about my work-line.'

'There's no such thing as a work-line,' I said, irritable through misery that he wanted to go.

'I know. Still, she was right in principle.' He bent and kissed the top of my head briefly. 'Good night, sweetie. Sleep well.'

I froze inside. It was the first time he'd ever called me sweetie. It was a term I hated – it had such a frighteningly casual ring. As if I were – but I was, I realized suddenly. I was his mistress. It was the first time I'd put it to myself like that. I'd never realized before just how vulnerable a mistress is.

Chapter 16

CHRISTMAS DAY started badly. To begin with, I'd spent part of the night dreaming about Father – one of those long, tangled dreams with occasional moments of such lucid clarity that you can remember them in detail for years afterwards.

We seemed to be running against each other in some complex obstacle race. It was terribly important that I should beat him, and I struggled desperately against the invisible forces that always prevent one running in dreams. Every now and then we'd have to climb a huge wall, or jump a ditch, or crawl through a barrel. As I battled my way over or through each obstacle I'd think: *I'll be ahead of him after this – he'll never manage this one.* But when we came into the straight again he was always beside me, running, panting, straining to get ahead just as I was. Then in the end we came to a river so wide I couldn't see the other bank; I felt frightened and thought this must be the end of the race, and I wanted to stop, but Father plunged straight in without looking at me so I had to plunge in too. The water seemed almost solid, and it was a heart-breaking effort to keep afloat, let alone swim; the heavy dark mass kept closing over my head. I was so sure I was drowning that I forgot about the race and screamed out, 'Father! Father!' Each time I stopped to catch my breath I could hear his voice in the distance shouting, 'Jane! Help! Jane!' – despairingly, getting fainter and fainter. At the same time I could see Terry standing close by, on firm ground. He had his back to me. I longed to call out to him to help me, but his name stuck in my throat. This part of the dream was like many others I'd had about him. I always woke up hating him for not turning round of his own accord.

This time John woke me. I was in tears and my stomach felt painful, as if I'd fallen and twisted a muscle.

'You don't sleep well,' said John gently. 'You best wake up, have some tea. Happy Christmas.'

I held his big black hand gratefully until my heart stopped hammering. Then we had tea together with me sitting up in bed in my dressing-gown. I often did this. It was odd, but I had no feeling of shyness or modesty in front of John; he never seemed to pay the slightest attention to how undressed I was. Recalling my dream, I thought it strange that, having gone to sleep wretched and fretting about Toby, I'd completely forgotten him as soon as I lost consciousness.

Now I was awake, though, he became all-important again. I could hardly wait to see him. Below, I could hear the spasmodic tap-tapping of Minnie, his typewriter. I listened anxiously. He would type about a sentence, slowly and painfully; then would come a swift, angry machine-gun rattle of repeated x's, followed by a long, long pause during which I found myself holding my breath, my mind forming wordless prayers. Then at last, when I was beginning to think he'd left his desk or gone out, the tapping would begin again. Several times I went to the head of the stairs, my longing to go to him was so strong. But each time I turned back. I knew I must leave him alone.

It just didn't feel like Christmas Day. Trying to awaken my slumbering festive spirit, I invited John to come in and open his present. As soon as he started to tear the paper off I had a wild desire to snatch it back, rush out and buy him a record-player; it seemed such a ludicrously inadequate present after all he'd done for me. Instead I had to sit and watch him produce the belt, and although he seemed pleased enough with it the incident left me even more empty of joy than before.

'I got a present for you, too,' John said, grinning mysteriously. 'Not ready yet. I give you tomorrow.'

When he'd gone I went back to bed. There didn't seem to be much to get up for. I just sat there, thinking about Christmases past.

When I was little, my two cousins and I used to spend the holidays with each other's families in rotation. Before we reached an age at which it was considered improper, the three of us used to sleep in one big bed and keep each other awake most of the night, giggling and speculating on the mysteries and wonders of Christmas morning. Our stockings were always huge – not real stockings, but big ones made of net stitched with tinsel ribbon. In the morning when we woke, the first awareness was always of their new and sumptuous heaviness lying across our feet.

One Christmas Eve I woke at the critical moment, and saw, not Santa Claus, but three familiar figures indulging in heavy horse-play at the foot of the bed. There were two more familiar figures (female) hovering in the doorway hissing 'Hurry up – don't wake them!' and 'Michael, stop breathing gin-fumes in the boy's face!' I lay as still as death. Next morning, with ghoulish relish, I shattered the already somewhat shaky illusions of my two cousins. We told no one what we knew, and kept our secret for a year, while we plotted revenge. The following Christmas Eve, we enlisted the aid of Addy, our friend and ally, and laid an ingenious Santa-trap. This consisted of a collection of kitchen equipment – saucepans laid in strategic positions on the floor, a roasting tin filled with cutlery balanced on the top of the door, kettles hung at face-level from the ceiling. The grown ups having gone out for the evening we then kept awake alternately for half-hour shifts by one of the boy's watches until at long last we were rewarded by the sound of creaking and thumps from the stairs, accompanied by slurry avuncular curses and 'shushes' from the aunts. The trap worked like a charm. The uncles and my father, jolly and unsuspecting after an evening's celebrations, blundered in with their sacks of bounty; the tins and cutlery crashed round their ears as they pushed the door open. Propelled forward by the shrieking aunts, who were bringing up the rear, they stumbled in, falling over the pots and pans and bumping into the dangling kettles, dropping their sacks and shouting and generally making the most satisfactory uproar imaginable. The lights went on; we leapt up and pounced on them, adding our howls of ingrate triumph to the general confusion – ending the happy myth not with a whimper but a bang, while Addy, the fellow-conspirator, leant against the wall and laughed herself to helplessness . . .

I got out of bed suddenly and fumbled for some money. I went downstairs to the phone in my dressing-gown, pausing only for a second outside Toby's door to listen for the typewriter, which was silent, and for another moment outside Mavis's to leave her snuff-box. At the phone I rang the operator and asked for Addy's number.

I wondered why I hadn't thought of this before. Perhaps I had thought of it, but just hadn't wanted to do it. Now it seemed like the only thing that would make Christmas tolerable. I waited happily for them to get through. There was no need to plan what to say; it would all be easy, as soon as I heard her voice.

'No reply, caller.'

Slowly I put back the receiver and climbed upstairs. It was a moment of despair.

Mavis came to her door. If I could have avoided her, I would, but it was impossible. She had my present in her hand and was smiling a merry Christmas-morning smile. To my eyes this made her look like a strip-dancer at a funeral.

'Who forgot to press button B?' she asked archly.

'Oh . . .' At any other time I'd have laughed at this innocent self-betrayal; just now it didn't seem funny, only irritating.

'Thank you for the lovely box, dear! Wherever did you find it?'

'Do you like it?'

'Like it? Of course I like it, I love it! Now come and see what I've got for you.'

Her room was an Aladdin's-cave of coloured balls and jack-frost. She had more Christmas cards than I'd ever seen for one person; every surface was a forest of them.

'How pretty,' was the best I could manage in my present mood.

'Yes, isn't it,' she agreed complacently. 'Here you are, then, dear, and a merry Christmas, in spite of everything.'

I couldn't help smiling at that; she still hadn't quite forgiven me for the fact that her remedy hadn't been effective. I unwrapped her gift.

It was a small book called *Baby and You.*

Good Old Mavis, I thought, suppressing a giggle; *she takes her defeats like a lady*. I said 'Thank you' in a choked voice and kissed her. She sighed.

'Well, dear, I'm only sorry it didn't work. I really can't understand it. You did do exactly what I told you, didn't you?'

'It doesn't matter now, Mavis.'

'But I don't like to feel I let you down, Jane.'

'You didn't let me down. Please don't give it another thought.'

She sighed again, but dismissively, a no-good-crying-over-spilt-milk sigh. 'Well now,' she said in a brisk voice, 'we must think of the future. What are you going to *do*?'

This is the sort of question people in my position come to dread. I think those under thirty find it difficult to accept the fact that some actions may have results which are final and inescapable. When you're young, everything seems reversible, remediable. Time will put everything right. Unkind words, ill-judged behaviour – stupidity, cruelty, it can all be made up for, cancelled out later. But now I'd done something which was forever. I still couldn't quite believe that nothing would ever be the same again.

'I don't know yet,' I said.

'If only Toby had a little money – or a proper job – he's a sweet boy, but – '

'Mavis, if you really want to help me – '

'Oh, I do, dear!'

' – you'll stop talking as if Toby's the father. You must know he isn't.'

Mavis's eager expression went blank, then turned hurt. 'I'm sure I've never dreamed of saying – '

'Mavis, dear, I don't blame you. Just, please, don't talk about me any more.'

Oddly enough, she wasn't offended. 'Well, I always was a gossip, always will be, it's in my nature. One has to come to terms with one's little weaknesses,' she said tolerantly, as if speaking of someone else's. Then she appeared to think of something else. She frowned for a moment, then picked up my hand and led me to the window.

'Yes, I thought so,' she said after a moment's scrutiny. 'This tall fair man I spotted last night – '

'Oh Mavis, for heaven's sake!'

'No, now you're very naughty to scoff.' She dropped my hand and looked at me. 'He's overseas, isn't he?'

It was probably just a lucky guess, but it shook me, and she saw it. Pressing her advantage, she hurried on: 'Why not write to him? Oh, I know, you don't like to ask him for anything – my dear, you don't have to tell me, I've seen it all before. But you've not only got yourself to think of . . .' She talked and talked. It was minutes before I could get a word in. The word I finally got in was 'No'.

She sighed resignedly. 'Well, we'll just have to think of something else, won't we?'

'It's not your worry, Mavis,' I said, I hope not rudely.

'No, but it's so much more interesting than any of mine,' she replied . . .

Cheerful crashes and bangs floated up from Doris's kitchen as I went back upstairs, and I could hear outbursts of raucous male laughter and pinch-induced shrieks. Charlie had evidently been forgiven, and was about to be fed. Somebody, at least, was feeling Christmasy.

Toby's typewriter was still silent. I stood outside his door listening for a long time; there wasn't a sound. I was well aware I should wait until he came to me. I let myself knock.

'Who is it?'

I went in. Toby was lying on his back on the bed, smoking. My eyes went to the desk. It was neat and bare. The typewriter was covered. A cold feeling ran over me. It was like seeing a room that's been tidied up after a death.

'I thought you were working,' I said.

'I was. I had to stop.' There was a curious note of finality in his voice.

I walked slowly to the bed and sat down beside him. The edge felt unfriendly and insufficient under me, and he didn't move to make room.

'What's wrong?'

'I don't know.' He didn't look at me, but stared at the ceiling, frowning against the smoke.

I felt as if he felt I was a stranger. After a long time I said, 'Do you want me to leave you alone?'

He shrugged and shook his head helplessly.

My hands and feet were like ice. 'It's Christmas Day,' I said stupidly.

'Yes,' he said, and now his voice sounded desolate. 'I know. I've nothing to give you.'

'It's not important – '

He jerked with pain and anger as if I'd laid a whip on him. 'It *is*!' he shouted. The shout startled me to my feet. I felt suddenly afraid of him, afraid to be too close to his pain, knowing I'd caused it. I walked to the door.

'Jane.'

I dared not turn and let him see my face. I stood facing the door and said, 'Yes.'

There was a long moment and then he said in a stifled voice, 'It's gone.'

My first thought was that he meant his feeling for me. Trust a woman to think of that first. I said nothing. My skin crawled, and I shivered a bit as I stood there, desolate as a child in a corner.

He went on talking. 'I know why, I think. It's because now there's a reason why I *must*. It's not just me any more, me doing what I want to do when I feel like it. Now it's me doing the only thing I can do because I have to make some money.'

I turned and we looked at each other.

'Not for me,' I said loudly. I was very frightened. This was what one person's needs could do, if inflicted on another person. 'You don't have to make money for me. I'm not your responsibility – I'm not anybody's but mine. And you're not anybody's but yours. I won't take the responsibility for you losing the will to write, or for shackling your motives, or anything else. We've no right to wish our problems on each other. That's the difference between being married and single – and we're single.'

I went quickly out and up to my room. I was shaking. I sat for a while holding the baby under my hands. Then I got up and took the two rugs by their corners and dragged them outside the door. After that I swept the pock-marked linoleum, and then washed it, working from the far corner under the bed right round the angle to the door, backing along on my knees. That took an hour, and made me so tired that I was able to lie down and go to sleep. I was numb, but it was a numbness that promised to give way to an agonizing pain quite soon.

I woke to knocking. In my warm, sleepy contentment I expected it to be Toby, the Toby of before. But it wasn't; it was Addy.

She stood in the angle, shapeless and erect in her aged but once-good suit with the fox-head-and-riding-crop brooch on the lapel; the well-pressed faded blouse; the sensible heels planted apart; the leather gloves softly slapping the palm of the hand – and of course, a new hat. She always bought new hats. This time she'd outdone herself. It was as ultra-fashionable as the suit was dated. It bestrode her severely-parted hair like a sequined circus girl, riding backwards on the solid rump of a matronly old mare.

'Merry Christmas,' she said with false heartiness. 'Or does the mere suggestion make you want to heave?'

I flung myself out of bed and into her arms. The fox-head pin scratched my cheek. The hat was so new it gave off a faint, expensive smell.

'Here! That'll do. No need to knock me for six. Let's have a bit of light on the subject.' She switched on the blue urinal and looked at it. 'What a curious shape! It reminds me of a hospital, for some reason . . . Well, let's look at you. Yes, you've got quite an interesting shape, too. Do you like my hat?' She adjusted it at a still more ludicrous angle in the mirror.

'I'm crazy about it,' I said fervently.

'Like to try it on?'

'Yes, please!'

I tried it on. Addy adjusted it fastidiously above my hollow-eyed, pasty face. My cropped hair stuck out bleakly. On me, it looked like the fairy on a Christmas tree which has shed all its needles.

'You need a bit of make-up to set it off properly,' Addy said thoughtfully. She opened her handbag and brought out an astonishing assortment of cosmetics, with which she daubed my face. They were all the wrong shades for me (for her too) and I looked like a tired clown by the time she'd finished, but on my previous appearance anything would have been an improvement. She didn't ask what I'd done to my hair. She sat back and said, 'There! That's more like it,' with a rich air of satisfaction, as if I were her masterwork. 'No, don't take it off just yet. It brightens the room.'

I sat curled on the bed in my shabby dressing-gown and Addy's spectacular circus hat, while Addy inspected the room.

'I like it,' she said at last. 'The rest of the house is unforgivable, but this room's fine. The white walls make all the difference.'

'John did those. He's the man next door.'

'The black one with all the teeth? Like a young Robeson, with that tremendously wide face, yes, I saw him as I came up. Fascinating. What about some tea? No, don't move, I'll do it.'

While she made tea with her usual haphazard efficiency, she put me into the picture. In casual, chatty tones, she told me that 'my news' hadn't penetrated to her Surrey retreat, and in fact hadn't reached her until an hour ago when she'd arrived, having heard nothing to the contrary since last year, to keep the traditional family tryst at my father's house. There she'd found him alone – 'pretending to have forgotten it was Christmas' – all the rest of the family having tactfully cried off.

'Your father thought one of the others would have blown the gaff to me – presumably *they* thought *he* had – the net result, as always when you leave it to George, being that nobody told me a thing. Not even you,' she added, with the first hint of reproach she'd used.

I opened my mouth to utter some as yet unthought-up excuse, but she stopped me. 'Don't bother,' she said, 'I can imagine – the old hide-your-head urge – well known to me. Well now, tell me why you're not living at home. On second thoughts, don't. I can imagine that, too. Silly old sod.'

Somehow this surprised me – not the word sod (I'd learned most of my swear-words at Addy's knee) but the word silly. It seemed out of place.

'Why silly?'

'Well, the old fool! Always bleating and moaning because he hasn't got a son – no one to carry on the Great Name of Graham –' She gave a short guffaw. 'So now you're going to have what might well prove to be a boy, very likely is from the way you're growing. Presumably you'll adopt it yourself?'

'Adopt it?' I asked, bewildered. 'But it'll be mine.'

'Yes, yes, I mean adopt it legally. Then it becomes sort of quasi-legitimate. You give it your name, and it's all above-board, or something. The law then pretends it's a waif or stray and that you're doing it a favour, and all is forgiven. The child becomes officially your adopted child, instead of irregularly your own.' I opened my mouth to speak, but she silenced me. 'I know, I know. The law's an ass. Never mind, what it comes to is that there may well be a sturdy little male to carry the name of Graham proudly into the future. Which there wouldn't have been, in the normal course of events. But William can't see that, of course. Oh, dear me, no. So he kicks you out and settles down to a nine-months' bender. Whack-o.' My aunt sat down suddenly, looking very tired and rather ill.

'He's – drinking?' I said with difficulty.

'Like the proverbial fish.' She slumped in her chair, her hands limp on her tweed lap, her head lolling as if she were asleep. It was so unlike her to slump that I felt a new alarm.

'Are you all right, darling?'

She straightened sharply, and grinned at me, but her face was pale and there were shadows I hadn't noticed a moment before. She had always been, in an aggravated way, very fond of my father, who was her nephew, the son of her twin sister who had died.

'Me!' she said loudly. '*I'm* all right! Good heavens! Speaking of drink, though, have you any? No, don't get up.' I directed her to the Glen Mist. She poured us both a generous tot, and drank hers rather faster than liqueurs are normally drunk, then gasped and blinked as sudden tears started to her eyes. 'It's been quite a day,' she said. 'Now. Tell me as much as you can tell to a maiden aunt, and let's see what can be done.'

I told her a cut-down (but not a Bowdlerized) version of the story, omitting Toby. I wouldn't have omitted him three hours before, but now it seemed I must face up to the situation as it was without him.

'And you're sure you haven't got a hankering for this Terry?' she asked at the end. 'Because if it's just pride, that's silly. But if you really don't want him – '

'I don't, I truly don't.'

'Pity, since he's doing so well.' Addy always had a severely practical streak. 'Still, we can manage. I'm scarcely rolling in money, but, like the margarine ads say, small amounts can be spread over oodles of bread.' She sat down on the bed and held my hand; all the flippancy was suddenly gone from her face. 'Will you come and stay with me for a while?' she asked gently.

Addy was one of those rare people who never makes a sacrifice. She didn't believe in them. The Aunts always used to say she was selfish because of this, but her argument was that as she never wanted anyone to do anything for her unless it gave them pleasure, she never did anything for anyone unless it gave *her* pleasure. The result was that sometimes members of the family or others who went to her for help came away empty-handed, however great their needs or deserts might be; Addy never used need as a yardstick. But on the other side of the medal were the occasions, such as this one, when she volunteered something you'd never have dreamed of asking for, and you were free to accept it because you knew she'd be disappointed, not relieved, if you refused. I didn't even have to make the conventional protests. I just squeezed her hand and said, 'Yes, darling. Thank you.'

Chapter 17

LEAVING the L-shaped room was a horrible wrench, because I hadn't had time to prepare myself for it. Addy saw it and understood, and dealt with it in her own way – by refusing to give me time to wallow.

'I'll come down to you in a day or two,' I hedged.

'No,' she said, with an air of finality. 'You'll come now or not at all.'

She had her car – an ancient Morris known as the Galloping Maggot – parked outside, and before I quite grasped what was happening my clothes had been haphazardly flung into a suitcase, the few of my possessions for which she saw any immediate need piled on to the afghan and gathered up like the bundle of some giant Dick Whittington, and while I dazedly dressed she was lugging these down the stairs and loading them into the boot.

'What about the rest of my things?' I said when she returned.

'How much do you pay a week for this room?'

'Thirty bob.'

'Would the old harridan take half that as a retainer?'

'I'll ask her.'

Addy went down ahead of me. When she'd gone, I looked round. The L-shaped room, partly denuded, already had a pathetic, don't-leave-me air of desolation. It struck me we could easily have taken everything now. There was no point in ever coming back since I was nothing but a hindrance to Toby.

But somehow I couldn't bear to sever connexions altogether. Not so suddenly and finally. Perhaps he would change his mind. Besides, it comforted me in my act of desertion to see some of my things left behind, as one gives one's glove to a dog when one has to leave it alone, as an earnest of good intention to come back.

On my way down I stopped outside Toby's door. It hurt me to think of him, but I couldn't leave without a word. I knocked. There was no answer. I tried the door; it was open, but the room was empty. I felt a sort of painful relief. I put a sheet of paper in the typewriter and wrote:

Dearest Toby, my great-aunt has appeared unexpectedly and is carrying me off to her home in Surrey. In view of the way you feel, this seems a good idea; it means you won't have to worry about me any more, so perhaps the thing you said was gone will come back. I love you and I don't want to be on your conscience.

If I'd been honest I would have added, '– or to have you on mine', but that sounded, even to me, as if I didn't really love him, and I wanted to believe I did and to have him believe it. The trouble was, I couldn't feel any love for him at the moment, only a pain like a black bruise. I left the letter sticking in the machine and went on downstairs.

Doris was in such an agreeable mood she'd have said yes to almost anything. She and Charlie were sitting amid the wreckage of Christmas pudding and turkey bones, cracker mottoes and beer bottles; they were somnolent and at peace with the world. Going off to stay with auntie, was I? That's right, well, have a nice time, dear. Had I enjoyed the party? That's good. The room? Yes, of course, anything I liked; yes, she'd keep it for me. Thirty shillings for two weeks in advance? Very nice of me, always useful around Christmas, a bit of extra. She didn't seem to realize it was less than usual, not more. I could almost see her totting up how many bottles of best mild Charlie could get for thirty bob as soon as they opened.

Then I climbed into the sagging seat beside Addy, and we drove into the country.

I spent two weeks in her little white cottage before she would even begin to discuss ways-and-means. 'Rest,' she said. 'Eat. Read books.' I protested for the first few days, but when I tried to talk seriously she simply put her hands over her ears and went about singing in a loud, discordant voice to drown me out. So in the end I put myself in her hands.

Her beds had deep spring mattresses which supported you as subtly as salt-water, and many pillows, and enormous billowing Continental feather-quilts. After the camp-bed, it was like sleeping in a cloud. Every floor was carpeted wall-to-wall, even the bathroom. Every room had an open fire, cheerily burning. All the walls were white, except where they were lined with books. The cottage itself constituted a small library, and my aunt's taste in books was catholic – there was something for every mood: thrillers, plays, dozens of biographies, philosophy, and just about every classic Penguins have ever brought out. There was even a pile of well-thumbed American comics, paper-backs full of people called Charlie Brown, Pogo and Li'l Abner. I had never met any of these characters, and sneaked the first booklet into my room as if it had been full of eroticism; but my feeling of guilt was short-lived. Addy discoursed freely on the social significance of Pogo, the psychology behind Charlie Brown and Snoopy, and told me that no less a person than John Steinbeck had recommended Li'l Abner as one of the great satires of our time.

After that I went through the pile like a dose of salts. I didn't find them very significant, but they were extremely entertaining. It was so long since I'd read anything, I found it useful to start in the nursery, so to speak; afterwards I got on to other things and soon found myself reading and reading until my eyes ached and I had to stop. So then I went for walks.

The countryside round the cottage was winter-stricken. It was too early for even a portent of spring; the trees were stark and without promise; round their roots their last year's covering lay clogged and rotting. Such birds as there were had a furtive air, as if they had no real business to be alive in those dead surroundings. The water in ponds and ditches lay rank and still, reflecting the lifeless grey of the sky.

My first walk, by myself, depressed me; like the ponds, I was so empty of colour that I reflected the January drabness of the scenery and had a feeling that this inner deadness was forever, that there would never be another spring. I crouched by the path and with a twig I dug among the cast-off sticky leaves, seeking something, some shoots of green to indicate hope, but there were none. I shivered suddenly, and put my hand inside my coat. I didn't seem to be getting any bigger. If my baby were to die in there, how would I know? My legs began to ache from crouching, and my coat-hem was getting wet. I stood up, threw the twig away and walked quickly back to the cottage.

But next time, Addy came with me. She wore rubber boots and a very old tweed coat, but no hat or gloves. Her white hair was as cheerful as snow against the bleak greys and browns of the woods. She didn't meander idly, as I had; she seemed to be heading somewhere. She strode briskly along, not talking much, humming tonelessly under her breath. In her hand she carried a long whippy willow twig, and as we passed the larger trees she would give them a whack with it; once she said absently as she did so, 'Wake up, can't you?' Periodically she would look round with an impatient air at the dead-seeming wilderness, or glare up at the waterlogged sky. Eventually she spotted a pussy-willow which seemed to be budding; she examined it with an air of slight mollification, like a housewife who inspects her home after the char has gone and eventually finds that at *least* she's cleaned the silver . . . I was so inwardly amused, watching her irritation with winter, so like my my own and yet so different, being positive and active instead of passive and defeatist, that I had no time to wonder if I were unhappy or not.

I thought about Toby; but now it hurt worse than thinking about Terry, and I tried not to. I thought about Father as well. I kept remembering what Addy had said. Once, I mentioned it to her.

'We can't just leave him there, drinking away all alone!'

'I've let him know you're down here with me. That should stop him worrying.'

'Do you think it's worry that's making him drink?'

'Partly. It's principally guilt.'

'It won't stop him feeling guilty – the fact that you've taken me over.'

'Well, I can't help that.'

'But we can't just – '

She turned to me and put her hands on her wide hips. 'So what would you like to do? Go and ring his doorbell and beg him to take you back?'

'No, of course not, but – '

'Suggest something then.'

I thought, while Addy went on with her cooking. She cooked like an angel. After two weeks I couldn't tell how much was pregnancy and how much was fat.

'Well?' she asked at last.

'Couldn't I – write to him, and tell him I – forgive him?' I faltered.

She stared at me.

'Tell him *you* forgive *him*?' she asked incredulously. 'Are you all there? The first rule about guilt, you poor fathead, is that almost no one has the courage to admit that's what's the matter with them. If you should ask him why he's drinking, he'll tell you it's because he's ashamed of his daughter. Have a little sense.' She bent and hitched a casserole out of the oven.

'When you say he's drinking – ' I began cautiously.

'I mean, oddly enough, that he's drinking. Now let's drop it. It takes a great deal of drink to do a man of William's constitution any lasting harm. Let's get an early night. I want you to help me in the garden tomorrow.'

But the thin edge of the wedge was in. Next day, clearing the broken brown stalks of old Michaelmas daisies, I ventured to bring up the subject of the future.

'I must try and find a job of some sort soon,' I said.

I'd expected her to reiterate her rest-eat-and-read injunction, but instead she stood with one booted foot on her spade and said 'Yes . . .' rather absently, fumbling for a cigarette in the pocket of her gardening apron. The smoke smelt pungent and good in the damp air; she sniffed it appreciatively. 'Let's have a bonfire,' she said suddenly.

'It's too late, everything's soaking,' I objected.

'We'll cheat,' she said. 'Rake it all into a pile over there.' She went into the cottage and came out again with a can of petrol. We threw the lighted match from a distance and the thing blew up with a satisfying whump. Gradually the blueness died out of the flames and the smoke began to smell as it should. We rushed about like children, finding dead things to feed it with. The smoke was half-steam and the fire hissed spitefully, but it burned, with the surreptitious addition of a bit more spirit. We stood and watched it, savouring the deep primitive pleasure of incendiarism. Addy rested her arm on my shoulder.

'Would you like to work for me?' she said at last.

I looked suspicious. 'No charity.'

'Work, I said. Real work. You can type, can't you?'

'Yes . . .'

'Did you know I'd written a book?'

If she'd said she'd built a planetarium, I'd have been less surprised. For all her keenness on reading, she had never struck me as being in the least literary, or in fact creative in any way. She wasn't even a good letter-writer.

'What sort of a book?'

'Just a book. It takes the form of letters.'

'Letters?'

'Love letters.'

I was more surprised than ever. I couldn't think of anything suitable to say to that. Addy was staring at the dwindling bonfire, abstractedly.

'It's all in rough,' she said at last. 'In my terrible illiterate scrawl. I never meant to do anything about it – I mean, in a way, it's rather private, like a diary.' My amazement grew. Could these letters represent some non-fictional chapter in Addy's life? So far as I had ever heard, she had never even nearly married. Now she was middle-aged – no, she wasn't, she was elderly. I'd never wondered about her age, as she never seemed to change, but now I did some mental arithmetic and it appeared, unbelievably, that she must be nearing seventy. I felt a sudden shiver of disquiet, the way a child feels the first time he realizes that parents are not immortal.

'Anyway, now it seems suddenly like not a bad idea. Of course, in all probability no one will be in the least interested. Still, the manuscript's sitting there. Who can predict the weird tastes of today? Some publisher might gamble on it . . .' She took a last drag and threw her cigarette into the fire. I was somehow reassured by the almost masculine strength of the gesture.

'I haven't got a typewriter,' I said.

'I have. It's older than God, but it works. I bought it in a rummage sale years ago for business letters.'

We watched the fire. It was dying; the smoke slunk away, keeping close to the ground like a cat that's stolen something.

'So, your idea is that I should go on living here, with you and on you, and take money from you as well?'

'Well, of course you can do that if you like. Come on in, it's getting damn' cold.'

We went in and made tea and buttered toast and sat in the bright living-room by the fire, listening to the rain which had begun to fall, relishing that peculiar feeling of security that comes from being warm and under cover during wet weather.

After two cups each, drunk in silence, Addy got up and fetched the manuscript out of her desk. It was a big, untidy folder, leaking odd bits of paper covered with Addy's thick, spiky writing. She sat down and began looking through it. Unexpectedly she said:

'How much do you miss that little room of yours?'

Up to that moment I hadn't been aware of missing it at all. But when she mentioned it, I felt a pang of remorse because I had been so revelling in the creature comforts of the cottage and making comparisons to the disadvantage of the room in Fulham which had sheltered me through so many trials. I thought of it, empty and cold and getting dusty and airless, and I felt the strongest sort of longing to get back to it.

'I'm missing it now,' I said.

'Glad you didn't give it up completely?'

I looked sharply at her. She grinned complacently.

'Give yourself another couple of weeks here,' she said, 'just to get you safely into the fifth month, and then I should go back, if I were you. Take this lot with you, and my antique machine; and get to work. I'll pay you either by the hour or by the page, whichever you like; and when you've finished that, we'll see.' She stood up, her hair like a snowy halo in the firelight. She held the folder in front of her with both hands. 'Perhaps you'd like to make a start while you're here,' she said. 'I'd like you to get through it as quickly as possible.' She frowned down at the folder, tucking a few of the untidy corners in out of sight; the movements of her hands were oddly tender, but gave an impression of exasperation, like a mother trying hopelessly to make her tomboy daughter look ladylike to meet someone. Then she thrust it towards me. 'Here, you may as well have a look at it. Just remember, I don't want your opinion. Unless it's favourable, of course. Well, I'm going to cook the dinner.'

I opened the folder with a feeling of apprehension. I wanted so much to be able to say something nice about its contents, which evidently meant more to Addy than I would ever have dreamed possible. But love letters! There was something – incongruous about the idea. Addy, who knew all about one sort of love, had always seemed to me completely immune to the other.

I selected a letter at random from among the assorted pages jammed inside the cover. It began without salutation, and consisted of a light-hearted account of a day's doings. It might have been a page from a diary, so uninhibited, vital and intimate was it; but there was an undercurrent – not very strong in the first sheet I read – of a second-person factor; on closer examination I noticed that the small inevitable disappointments and set-backs of the day were glossed over humorously, as if to spare the reader worry; the highlights were brought out the way an actor 'points' certain lines to get a laugh from his audience.

I picked out another sheet. This was longer; its tone was immediately more serious. A totally different phase in the life of the writer was being described. There was no attempt here to disguise the pain behind the words, caused by some unspecified sorrow. Here the feeling I got was of a willing opening-up of the heart, an essential sharing of sorrow in the sure knowledge of understanding and comfort. The words 'I know you will understand how I feel because you always do,' did not appear; that was simply the assumption behind the letter; it needed no stating. In fact, it soon proved to be behind every one, the gay, the serious, the tender – the perfect security of perfect sympathy.

I thought this would make for dullness after a while – was there to be no conflict between the two lovers, the voluble sender and the silent, reflected receiver? But soon I discovered that the conflicts came in the writer's life, and, later, that the conflicts were, in some odd way, resolved in the letters. Most of the writer's troubles were self-made, as in real life; they were the self-created hells that a sensitive, emotional woman will always encounter in her everyday dealings with herself and with other people; it was impossible not to believe in them as I read. And I marvelled at the way that explaining them to the recipient of the letters, getting outside them sufficiently to avoid alarming him, yet safe in the knowledge that this was a token act of kindness because he would know quite well how desperately important they seemed to the writer – these factors, together with the vital underlying one that basically nothing mattered too terribly except the fear of losing the one who was loved, made for a sense of balance and light-hearted courage in the face of life which I found so moving and exciting that I kept reading, one letter after another, avid to see how this magic formula would affect the wide range of life-like situations the writer found herself involved in.

I soon stopped associating the writer with Addy. This was evidently a woman in her early thirties, living a life full of mental and physical activity in the heart of some big city. The reason for her separation from her lover was never made clear – there were glancing references to it as something inevitable which would end one day – in some of the happier letters it seemed that they were about to meet; only in her rare moments of despair did she allow herself to hint that they might never be together again. But generally one got the impression that the relationship could scarcely be improved. That was what was so clever about the letters. They created two people, two rare people complete in each other – no, more than that. The writer was complete in herself. I recognized this with a shock when I realized that there was never even a reference to letters received.

I was still reading haphazardly and greedily when Addy came back into the room. It must have been two hours later. The fire had sunk to embers and I was a long way away; it was an effort to come back and reconcile the young woman writer with the old woman aunt. I blinked up at her as she moved about laying the table with brisk, graceless efficiency. I looked at the shiny, lined face, the cropped white hair, the lumpy figure and stumpy ankles and bony, direct hands. Was the warm, temperamental, essentially feminine young woman, whose words I'd been reading, still shut up inside that other body, like the thin man in the fat man, and were these jumbled pages on my knee her way of getting out?

At last Addy, the solid, seeable Addy, stopped busying herself with the table and looked at me. It was a look I'd never seen on her face before – a vulnerable, eager, apprehensive look. I realized in that moment that she had never shown this work to anyone before and that she cared, very much, what I thought of it. But I couldn't find the words to tell her. So I just nodded.

'You like it,' she said. What happened to her face then was wonderful. I got up and kissed her.

'Of course they're not in order,' she said. 'I shouldn't let you read them all jumbled up like that.' She took the folder from me and began looking through it again, eagerly, as if finding someone else who liked it had made it more exciting to her.

'But I want to ask you something,' I said. 'Why does he never write to *her*?'

She looked up at me, a look I could hardly interpret. It was partly a sort of kindly impatience with me for not having understood, and partly rue. 'Because he doesn't exist,' she said matter-of-factly. 'Men like that never do. They always have to be invented.'

Chapter 18

IT took me all of two more weeks to get the hang of the typewriter, a foot-high erection of jangling steel with a temperament behind every lever, and to sort the letters which made up the book into some sort of order. Addy herself grew infuriated, saying she'd had no idea they were in such a muddle, she'd just written them at odd times and stuffed them into the folder, never seriously intending to 'do' anything with them. 'If ever a work of art was untainted by considerations of commerce, it's this one,' she said grimly, as we knelt on the floor together with the innumerable sheets of paper spread out round us like the sea round a pair of islands. The pages ranged from foolscap sheets to perforated scraps torn off a small shopping-pad; most of the writing had been done with a blunt pencil. It was fatal to let Addy start re-reading any of it, because she immediately started making extensive corrections. 'That was all right as long as it was just for me, but if other people are going to see it . . .' I teased her and said real artists were only concerned with the impossible task of satisfying themselves. 'What bosh,' said Addy contemptuously. 'I'm easy to please. I think every word I write is inspired. But I don't expect others to regard it with my biased eye.'

At last I was ready to start the fair copy, and Addy went off in the car and returned with reams of quarto and boxes of carbon, rubbers, rubber thimbles, and a box containing a fascinating lump of something like plasticine for cleaning the typewriter keys. (It wasn't much good for cleaning anything when we got finished playing with it.) Then she established me at a large table with everything neatly arranged within reach, and left me to it.

But not for long. She couldn't keep away. She kept making excuses to come into the room and would edge her way over to me and stand, breathing heavily, mesmerized by the sight of her hectic scribble being translated into beautiful clean print on the uniform white sheets. As soon as one was free of the machine, she would pounce on it and set about ravishing its virgin perfection – slashing great lines through it, writing inserts in the margin and indicating their intended positions with balloons and arrows and crosses. As I retyped it, she would suddenly twitch and gag behind me as she saw something else that needed changing.

After a week of this I had typed a total of fifty-two pages. Forty-one of them were waiting to be retyped, twelve for the second time, eighteen for the third.

'Darling,' I said at last, 'whether you're paying me by the hour or by the page, you'll be broke very soon if I don't take the whole issue out from under your thieving hands. Let me go home and do you a fair copy and send it to you, and then you can make ALL your alterations at once.'

With the greatest reluctance, she agreed. 'It's like sending your only child away to boarding-school,' she said fretfully as she drove me to London. I smiled secretly. I knew she didn't mean me.

I think she had almost completely forgotten, during the past three weeks, that there was a bona fide child involved in any of this.

But I hadn't.

Prior to Addy's remark about the likelihood of its being a boy, I hadn't cared, one way or the other; now I wanted a son. This was irrational, since obviously I was more nearly capable of rearing a girl by myself than a boy – I knew almost nothing about little boys except that their need of a father was imperative if they were not to grow into Oedipus-riddled weaklings or even outright homosexuals. I had also heard that if you allowed yourself to think of your unborn child as positively one sex, and then it turned out to be the other, the pre-natal influence of your wrong conviction had a most undesirable effect – you found yourself landed with an effeminate boy or a brawny hairy girl, thoroughly unbalanced and with every right to blame you.

In any case, I was rapidly reaching the stage when I suspected that every passing thought about the baby could have a positive and permanent effect on it for good or ill – as if it had been made of very soft clay and each thought was a fingerprint. I endeavoured to think only beautiful but strictly neuter thoughts, but this was difficult, since I was considering it more and more as a potential human being, and almost all humans are so unmistakably one sex or the other. It was relatively easy to think about a neuter baby, but almost impossible to envisage a neuter child or a neuter adolescent. So eventually I evolved a system where, to be fair, I followed each boy-fantasy scrupulously with a girl-fantasy. Only as the boy-fantasies invariably came first, the girl-fantasies were always faint and unconvincing repetitions, to be raced through like homework in order to return to the ever-strengthening image of a boy.

The house looked, and smelt, just as usual. Addy sniffed ostentatiously as I let us in. 'I smell bugs,' she said.

'You're right,' I said, 'though I'm surprised you know what bugs smell like.'

'I was a nurse in the fourteen-eighteen war,' she said succinctly.

The house was very quiet. It was the middle of a week-day – but even allowing for that, it was *very* quiet. We toiled up with my things from the car. The L-shaped room had an air of damp neglect, and (as it were) hardly looked up when I came in.

'There's a funny smell in here, too,' said Addy.

I sniffed. It was a faint staleness; vaguely familiar; I couldn't identify it. 'Just being empty,' I suggested, hurrying to light the gas and open the window.

'That's unlucky,' said Addy, pointing to the Christmas tree, a pathetic little object bedecked like a corpse at a mortician's. Underneath it on the table was Toby's present, the paper and carbons. They were almost buried under a layer of pine-needles. The sight sent a cold pang through me. I'd been, for five weeks, an escaper to another world; now, faced with the tree he'd helped me to buy, the memory of the Christmas that had gone so bleakly wrong came back as clearly as one remembers last night's painful experience on waking from a deep, exhausted sleep.

Addy was watching me closely. 'Perhaps I was wrong to bring you back here,' she said. 'You look funny. Are you going to be all right?'

'Yes, I think so,' I said. 'I've got something to do now.' I spread an old newspaper on the floor and lifted the dead tree, with all its trimmings, on to it.

'Oh, save the decorations for next year!' Addy said.

I shook my head. Separating the tree from Fred's pot, I carried the sad remains down and out to the dustbin in the front. Addy came with me, and handed me the manuscript through the window of the Galloping Maggot.

'Take care of your little self,' she said, fixing her young blue eyes on me. The 'little' touched me; sentiment was unusual from her. I blinked and nodded. Our eyes stayed locked for a long moment, hers stern and tender at the same time. Then she let in the clutch and the car bounded forward.

'Thank you for everything!' I suddenly remembered to shout after her. Her hand appeared through the window and made a rude gesture to my thanks. The car turned a corner and I had a quick glimpse of her stern profile, her gay white hair blowing. Then she was gone.

Now it was she who seemed unreal, she and the cottage and the last five weeks. But the manuscript was left; it gave me an incredulous feeling, like a solid trophy brought back from a dream.

I went slowly upstairs again. This time I let myself stop outside Toby's door. I stood on the landing, thinking how we had met there when I came out of hospital. My heart was beating painfully. *He will always be important to me*, I thought with sudden doomed certainty.

I knocked. There was no answer; I hadn't expected one. It was too quiet. I tried the door – it was locked. That gave me an uneasy jolt. Toby never locked his door. He always said there was nothing to steal except Minnie, his old typewriter, and he added that if anyone stole her he would personally murder the thief.

I went up the last flight to my own floor. The silence began to seem slightly uncanny. I tried John's door; he was nearly always in at this time of day, but he wasn't in now. As I opened the door, a stench came out and hit me in the face. It was the mother and father of the faint smell in my room, and was compounded of stale air, unwashed linen, John's own personal smell – and, to my surprise, rum.

Uneasily I closed the door and went into my own room. It had perked up slightly already. I set myself to work, washing curtains, dusting and cleaning. It was much later that I made a tour of the house and found that, though it was now after eight o'clock at night, it was still quite empty.

And it stayed empty.

Actually I expect Jane and Sonia were in the basement, but somehow this didn't count. The house was hollow and silent beneath me. I'd never been the nervy type who minds the dark or being alone in an empty house. Perhaps because I'd never *been* alone in an empty house for any length of time.

During the days it was all right. I worked on Addy's book, and went to the doctor's, or shopping. I ate out sometimes. Often I went to Frank's for coffee and toast. Every time I'd been out I hurried back hoping to find lights on and the house full of the small comfortable sounds of inhabitance. I wouldn't let myself admit, at first, how much I dreaded the dark crouching quiet of the night.

It seemed to get worse, not better, as the days passed. I felt a sense of unreality, as if I had been left alone in a condemned house. Where were Mavis and Doris? Where on earth was John? – and Toby? Were they all dead? Had the house been sold? Ludicrous things comforted or upset me. It was a disproportionate relief to find the pilot light in the bathroom Ascot still burning. It gave me a feeling of shivery disquiet to see the piles of '3d. Off – Buy Now' throw-aways mounting on the door-mat. Doris had always pounced on these, and never let them filter through to anyone else.

At night I lay in bed and found it increasingly hard to sleep.

The weather was freezing, and the cold seemed to permeate the corpse-like house. It was only by burning my gas-fire nearly all the time that I maintained my little beach-head of living warmth against the encroaching rigor mortis that I imagined was gripping the house.

My imagination was working overtime. All the womanish terrors which I had always felt myself to be above, came creeping over me as I lay alone. I thought of everything – prowlers, burglars, murderers, maniacs – even ghosts. I was disgusted with myself, but I couldn't help it. I got so that I even imagined small sounds, and frightened myself half senseless by my interpretations of them.

One night about a week after my return, I imagined I heard a door close, far below. It was nearly midnight. I had been lying there since ten o'clock, fighting the urge to switch the light on. I lay absolutely still, listening. Had it been the door? I now thought I could hear more faint sounds. They seemed to get louder and nearer. Footsteps coming up the stairs . . . I began to sweat. I tried to get hold of myself. In the morning it would seem senseless and babyish. But now I was sure I could hear something. Traffic outside and the roaring of fear in my ears prevented my being sure until the footsteps were on the last flight.

Now it was unmistakable. It was a slow, irregular sound – a few steps up, then a pause, then a few more steps. My body was rigid in every muscle. I hadn't bolted the door. I had no weapon. I was alone in the dark and in this neighbourhood could probably scream myself hoarse and no one would come. I don't think I've ever known such physical fear. It was at its peak long before I heard the footsteps stop outside my door and someone fumbling at the handle.

I didn't even hear my own scream as the intruder came into the room. I knew I had screamed only when a hand clutched at my mouth and a voice said urgently, 'Don't – don't!'

It was the familiar smell that reached my frozen senses first, and then the softness of the hand, and then the voice. Slowly I relaxed as my fear receded, leaving me as limp as a sheet thrown over the pile-driver of my heart, nearly bursting through my ribs.

John was slumped on the floor by the bed, his hand still holding my mouth, but loosely, as if he, too, had suddenly lost all his strength. I moved it and said in a shaking voice, 'You stupid bloody great idiot, you nearly made me die of fright!'

He grunted and shook his head.

'Get up and turn the light on, for God's sake.'

He obeyed, finding the light after a few moments' blundering about. Reality and sense and comfort returned in a split second. 'Tomorrow,' I said grimly, 'I shall go out and buy some night-lights. Now will you kindly tell me what the hell's the idea?'

He really looked worse than I felt. He was unshaven, his frizzy beard stuck to his chin like black crêpe-hair. His clothes were filthy and torn and he had what on anyone white would have been a black eye. He was shivering like a wet dog and tears were running down his cheeks.

'I sorry,' he began. 'I sorry, I sorry – '

'Okay, that'll do,' I interrupted hastily. 'Never mind being sorry, just tell me where you've been and what's been going on around here. And what you meant by coming in here in this state,' I added severely. I could see he was full of rum to the gills.

He came back to my side, almost fell on to the floor again and put his head down on my knees.

'You go away,' he sobbed. 'You go away Christmas Day, never say good-bye – you just go. Then later, Toby, he go too. Same as you, one time he there, next time he gone. Not say nothing, not say good-bye or comin' back or nothing. I felt all alone with them two old women. They never like me. That Mavis, she say black men smell. I hear her. She mean me to hear. And Doris, not let me play my guitar for keep myself company. So I go to the club and I get drunk.'

He lifted his head and stared at me angrily.

'I get so drunk I fall down. I can't play. They sack me. I been there three years, best guitar they could have, they sack me first time I ever get drunk. I fight with boss. I hit him, then they hit me many, many. They throw me out in the gutter.' His big hands played with the afghan and he stopped looking at me.

'So then what?'

'I come back here. I got nowhere else to go. In my room I get more drunk. I bust your cradle.'

'My what?'

'I make you baby-cradle, like I promise. It was for your Christmas present, not quite finished, but then you go away before I can give it to you.'

'And you – broke it?'

He nodded. 'Broke it all up. It was a good cradle, best thing I ever make.' He started to cry again. I began to cry myself. The pain one could inflict, just by forgetting to say good-bye! I could hardly bear to think of him breaking the cradle, his big gentle hands gone savage and destructive on the thing he had made with such care and love. It nearly broke my heart to think of it.

I tried not to cry; I knew it would only make him worse. 'But how long ago was all this?' I asked, trying to be practical.

'Long time, days and days. Then I hate myself and I hate you and Toby and them old women, and I got to get away. I go all sorts of places. I get drunk at night, sleep in park, or where I can. Police catch me, I spend a night in jail – everything. Get in fights. See terrible things, terrible people – bad people. Me bad too. Me rotten bad right through.' Then he raised his head and said in a slightly less self-abusive voice, 'Not bad like them others, though. I not go with them bad women like all them others.'

'That's good,' I said. I stroked his head and he rested it on my knees again. He seemed more peaceful now and my own heart had calmed down. 'And why did you come in here?'

'I dunno,' he mumbled tiredly. 'Just want to be in your little white room. You scare me to hell when you scream. I not think you ever come back.'

We sat quietly for a long time.

'Come on,' I said at last, when both my legs were going to sleep. 'Let's have some hot coffee and I'll bathe your eye.'

Chapter 19

I WORKED through the following morning with a light heart. Fear and the anticipation of fear had lifted like a shadow now that John was next door. I could hear him shuffling about, tidying his room, humming to himself. Once in a while we'd shout through the partition to each other. After a while he began to play his guitar. It made a good background.

The letters were falling into sequence. As I typed, I felt the now familiar sense of satisfaction at having a part in something that seemed more and more good to me as I went along. The typewriter and I had called a truce; or perhaps I'd mastered its senile vagaries. Anyway, I no longer had to drive myself to the table in the same way as before. And while I was working I wasn't thinking with longing about Toby, or with hate about Terry, or with anxiety and guilt about Father. I was thinking solely about the letters, getting completely immersed in them.

At noon, I heard the front door slam, and voices came up from below. I went out on to the landing and leaned over; it was Doris and Mavis, and someone else. I went down and met Mavis toiling up the stairs with a suitcase and the cat in a basket. She looked cheerful and bright.

'Hullo, dear!' she said when she saw me. 'You're back, are you? That's nice, we are too! Lovely time we've had. Here, could you take kitty for a minute?' She thrust the jerking, heaving basket into my hands. Low growls of outrage issued from it. 'Poor kitty-kitty,' cooed Mavis through the wicker. 'She doesn't love her mother, does she then?'

We went into Mavis's room. 'How long have you been back?' she asked, fussing about blowing dust off her trinkets while poor kitty-kitty cursed ominously.

'A week. Shouldn't the cat be let out?'

'Oh yes, will you dear? Now, where was it you went? *We* visited Doris's sister in Folkestone. Such a kind soul, but what a lot of little rugs! Charlie came with us. I'm afraid I'm no use as a chaperon . . . Oh dear, has she scratched you? Naughty girl! She's apt to do that when she's first let out. Like a cup of anything?'

'No thanks,' I said, sucking my wrist where it had been savaged by vengeful claws.

'Doris didn't expect you back . . . poor ducky, have you been here all alone?' But she obviously wasn't interested in my fate. She was bursting with news. 'I'll give you three guesses what happened at Folkestone!'

'I didn't think anything ever happened at Folkestone.'

'Oh yes it does! Go on, guess.'

'I couldn't begin to. Do tell.'

Mavis looked roguish.

'If I whisper Doris and Charlie – then couldn't you guess?'

'Don't tell me they eloped!'

She chortled with glee. 'Gave me the slip! Didn't tell a soul!'

'But I can hear Doris downstairs now – they can't have gone far.'

'Just to the local registry office, dear, and home in time for tea. Only of course we didn't have *tea*. Isn't it thrilling? Fancy her, at her age! She's potty for him. Just like two love-birds, weren't they, mother's little angel?' she asked the cat, who gave her a look of contempt and retired under the bed. She went on to me: 'So we'll have a man in the house again. I've missed one since Toby went.' Her glance narrowed as she waited for my reaction.

I felt a momentary dislike for her. It was grim to be dependent on someone like her for the news I needed so badly.

'Go on then, Mavis.'

'Go on, dear? What about?'

She must have her pound of flesh. 'I want to hear about Toby.'

She smiled her smug little cat-smile and snuggled her hips into the chair.

'Well, dear,' she said, 'it's my belief it was all your doing. Terribly lonely and miserable he was, after you'd gone. Didn't do any typing, never went out, just stayed up there smoking and reading . . . very unfriendly too, any time I went up to see him. Just wanted to be left alone, he said. I got quite lonely myself; I had to spend my time with Doris, only Charlie came round a lot, and two was company, you could see that a mile off. Well, two days before we was due to go to Folkestone, Toby came to see me. First time since before Christmas. Looked bad, poor boy, quite peaky, worse than for a long time. Said he was thinking of leaving. He only said it casually, I never thought he meant so soon. Where will you be going? I said. Well, he didn't know, just to somewhere different. Said the place was getting on his nerves. He said had I heard anything from you, and when I had to say no – why ever didn't you write, Jane? Poor lad, you could see he was pining for you – he said if you ever came back, would I give you this.'

She took an envelope out of a drawer and I turned it over. The back was slightly wrinkled from where she'd steamed it open, but I let that pass. Inside was a short note.

If it's any satisfaction to you, I can't write any better when you're not here than when you are. You've become part of this hole of a house – the only good part – and it seems I'll have to leave the bloody place to get away from you. I wish I hadn't said or felt what I did when I last saw you. But the next day my mood had changed, and I wanted you like hell, but it was too late. Serve me right for visiting my personal failure on you, or blaming it on you. I'm sorry.

Toby

P.S. If I thought I could do you any good, I'd stay and wait for you. I feel a bastard for going, but what the hell, you'll probably never come back anyway, why should you.
P.P.S. By the way, I'm a Jew. So you probably wouldn't have wanted to marry me anyway.

Everything about this brought him back to me so powerfully it was as if he were in the room. It seemed incredible that I couldn't immediately start arguing the points in the note, one after the other. How dared he go off and leave a provocative thing like this, so full of what seemed like deliberate misconceptions? I felt a welling fury within me that he was out of reach of my answers, my reasoning, my sudden agonizing longing for him.

It was the final P.S. that was the hardest to bear.

'What the bloody hell makes him think that!' I exploded nearly in tears of frustration. 'I've never said a word against the Jews! I *like* the damn' Jews, god-damn it! How could he do this?' I looked up and saw Mavis's avid, absorbent face upturned to catch my emotion. I stifled my outburst with an effort. 'Well, so what happened?'

'Nothing, dear, only next morning he'd gone. Left a note for Doris saying he was sorry he couldn't pay her, but that he was leaving something to cover it. Doris was ever so put out. I told her she should think herself lucky – worth far more than he owed, I said, but she said she didn't want the bother of finding someone to buy it –'

'What? What did he leave?'

'Didn't I tell you, dear? His typewriter.'

His typewriter! My heart grew cold.

'Has she sold it yet?'

'Not so far as I know, dear. It's still up in his room.'

I went down and chatted to Doris for a while and then casually offered to buy Toby's typewriter from her. She tried to drive a hard bargain but I knew she wanted to be rid of it so all the big guns were on my side. I got it for a fiver, and she gave me the key of Toby's room.

It gave me a strange feeling to go in there and see it like that, with no trace of him left except the typewriter and some cigarette stubs in a saucer. I took the machine upstairs with me; I felt as if it were the one thing saved from a disaster. I thought of using it for Addy's book, but decided not to. For one thing, the type would be different. For another . . . well, I happened to be its technical owner at the moment, but it was really Toby's.

It frightened me to think of Toby, somewhere, working at something that wasn't writing. I tried not to think of the typewriter left behind, as a symbol of defeat. Whether it was my fault or not hardly mattered. What mattered was he musn't give up.

I shut my mind and went back to work.

But my mind wouldn't stay shut. With the letter, a tangible inheritance, lying beside me, my desire for Toby – his companionship, his love and his dear silly face – came back like a boomerang and hit me hard, leaving me breathless and unable to concentrate. I felt astonished that I had endured life without him for so long. It must have been because our last meeting had left such a cold, loveless imprint on my mind that it sealed off everything that had happened before. Now, that ending seemed dim and unreal; all that mattered was the rest. Our long evenings together in this room, with him sitting on the floor talking endlessly about himself and making me laugh; our first incredible night together; our fraught meeting on the landing when I came home from hospital; the next day, strolling through the market with that sense of reckless happiness and completion; the moment when he said, 'Am I a failure as a writer?' Was it something I said then that started the chain of estranging incidents? It had all begun, and ended, so quickly. Not surprising, really; it was a law of nature that if a growing thing had no chance to put down roots, to take a grip on life and reality, it couldn't withstand the first hot sun or downpour of rain. I felt the impact of our failure on each other and sat staring dry-eyed at the letter that proved it so inescapably.

Life without Toby became like life minus an arm. It seemed I couldn't possibly go through with having the baby without him. No purpose, no prospects seemed really to matter very much when I had no equal and ally to share them with. Loneliness settled on me again like a recurrent disease. Perhaps it would lift for ever when the baby came; but I had an uncomfortable expectation that this would not be so. A baby, more than most things in life, needs to be shared.

I wanted to find him but I didn't know where to look. It was terrible. Often I raged at him inwardly for inflicting this sense of helplessness on me. Other times I would go out walking the streets in a futile hope of seeing him. Sometimes there would be men who looked like him. The disappointment never stopped hurting.

The weeks passed – the longest of my life. John and Mavis shared them with me. John was out of work for a long time and we shared food as well as time and worries. John's simplicity about my problems amused and touched me. He would say, 'Every woman have babies. Not to have babies is sin against the Lord. He help you; He better than a husband.' I smiled, but it helped somehow. When he was in his own room I heard furtive hammering and sawing – I pretended not to know what he was doing.

Mavis made a very practical contribution. In a way she regarded the baby as her fault, and to make amends she would appear about three times a week with some delicately-made matinée jacket or tiny nightgown, all exquisitely smocked and embroidered. I was embarrassed at first and implored her to stop, or at least to let me pay her, but she became offended at the mere idea and said she enjoyed doing it. In the end I persuaded her to let me buy the materials. Actually I was extremely grateful. My own laboured efforts produced an average output of two pairs of bootees a week.

Addy's book of letters progressed. I sent off instalments to her each week, and she would promptly send me a postal order for the precise amount due, calculated by the page. It was surprising how much I earned in this way – not great sums of course, but enough to save on, as apart from food for John and myself I was spending almost nothing.

I knew I should be going to classes, doing relaxing exercises, watching my diet, planning for the future. Instead I stayed in the L-shaped room, regarded the descent to the bathroom as sufficient exercise, lived on oranges and eggs and coffee, and dreamed about Toby and the baby – dreams so divorced from reality that they should have made me wince.

Once a week I went out. I shopped, I mailed Addy's envelope, I went to the doctor's. Each week I noticed that my coat fitted me a little less comfortably, that Dr Maxwell's questions about my plans and current activities grew a little more pointed, and that I was a little more tired when I got home. I also noticed Spring was coming. Minute green buds appeared among the soot-blackened old leaves that flanked our front-yard dustbins. On the creeper that spidered its way over the doctor's house, the buds were pink, like small insolent tongues stuck out at the Winter. Often the air was as bland as warm milk, and aeroplanes rumbling across the blue skies reminded me of the summery sound of bees.

The Spring can be more painful than any other time of the year. Summer is lazy and indifferent; Autumn is demanding and invigorating; Winter is numb and self-contained. But Spring has none of the palliatives. Every emotional nerve is close to the surface; every sound and sight, every touch of the air, is a summons to *feel*, to open your doors, to let life possess you and do what it likes with you. To refuse to take part in the sharing and feeling and growing that the Spring demands with such gentle imperiousness is punished by a painful awareness that you're betraying something – the sort of guilt a religious person would experience after committing blasphemy.

And I was refusing. I was escaping again. I had accepted the idea of the baby, but only, it seemed, in terms of fantasy, not reality. Without Toby to hold me down to earth, I might as well have been living in a pink cloud as in a small L-shaped room up five decaying flights of stairs.

The book was nearly finished. I was beginning to wonder what I would do for a living after I had written 'The End' and sent off the last sheets to Surrey. Addy had said 'We'll see' – perhaps she knew other authors who wanted scripts typed. I wrote her a letter with the penultimate week's copy.

Darling Addy,

This is almost the lot. I'm prepared for lots of retyping – I expected some returns from you before now – but those shouldn't take much longer than a week. I must tell you yet again how tremendously good I think it is.

Have you found an agent or anyone to act for you *re*: The Book? I believe it's a necessity. There's a woman I've heard of called Billie Lee; I hear she's very good and 'knows everyone' in the publishing world.

When are you coming to see me? I don't mean you should get worried and rush up before you feel like it, but it would be good to see you again. The fact is, though I'm perfectly well physically, mentally I feel like a jellyfish. I just seem to drift through the days with no real sense of purpose or definite plans for the future. Nothing seems very *real*, somehow . . . I wish it were possible to go and buy oneself a couple of yards of backbone, a pound or two of decisiveness and courage . . .

Sorry I sound so wet. I've no one grown-up to talk to except you. As I say, there's nothing to worry about. But any pep-talks you can dish up will be well received.

Any news of Father?

Addy was always a bad correspondent. Aside from the weekly postal orders, she had written only one brief note since I came back to London. So I was very surprised to get a long letter back this time by return.

Her writing was a good deal less legible even than usual; the words sprawled haphazardly across the pages, sloping downwards so steeply that a large triangle at the right-hand corner of each page was blank.

Darling, thanks for letter, script, *et al*, *many* thanks, sorry haven't before. Things have been tricky, I note what you say about an agent, how clever darling, I never think of things like that. Can you ring her, sorry to ask but you'd do it so much better and are on spot. Do it *quickly* and let me know. Don't plug book too hard, we're prejudiced, we don't know if outsiders may hate it. Haven't done corrections yet, do you think at a push the ms might do as it is? Your editing has improved it so much. About you. *Wish* I could come, impossible now. I know what's wrong, you haven't decided WHAT YOU WANT. (She'd underlined this many times.) Terribly important to draw up a balance-sheet every now and then, debits and credits. Decide what you want, what's worth fighting for. Don't drift, ever. Decide – then act. If you fail, well at least you tried. Don't know what you want so can't advise you how to get it, but don't let life push you about. About William. He's still at it. Again you must decide. Just one question: You say you were unhappy at home. Why didn't you leave when you could afford to – long before you did? Perhaps you love him more than you think. You're not a jellyfish darling, you're like me, you need another person. I invented mine. Those of us who aren't self-contained need other people as 2-way channels, to feed us with a sense of reality so we can pour ourselves out into life. *Through* them. My person was in my imagination. That's the lonely way. I hope yours is more solid, darling. One other thing, don't listen to people who tell you not to be ashamed. Without shame sometimes, we'd go on making the same mistakes over and over. On the other hand don't overdo it. It must never touch your basic self-respect, without that you're done for, and as far as *your* 'shame' is concerned, Claudius was right, 'Sure it is no sin, or of the deadly seven it is the least.' It can represent the best or the worst in us; I never found the best in a man and I couldn't compromise but I'm not saying I haven't regretted it sometimes. But the best must be worth any discipline, well, I must stop wuffling. Be kind to William and darling, tell the baby when it asks, don't put it off, don't put anything off. So glad you like the book, it's made such a difference, I have real hopes for it now. Don't worry too much about money. I love you. Addy.

It took me ages to puzzle out all the illegible bits and interpret the non sequiturs. Something about the scattiness of the style troubled me. The contrast between it and the clear, lucid prose of the letters of her book was staggering, though often in ordinary correspondence she was careless and let her mind jump from one thing to another. But this was worse than I had ever known.

I went to the telephone with a feeling of undefined reluctance. I had a dim, unreasoning fear she wouldn't answer, but she did, and the fear lifted sharply, like a blind snapping up to let the sun in.

'Addy – it's me – '

'Yes, darling? What is it?'

'Oh – nothing – I just wanted to thank you for your letter . . . I felt foolish in my relief.

There was a long pause, and then her voice came faintly, as if she were only half paying attention to the conversation, 'Oh good . . . sorry to be so unhelpful . . .'

'Is this a bad line? I can hardly hear you.'

There was another pause and then she said, 'Is that better?' It was. She went on, 'I'm glad you phoned . . . have you finished the book yet?'

'Yes, I finished it last night. I'm sending it off today.'

'You're wonderful . . . so quick . . .' The conversation petered out again.

'When will you be coming up? Why did you say it was impossible?'

'Did I?' she said vaguely. 'Oh – well, I'm tied up at the moment – and there's the garden – I hate to leave it at this time of year, just when everything's trying to grow.'

'Would you like me to come and help?'

'No, thank you,' she said with sudden firmness.

I felt rebuffed. I hadn't meant it to sound like fishing for an invitation to stay. She seemed to sense it, and went on quickly, 'You can help me best by contacting the Willie woman, that agent. I'm going to send the whole manuscript back to you, just keep one copy for myself, it looks so nice, all typed, bless you . . .'

There was another unaccountable silence. 'Addy?'

'Yes, dear?'

'I wondered if you were still there.'

'Just lighting a cigarette . . . Has the baby started to move yet?'

'I think so – there've been little movements for a month or more – not real kicks though. The doctor says that's all right. Some babies are more peaceable than others.'

'How long will it be now?'

'Three months . . .'

She said, 'Oh . . .'

'What's the matter?'

'Matter? Nothing, why?'

'You sounded funny . . .'

'I'd got it muddled. I thought it was due sooner.'

Something in her tone made me stick my neck out again. 'Are you sure you wouldn't like me to come down?'

'Quite sure, thank you,' she said briskly. And then, on the same note: 'Well, I must be off. Things to do. Take care of yourself.'

I barely had time to say good-bye before she'd hung up.

The last note struck in the conversation left me slightly reassured. It sounded like her usual self. I went and got the last of the manuscript ready for the post. At the last moment something made me write a note to her: 'You sounded so strange and far-away on the phone today – you're not ill or anything, are you?' But as soon as I had the words on paper I tore it up quickly. It was a stupid idea. I refused to let it take root or give it the least encouragement to be true.

Chapter 20

The day Addy sent the completed manuscript back to me I telephoned Billy Lee and made an appointment. She was a flashy, hard-bitten little woman with many jangling charm-bracelets and dyed red hair. Why I should immediately have liked her I can't think, but I did. Perhaps because she didn't waste time or make any false promises.

'I'll read it quickly,' she said. 'I can't say more. Publishing's costly and first books by old people are very hard to sell.'

When I got home John was waiting for me with a grin across his face which shone like a new moon through the darkness at the top of the stairs.

'I got something for you,' he said. 'Two things.'

One was the cradle. It was a long box with a roof-like hood at one end, on rockers. It had all been carefully sandpapered and painted white, and there was a flower-carving on each side. Hanging from the peak of the hood was a bottle of Guinness.

I let out a hoot. 'John, it's perfect, but what on earth's that for?'

'That for us – not for the baby,' he said. 'You like it? Really?'

I rocked the cradle. It swayed smoothly from side to side without any bumping. 'It's a beautiful cradle,' I said. 'And a beautiful Guinness. Let's have it now.'

'Good.' He poured it into two glasses and held his up. 'Now you got to drink me good luck,' he said.

'I do – I do!'

'But special. Something good happen today.'

'Hooray! What?'

'Wait there,' he said.

He went into his own room and shouted, 'Listen now!' After a moment I was astonished to hear a trumpet solo with a full orchestral background, playing *St Louis Woman*. Hurrying after him, Guinness in hand, I found him crouched over a small but brand-new record-player.

'John! You got one!'

'Yes. And tonight, I buy the dinner, and cook too, while we listen to all my records I never played.' He beamed up at me. 'I got me a new job. Bloody good. Better than old one – I play solo now, good band, no more club, not work all night, Union rates.'

'Marvellous!'

Suddenly I staggered and dropped the glass. John jumped up and held my shoulders.

'What's the matter?'

It was the most extraordinary sensation. It had to happen twice before I realized what it was. Then I wanted to shout with excitement. 'Feel! Feel!' I cried, holding his hand over the baby. A second later he snatched it away. He danced about pretending it was hurt.

'Boy, he kicking like a footballer!'

And he went on kicking.

His hitherto gentle stirrings within me had merely reassured me that he was there; they hadn't served to remind me, as the recurrent kicks now did throughout the day and most of the night, that he was not only there but alive, growing, fighting towards the fast-approaching day when he would plunge head-first into life.

This tangible life-force drove me, literally, from within. Addy's letter had its intellectual effect, but the kicks and blows from my inner mentor were probably the deciding factor in my abrupt emergence from lethargy.

I began, belatedly, to go to classes, to take exercises; I was told reprovingly that it was probably too late to save me much 'discomfort' at my confinement (the word 'pain' is avoided so strenuously at pre-natal clinics that one becomes over-conscious of it by its very absence); but none the less, I was encouraged to persevere – 'for baby's sake'. It never failed to grate on my nerves when well-meaning people referred to 'baby' instead of 'the baby' or 'your baby'. It seemed, somehow, an unwarranted familiarity if not a downright twee-ism. But the very irritation I felt at small things of this sort encouraged me. It was a sign that I was fully alive and aware again.

I removed the cheap kilt-pins and bits of elastic with which I had been carelessly enlarging the plackets of my ordinary skirts, put them away and bought two inexpensive but quite passable sets of maternity 'separates'. I dug out the dog-eared list of books that Dr Graham had given me months ago, got them out of the library and read them carefully. One of them thoughtfully supplied a list two and a half pages long, of 'everything you'll need for your baby'. Because it said 'your' baby I was prepared to give it serious consideration; but if I had bought everything on it, not only would I have had to go deep into debt but I would have been left with no living space. I took it to Dr Maxwell, and he roared with laughter and put a check-mark beside about one-fifth of the items, and query beside another fifth. The checks were musts; the queries were things it would be helpful to have, if I could afford them. The pram, the bath and the crib came into the second category.

'He can sleep in a nice clean drawer and be bathed in a nice clean sink,' he said briskly. 'Only don't close the drawer by mistake, and mind the taps.' I was rather shocked and asked him if he were joking, but he looked put out and said certainly not. 'Of course, if he turns out to be delicate, that's different. But normal babies are tough as old boots. Give 'em plenty of love and they don't give a damn if you put 'em to bed in a window box and bath 'em in the rain-barrel.'

'Won't I need a pram to exercise him?'

Maxwell snorted. 'Ever stop to figure out how much exercise a baby gets, lying in a pram? It'll be high summer when he comes – take all his clothes off and lie him in the sun on a groundsheet.'

'But when I go shopping?'

'Carry him on your back like the Indians.'

I laughed. 'I can't do that!'

'Why not? Well, get a pram then, an old one. Now I come to think of it, we've got one at home somewhere, probably up in the attic if my wife hasn't chucked it out. May be a bit cobwebby, after all we haven't had a baby for ten years – and it's done for three of mine – perhaps it's a bit battered, too. Still, if you don't mind a few snooty looks from the nannies in Kensington Gardens . . .'

It was a perfectly wonderful pram. Nor was it either cobwebby or shabby, by the time the doctor's wife and eldest son got through cleaning and painting it. They even offered to keep it for me until I was ready for it.

I bought the rest of the things the doctor had checked, plus some of the 'queried' items. I regarded these as semi-luxuries, and made amends by cutting down on essentials – a nightie here, a dozen nappies there. (Why should any baby need four dozen nappies, for heaven's sake?) I enjoyed the shopping very much. Everything I bought added to my growing sense of the reality, the exciting imminence of the baby's arrival. When he kicked me now, I would say, 'All right, all right – what the hell more do you want?' and feel a surge of physical joy go over me that was like being bowled over by a warm wave on a summer beach.

Perhaps I would have enjoyed the shopping even more if I had bought a ring to wear. But I didn't; somehow it seemed too big a lie. I let people give me looks, and returned them with interest.

The woman at the clinic was surprised and rather annoyed by the progress I made in learning to relax. I did work hard at it, but I think my success was partly due to having learned to breathe properly for the stage. My diaphragm and various other muscles seemed to be well under my control, whereas a lot of the other girls couldn't seem to locate theirs mentally – it was like trying to wiggle their ears. I felt so bursting with confidence from this small triumph that I asked Mavis to teach me smocking, and I learned it in a week.

I felt transformed. It was like having lain frowsting in bed, unable to summon the energy or enthusiasm to get up, and then at last rousing oneself, having a refreshing bath, making up one's face and getting cracking. One invariably wonders why the sleazy, rumpled bed seemed too attractive to leave.

I put an advertisement in the newsagent's frame to say that I would type manuscripts, letters or anything else anyone wanted typed. The old man I had talked to on my first day in the house shook his head when he read it. 'No one round here writes,' he said. 'They can't, poor ignorant bleeders.' Still, he put it up, and about two days later telephoned me. 'Well – shows how wrong you can be,' he said. 'I got something for you. I'll bring it round on me way home.' I knew he lived behind the shop, and felt grateful as well as excited about having some work to do.

It turned out to be a television play. It was pretty appalling, but who was I to worry? Before I'd finished with that one, there came another. The little newsagent waxed cynical as usual. 'You make what you can out of 'em,' he advised me, sucking his teeth. 'They watch the thing a few weeks, think they know all about it. Television plays! Most of 'em couldn't write a laundry list.' But I'd have typed even laundry lists for money, and my new customers didn't seem to be short of that. The newsagent fought my corner and insisted on cash in advance.

I still had spare time on my hands. I spent a lot of it walking. The doctor had told me this would be good for me, providing I got on a bus the minute I felt tired. I could usually walk several miles before this happened.

One day I walked to Drummonds; or rather, most of the way. I took a bus the last few miles. I stood looking up at the corner window of what had been my office. A rather smart young man in a bow-tie kept peering impatiently out into the street as if expecting someone. He had dark hair and a thin black moustache and small, discontented eyes. He looked Jewish. He was the first Jewish person I'd ever disliked on sight.

Several times I found myself walking towards home – my father's house. I always turned back before reaching the river. I had a superstition that the magnetic field would be too strong for me once I set foot on the bridge.

Days began to pass more slowly, to lose their individuality. Events like the arrival of James with the promised armful of nappies and some flowers – plus the welcome gift of a year with a nappy-washing service – stood out like bas-relief on the uniform flatness of the days. Also, we were having a spring heatwave. I moved slowly through long soporific days of sweet drenching sunshine, filled with an unreasoning contentment. Sometimes it seemed too hot to move. But I did my exercises every day. If I tried to skip them, the baby's kicks seemed to accuse me.

One evening when I was idling slowly along the eight-o'clock-quiet street, my back began to ache a little and I turned into a small public garden where there were some benches and a show of tulips and wallflowers in the litter-patterned flower-beds. I eased myself down on a bench and closed my eyes. The litter, the dusty flowers, the ugly rearing walls surrounding the tiny ineffectual oasis in the concrete, vanished. The sounds and scents remained. The wall-flowers' perfume was untarnished by their coating of soot. There were birds somewhere, closer to my ear than the traffic. My tired muscles relaxed; the baby was asleep inside me, and peace wrapped me round, as uncomplicated as it must be for animals, resting their tired bodies and conscious only of the elementary pleasures of warm air and safety and no loud, sudden sounds. I drifted off to sleep.

I barely seemed to touch the bottom before starting to rise towards wakefulness again; but it must have been longer than it seemed, because when I opened my eyes it was almost dark. My earlier light sweat made me damp and chilly now. The walls of surrounding buildings climbed unlit into the gloom; there was a feeling of being down a well. I shivered a little and stood up stiffly.

As I left the garden to get back on to the road, I thought I saw a figure detach itself from the shadow on one of the other benches. A little way along the street, I turned to look back. A man had come out of the garden and was walking along after me. He was tall and lanky and wore a pulled-down hat. He had his hands in his pockets, and looked so much like a traditional film stalker that I felt no more than a trivial, fictional alarm. But just to amuse myself I pretended that he was following me. Every now and then I looked back and when he was still there, I felt almost pleased. I began to plan how I would snub him if he spoke to me. But of course he wouldn't; I was so very obviously 'married'. I nearly giggled at the idea of anyone trying to pick up a girl as pregnant as I was.

However, when I'd been walking slowly for ten minutes and he was still behind me, I began to get rather tired of it. I turned into a crowded coffee-house seeking warmth and the security of numbers. Not that the numbers were very comforting except in their quantity . . . they were nearly all Teddy-boys. One of them looked me up and down and remarked with a snigger, 'You can see she's got the right stuff in her,' and another one called to me, 'Carry yer luggage, lady?' at which they all tittered idiotically. One of them stood up and said, ''Ere, ma, 'ave my seat, you got more to carry round than wot I got.' His girl-friend kicked him and went off into shrieks.

It was like a nightmare in which one gets lost in a zoo. I wanted to get out again, but that would have called forth more inane jeers. I put my head down and walked to the far corner of the café, where there was an empty table. I sat down and stared at its coffee-smudged red top. I wished I smoked, it would have given me something to do with my hands. I felt spotlit; there was a sort of horror about the faces I had seen as I came in – thin, meaningless, unreachably stupid. I felt the baby kick protestingly against the sudden tension within me, and it hurt for the first time.

Someone came to stand by my table. I said, 'Coffee please,' without looking up, but the figure didn't move. I felt an unthinking panic, as if those simian creatures were closing round me; it rose to my throat and I thought wildly, 'It's bad for the baby for me to feel so afraid,' I stood up sharply, meaning to push through at any cost and get out. Face to face with me was Terry.

He took off the pulled-down hat and his fair hair dropped on to his forehead, giving his sharply-angled face a look of ineffectual youngness. His eyes wavered, met mine, as if accidentally, and then swivelled off again. He looked like a child who expects a beating.

I stared at him with unbelief. I had hardly thought of him for months. At one time I used to feed myself perpetually with fantasies of this meeting. Lately, I had always imagined meeting Toby. By now I was thinking, even in dreams, of Toby as the father of the baby. The truth of the matter swept in on me shatteringly now. This thin, intelligent face – that rather small mouth, those blue eyes, that nicely cleft chin and narrow, angular jaw – all these my baby might have. It was incredible. I couldn't relate the seed of that body to the body within me, any more easily than with any other man I knew, or didn't know. I felt no pull, no pang of affinity. I scarcely felt recognition. Only a remote mental astonishment.

'Hallo, Terry,' I said. The astonishment echoed in my voice.

'Hallo,' he muttered.

I became aware that the Teddies were murmuring and guffawing.

'What a place to meet!' I said. 'I ducked in here because I thought there was a stranger following me.' It shocked me anew to realize how right, in one sense, I'd been.

'I saw you asleep in that garden,' he said. 'I've been sitting there for an hour, looking at you.'

Our eyes met. 'Just please don't ask if it's yours,' I said.

His fair skin flushed darkly. 'I wasn't going to,' he muttered.

He reached out hesitantly and took my arm. 'Let's go somewhere civilized where we can talk,' he said indistinctly. Stares and whispers followed us as we went out. I wondered if something intuitive deep in those untouched shaggy brains told them, as intelligent observation could not have done, that we were not an ordinary married couple.

Out in the lamp-lit street we walked along aimlessly. Terry had dropped my arm uncertainly as soon as we were outside. I was aware as I hadn't been before of the weight of the child, and my own waddling, head-back gait. I tried to think of something to say, but the situation was so unexpected I couldn't.

'Let's get a taxi,' said Terry.

'That'd be lovely,' I said politely.

In the taxi I made myself relax. My legs and back ached painfully. I closed my eyes and enjoyed the padded movement and the pattern of passing lights on my eyelids.

'Are you all right?'

I reluctantly forced my mind to function. 'Yes, just tired.'

He was sitting in the far corner of the taxi, looking at me with the same helpless, expectant expression.

'Where are you living?' he asked.

'In a room in Fulham.'

'What's it like?'

'Quite all right.'

'What's the address?'

I told him. I felt as if I were floating on a tide of events it was pointless for me even to try to control or fight. My back was still aching; I shifted about trying to ease it.

Nothing more was said till we reached the house. Terry paid the taxi while I stood on the pavement. Then he turned, almost apprehensively, and looked up at the house.

'It looks pretty shabby,' he said.

I laughed. 'You should see it by daylight,' I said.

He hung back. 'Couldn't we go somewhere else?'

I understood his guilty reluctance to see the details of the situation he had placed me in. 'It's not all that bad,' I said, thinking with unexpected hardness, *Let him see it. Why should I let him off?* 'Come on.'

He followed me silently up the long flights of stairs. 'Isn't it very bad for you to climb all these stairs?' he asked. He seemed unable to help rubbing his own nose in it. My hardness disappeared. I felt sorry for him. After all, what a shock it must have been for him to see me sitting in that depressing, grimy little garden, my hair lank with heat, my smock unmistakably bulging, probably asleep with my mouth open ... He must have recognized me, started towards me perhaps, and suddenly – seen; stopped short; calculated with numb horror – and then, how much easier to run like hell than to stay! I stopped at the top of the fourth flight and tried to get my breath without panting.

'It's good exercise if you go slowly,' I said casually.

'God, not more!' he exclaimed anxiously as we started to climb again.

'Only one flight.'

The L-shaped room welcomed me as usual, its flashing whiteness leaping outwards from the lamp as I switched it on, its patches of bright colour pleasing my eyes. James's flowers were still not finished; they fanned gaily from one of the bakelite mugs, flinging exotic shadows. I moved a plastic bath-bowl filled with a jumble of baby-clothes and talc so that Terry could sit in the arm-chair.

He sat, as if dazed, but jumped up again guiltily as I began to light the fire. 'Here, I'll do that – ' I handed the matches to him silently, watching his hands tremble over the business of striking them. He took longer over it than necessary, putting off the inevitable moment when we would have to talk. I felt sorrier and sorrier for him. I wished now I could have spared him. After all, what possible good would it do?

'Would you like anything – coffee?'

'No, heavens, no, please!'

I sat on the bed resting my back. He sat again in the arm-chair. After a while he met my eyes.

I found it easy to smile at him. 'Don't look so anguished, darling – it's serious, but it's not a Greek tragedy.'

It seemed natural to call him darling. It was more a theatrical than an emotional term of endearment. But it seemed to stick a further barbed dart of guilt into him. His hang-dog expression was almost comic on his long, thin face. I hadn't realized how well it lent itself to lugubriousness.

'I can't seem to get it into my head,' he mumbled. 'I sat there in that garden, trying to get it into my head,' He licked his lips. 'Why didn't you get in touch with me?'

I forbore to mention that he hadn't left me his address. 'Because it seemed such a cheek – presenting you with a bill like that for something you hadn't even enjoyed.'

There was a silence and then he said with an effort, 'You didn't enjoy it either, so why should you pay the bill all by yourself?'

'There was no alternative for me.'

'Wasn't there?'

'No, there wasn't.' I winced from my own dishonesty, remembering the night I had panicked and made that unkept appointment with Dr Graham. But there was no need to mention that now, I felt.

'Did you never even think of telling me?'

'No.'

'You could have found me if you'd wanted to.'

So he remembered about the address. 'Yes, but I didn't want to, Terry.'

He stared at his knees. 'Was I so – did I behave so badly?'

'I understood how you felt.'

'It was just that it was all so – '

'I said I understood. I felt the same way.'

'Everything was spoiled. It was so much my fault that I couldn't face you, remembering how I'd felt before, and how I felt afterwards – '

'Terry, do shut up about it,' I said quite gently.

We sat silently. At last he roused himself.

'Jane, I can't tell you what I felt when I saw you asleep there, and realized . . . You looked so tired and alone. What you must have been through all these months – I don't want you to tell me about it, although I know I deserve to have to hear it all – I just can't bear to think of it.' I said nothing, and he said with difficulty, 'Did your father – '

'Terry, don't do this to yourself. What on earth good will it do? It hasn't been so bad. I haven't been alone all the time. I met a boy – in this house – in fact, I made quite a lot of new friends. It's been interesting and good for me in lots of ways.'

He was staring at me. 'God, how you've changed!'

'How?' I asked, interested.

'Don't you want to – to hurt me in some way – punish me for all you've gone through?'

'No. Well, only a little. If you'd come back a few months ago – but I feel different now. More peaceful about it.'

'Jane – ' he leaned forward. 'Tell me how you feel now. Bitter? As if you were caught in a trap?'

I shook my head. 'Not a bit like that any more.'

'How, then?'

'I'm quite excited about it. I can't wait to see what he'll be like.'

A look of gratitude and relief flattened out his face for a moment. His mouth relaxed open and he stared into my eyes.

'You mean it,' he said at last. 'Thank God, you really mean it.'

'Of course I mean it,' I said lightly.

Chapter 21

AFTER he'd gone, I sat quietly on the bed. I could hear John's record-player through the wall; he had on his favourite, the cracked old 78 version of *St Louis Woman*. I closed my eyes and let its harsh melancholy notes spin over me. After a while, I opened them again. The late evening light was gentle with the shabbiness of the room, giving it a look, almost of elegance – if you didn't look at the stove, whose bared tap-teeth snarled unconcealably. I looked round with pride and affection. The pain in my back had gone; the relief was wonderful.

The baby stirred. I had often thought I could detect his mood from the way he moved; now he seemed to me petulant, reproachful. I put my hand down and felt the blurred outline of his head.

'What's your trouble, my lad?' I asked aloud. 'Should I have taken the money he wanted to give us? Why not, you ask. A good question.'

Well, why not? He hadn't offered it out of a sense of duty. Or had he? I didn't much care. What mattered was that I hadn't wanted it, from him any more than from James. 'It would have given him some claim on you,' I said to the bump under my hand, 'and such claims can't be bought with money.' But I knew that wasn't the only reason. I looked at the stove, snarling like the part of me that had wanted Terry to see all this – the five long flights, the darkness, the smells, the landing taps; I had wanted to punish him. But that feeling had gone – so quickly. I drew back my lips and snapped my teeth happily at the stove. I felt pleased with myself. It would have been so easy to hate Terry, to take advantage of his vulnerable position; it would have been so easy to take the money, and to justify taking it. I wasn't pleased because I'd resisted the temptation to take it. I was pleased because I hadn't wanted it.

Now, if it had been Toby . . .

The happy feeling went. The light was fading and the Satchmo trumpet-notes seemed to stain the air like streams of ink. Desolation laid its hand on me. I wanted him with a pain like cold steel.

Terry's words came back. 'If there's *any*thing I can do . . .' It had been a plea. He needed to help, somehow. When you break something irreplaceable in someone else's house you want to pay something. The hostess is cruel if she doesn't let you. Well, paying was out of the question. But perhaps –

I rested for half an hour, stifling a growing feeling of impatience. It was good relaxing practice. Then I got up and went down to the phone.

He answered at once. His voice still sounded strained.

'Terry, it's Jane.'

'Jane!' His voice went light and high. He sounded very glad, not discomforted. 'You rang! I'm so pleased – did you change your mind about – '

'No, darling. But I thought of something you could do for me.'

'Of course! Oh, bless you for thinking of something – I'll do anything – '

'It won't be easy – you may not be able to do it at all.'

'I want to try,' he said eagerly.

I couldn't help being warmed. He had a kind of fundamental sweetness. I began to remember what I had loved about him.

'You remember I mentioned a man I'd met who lived in the house here?'

'No – I mean, you probably did, but – '

'Well, his name's Toby Coleman. Actually I think it may be Cohen.'

'Jewish?' Terry's tone chilled perceptibly. I'd forgotten this about him.

'Yes. He's left here and I've no idea where to start looking for him, but I want to find him. He's a writer. By this time he may well be trying to interest publishers in his first novel. Do you think you could ask round for me?'

There was a silence. I thought he might say, 'Hell, I'm not a detective,' or 'There must be about a hundred thousand writers trying to flog first books,' or even 'What do you want with some little Kyke?' I could sense all those thoughts going through his mind while the silence dragged on.

'All right,' he said at last. 'I'll do my best. Just a tick while I write the name down.'

A letter came from Billie Lee. '. . . Not at all what I'd expected, and *not* the sort of thing one can be certain of selling. But personally I like it so much that I am prepared to push it. It's written as if the author had never read a book in her life, but in some mysterious way it's none the worse for that . . . I'll let you know as soon as there's any news, but it may be months, so be patient. I believe it will be a winner.'

This seemed enough to start getting excited about and I rushed to phone Addy. I was childishly disappointed when I couldn't get a reply. I felt almost irritated with her for not being there to be told. I tried several more times that day to phone her, but she was never in. Eventually, feeling rather cheated, I wrote to her, enclosing

Miss Lee's letter. She was a terrible correspondent and I hadn't heard a word since our last phone call, but I was sure this would get a rise out of her. But days passed, and not even one of her scrawled postcards came.

A week went by, and another. I knitted. I walked, I typed terrible plays for television. I had a little money, my body was healthy and responsive, my baby seemed to think he was in a gymnasium. I stayed fairly quiet; my mind was alert, but peaceful. I knew only now how the bitterness against Terry had been undermining me. It must have been mainly subconscious, but it was as if an abscess had been lanced; the poison had drained out, the strange internal pressure relieved.

There were suddenly only seven weeks left, and I woke up to the fact that I had nowhere for the baby to live. It was Doris who brought it home to me. She came shuffling up one evening, breathing hard and crossly with a noise like snoring.

'Are you there, dear?'

I asked her in and offered her tea. She didn't answer. She was staring round the room, her mouth ajar.

'Gawd save us,' she breathed at last.

'I'd forgotten you hadn't seen it,' I said, waiting for an explosion of wrath.

She groped for a chair and sat down heavily, her eyes never ceasing to dart hither and yon, sharp with disbelief.

'Well!' she got out. 'Well, I never. I wouldn't have known it!'

I decided to brazen it out, though I didn't really hope this would prevent a frightful row. I was only thankful that my-sister-made-that-rug was still in the place of honour before the fire.

'It's nice, isn't it?'

I expected an outburst of protest as soon as Doris had mustered sufficient words of withering scorn. To my utter amazement a slow smile spread over her large (and, since her marriage to Charlie, placid) features. 'Takes a bit of gettin' used to – all that white – fair dazzled me eyes at first. But – well, I don't know. I just don't know.'

I hastily made the tea before this mood wore off.

Doris looked round again, and now her eyes narrowed. One could almost see the £ signs ring up in them like a cash-register.

'Nice-looking room, this,' she said speculatively. 'Best in the house, in some ways. Away from the traffic noises, nice and bright

– tasteful. That's what Mrs Williams always said. A nice, tasteful little room.' I could see that she was already getting used to the transformation. Quite soon, as far as she was concerned, the room would always have looked like this. 'You have to own it's good value for thirty bob,' she said, looking me straight in the eye.

I tried not to laugh. 'Oh, certainly,' I agreed solemnly, not seeing the trap I was heading for.

'Of course, I let Mrs W. have it for that; but then, she was living on her widow's pension.'

'I thought she had it for nothing.'

'At first, that was,' Doris said quickly. 'In the end, she insisted. Such a lovely, bright room, she said to me. I must pay something. So I let her have it for thirty bob. Just, like, a token rent.' I saw the trap yawning, and tried to dodge, but it was too late.

'I haven't even got a widow's pension,' I pointed out.

'Ah, but you're *young*, dear, now aren't you?' She smiled blandly. 'You can *work*. You *do*, of course, I've heard you typing away up here, ever so industrious. She's a worker, whatever else she's not, I've said to Charlie. Besides . . .' And now she allowed her eyes to drop. 'Quite soon there'll be two of you – won't there?' She smiled archly to show that her mind was broad. 'Make no mistake, dear, I'm not saying anything. You're welcome to stay, but really what I come up here to say was, well it doesn't make it easier to find tenants, having a baby in the house, crying and that. So, I was wondering . . .' She stopped to think. It was obvious the look of the room had made some quick reassessments necessary. 'I was wondering if you'd like the bigger room downstairs, the empty one on the first floor. Fewer stairs for you to climb,' she coaxed, 'it's only three-ten a week.'

'Thank you, but I'm fond of this room. I'll manage somehow.'

'Ah well, but that's the thing. I've had rooms empty so long, I'll have to raise the rent on this one – well, bring it back to what it was, like, before Mrs Williams. Two-ten I used to charge for it then, plenty of people glad to pay it for a nice cheerful little place like this.'

'I see,' I said. All desire to laugh had left me.

'Well, you think it over, dear,' she said comfortably, heaving herself out of her chair. 'Two-ten for this room, or three-ten for the nice big one on the first.' At the door, she stopped to say, 'I dare say you'll want to fix it up a little, according to your own taste. *I* don't mind, dear, not a bit. You just do what you like.' And when I've done what I like, I thought, I'll get kicked out of that one into another, in the hope that in due course I'll transform the whole bloody house.

When she'd gone I sat still. My heart was pounding and my hands were sticky. I looked round my room. I wondered why it hadn't struck me before that I would have to leave it. I'd grown to love it and depend on it so much that perhaps I'd worked on the basis that it would magically stretch to accommodate the baby. Now I saw that it was only a little room, really; it had just seemed adequate to all contingencies because of its importance to me.

I got up heavily and walked the few steps needed to traverse my kingdom. I touched the table whose scars had been decently hidden by a tablecloth ever since I arrived. I patted the walls in their proud new whiteness; I stood on my-sister-made-that-rug and stroked the friendly afghan. I thought that Doris would get a shock when she saw it without the trimmings which were mine – the flowers, the chair-cover, the curtains, the picture. Despite the walls and the wardrobe shelf, it would be a scant thirty bob's worth again. I would have thought this funny if it hadn't been for the sudden clarity with which I could picture the denuded room, as it would look when I left it.

I went to an estate agent and obtained a long, deceitful list of flats. I walked my feet off. I told my first real lies, the lies implied by the situation, the lies made necessary by the innocent recurring questions.

'What does your husband do, madam?'

'Where's your husband, dear? He shouldn't let you do all the walking, should he?'

'Oh, it won't be big enough for three, madam.'

I told them I was a widow. I got overwhelming sympathy which was worse than being despised. But I justified it to myself in a hundred ways until one day I went to look at a flat in a private house. It was far better than anything I had seen until then – it was lovely, in fact, but rather too expensive. The lady who owned the house was gracious and charming. She didn't ask questions, just took it for granted that I had a husband; she spoke about him without a suspicion in her mind. I told her what I'd told the others. She didn't doubt it for a second; but she became much more gentle and kind –

even offering me the place at a ludicrously reduced rent, offering to look after me and the baby. She was making all sorts of plans in her kindness and sympathy, while I just stood there, facing my lie in growing agony.

At last she noticed my unresponsive silence; she was too sensitive not to notice.

'My dear, I'm so sorry,' she said, 'I'm making you unhappy with my fussing. Frankly, I don't know how you can bear the situation at all; you're the bravest person I've ever met. You must come here, that's all I'll say now. You will come, won't you, and let us look after things, just at first?'

She looked at me with her calm honest eyes, seeking so sincerely to help me, and I think she guessed the truth before I told it, because her face changed a little just before I began to speak.

When I'd finished, she still looked at me, and not all the sympathy had gone. She thought for a little while, and then said: 'You're still welcome to come here.'

I wanted to cry, but she was so dignified and so ready with sympathy that I felt it would be like begging. I told her it would be impossible now. 'Perhaps if I'd told you the truth at first . . .'

'Yes,' she said sadly. She even understood that.

At the door she shook hands with me and wished me luck. 'May I give you a piece of advice?' she asked gently. 'I know how difficult it must be to tell people the truth. But do try. I'm sure it's better.'

I'd known all the time that it would be. But one always has to try the easy way, to prove that in the long run it's harder than the other.

I came home that day rather more tired than usual. It was two weeks since Billie Lee's letter came – a month since I'd met Terry. I had been expecting to hear from Addy or Terry from day to day, but there'd been no word. I had been counting on finding a letter from Addy today. I was so sure there would be one that I'd let myself look forward to it. I hurried eagerly to the hall table before I had even closed the front door. There was nothing for me. I felt preposterously disappointed and hurt, as if Addy had let me down on purpose.

The toil up the stairs was really a burden now, especially at the end of the day. I sat down several times and had trouble getting started again. I had a silly weak feeling that there was no point in going any further. Suddenly I was unbearably depressed. How *could* Addy not write? Now I stopped to think about it, why hadn't she written ages ago, or come up to see me? Perhaps she'd been up, but hadn't come by. Nobody ever came. You couldn't blame them, but the fact remained – I hadn't a single friend in the world, not one.

I was sitting in despair half-way between the fourth and fifth landings when John started down the stairs and nearly fell over me.

'Hullo, Janie,' he said. 'What you doin' sittin' there?'

'Just sitting here,' I said in a muffled voice.

He bent closer. 'You been cryin'?'

'Yes.'

'What for?'

'I don't know,' I said drearily.

He sat down on the narrow stairs beside me. 'You feelin' lonesome?'

'Yes,' I gulped.

He put his big arm round me. 'Why you don't come in to me when you feelin' on your own? I play you my records, you see, cheer you up.'

'I thought you didn't like me any more,' I said childishly.

'Who say I don' like you?'

'You never come to see me – nobody ever comes – ' I caught my breath in huge self-pity and began to weep afresh.

He squeezed me in a brotherly way. 'You silly. Someone come today.'

I stopped crying and blinked. 'What? Who? When?'

He grinned at me. 'You have a guess who.'

I stared at him, Toby's name forming in my mouth. But any mention of Toby always seemed to upset him, so I said instead, 'A man or a woman?'

'A man.'

Could it be? 'Toby?' I asked tremulously.

'No,' he said, his face going sad. 'Toby don't come back to us no more.'

'Then who?'

'Your father.'

It was the utter unexpectedness of it that knocked me endways. I couldn't speak. I sat staring at John blankly, trying to take it in.

'My *father*?' I echoed at last, unbelievingly. 'He came *here*?'

'He come up the stairs, knock on your door. I come out of my room. Boy, was he surprise to see me! If he sees a elephant behind him, he couldn't be more surprise!' John evidently was not offended. He choked with laughter at the memory.

'What did he want? What did he say?'

'He say he want to see you. Say he's your father.' He stopped.

'Well? What else?'

'Nothin' else. I tell him you out, be in later. He go off again.'

'Didn't he say anything? That he'd be back?'

'Didn' say nothin' else, just went.'

'How did he – did he look – ' I realized the futility of asking John that sort of question. I got to my feet, with him helping me solicitously. I still couldn't quite get used to the idea.

'I wonder if I should phone him.'

'Why not?'

Why not indeed? But I didn't. I sat around all evening waiting for him to come back, or telephone me, or something. Nothing happened. I couldn't really believe it, without the evidence of my own eyes. Suppose John had made a mistake somehow, or invented it out of a wish to cheer me up – if I phoned, what a fool I should look! Father would think I was crazy. On the other hand, if it were true – if he really had made the first move . . .

I slept at last, but uneasily, waking up every now and then, half-thinking I'd dreamed what John had said. In the morning I thought of something.

I knocked on John's door. He appeared, baggy-eyed and in his underwear, still half-asleep.

'The man who came yesterday – what did he look like?'

'You don' know what your own father look like?'

'I'm not sure it really was my father.'

'I don't remember much – he was just a ordinary-type man.' He rubbed his hand hard over his thick frizzy hair. 'Nothin' special about him. Oh – 'ceptin' his ears. Real big stickin'-out ears he had. It was that made me reminded of a elephant.'

Chapter 22

It was time to go home.

Suddenly I was in a hurry – an almost unendurable hurry to get there. But I made myself walk. Buses kept passing that would take me to the door, but I let them go. I must go slowly. I had to think, and be ready. I'd already made enough mistakes to be getting on with.

In my pocket was the note Father had written me soon after I had gone to live in the L-shaped room. It still carried the myriad creases I'd inflicted on it in my self-pitying hurt because Father hadn't crawled all the way to Fulham on his stomach to fetch me home. When I reached the Bridge – the boundary of home territory – I stopped near the middle and read the note again.

Dear Jane,

As you can imagine I find this letter hard to write. We haven't been very close these last years, which may have been my fault, I suppose, though I don't see where I went wrong . . .

I looked out across the river. It was such a familiar view, the green towpath on one side, the old houses and angular blatant factories on the other. Above my head, gulls wheeled about the grey graceful spires. A bus rumbled across behind me, making the Bridge jog gently. I closed my eyes, and the sounds and smells – the rank mud, the yeast from the brewery – were more familiar still, carrying me back into my childhood. It took no effort of memory to shrink till my head was below the level of the rail, my hand firmly embedded in Father's. He was telling me a story – my favourite story, the one about the brass plate.

In his slow, serious voice he would read out, from the unpolished plate screwed to the wooden rail, the brief memorial to the brave South African lieutenant who had dived 'from this spot' into the Thames to save a woman's life. 'From this very spot?' I would always ask, awed by the pinpointed locale of tragedy. 'Yes,' Father answered gravely. 'Here he stood, and saw the woman float out from under the Bridge, shouting for help, and without even stopping to take off his coat he dived straight in.' For years I thought Father had been there at the time, so convincingly did he invent details in response to my importuning. 'He couldn't swim very well himself, but he managed to get the woman to the bank, and then he died.'

'But *why*? *Why* did he die?' I remembered feeling almost frantic with anger that God should have let him die and spoil the story.

Father never hid the facts of life or death from me. 'Perhaps he'd swallowed a lot of water, or perhaps he had a weak heart. Anyway, I don't suppose he minded dying,' he would add to comfort me. 'After all, not many people get a chance to save a life and be remembered for ever.'

My eyes were still closed and I found my hand clenching hard on itself, as it used to grip Father's, happy because it was the mythical lieutenant who had died and not anyone I really loved. The pattern of feeling came back to me so clearly, it was impossible not to remember at the same time how much I'd loved Father in those days – completely and trustingly and without complications.

I tried to remember when I first began to feel he was failing me – or I him, because now I was no longer sure which was at the bottom of my resentment. It must have been when I left school without matriculating. I wanted to be an actress, and anyway I was bad at almost everything at school and so hated it. Several of my friends wanted to leave early too, and aggrievedly compared notes about their parents' reactions – which were all along the lines of how much we would regret not getting a proper education. I boasted that my father was different; he would understand that I was an artist and that to stay on at school would be a fruitless waste of time. But when I confidently put this theory to the test, I got a terrible disappointment. Father refused to understand. His reaction was the same as all the other parents'. I was ashamed and angry, and from then on nothing went right. Everything I wanted to do, he seemed to disapprove of. Every time he proved to have been right, I resented him more. Any time he proved wrong, I scored a point for myself.

So whose fault was it? Who started the race, who kept it going? I glanced at the note again.

'I've always done my best . . .' That had sounded so self-pitying when I had first read it. Now it seemed no more than the simple truth. 'I think any parent would have felt as I did, being told a thing like that without any preparation. You almost seemed to enjoy telling me . . .'

I had enjoyed it. It had been another point scored, the decisive victory. It had proved hollow immediately, but at the moment of telling, I'd relished it. It had been war between us for so long. Or perhaps I'd been fighting alone . . .

Was it possible that I had formed a disillusioned mental picture of Father and fed it with misinterpretations of everything he did and said from that time on? Once I'd got it into my head that I was a disappointment to him, that he disliked, patronized, begrudged me . . . might not everything that happened tend to feed that belief? Had I, perhaps, *wanted* to feel ill-used, misunderstood? I read the last part of the letter.

'I am still your Father and I don't enjoy thinking about you alone somewhere. Your home is here and if you want to come back to it, you should feel free to. It's not right for you to be among strangers. You are still my responsibility . . .'

It was difficult to understand why I'd been unable to see anything in this but frozen patronage and a loveless charity. Now I could see nothing but an undemonstrative man struggling to pull his world together, with pride and prejudice on one side and love on the other. Before, I'd always imagined he saw me as the murderer of my mother. Now I realized that never, in reality, had he indicated that he felt this. Wasn't it more likely that he regarded me as something saved from a disaster, all the more to be cherished and perfected because I was all he had left?

I left the plate and walked on across the Bridge. I was getting tired now; I knew I should get on a bus, but it wasn't far to go. I walked on, past the shops, past houses and pubs, past a montage of faces and gardens and windows and dogs, most of which I recognized remotely, like recollected bits of dreams. At last I came to the house, the house I'd been born in, as solid and brown and honest as ever, with its windows and front door so symmetrical and square-set, still making a face – a shocked, comically reproachful face – which I made back at it from force of old habit. '*Don't you say "Oh!" to me!*'

The front garden was, as always, tidy and well-dug; the drive was clear of bus-tickets and weeds. Only in the windows were there signs of neglect. The white net curtains were yellow, their ruffles limp. They gave the eyes of the house a tired, morning-after look.

My mind winced from the prospect of this difficult meeting; but as soon as I came through the gate I couldn't have turned back. It was like being passed from hand to clutching hand between two lines of people. As I climbed the steps heavily I found the right key ready in my hand.

But I didn't have to use it. The door was opened from inside and my father stood in front of me. He seemed very tall because he was two steps up from me, and his face, in the shadow of the doorway, looked only half familiar and much, much older than I remembered. He was not dressed for the office and for the first time it struck me that I shouldn't have expected to find him at home on a Thursday morning.

'Jane,' he said without surprise.

'Hallo, Father, aren't you at the office?' I could hardly speak, I found. The fatuous words barely seemed audible over the beating of my heart.

'I stayed at home, hoping you'd come,' he explained simply.

He stepped back and I came into the hall. It was dim in there after the hard bright sunlight; dust-motes moved lazily in the ray from the fan-light. Everything had that only half-recognizable look. Nothing was actually changed, but there were no flowers; the mirrors had films over them, the carpet looked grubby and faded.

'Place needs doing,' said my father vaguely, seeing me glance round. 'Come into the garden, I haven't let that go.'

He had always been a good gardener, loving the dullest chores and often, I remembered, boring me over meals with details of manures and blackfly and suckers on the lilac. Now, after so long without a garden, I felt a rush of nostalgia as Father led the way down the steps at the back and I saw the clusters of narcissi and tulips growing straight out of the grass under the blossoming pear, and the clumps of new green on the cut-back perennials, standing out sturdily against the well-turned earth. As we walked along the path I picked a sprig of baby mint and rubbed it in my fingers to breathe the soft spicy smell of coming Summer. As I straightened again, with difficulty, I saw Father look quickly away.

'I thought that late frost would be the finish of the bulbs,' he said, 'but it just kept them back a bit. Look at those tulips. Not a curled leaf among the lot. Same with the hyacinths.'

'They're lovely.' I bent again to smell the bushy spikes, but Father stopped me by stooping quickly and snapping one off to give me.

'Oh, don't pick it! It seems so sad – '

'We'll put it in a glass of water. House needs some flowers.'

We wandered round and he told me what he'd been planting and transplanting. Before long he said, 'Let's sit down, you look tired.' There were two canvas chairs arranged under the trees. 'It's not too cold for you?'

'No, it's fine.'

We sat down. I couldn't get over him not being at the office. It seemed unnatural, somehow.

'It's good to see you,' he said.

'You, too.' We smiled at each other. 'Why did you come yesterday?'

'Never mind that just for the present. Are you well? You look very well, I must say. Nice little frocks they make now.' He reached out to touch the material of my smock and I noticed his hand shook. He saw me looking at it and met my eyes with a wry smile.

'Getting to be an old man.'

I watched him covertly while we made fumbling conversation. The drinking had left its mark on him. Not just the shaking hands but in his eyes and under them and in the colour of his skin. I wondered whether to broach the subject but it seemed an impertinence. Evidently he felt the same about the change in my appearance, and the cause of it. The baby was not mentioned.

'Would you like some lunch?' he asked at last. 'It's well after two. You must be hungry.'

'No, not terribly. What about you?'

'I could do with a bite of something. You stay out here in the fresh air and I'll bring you a snack.'

'No, let me come and help.'

We went back into the house. Our mutual courtesy and restraint seemed quite natural inasmuch that we were strangers to each other. But there were so many important things to be talked about that I felt we couldn't go on like this. Only I didn't know how to begin.

'Funny sort of house you're living in,' he said suddenly while I was laying a tray.

'But you didn't see my room. That's quite different from the rest.'

'Don't like to think of you being in a house like that. That coloured fellow – '

'He's been very kind to me.'

'Say coloureds don't smell different from us. That one did. Smelt like a polecat.'

'Oh, come now, Father,' I said, not able to help laughing. 'Polecats smell vile. John doesn't smell at all like one.'

'Awful old witch of a landlady, too. Surprised you haven't had trouble with her.'

'I have, now and then.'

'Thought as much.' He was bent over the stove, painstakingly stirring bits of parsley into a warming saucepan of tinned soup. 'You say your room's all right – can't be very big, though. Not big enough for more than one person.' It was his first even indirect reference to the baby.

'No.'

He straightened up and looked at me with his tired eyes, yellow like the curtains in the front windows, the soup-spoon still in his hand. 'Better come home, hadn't you?' he asked. The words hung sparkling in the air.

'You wouldn't mind?'

'I want you to.'

'You don't owe me anything, Father. On the contrary – '

'Who said anything about owing?'

'Then why?'

'The question is, why I ever wanted you to leave. It's a question I find it more and more difficult to answer.' I watched the stooping figure bend over the stove again. He was, I noticed now, thinner than before.

'Have you been eating properly?' I asked, sharply, as if he were my child instead of the other way round.

'Oh yes . . .' he said in the vague way that was quite new with him. I felt that if I asked him when his last meal had been, he wouldn't be able to remember.

'You don't look awfully well,' I ventured.

'I've been drinking too much,' he said with an indifference that shocked me more than the words. 'It doesn't do one any good.'

'Then why do it?'

'Because one keeps hoping it *will* do one good, I suppose,' he said with a shrug. 'This is ready now.' He poured the soup carefully into a tureen.

'It smells good,' I said automatically.

We carried the food out into the garden. Outdoors my father straightened his body and his manner and speech became more positive and vigorous.

'The house gets you down a bit, doesn't it?' I suggested, shooting in the dark.

'I can't seem to get around to cleaning it,' he said apologetically. 'It does depress me. Specially at night.'

'I'll serve,' I said, reaching for the soup ladle.

'No, please. Let me. You sit still and rest.'

I watched him ladling out the soup into the first soup plate without noticing that it was dusty from months of sitting unused on a shelf, and it came to me very clearly that there was nothing wrong with my father except being alone. He had been alone, I realized, not just since I left, but for as long as I'd known him, as I would be, even after my baby was born. Everyone who is without a mate is basically alone. It's a special and very destructive form of loneliness.

'Perhaps you don't want to come back,' he suggested calmly as he passed me my soup. 'If so, I shall quite understand. Independence is a very important thing.'

We drank our soup. Father held his plate high so that the shaky journey of the spoon between it and his lips would be as short as possible. His eyes travelled round the garden as someone might cling to a good-luck charm during a moment of crisis.

'I had thought of moving into a larger room,' I said, keeping my voice steady and matter-of-fact. 'Of course, there are difficulties.'

Father rested his plate on his knee and stared at the tulips. 'Financial?'

'Not at the moment, though I suppose before long – '

'No need for those.'

'I couldn't, Father.'

'Couldn't what?'

'Take money from – '

'Me? No. I see that. I've been a little grudging in the past, I know. Spoiled my chances of helping that way for the moment. No, it would be from – another source.'

'What do you mean?'

My father put his soup plate back on the tray slowly.

'You haven't finished your soup,' I said.

'I'm not hungry.'

'You ought to eat it, you're looking thin.'

He suddenly turned and looked at me. His hand came and covered mine, pressing hard so that I shouldn't feel the trembling, but I could feel it. He smiled at me, but his eyes were full of tears.

'I've got something bad to tell you.'

My mind jerked back and I heard myself saying, 'No.' Father kept his hand on mine and kept looking steadily at me, and after a moment I said, 'Go on.'

'Your Aunt Addy's dead.'

There was only a short moment of sparkling numbness inside my head before a wave of grief engulfed me. There was no intervening stretch of shock before I could feel anything; in some part of myself I must have been expecting it. I felt as though sorrow had fists and used them to beat my heart. I sobbed with pain at the pictures that came – Addy in her funny circus hat, Addy pouring petrol on to the soggy bonfire, Addy holding her manuscript as tenderly as a child. I remembered the last phone call, how she had refused to let me come . . .

Father was standing beside my chair, holding me tightly. I pulled back from him and said, 'Was she all alone?'

'No, she was in the local hospital.'

'But no – friends, none of us?'

'Nobody knew. She didn't let anyone know.'

'The hospital – they should have told us!'

'She wouldn't give them any names. She must have *wanted* to be alone, Janie.'

I didn't say what we both knew. Nobody *wants* to be alone when they're dying, or when anything important is happening to them.

'She's left you everything – the cottage and all her books, and the rights to some manuscript or other.'

I sat dumbly. I had no more tears for the moment. Father sat down again, drawing his chair closer to mine, still holding my hand.

'So you're a bit more independent now. You could sell the cottage, or if you'd rather, you could keep it and live there, after the baby's born.' He said this without effort. It was easy and natural to talk about the baby now. 'Only I don't like to think of you being so far away – it's a desolate spot. I'd rather you were near me at first. If you could stand it.' He took back the handkerchief he had lent me and wiped his own eyes. 'I'm being entirely selfish about this.'

'If I come home, it'll be purely selfish on my side, too.'

Our hands tightened. The two lies cancelled each other out.

Chapter 23

I TOOK a taxi back to the house in Fulham. Father had insisted I should take taxis from now on.

He had wanted to come back with me immediately and help me move, but I told him I wanted to do it myself, in my own time. It would be difficult for any man, and more especially a man like Father, to understand my irrational feeling for places. It wouldn't be possible to say good-bye properly to the L-shaped room if he were there.

I let the taxi go, and stood looking up at the house in the twilight. The heatwave had passed; the sky was cloudy and the air was heavy with coming rain. The house looked just as I had first seen it, that wet afternoon in October, except that now it didn't seem ugly.

I saw a curtain stir on the ground floor, and Doris beckoned. I went up the shabby steps past the overflowing dustbins. Charlie had been doing something to the hedge; it was not exactly trimmed, but its disorder was now angular instead of bunchy. Looking down into the area as I felt for my keys, I noticed that he'd been putting a touch of paint on the basement window-frames, too. I smiled as I remembered the late Fred's happy relations with the other Jane, and wondered if history would repeat itself.

Doris met me in the hall. 'How are you, dear? Have you made your mind up yet?' I hadn't had the heart to tell Doris before that I was leaving.

'I'm going home, Doris,' I said. 'My father's asked me.' They were wonderful words. I listened to their echoes with warm pleasure.

But they gave no pleasure to Doris.

She drew her mouth in at the corners and folded her arms. 'Oh. Well, that's nice, I'm sure,' she said sourly. 'When are you going, then?'

'Right away.' Then, as she opened her mouth to protest, 'Of course I'll give you a fortnight's rent in lieu of notice.'

Her mouth softened a little. 'I suppose it's quite right, your father takin' you in,' she said, her hand twitching as I opened my wallet. 'Often wondered whether you had no people or what. Just as well in a way, what with the noise and nappies and everything,' she added in one of her classic non sequiturs. 'Funny, someone come after a room today – couldn't afford the first-floor. Young lad he was, bit of a Ted, Charlie thought, but I don't know . . . Ta, dear.' With the money in her hand she became all affability once more. 'Anything we can do to help? Bags down the stairs or that? Charlie'll come up in a few minutes and see how you're gettin' on. Tata for now, dear.'

Just as I was starting slowly up the long flights, she called after me, 'Oh, there – I almost forgot! There's someone waiting for you up there. Told him I didn't know when you'd be back, but he would wait – I let him have my key, dear, I didn't think you'd mind.'

It was Terry. He rose from the arm-chair as I came in, panting from the climb which seemed suddenly to have doubled in height.

'Hullo, Jane,' he said, keeping his eyes resolutely fixed on my face in a way which would have made me laugh if I'd had the breath to spare. He took a step forward awkwardly, not knowing what to do with his hands. Odd how Englishmen always want to shake hands. To me it would have seemed more natural to kiss him. I sat down on the bed, trying not to puff too obviously.

'Waiting long?' I asked.

'About an hour.' He stood in the middle of the room, his lean height looking stooped and crane-like under the sloping ceiling. 'I'm sorry I haven't kept you posted on the search for your friend. I wanted to wait until I had something definite.'

My breathing stopped for a moment and then went on raggedly. 'Have you something definite now?'

'Well, yes. I put everyone I knew on to it at once; there were a couple of publishing houses where I didn't know anybody, but I passed the word round through friends. Surprising what a little world within a world publishing is – its own grapevine and everything. Cigarette? Oh no, you don't, of course.' He lit his own. 'Well, I phoned most of them every day, but nothing happened for a month. Then a chum of mine in Hutchinson's got on to me – day before yesterday, this was. Said a script had come in of a first novel by someone called Cohen. First name Tobias. Sounded right. I had a bit of trouble getting his address out of my friend – ethics or something – anyhow, I persuaded him I wasn't going to steal a potential source of revenue. Which it seems your young author may be, by the way – the first novel appears to have something, even if it is mostly in longhand.'

My backache was nagging. My hand moved of its own accord to rub and ease.

Terry was pacing. Now he stopped and looked at me. 'Listen, Jane, before I go any further, just how important is this chap to you? I know I've no business to ask, but apart from the tentative promise of the manuscript, he didn't strike me as a particularly – well, what I mean is, there's not much security for you there. Sorry if I'm talking out of turn.'

'Go on with the story.'

'He's living in Holland Park – a little cellar, you couldn't call it a flat. First sight of him gave me a jolt – looked like a scarecrow, hair wild, unshaven. Room's like a monk's cell. Bed, chair, table, suitcase. Stacks of paper. Nothing else ... I shouldn't think he's been out of it for weeks from the look of him.' He stopped.

'Did you tell him you'd come from me?'

'I asked him if he knew you – to make sure it was the right person. He said yes. Pretty guarded about you; I couldn't get him to say much. Asked how you were. When I said you were back here again he seemed very surprised – well, upset, almost. He said he thought you were with an aunt in the country.'

For a second the mention of the aunt brought Addy into the room; sitting beside me, saying, 'Would you like to come and stay with me for a while?' ... My glance went automatically to the place she had sat as she said that. My eyes were stopped by the hunched bulk of Toby's typewriter, covered by its black hood.

Terry went on: 'I said you were looking for him – wanted to see him. He didn't say much – just stood still and stared at me through all that hair like something peering out of a jungle. By God,' he said, unable, I saw, to help himself, 'he is a Jew, and no mistake – that beak! Wonder why he changed his name – and then changed it back again?'

I thought, *He changed it because of people who feel like you, and he changed it back because* – but there was no sure answer to that yet. Until I saw him, it was nothing but a hopeful symptom.

'So – is he coming?'

'Couldn't tell you. It's up to him, isn't it? He knows where you are – he knows you want to see him . . .' He spoke almost sulkily.

We sat in silence for a while. My backache was worse. I kept curving and straightening my spine to ease it.

'Well, thanks,' I said at last, lamely.

Terry took this as a dismissal. He got to his feet with an air of relief and yet reluctance, as if he hadn't completed his business and didn't look forward to doing so. 'Is there anything else I can do?'

'No, bless you, I'm very grateful to you.' I realized this was a little ironic, and glanced at him to see if he'd noticed. He was looking at me oddly, a frown between his eyes. 'What are you thinking?' I asked curiously.

'I was wondering what that Cohen bloke would have done if I'd suddenly said, "I'm the father of Jane's baby." '

I said nothing. It was an intriguing thought.

'I've been thinking a lot about you, and everything,' he went on, stumblingly, as if driving himself. 'God knows I haven't enjoyed thinking about it, but I felt I had to. Even though it couldn't do any good. Perhaps *because* it was unnecessary – I felt I ought to share a bit of what you've been through.'

He had such an unconscious air of self-conscious virtue that I almost laughed, but one couldn't very well laugh in the face of such solemn earnestness.

'I've always thought it pretty lousy, the way a lot of men divide women into two groups – you know, the good and the bad, the wills and the won'ts, marriage or the mantelpiece. I've argued against it a hundred times with chaps I know who despise the girls they've been to bed with. But you can't imagine how frightful it is to come up against the unexpected realization that underneath, one's exactly the bloody same oneself.' He glanced at me from under his eyebrows and looked quickly back at his hands. 'After that night in Collioure I despised you. There was no earthly reason for it – I mean if one looked at the thing rationally – except that I knew I hadn't been any good for you and I felt rotten so I told myself that it was you who hadn't been any good. And during the week after you left, that idea somehow got changed a bit until you were just no good, full stop. You were *that* sort of girl. I kind of dismissed you in my mind because I didn't want you any more. I simply never thought about the possibility of *this* happening. Funny how one thinks of sex as if it were just a thing by itself, without any build-up or results . . .'

There was a long embarrassed silence. I took up in my thoughts from where he left off. You don't think, at least not when you're pursuing love greedily and selfishly, that your goal may be the start of something. The night which started this was suddenly vivid in my mind again as the beginning of what would be a man or a woman, who would some day beget more children, who would never have existed except for one moment when Terry decided that he couldn't hold on for another second and that it would be safe enough – not really either knowing or caring. I wondered, and I think he did too, now, whether either of *us* had descended from some moment like that – self-indulgent, shallow and meaningless . . .

Terry suddenly said, 'I suppose there's not a chance you'd marry me?'

It came out in a mumbled, apologetic rush. I caught a glimpse of his eyes before he turned them away; I almost said yes to see the desperate appeal for a refusal in them turn to panic. But he hadn't really deserved that, so I shook my head.

'Can't really wonder,' he said, concealing his relief admirably. He rubbed a hand hard all over his face, as if the skin literally itched with embarrassment, ending by pulling at his nose. It was a gesture of his that fitted into a years-old memory groove. I wondered if that sort of personal idiosyncrasy could be inherited. It would bring a special pain, in the future, if your child suddenly rubbed his face like that, and pulled his nose; to have nobody to rush to and say, 'He did that thing of yours, you know, that you do when you're embarrassed . . .'

'What's the matter?'

'My back hurts.'

'I'll rub it – '.

'No!' That was what husbands did. There must be none of that.

'Well – ' he stood awkwardly. 'I don't like to leave you.'

I told him about Father, and he immediately became gay with relief. 'I'll help you pack!'

I meant to say no, but I was lying down now, my hands under me holding the ache, and I wasn't at all sure how I was ever going to get up again, so I said, 'Thanks, darling.'

Half an hour later, when the rug was rolled, the curtains down and folded, the breakables wrapped in newspaper, and my suitcase lying open on the pock-marked floor, somebody came up the stairs and knocked on the door.

'That'll be Charlie,' I said, 'come to help down with the cases.' Terry said, 'I'll let him in,' and disappeared round the angle. I heard the door open and a long, unaccountable silence. Then Terry's voice said shortly, 'Wait there, will you?' He came round the angle; his face was set. 'It's Cohen.'

I closed my eyes for a moment and pretended it was only Charlie. I was too tired; I couldn't cope with all I should be feeling. Then I put my feet on the floor. My back gave a mighty stab that made me grimace with surprise, because the pain had stopped ten minutes before.

'Do you want me to go?' Terry asked.

'Yes – no, wait. I don't know.' I tried to pull myself together but everything kept sparkling in front of my eyes. My hands were shaking.

'You're white as a sheet.'

'Toby!' I called unsteadily. 'Come in, will you?'

He came in hesitantly. Despite Terry's description I was expecting him to look as I'd last seen him, but he was quite changed and it gave me a shock. To begin with he had a beard. It made him look ten years older, and completely did away with his vulnerable, baby-blackbird look. The reddish shadows on his face were more marked than ever; his hair was too long, and his jacket – the same green corduroy one – was now worn almost transparent. He had on a clean shirt and tie, but even across the room I could see the frayed cuffs and collar.

We looked at each other. I don't know how it would have been if Terry had not been watching. As it was, there seemed nothing we could safely say.

'How are you?' Toby asked at last. He didn't so much as glance at Terry, but kept his eyes gravely fixed on me.

'Fine,' I said inanely.

'You don't look it. You look frightful.'

'Really, I'm all right.'

'You wanted to see me.'

'Yes.'

Again there was silence. This time Toby did look over at

Terry – a sharp, dismissive glance. When Terry didn't move, he said: 'It'd be easier to talk if we were alone.'

Terry said, 'Is that what you want, Jane?' Before I could say anything, he went on, 'Because I can't say I like leaving you alone with–'

Toby said to me, 'Is this a friend of yours?'

'Yes, I am,' Terry said. He sounded suddenly aggressive, and when Toby turned to him his expression answered the note in Terry's voice.

'If you are,' Toby said slowly, 'you'll clear out for a while and let me talk to her. You came to fetch me, after all; you can't be very surprised to see me.'

'I'm just surprised by Jane's desire to locate you,' said Terry.

'Oh? Why?'

'If I'd lost you, I'd let you stay lost.'

I was dazed by the abruptness of the antipathy between them. They stood glaring at each other across the narrow room, their eyes full of cold, masculine fury. An unreasonable panic took hold of me – the panic one feels when two dogs stand facing each other, their hackles up, growling low in their chests. The pointless, primitive fighting instinct of the male . . . I watched Toby's knuckles whiten and sensed my own helplessness.

'Don't,' I said. Intended as a command, it came out weakly as a plea.

But to my surprise, Toby paid attention. I saw him forcing himself to relax. He was turning away towards me when Terry suddenly said, 'I know what you're thinking, and you're right. I did it to her. So what do you say to that, Jew-boy?'

I saw Toby's face sag in astonishment and then tauten in blind anger. He turned back to Terry and swung his fist at him in the same movement. Terry didn't even put his arm up to defend himself, though Toby didn't take very careful aim and he must have seen it coming. The blow landed badly, on Terry's cheek, and he lurched sideways, then straightened up again.

I said something sharp and meaningless which neither of them noticed. Toby hit Terry again, this time more carefully, and still Terry didn't resist. He went backwards and fell over the suitcase, and I felt a hysterical desire to laugh because it looked so unreal – a comic stage-fight in which every move is planned. Toby stood waiting while Terry got up. This time as he moved forward he did bring up his fists in a defensive attitude, but half-heartedly, without intention. Toby kicked the suitcase aside and it skidded against the wall. This time he struck out with his left fist, and I stopped wanting to laugh, because this blow landed squarely and made a shocking sound – I heard Terry's teeth grind together with a horrible squeak as his head went back and he staggered and fell hard against the stove. I could almost feel the sharpness of the gas-taps in a stabbing pain in my own back. One of them must have caught in his jacket because there was a tearing noise as he slumped on to the floor.

There was a moment's dead silence, making me realize for the first time what a series of loud sounds the fight had made. Then I heard footsteps pounding up from below, and Doris's shrill, querulous voice.

Toby stood looking down at Terry. He was breathing hard and his face was white under the shadows.

'Why didn't he fight back?' he said numbly. 'He asked for it. Why didn't he fight back?'

We crouched beside Terry. Doris and Charlie were banging on the door. Just as we rolled him over they burst in.

'Nah then, nah then, what's going on 'ere?' said Charlie, looking and sounding like a ponderous policeman in civvies. Doris was more practical. 'Help us get him on the bed,' she said briskly, pushing past me to pick up Terry's feet. 'I should've thought any fool could see what's been goin' on, even you.'

Terry was groaning and his face was starting to swell. I stood looking down at him, trying to analyse the searing confusion of feelings within me. The pain in my back returned deafeningly. I closed my eyes but that shut me into a dark roaring world of pain.

I groped through the shouting blackness for Toby's hand, as I had once before, but there was no answer. I opened my eyes. A number of people I knew were standing round the bed. It took me a moment to recognize them. As well as Charlie and Doris, Mavis was there, and John; Toby stood to one side rubbing his knuckles dazedly. I wondered why they all seemed so far away – tiny, insect figures, distant in importance. The important thing was the pain. It was gone for a moment, but it would be back. I knew because it had all happened before.

I tried to call out, but the microscopic little people couldn't hear me across the vistas that separated us. For a second I knew what it might feel like to be alone in the world.

Then the pain came back. When it had gone the crowd round the bed was vast and close. There seemed to be hundreds of huge figures moving cumbersomely in slow motion. This time if I spoke they couldn't help hearing, but now my teeth seemed locked together and I couldn't utter a sound. I was afraid of the next pain, and I was afraid of this sense of being alone. The nearness of this crowd of lumbering, mumbling giants, did nothing to help it. They were all strangers, unaware of me, and obviously uncaring – for it now seemed to me that all the people in the world were packed into the L-shaped room, and that every one had his back turned towards me.

Chapter 24

I WITHDREW into a private world. Sometimes it was dark and quiet. Sometimes it whitened like hot steel and there was a thin, high sound above the whitening. My own body was the steel, thrust into a furnace. The whiteness would dim to red, and to black again, and the thin sound would stop, and for a while there would be silence and peace.

There was movement and hands lifting and pressing the molten steel; it seemed that every touch sank into my flesh and would leave deep holes when it cooled. Sometimes there were voices, but they were just alien sounds. Once there was a long period of jolting and roaring, a sense of motion. I thought that the piece of flaming metal that was my body was being carried along on a conveyor belt towards machinery that would beat and cast it into some strange new shape.

I opened my eyes to see lights passing overhead one by one. Then they stopped and a face blocked one of them out as it hung over me. It was the face of a man with a beard and he said, 'I've rung up your father; he's coming.' I wanted to tell him I had no father, but then I wasn't sure whether it was a father I lacked, or somebody more important. I didn't know clearly who the man with the beard was, but I smiled to him, and then the lights started moving again and I closed my eyes.

The next time I opened them there was another face overhead. This one, strangely, I recognized at once. It belonged to Dr Maxwell.

'Well, well, this is too bad,' he said crossly, as if I'd got him out of bed. 'What have you been up to this time?' I felt terribly ashamed and my eyes filled with tears because he was angry with me. I didn't stop to ask myself why. Then suddenly he did something that hurt and my shame turned like lightning into fury. 'What the hell are you doing?' I shouted wrathfully.

'Such language,' said a woman's voice above my head.

I strained my eyes upward to see who was there, but all I could see was a white blur.

'Addy swears,' I said by way of self-excuse.

'Then she's very naughty,' said the maddening, unseeable woman complacently.

'You don't know anything about it, you silly cow,' I said loudly, to shock her into silence.

'Keep quiet and bear down,' grunted Dr Maxwell.

'What?' I asked stupidly.

'Bear down. You know how to bear down, don't you?'

The significance of this came sharply into focus.

'Am I having a baby?'

'I hope it doesn't come as a complete surprise to you?'

I struggled to remember through thick layers of padding round my brain.

'But it's not due yet!'

'No, not for another month.'

'Then what are you doing, making it happen now?' My mind suddenly burst through into lucidity. I clearly remembered that eight-month babies often die.

'It's not my idea, I assure you. Now, kindly keep your mind on what you're doing. You've just missed a good one.'

To bear down in the middle of a pain was akin to biting hard on an abscessed tooth. I winced and wouldn't.

Dr Maxwell grew exasperated. 'Oh, come along,' he said at last. 'You're not being one bit of help. Remember your exercises.'

'Sod my exercises,' I said between my teeth.

'Such language!'

But when they offered me gas and air my language grew worse than ever.

'Then what *do* you want?'

'I want to hear it cry when it's born.'

'Well you won't until it is, and it never will be unless you push. Come on – *now*.'

I clenched my jaw and pushed. I felt the baby move inside me. He was kicking, fighting to get out. He wasn't dead then. I pushed again.

'No, stupid, not in between. Wait for it.' But Dr Maxwell sounded less annoyed with me, and the nurse wiped my face from behind.

'Is he the right way up?' I asked.

'Yes – head down like a diver. Next one – '

I pushed. It really did hurt.

'Sure you don't want a whiff of this?'

I wasn't at all sure, but I was too occupied to answer. The contractions were coming quickly now, and I knew it couldn't be too much longer. Silly to give in right at the end.

As a matter of fact, it wasn't nearly the end, but as long as I believed that every pain was bound to be the last, I could always put up with just one more. And certain background aspects of it I liked. I liked the way everything else, receded into the distance. When I'd made love to Toby, nothing else had mattered – nothing else had seemed to exist. Tomorrow's problems, other relationships, discomfort, guilt, money worries – all were suspended. And that was how I felt having the baby. It called for the same complete concentration – dedication, almost. I felt as if I were projecting myself into a new dimension, and it was so important that everything else acquired a new and relatively tiny perspective.

After a while, though, I got so desperately tired that the sense of elation disappeared. I felt I *must* stop, I *must* have peace, and I got a panicky trapped feeling because I had to go on and on. I tried to think about Toby – Addy – my father. Nothing and no one helped. I had only myself. There was a strange, out-of-this-world moment when I understood with absolute clarity why I'd run away to the L-shaped room. I can't recapture it now, quite, but it was something to do with mirrors. It was as if I had hated my own face and wanted to escape from the mirrors which reflected it . . . only the mirrors turned into people, and it wasn't my face that was ugly, but me, as a person. Now that was changed somehow, and the L-shaped room had served its purpose – as a mirrorless house would no longer be needed by someone whose blemish had gone.

Then the moment of clarity clogged up with meaningless circles. The circle of the light overhead; Dr Maxwell's glasses; the white blurred circles of faces and bowls and wrist-watches. Even voices made circles of sound in my head.

'One more, now, you're doing fine . . .'

The push was a small red circle of pain with a big white circle trying to get through. But the thing was impossible – mathematically impossible.

'I can't do it – '

'Yes you can. You almost have.'

Another circle descended, dark and dome-like. 'Just take one little whiff . . .' said a wheedling female voice.

I was struggling now, with a full and ecstatic awareness. This was the moment – now – now! I pushed the mask away with a fierce gesture. The stupid cow wanted me to have gone through all this and then be cheated at the last moment! I told her what to do with the mask.

'Such language!' were the first words my son heard. At least I hope so.

Chapter 25

It was about the time the baby should have been born that I went back to the house in Fulham for the last time.

I rounded the corner, pushing Dr Maxwell's pram with my son lying in it. It was only the second or third time we'd been out together, although he'd made a quick recovery from his early birth and now weighed nearly ten pounds and was extremely attractive in a still-slightly-shrimplike fashion. He had a lot of dark hair (not all in the right places, but that would soon go, I'd been assured) and the most amazing little hands and feet, which I never got tired of looking at. His nails in particular fascinated me. They were as small and perfect as pearls. I'd called him David. I'd thought about various names, already held by various people, but in the end I'd called him David. You can't please everyone.

I stood looking at the house. I wondered if anyone was at home. I listened in vain for the sound of *St Louis Woman*. John had stayed at the hospital all night when David was born. So had Toby and so had Father. They must have made a bizarre trio, sitting in the waiting-room hour after hour; it made me want to giggle to imagine what the nurses made of it. They were nearly all Irish girls, and I heard they had bets as to which of my male visitors was David's father. I don't suppose the odds were very high on Terry; for one thing, he came on to the scene rather late, having been confined (during *my* confinement) to another part of the hospital with a cracked jawbone. When he came along at last, in the second week, I was disturbed by my inability to feel that he was any more part of the baby than Toby or John. They had had so much more to do with my getting through those dark months; it seemed they were more entitled to a share in David than Terry was.

He was very diffident and quiet, standing beside the bed making awkward conversation. He kept repeating 'You're sure you're all right, then?' and when I said *I* was all right, what about him, he rubbed his bandaged jaw and said 'That chap of yours packs quite a punch – didn't even see it coming.' But the note of satisfaction in his voice gave me the clue to the mystery of the one-sided fight, and my impression was confirmed by the fact that Terry no longer seemed guilty, nor talked about marriage. The simple public-school standards relating to crime and punishment can last, I saw, through life. He had allowed himself to be 'beaten'; the score, in some fundamental, immature way, now seemed to him to be settled.

That was all right with me. His proposal wasn't any sort of compliment, when you came right down to it; it was simply an attempt at expiation. I was fond of him, but I didn't respect him, any more than he did me. Which wasn't much, whatever he might say. To him I was irretrievably *that* sort of girl for ever.

It was borne in upon me that I would be *that* sort of girl in most men's eyes from now on. This didn't alarm me unduly, partly because Toby didn't regard me as *that* sort of girl, and partly because nothing was alarming me at the moment. David, who was creating the causes of alarm and despondency, was also neutralizing them at source. One look at him grinning gummily up at me made the world and its judgements recede. This wouldn't last, I knew, but while it did I saw no point in arguing.

I rocked the pram gently, remembering how tenderly John's enormous hands had scooped the baby out of his hospital crib beside my bed. He held him as surely and firmly as one of the nurses, cradling the tiny head in a giant paw that could have crushed it like a walnut. As he held David in his arms, a wide grin splitting his broad black face, I realized something I hadn't grasped before about John. It gave me a shock, but not an unpleasant one. I waited for a change in my affection for him, the faint revulsion I had felt for Malcolm and others like him in the past. But there was no change. I knew what I owed to John, and that he couldn't have helped me in the way he had if he had been any different.

Father had stood by while John played with David. I could see it was a peculiar kind of torture for him, but he didn't interfere. He himself didn't touch the baby for a long time. It was as if he just wanted to see him, to know that he was there and real, flesh of his flesh, and to examine his own secret pride; that seemed to be enough. Also, I think he was a little nervous that he might damage him somehow.

Dottie came, as she had come before, upbraiding me for not contacting her, her good-natured abuse dissolving into enchanted gurgles every time her eyes fell on the baby. I asked her to be godmother. She accepted with joy. The godfathers, of course, were to be John and Toby. 'The christening,' said Dottie succinctly, 'should cause quite a stir.'

And of course, Toby came. He had shaved the beard off, but I discovered it was not that which made the change in him. The fledgling look was gone for ever; the darting, restless eyes and nervous hands were calmed and still. He'd learned to live alone, to discipline himself and to write. The novel, he told me, had started moving again only after weeks of miserable loafing about, missing me desperately and unable to come to grips with anything. Then one night he had come in from a particularly insipid and boring film and had sat down in front of his table, picked up a pen and said to himself 'I will write fifty words. Just fifty. It doesn't matter how bad they are, and I'll stop after fifty words even if it's the middle of a sentence.'

He wrote two thousand words that night, and after that he was afraid to stop. He forced himself to work between certain hours each day. He had a superstitious fear that if even one day passed without his adding to the book he would lose himself again in that drab labyrinth of un-doing. He didn't even give himself a break after the first novel was finished. He sent it off to a publisher at lunchtime one day, and the same afternoon he started mapping out the next.

'So now you're not blurred any more,' I said when he'd finished telling me.

He stared. 'Fancy you remembering that,' he said. 'It's started to be true. I can't tell you how wonderful it is to be so *totally* absorbed in one's work that nothing else impinges at all.'

I thought of the feeling I had had while David was being born, and nodded.

'Why did you send that character to find me?' he asked suddenly. I sensed his unease. I think he was afraid I'd make some demand on him which would lure him away from his new-found singleness of mind. I hesitated. If I answered 'Because I love you and need you and feel like half a person without you,' he would probably respond with the corresponding need in himself and the whole thing would start again. I wanted it to, and in a way I think he did. But it would be a risk. Later, perhaps, when his new disciplines were more firmly established, it would be possible to add a full-time love relationship. As our hungry need for each other diminished, and we grew stronger as individuals, we'd have more to give.

'Well? Not that I wasn't glad? I've never stopped wanting you.'

'I've got something of yours.'

'What?'

'Your typewriter.'

It was lovely to see what happened to his face. All the serious grown-up lines lifted at the edges and his eyes lit up with incredulous pleasure. Even the neatly brushed hair seemed to spring on end as of old.

'You've got Minnie!' he exclaimed joyfully. 'You angel!'

You darling blackbird, I thought, yearning for him, my treacherous female arms longing to imprison him for ever.

'Fancy you saving old Min!' he kept saying happily. 'I always felt like a traitor, leaving her in Doris's bovine clutches. How is the old duck, by the way?'

The moment of weakness – that one, anyway – passed. We gossiped and shrieked until a nurse came rushing up to chase Toby away. I watched him go with a painful stab of advance loneliness. Once he'd asked me if I would love him more if he were successful. Now he was successful, in the way I'd meant when I'd answered 'yes'; but I realized only now how *much* more I'd love him, unblurred. I longed for the time when we could safely and unpossessively lay claim to each other. But I felt so happy about him, it didn't matter too terribly that he wasn't mine yet, and might never be.

When Father came to fetch us home, I rode in front beside him holding David in my arms. He smelled warm and milky and stared up at me with bleary eyes. Father's glance kept leaving the road. On the way from the car I said 'Hold him a second while I get the things out of the back,' and dumped him unceremoniously into Father's arms before he could protest. David clutched his finger in a strong, trusting grip. When I wanted to take him back, Father said 'Do you think I'm going to drop him or something? I'll carry him upstairs.' The next evening he was demanding bath privileges.

The yellow look was gone from Father's eyes. It was gone from the net curtains, too, because I had washed and bleached them. It seemed easy to apply what I had learned in the L-shaped room to the wider field of Father's house. It was recovering – and so, more slowly, were its inhabitants – from the exigencies of the past eight months and the past twenty-eight years.

But I missed the L-shaped room. Each morning I woke expecting to find myself in it. To have been wrenched away from it so suddenly made me feel like a snail with a broken shell. I was sucked back irresistibly for one last look.

And now here I was; and I could only stand on the pavement and stare upwards. I couldn't bring myself to knock and ask Doris if I could see the room. It was rented again, I knew. My things had been collected weeks ago, after I'd been taken to hospital, and Doris had lost no time in getting a new tenant. A young lady, John had reported. I wondered if she might be another like Jane and Sonia. But no; customers would never walk up all those stairs. I was filled with curiosity about her, whoever she was. Had she been adopted by Mavis? Had she been frightened by John's black face in the little window? Had she mastered the bathroom geyser? And most important, what had she done to the room?

Well, it was no good. I would never know. Better that way, perhaps.

I turned the pram round to head for home. My heart was heavy.

I hadn't said good-bye to the room that had sheltered me and taught me so much, and now it was too late and it would have to go on nagging.

At the corner I looked back once more. Mounting the steps was a girl, a stranger. Without stopping to think I called out and she stopped. I bowled the pram at full speed back to the foot of the steps.

There was nothing special about her – just a rather plain girl in her middle twenties with mouse-coloured hair. She carried her shopping in a string bag. Onions, I noticed. Doris won't like that.

She was looking at me indifferently.

'Yes?'

'Excuse me – but do you live in the top front room?'

'Yes?'

'I used to live there – before you.'

'Yes?' she said again. It was plain she needed more explanation than this.

'I was wondering – could I see it?'

Puzzled, she frowned. 'Did you leave something?'

'No. I just . . .' Either one understood that sort of feeling or not. 'I just wondered how you were getting along in it.'

'Me?' She was beginning to look at me sharply, suspecting there was something funny about me.

'You like it?'

'It's all right,' she said with a shrug that chilled me.

'I was there for seven months,' I said uselessly.

'Were you?' Her voice was flat and withdrawn. Her eyes wandered and encountered David. In the same flat voice she said, 'Is he yours?'

'Yes.'

She stared at him. 'What's wrong with his ears?'

'Nothing, except they stick out a bit. I keep them taped back.'

'That doesn't do any good,' she said unexpectedly. 'There's an operation for it; they cut a little cartilage and then they lie flat.'

'Have you got any children?'

'I had a little boy. He got run over.'

I became numb in my refusal to imagine such a thing happening to David. The girl came slowly down the steps and stood over the pram. She offered her finger to the baby, who was awake now. He couldn't focus on it, but when he felt it touch his hand he immediately took hold of it. The girl smiled. When she smiled she looked older; I could see she might be nearer thirty.

'He's a dear,' she said at last. She looked up at me. Her pale eyes were pink-rimmed, but she still smiled and let the baby hold her finger.

'Were you living in that little room all by yourself, before you had him?' I nodded. 'What about your husband?'

'I'm not married.'

She looked down at David's face and said, 'But you're lucky. At least you've got your baby.' She drew her finger gently out of his grasp and tucked his small hand under the blanket, lingering over the movement. 'Why did you want to see the room?'

'I was fond of it.'

She looked at me incredulously. 'Fond of it? That poky little place? With that black man next door, and the landlady and everything? And the house all dark and smelly – and those two women in the basement – ' I felt depression swoop on me. It was all quite true, and how I had seen it myself at first. 'Still,' she said reluctantly, 'you can come up if you like. I don't think anyone's in.'

I left the pram in the hall and carried David up the long, musty-smelling flights. Again, my awareness of the smell was renewed by absence. 'Can you smell it?' the girl whispered.

'Yes.'

'It's horrible. Hits me in the face every time I come in. And all these stairs!'

I felt a stirring of unreasonable irritation, a defensive feeling for the house. 'You get used to them,' I said, shortly.

But indeed I wondered if I ever had. By the top I was exhausted; my legs ached and the baby felt like a ton weight.

It seemed strange to have someone let me in with my key. And the room gave me a shock. I should have expected it, but my eyes anticipated the room I'd left, and it was completely changed. In many respects it was as I'd first seen it. The plaster Alsatians were back in position, their badly-painted orange faces staring stupidly on either side of the cottage garden. The poor pock-marked floor was again exposed. The brown curtains were drably back. Only the white walls and the afghan struck a familiar note.

'It needs things doing to it,' the girl said more defiantly than apologetically. 'Only I'm not going to do them. I can't be bothered.

Why should I? It doesn't matter, no one's ever going to see it. I've been here a month and you're the first person's ever been up here.'

'Not Mavis?'

'Who? Oh, the old duck downstairs. She's come knocking once or twice. I haven't let her past the door. She's all right, it's just that I don't want to get mixed up with anyone in the house. I don't want to get mixed up at all, with anybody, any more. Oh, sorry – keeping you standing there. Here, put the baby on the bed and sit down for a minute.'

I obeyed. David lay framed by the garish squares of the old afghan and gurgled. I think he could see the bright colours out of the corner of his eye.

'He likes that old woolly thing,' she said, watching him. 'I like it too. It's about the only thing in the beastly little room I do like.'

I sat in the arm-chair. The cover I had had made for it had come back with the rest of my things. It was naked and greasy-brown again.

'That arm-chair ought to have a cover on it,' said the girl. Then her mouth tightened as if the words had slipped out in spite of her. 'Not that it matters.'

'I've got one you could have,' I heard myself saying.

For a minute she hesitated. Then she said firmly, 'No thanks. Once you start turning a room into something there's no stopping. I'm just not bothering.' She seemed to be embarrassed by my being there. Everywhere I looked she would follow my eyes and say, 'Yes, those curtains. They're horrible. Dirty, too. Still, I don't care.' Or, 'It's gloomy at night – needs another lamp, really.' Or, 'Yes, the floor's awful. Needs something on it, besides that horrid little rug.'

'My-sister-made-that-rug,' I said automatically.

'Your sister did?' she said incredulously.

'I mean, Doris's sister.'

'Oh.' We sat in silence for a while. Then, as if driven to give some explanation for her being there, she said, 'I wouldn't have taken a nasty place like this if I could've afforded better. My husband left me after the baby died. Mind you, I think £2 is too much. She wanted two-ten, but I wouldn't give her that. Old Scrooge,' she added bitterly.

'So you haven't met anyone else in the house?'

'Oh, I've met them,' she said. 'You can't help it. That John.

He looks after me like he was my mother or something. I was afraid of him at first, but he's so kind you couldn't hurt his feelings. And there's an old married couple on the first floor – they're always sending little notes asking me to have supper with them. And then, there's a chap just underneath me. He works in a garage. He looks quite nice – must be miserable for him there, doing for himself. But I'm not going to get mixed up with them. I'm just not. It's like with doing up the room. Once you get started there's no end to it. They get friendly and soon they find out all about you, and your life's not your own any more.'

I sat there, savouring an uncanny feeling of omniscience. I could see the future as clearly as if I were sitting through a film for the second time.

'I suppose you can't understand how I feel,' said the girl defensively.

'Oh yes I can.'

She was watching me now. 'It must be funny for you, seeing me in this place. Though I don't know how you could ever have been *fond* of it . . .' She glanced round with distaste. At the same moment her foot was unconsciously straightening the rug.

Just before I left, the girl faced the mantelpiece and said with sudden vigour: 'One thing I am going to do, and right this minute, is to put those awful dogs out of sight. They really upset me, they're so ugly.' She was putting them in a suitcase under the bed as I said good-bye.